DOUBLE-CRO$$ED
FOR
BLOOD

O.J. SIMPSON'S
CONSTITUTIONAL DISASTER

HENRY S. JOHNSON, M.D.

6/14/2

To Chef Youngblood

THE SUPPRESSION OF EVIDENCE
& PERVERSION OF JUSTICE IN AMERICA

You are wonderful to help.
Please don't stop!

God Bless   Doc

Published and Distributed by:
Milligan Books
an imprint of Professional Business Consultants
1425 W. Manchester, Suite C,
Los Angeles, California 90047
(323) 750-3592

First Printing, February 2002
10 9 8 7 6 5 4 3 2 1

ISBN: 1-881524-88-4

FOR OUR STRUGGLE IS NOT AGAINST FLESH AND BLOOD,
BUT AGAINST PRINCIPALITIES,
AGAINST POWERS,
AGAINST THE RULERS OF THE DARKNESS OF THIS WORLD,
AGAINST THE SPIRITUAL FORCES OF EVIL IN HIGH PLACES...

EPHESIANS 6:12

About the Author

Henry S. Johnson, M.D. an American Board Certified Internist, practices in Los Angeles. He graduated from the University of Minnesota with a bachelor's degree in 1976. Dr. Johnson received a medical degree from Meharry Medical College, Nashville in 1980 and moved to Los Angeles to complete an internal medicine residency at Martin Luther King, Jr./Charles R. Drew/ UCLA Medical Center.

Dr. Johnson has volunteered as a visiting attending physician at King/Drew Medical Center. He was Chief Resident, Department of Internal Medicine in 1983/1984. Dr. Johnson is Past President of the National Medical Association's Los Angeles affiliate—Charles R. Drew Medical Society. He is a past-member of the Drew University Board of Directors.

Dr. Johnson has been in private practice in Los Angeles since 1984 with an emphasis on medical review of case management, testifying as medical expert. His areas of expertise include, critical care and emergency medicine, sports medicine and rehabilitation. His extracurricular activities have included medical supervising, coaching in kids' sports programs and participating on several non-profit executive boards.

Dr. Johnson formed Ocean Medical-Legal Investigation Group in 1998, to expose the fraudulent phone records used to frame O.J. and identify the real killers. Dr. Johnson has appeared on the *O'Reilly Factor, Fox News Channel, Court TV,* local and national television networks, *KABC Radio, Pacifica Radio network, Voice of America* and a host of radio interviews across the nation. Dr. Johnson was instrumental in filing the federal motions to produce the missing phone record evidence in Mr. Simpson's appeal, but was denied; he co-authored O.J.'s petition to the California Supreme Court.

CONTENTS

ACKNOWLEDGMENTS

This writing is dedicated to the recent memory of three people, without whose sacrifices it would have all been impossible—my parents, Henrietta and Thomas H. Johnson, M.D., and Mrs. Eunice Simpson. I have been very fortunate indeed in receiving encouragement and the insight from many people over the course of the past 7 years.

To help focus my analysis, I had several interviews primarily on listeners' supported radio across the country, and I am very grateful for the interest shown by many who heard me on the topic. Furthermore, I am indebted to those that E-mailed me, posted in Internet chat rooms, or sent information to my attention. I want to pay special recognition to the daughters of both families—Beth, Linda and Sharon Johnson, along with Shirley and Carmelita Simpson (with all due respect to their husbands) for making the final years of their elders safe and comforting.

I cannot let it go unnoticed that my right-hand, my medical secretary Juanita Parada, kept me in touch with reality, balanced with an unconditional faith in my mission and professional diligence during the course of this project. My transcriptionists—Carole Lewis, Tracey Flores, and June McClure—cheerfully accommodated my impositions with dedication as well. John Parada, with the eyes of an eagle, made sure this self-published edition maintained its literary integrity. I have listed below only a few of those who were instrumental in helping to sustain my conviction to enlighten the public:

Richard Johnson, Mark Adzick, Judge George Adzick, Ret., John and Concecion Retamosa, Ralph Russell, Charles Dudley, Larry Edwards, Frank Ivey, Tony Little, Spike Moss, Lori Winkelman, Samuel Young, Gaynell Marrero, Don Denson, Irene

Martimianakis, Eric St. James @ *WOL*, Ron Brewington @ *KJLH*, Armstrong Williams, Aaron Booth, Atty., Gary Randa, Victoria Boone, Miki Gaut, Thomas Warner, Atty., James Mayes, M.D., Rev. Richard Byrd @ *KPFK*, Doris Spann, Hilda Anderson, Hazel Colbert, Kay Kelly, John Jefferson, Art Whaley @ *WLIB*, Gary Johnson, Luis Quijano, Najee Williams—Tech Support, Juan Medina, Wesley East, John Settles @ *KMOJ*, Dottie Wright, Henry Williams, M.D., Kamuel Presley, Edward Puckett, David Camp, Harvey Johnson, Al Rantel @ *KABC*, Claude Rogers, Tony Takvoryan, Felipe Telona, Johnny Sample, Larry Brookins, Artis Woodard, M.D., Eugene Christian, M.D., Dr. Rosie Milligan, Linda Deutsch @ *AP News,* Christian Boone @ *APB News*, Boko, Delvin Campbell, Tony Calloway, M.D., "Big Money" Griff, Jeep Swenson, Cyrus Green, M.D., Kenya Boone, Charlotte O'Malley, Richard Williams, M.D., Derick Balenger, and Lisa Parada, for her loving and patient spirit.

To my brother, Thomas Johnson III, for being the warrior and solid rock of support that I needed, especially in helping with the investigative work, the legal theories and briefs.

My son, Jonah, came through for me, like a champ, creating the cover art for this book. Lastly, I ask those who are my foundation— my wife Andrea, my children Jesse, Jonah, Judah, Jianni, my grandson Milan, and my extended family—to forgive me for the time I took away from you to make my own selfish dream to publish this book, a reality. Thank you for your patience and all your support. I love you all so very much.

God Bless You All, Henry S. Johnson, M.D.

FOREWORD

The so-called "Trial of the Century," which would be better described as the "Scam of the Century," spills into the new millennium with this book, an examination of the corruption that ran through all aspects of my trial(s).

Dr. Johnson's work debunks the hype surrounding my persecution with such clarity, it is frightening. His conclusions demonstrate essentially how the "American Dream" gets sabotaged, when the protections we take for granted as citizens are annihilated, while sanctioned by a racially distorted media.

Doc Johnson, whom I consider a sincere friend, remains an independent thinker. I am grateful to his commitment to expose the fraud and help me. His work sheds light on situations which most people find too stressful to consider openly. Dr. Johnson's ability to focus on social issues, impacted by the media spin on my pathetic trials, sets this book ahead of "all the rest." I found reading about his experiences enjoyable and insightful.

If you take anything away from this provocative, yet sensitive story, consider the point made about the rights of all Americans, and the fact that if my rights can be trampled, whose rights are protected, whether they be Black, White, rich, poor, man or woman?

Dr. Johnson has placed me in an awkward position, which my instincts propel me away from, yet my curiosity draws me near. I have always looked for the finer qualities in people, kind of a silver lining behind the cloud. No matter what Dr. Johnson's theories prove or disprove, my family, friends, fans and those whom I trust and trusted know, as God is my witness, I would never shun the burden imposed on me by compromising my integrity. My fight is still in front of me, but "Doc" and his team have shown me some daylight—a seam to run through. History will record that which is self-evident.

First and foremost, I have always maintained my innocence, and truth is the "Rock of Ages." It can never be tarnished, despite every effort to beguile through clever designs. Dr. Johnson has impressed me and I know he will impress you. Anyone who knows me knows, I'm not one to fall for the okey-doke. Everyone has the capacity to fall prey to love, forever hoping that our wishes and dreams would somehow be fulfilled. Throughout my career, having basked in triumph, cherished the adulations of adoring fans, and shared the congeniality of world leaders, I have experienced loss as well, but never accepted defeat. I have been pegged as a murderer, a brute, a wife-beater, money-launderer, porn star and a drug dealer. They have plastered my face and name across tabloids and the media for the past several years, making billions of dollars—illegally, mind you—at my expense. During holidays and times of celebration, the same tired stories of my trials are rehashed, to re-enforced the "beliefs," lies and distortions about me and my supporters, imbedded in the minds of the average John and Jane Q. American.

I am just so proud of how my children have held up to endure the undeserved public humiliation of their father, in the face of the tragic loss of their mother. No matter, as a man in this mortal world of flesh and blood, whether I am able to convince the skeptics of my innocence, as a Christian, I know my account with God will be acceptable in His eyes.

Despite having set records of speed and strength on the field of competition, and having been loved across the world yet hated in my own country, in the final count I remain simply, Eunice Simpson's son—O.J.

In the face of my continued vilification, it is reassuring and refreshing to read an honest commentary about my trials. As a prisoner of persecution, I watch along with the multitude the sensationalizing of the most trivial and insignificant things in my life. This makes me appreciate someone who staid the course, and remained objective, in a critical analysis of the medical facts surrounding the deaths of my ex-wife and Ron Goldman.

Dr. Johnson has given us a road map, his interpretations, and a key to future generations who may unlock this epoch in history, searching in earnest for a resolution to eternal conflict. Who in recent history has suffered the amount of humiliation and stigma I had to put up with, when it seems all the facts which supported my innocence—the lies told by the LAPD, the prosecution misconduct, and judicial bias—have been totally ignored. Yet the media can be a blessing and a curse. I have tasted both the honey and the vinegar. Despite what I would consider a continuously biased presentation of the facts surrounding my life and legal challenges, publicity remains to me a skewed consolation.

Due to the constant media barrage, there will always remain a curiosity of sorts. The prosecutors never proved their case against me and I was denied the opportunity to prove my innocence, leaving two questions in most people's minds—did I do it or didn't I? It would be foolish for you to believe conclusively in either perspective if you were not factually informed. Whatever you believe, guilty or not guilty, it behooves you to examine how Dr. Johnson so vividly, yet with common sense, fillets issues which have always haunted America and impacts our daily existence.

It is comforting to know a rational explanation of the evidence and events surrounding the crimes I was acquitted of, has been produced for the public and posterity. More than a question of my innocence or guilt, Dr. Johnson forces the reader to look at his or her personal insightfulness (or lack thereof), how your beliefs were manipulated, and begs the question, what in the media can you place your faith in, particularly during stressful times.

Don't worry about me, I didn't do it and Dr. Johnson all but proves it. Forget about the "Mountain of Evidence," just consider the implications when I'm allowed to completely exonerate myself. Then you will realize that freedom is a figment of the imagination to those unwilling to protect the rights of every American—who's next?

I support Dr. Johnson in his endeavor, as he has supported me.

O.J. SIMPSON

Chapter One

WHY I WRITE

At the end of the millennium in Tinsel Town, the mecca of dreams and disasters, a sham of colossal proportions was staged. Played out in democracy's premier legal system, the world would bear witness.

Through means of constitutional perversion and a total disregard for the moral virtues of America, O.J. Simpson would be prosecuted, persecuted, symbolically lynched and castrated to satisfy the lust for revenge from a brainwashed segment of society.

The outcomes of the verdicts have left Americans polarized, primarily along racial lines. Neither Blacks nor Whites will trust each other because the truth has been hidden from both. The disharmony promoted by media distortion and indoctrination created increased tension among Black people and has had an almost imperceptible, but dramatically negative impact on Black social stability.

No matter how incredible it may sound, investigators knew from the outset that O.J. Simpson should never have been charged for the double murders in Brentwood. Critical factors supported the initial statements of Nicole Brown Simpson's parents, that Nicole spoke to them by phone around 11:00 p.m., the night of the murders. In other words, the victims were still alive as O.J. buckled up in first class on the red-eye flight to Chicago. However, the telephone records of the Browns' and Nicole's were sealed by the court, and never permitted to be offered as evidence.

In a time of widespread scandals and corruption in politics, never would one imagine that such a Machiavellian bastion emerge, from the Los Angeles Police Department to the California Supreme Court. In a nation that inadvertently prides itself on the destruction of human life through draconian and selective law enforcement, when O.J. was acquitted, White America's vengeance rampaged through the media, society and the courts. Their perception was that a jury of Black women allowed a Black man, guilty of murdering two White people, to walk free in reaction to years of supposed racial intolerance and discrimination.

On the other hand, people around the world from Chile to China celebrated, along with the majority of African Americans the victory of justice that our world-renowned judicial system actually worked. To suggest the majority of people in the world, including Black Americans, were sympathetic to a Black man for "getting even" with White folks is a narrow-minded, paranoid delusion.

The status quo of racism and bigotry would prevail, however. O.J. Simpson would not escape the wrath of White America's superiority complex, particularly if the media had anything to do with it. O.J. would be tried, convicted and sentenced in the minds of the gullible before going to face an all-White jury in Santa Monica. Black society as a whole and Black children, in particular, would be made to pay for the "sins of twelve" seemingly dense and amoral Black women jurors, as the media would depict them. Even prosecutor Marcia Clark got in on the act, describing the jurors as "Moon Rocks," eliciting a chuckle from Oprah during a guest interview.

The dysfunction portrayed in our courtrooms only seeded discontent. Faith in the judicial system must be restored and not forced. When one group delights in seeing another suffer from depravity, we are not a unified country, and America must be defined in this context. With the suppression of crucial and relevant evidence that would completely exonerate O.J., the conspiracy against him took on a new life form. It would employ a loophole to circumvent the spirit of the double jeopardy clause in the Constitution, and hold him accountable twice for the double homicide. Never before in the history of American jurisprudence has a defendant been acquitted of murder, voluntary manslaughter, involuntary manslaughter or accidental death, and then held accountable for the same offense in a second trial.

People may argue that there is a distinction between criminal and civil prosecution, but that is only splitting hairs when the charges are the same. The Fifth, Seventh and Fourteenth Amendments of due process and equal protection, guarantee against such blasphemy. However, in the Santa Monica Courtroom, just like Supreme Court Chief Justice Roger Taney ruled against Dred Scott in 1857, *"The founding fathers never intended to include Negroes as citizens in the Constitution...therefore, a Black man has no rights that a White man is bound to respect."*

Despite this ruling never having been repealed, as well as the metamorphosing of our constitutional protections, one thing remains clear—the autopsy reports of Nicole Brown Simpson and Ronald Goldman shroud the secrets to O.J.'s innocence. The Los Angeles Police Department knew this, the "Dream Team" knew it and the California Supreme Court knows it too. Yet, when O.J. petitioned the California Supreme Court to release this evidence, they reacted like a star chamber.

When the California Supreme Court examined the evidence in

O.J.'s petition, they could not find O.J. guilty of any charges against him. However, they knew they would enrage the masses and lose powerful friends should they do what was just. Instead, they would demonstrate their weakness, washing their hands like Pilate to satisfy the crowd, and condemn O.J. by willfully acting to conceal the conspiracy that every agency from the United States Justice Department to Scotland Yard was intimately aware of.

These professionals knew, based on the autopsy findings, that more than one killer was involved. Only a veritable jackass would assume one guy stealthily killed two people in record time, with hardly a trace. Yet, through the designs of the media, a society could be densely brainwashed to assume the impossible, that not only could O.J. commit a double-murder—*"the immaculate deception"*—but that O.J. could be in two places at the same time.

The most unsettling thought about the "Trial of the Century" is, what made it so easy for completely divergent opinions to manifest themselves along ethnic lines in America. People must ask themselves, how did you get bamboozled? You must do a thorough self-evaluation.

Compelled to resist the dogmatic perceptions of the so-called "mountain of overwhelming evidence" led to the natural conclusions that culminated in this book. Motivated to write these passages as a means to disseminate facts over fiction, my ultimate desire is for greater cultural understanding. When a disagreement arises and goes unresolved, it breeds distrust and hostility, as well as isolation. The world is too small—and getting smaller by the day—for hypocrisy to thrive.

One must approach all confrontation with temperance in order to maintain balance and control. America could ill-afford to consider O.J. anything but guilty. Perish the thought of his innocence. It wreaks havoc on the collective subconscious, and indicts the very process by which all red-blooded Americans define themselves. You cannot hide the truth nor can you hide from the truth. Fear of the truth is of greater detriment than fear of the unknown.

Fear is a natural emotion. It is your internal alarm when your sense of well-being is threatened. However, unbridled fear is incapacitating or worse, self-destructive. If not recognized for what it is, all decisions which follow become random and chaotic. Now, if we genuinely search for the truth, facts which lead to improve chances of discovery, put us on a clear path to success and we are very much ahead of the game.

The world builds civilization on the successes and failures of our predecessors. To encumber our future generations with the burden of our mistakes, to inherit a dismal plight because of our selfish paranoia, imperils their future. Fearing other cultures, we do not strive to communicate and understand the spirituality of our respective heritage. We must avoid subconsciously allowing our inclinations to control our outward display, as inclinations are habitual, without reflection, and do not benefit society as a whole.

To be in a perfect state of selflessness should not mean inevitable martyrdom. We all have imperfections to redress, but in a White male-dominant society, one feels misguided, focusing his attention on personal improvement rather than protecting himself or his acquisitions from aggression. Thus, we move away from the idea of freedom of choice: religious, philosophical or political.

The church, as well, is in no way free of this influence. Preaching and politics seek a balance. First, to assume church and state disassociate by statute would be dangerously naive. They are intertwining enterprises, and rely on the same money to exist. They share currency, tend to be symbiotic, and operate as if there is no fault short of practicality. The church must work harder as the spiritual conscience of this nation, to lead as it has been pre-ordained, with a voice of compassion.

Lead does not mean an obsession with fornication, but to enlighten and not fall prey to pragmatism, money and power. The understanding to be achieved when an honest effort is put forth will be a great asset in our quest for prosperity and serenity. The toll that ignorance takes is more malignant on the individual than on the community. It shortens our life, diminishes our vigor and our ability to thrive. It entombs us with periods of despair. There can be no resolution to conflict without careful guidance and navigation. We can remain true to the tenets of this great country's foundation by making the effort to always remain circumspect.

We must focus on developing and cultivating more positive attitudes towards each other. This alone will be the best guarantee that the future generations will not succumb to the same transgressions that remain to us so unavoidable. You would suffer less anxiety if you accepted the status quo. If you are fatalistic, you can stop reading because this book is not about the failure of man and society, but about the future and how to enhance the brightness. We all know life was procreated in darkness but materialized in light. So we must be thankful that we can distinguish the two, push to bring forth illumination and extinguish ignorance.

The trials of O.J. Simpson maintained a certain fascination for the world at large and America in particular, because of the racial overtones encompassing romance and murder. Whites and Blacks were predisposed from historical and cultural influences to operate from opposing perspectives.

A higher percentage of Black people watched the live airing of the trial in contrast to the larger percentage of White folks, who were informed and persuaded by the media pundits. Furthermore, White Americans are more inclined to place an unwavering faith in the structures which meld our government into the system that it is. This is done consciously or subconsciously without regard to inequities.

African Americans, on the other hand, who have dealt for generations with the American legacy of discrimination, have remained suspicious and skeptical of a system which is supposed to guarantee life, liberty and the pursuit of happiness. Not to say either perspective is wrong or right, only that they are fashioned from historical perceptions and daily experiences. It has left a vacuum in America, a void destitute of understanding.

A large percentage of Blacks have been convinced of Simpson's "guilt" subsequent to the civil trial, having changed their opinion from that fateful day they were celebrating, October 3rd, 1995. Notwithstanding, many Whites have not forgotten nor "forgiven" African Americans, for the most part, for rejoicing as a Black man they felt was guilty of a savage act, perpetrated against a White man and woman, was set free. Hence, there exists an ongoing sentiment of distrust drawn mostly along ethnic lines. For Whites to believe in O.J.'s innocence, they would have to forsake their confidence in the system which defines their priorities. There are no practical solutions. Black people are more inclined to question the validity of the ambiguous. They sympathize with the plight of a fallen Black hero, if even mistakenly.

What appeared to be a gross cultural aberration to most Blacks i.e., a Black man gruesomely slaughtering the mother of his children, seemed a rational expectation to Whites. Contrary to what a collective, guilt-ridden and paranoid subconscious might project, Black people do not ruminate on retribution for the brutality inflicted on our ancestors, and the remnants thereof, which have negatively impacted our present day society.

Compared to centuries-old regional conflicts and fighting in the world, Black Americans are perhaps the most forgiving of all people. Frankly, the African American is probably the closest friend and ally that White Americans have; notwithstanding, the decades of racism and bigotry experienced. Just look at the world around us. The term ugly-American applies to White Americans who tend to be scorned, envied or ostracized outside of this country. However, our love-hate relationship is mitigated by race mixing, of which the offspring thereof, have taught us how to live peaceably, with temperance.

A man singularly in his heart, irregardless of race, finds it indomitable to sacrifice his own blood kinship, irrespective of its mixing with another kind. In the final analysis, isn't this the kind of world we all wish to thrive in? One of love and understanding? We can only achieve this through knowledge and wisdom of which is like medicine to the soul.

Good medicine is always healing. The social affliction left from the aftermath of the verdicts is in need of a strong poultice. Sometimes medicine is painful, but the lasting effects gained from prudent and benevolent application far outweighs the transient adverse reaction. Medicine, and the knowledge achieved from it, would help to cure some of our social ills. It will expose others as the poultice draws out the pus and toxins from the disease of deception.

It is for the masses to decide what to do with the elucidation of this information. I felt obliged to write an analysis and share my perceptions with those less knowledgeable of the facts, because of my similarities to Simpson. We are or were both in interracial marriages and have produced offspring from those unions.

A pall was cast on interracial relations early in the investigation, of which I took personal. Our research started long before I met O.J. Simpson. I was disinterested in proving his innocence or guilt. As a scientist and a neutral party, I wanted to present the facts as I saw them. If they helped O.J., more power to him. If they condemned O.J., *lo siento,* it made no difference. The courts and media dodged these issues but O.J. was open to deal with them. Despite the "Dream Team" never sitting down and knocking heads with me, O.J. invited me into his living room where we could look eye to eye.

During the football season of 1998, we developed a mutual respect. Every Sunday, O.J. made commentary between plays as he impressed us with his satellite TV. There was a constant parade of guys bringing beer, chicken and barbeque. Between O.J.'s incessant comments, jokes and camaraderie, he realized we were really on to something. O.J. is quick to analyze, plays his hand close to the vest and every move is calculated. Don't fool yourself, the guy is a master at what he does and he never ceases to amaze you with facts or folly. Despite O.J.'s gigantic ego, I appreciate that he was humble enough to say, *"Thank God for what you have done."*

My interracial marriage, just like most other marriages, has its highs and lows. I have dealt with the begrudging stares from all races and have remained, for the most part, in a fish bowl. At best, I am forgiving of the gawkers, circumspect of confrontation, and at worst potentially ruthless. Besides, Hollywood portrays Black people in distorted images, so I never expect to be treated any differently simply because I'm married to a beautiful woman who happens to be White.

Ironically, interracial relationships are analyzed and discussed most frequently by "experts" who are not in an interracial relationship. In contrast, I espouse my viewpoint from within. It tears my heart out to see the pseudo-mentality leading to fissures in race relations. There are issues too pressing to allow a setback in racial understanding to undermine our progress. Besides, it is the children who suffer the most from our insolence. I am uncomfortable looking people in their eyes while their smiles belie their true feelings. I detest a hypocrite nor do I care to be contrite or patronized. I just want the chips to fall as they may and deal with it. So in an effort to level the table, I will share with you the fruits of my medical investigation.

I wanted it to be clear in my mind if O.J. was guilty or innocent. To address issues which lead to duress, it remains essential that people from different social, sexual and ethnic backgrounds strive to communicate. I hope that you will remain objective as we reason through the analysis. It is gratifying that you have taken this opportunity, which you may find reaffirming, to consider an explanation, and compare it to your personal beliefs and what you have been told.

The thrust of this book is not about the guilt nor the innocence of O.J. Simpson, but about truth. Many may find my allegations irascible, while some may find them stupendous. They are guaranteed to provoke contemplation, and I just ask that you consider your position or your intransigence. Question whether your personal discord diminishes your ability to make concessions.

I am ninety-nine point nine (99.9%) percent sure the medical evidence is more consistent with a two-assailant theory, with one assailant left-handed; yet, this was never proffered by the Coroner during the trial. I brought this to the attention of the Superior Court only to be denied access, while in the meantime, erroneous information continued to be postulated.

This story needs to be revealed because the impact of this trial is profoundly connected to all of our daily lives. American subconscious rigmarole has come to the surface. Issues of a critical nature cannot be ignored solely because they are uncomfortable to address or politically incorrect. We should always pursue mutual understanding if "trust" must not be compromised.

I am energized to see these conclusions brought to light, and I'm not worried about mishaps, booby traps and skullduggery. As I surge forward to bring awareness to the material, our efforts have been primarily two-pronged, the Superior Court and the court of public opinion.

The media has been reluctant to entertain these issues, and its ability to publicly censor has been my *raison d'être* to aggressively pursue exposing this fraud. The guardians of the public's First Amendment liberties—the omnipotent media—has concluded what is politically appropriate for the average American to be knowledgeable of. First Amendment rights are principally defined in terms of freedom of speech. Speech is meaningless, however, if it is not heard or understood; for instance, if you didn't speak English or were deaf or dumb. Freedom of speech is better defined as communicating. Communication by definition includes more than one person. In order for one to understand, one must receive. This extends the spirit of the First Amendment to signify that one has a right to receive information, concomitant with the right to disseminate information. If the means of communication are abridged, then the rights of Americans are repressed to receive this contrasting theory or opinion.

My second concern is the wasteful spending of our resources without accountability to taxpayers. The challenge pitted against Los Angeles County has dangerous implications. The fact that my own findings tell me there is some other killer or killers still on the loose causes me some trepidation as well. No one in either trial wants to take responsibility. This information is widely transmitted, and I know, for a fact, people in pivotal positions and in the media have been convinced of my findings but refuse to come forward. To deny the truth and remain silent in the face of a gross injustice belittles the respect that hard-working, honest people have towards American ideals.

There is another issue. The pundits and talking heads have enhanced their persona by denigrating the social order in the African American community. Now comes a Black physician who knows what he is talking about, like a sword to slay the dragon. Who am I to confront the *status quo* and prevailing authorities? What is it worth? What is the end point? Why get involved? White people are not going to change, Black people can't change.

A significant part of the time, I wanted to concentrate solely on the medical evidence, but this in itself does not excite anyone to look at the real issues. Black people seem resigned to the opinion that White Americans have distorted perceptions regarding how they saw the case unfold and how Blacks perceived it. Whites, at the same time, have been immovable about their beliefs, and are ill at ease when pressed to look at the probable conclusions.

There are no significant challenges to the two-assailant theory, and the tactics used to counter these allegations are to ignore and suppress them. Is it coincidental that all media outlets would not show this presentation, or are they so universally convinced of

Simpson's involvement that they would rather lynch him than give him a fair hearing?

Have we reached a point in civilization where the senses we genetically inherit and have in common with each other are no longer relied upon for social progress and survival? If nothing else, I hope you may be shaken enough to awaken to factors which mold your mind-set. You must constantly do reality checks and guard against ambiguity, confusion and apathy.

America's indulgence is in conspiratorial theories. The end-points, which constantly change, tend to be viewed as inconsequential. These conspiracy theories take on a historical perspective and then become fable. Now we have the O.J./D.A. conspiracy, an example more meaningful because it is about as close as we have come to solving any of the conspiracy enigmas—that are so endemic.

Unjustifiable perceptions have eroded into the prospect for meaningful dialogue and relationships. The dilemma is how to undo what has been done. Step off the treadmill of homage to an unattainable solution and consider how to bring forth a realistic explanation. The trick is how to maintain credibility while confronting the disquieting tone of mob mentality.

Will the media gracefully broach the true nature of events or will it continue to sustain its momentum on the fears and ignorance of public hysteria? Will its mystique wear off, leaving the Emperor with no clothes? I cannot remember a time when public opinion was so patently patronizing and self-aggrandizing without basis.

A similar phenomena occurred during the anti-Vietnam war movement. We marched off to war, feeling it our patriotic duty, until people started to wonder if patriotism was the impetus behind support for a war most inductees were not sophisticated enough to consider what the fight was about. Although the immediate implications of the O.J. trial are not as glaring, it is what makes it all the more pernicious.

How often does one lying to you prove beneficial? That is a

distinct possibility in this case. How long must we wait before someone shows the courage to engage this topic in a public forum? All the mighty and powerful forces of social organization and media are being evasive and it looks worse in world opinion. The charade continues to play to standing room only at a premium, and the resolution is at best anticlimactic.

It has been several years since we began this work, and the resolve is as strong as it has ever been to expose this fraud for what it is. The preoccupation is finding a way to compel the media to confront this publicly, and to answer why the charade was perpetrated, knowing full well the more credible theories cannot be reconciled with the prevailing views.

Some people have said it may take twenty years before the media would ever embrace this information. Just like Muhammad Ali, the pendulum has swung back to him from being "persona non grata" during the Vietnam era. Muhammad showed the courage to refuse to fight in a war that he did not believe in, which foreshadowed the anti-war movement. More recently, and methodically pandered to, it trivialized the toll on American lives and the lives of other people around the world. Now, at the turn of the millennium, Ali is the public's hero and is celebrated for his greatness in the ring and statesmanship, without changing a beat.

Because the media has a one face presentation of O.J. Simpson, it makes you acutely aware that a balance would strike to the heart of virtues of our great society. Suddenly, an unbiased approach becomes irrelevant. Talk show hosts giving these facts scant recognition, appear to have an uneasiness when discussing the nuances of these accusations, appearing more petrified than impervious.

The real mystery is why (they all) subscribe to an illusion. Does one ever tire of being phony? Does the chronic liar ever measure his worth to society? Is there a sentiment that propels one to steal and hoard in the face of abundance? What kind of examples are being set and are they stable enough to sustain the hoax? All the energy wasted with the hope that all these accusations will fade and save face.

If indeed this case was false at its inception, then all the evidence put forth must be reconsidered, and validated or disposed of. The FBI, through Interpol, identified that the bloody footprints were allegedly produced by Bruno Magli's. The District Attorney's office was aware of this, but they, for some rational motive, chose not to pursue the connection of the footprints. Bruno Magli footprints are more probable than irrefutable physical evidence. Perhaps it would have been more meaningful if O.J. was found to own a pair of Bruno Magli's, and demonstrated that his Bruno Magli's caused the footprints. This would have given more credibility to their photos. Furthermore, the Justice Department should have launched an independent investigation if any evidence showed inter-agency collusion, evidence tampering or FBI involvement.

First Amendment rights issues arose again for Americans guaranteed an opportunity to examine the facts of the case, particularly since tax dollars underwrote the investigation. If the general public finds this subject intriguing, then why avoid it? The discussion should be open for the sake of racial understanding and harmony. It is a disgrace that media moguls worked in concert to deceive the public, but more distressing that all people were nearly fooled.

Race has been a subterfuge throughout the trials and media presentation. Yet during the civil trial, you were constantly reminded that race was not an issue. Racism says, the Black man and White woman are a no-no, the great American taboo. Racism says, Whites trust police while all others distrust the police. Racism says, an all-White jury is a symbol of domination. Racism says, one group may revel in another group's pain. Paranoid imagination says guilty. Hysteria supervenes and the end result is cataclysmic—a quiet riot.

Every improbability is unconsciously made to fit, until you run out of explanations, then you realize you have a menagerie of inconsistencies with no reasonable deduction.

In the autopsy reports of Nicole Simpson and Ronald Goldman lie dark secrets. Secrets that strike a sinister chord through the Los Angeles County Coroner's office to the "Dream Team." The question I have never been able to answer is, why would the D.A. concoct a bogus prosecution? What is apparent from the autopsy reports is that these crimes could not have been committed as they were detailed in the trials. What becomes obvious after thoroughly examining the autopsy reports is that there had to be more than one perpetrator, and not only that, the main killer was left-handed. Furthermore, they used two distinguishably different knives. The question is how could all the investigators miss this point or why did they choose not to divulge it? It suspiciously appears that the Medical Examiner and the District Attorney were both acutely aware that two knives were used. Irwin Golden, M.D., the Los Angeles County Deputy Medical Examiner who performed the autopsies on Nicole Brown Simpson and Ronald Goldman, suggested at the preliminary hearing that two knives were involved in the murders.

I don't know if the "Dream Team" went fast asleep on this point, but to a conspiracy theorist, a plot would seem to have hatched during the pretrial testimony of the Medical Examiner.

Dr. Golden, peculiarly and inexplicably, did not testify in the criminal nor civil trial. It is supremely extraordinary for a doctor, who renders service or performs the work, not to testify for himself at trial. I have never seen this done in my experience of over 20 years in the practice of medicine. Furthermore, Dr. Cyril Wecht, one of the most esteemed forensic pathologists in the world, and a media consultant during the criminal phase of the Simpson trial, declared it unheard of.

Now if you take into account what took place and was said at the preliminary hearing, it may raise hairs on the back of your neck. Taking a look at a synopsis of the courtroom transcripts taken during Dr. Golden's testimony, you will realize what is unspoken, speaks volumes louder than what was said. Here is an example of what I mean:

EXCERPT OF THE PRELIMINARY HEARING TRANSCRIPT

TITLE: THE PEOPLE OF THE STATE OF CALIFORNIA, PLAINTIFF VS. ORENTHAL JAMES SIMPSON, DEFENDANT.

TOPIC: OFFICIAL TRANSCRIPT, PRELIMINARY HEARING.

DOCKET #:   BA097211.

VENUE: MUNICIPAL COURT LOS ANGELES COUNTY DEPARTMENT 105.

YEAR: FRIDAY, JULY 8, 1994 1:30 P.M.

JUDGE: HON. KATHLEEN KENNEDY-POWELL.

APPEARANCES: FOR THE PLAINTIFF: MARCIA CLARK, WILLIAM HODGMAN, DEPUTIES DISTRICT ATTORNEY. FOR THE DEFENDANT: ROBERT SHAPIRO, GERALD UELMEN, PRIVATELY RETAINED COUNSEL.

TEXT:
IRWIN L. GOLDEN, M.D. HAVING BEEN PREVIOUSLY
DULY SWORN, RESUMED THE STAND, WAS EXAMINED
AND TESTIFIED FURTHER AS FOLLOWS:

Robert Shapiro: Dr. Golden, would you say that one of the most
important roles of your job as Deputy Medical
Examiner is to ascertain the time of death in a
homicide?

Dr. Golden: I would say to help determine a range of the time
of death.

Robert Shapiro: Are there other officials who work with you in
forming those conclusions as part of the investigation?

Dr. Golden: Yeah, the Deputy Medical Coroner,
the Coroner Investigator, and the fire department.

Robert Shapiro: And those people have filed reports, that are
included as part of the official autopsy protocol?

Dr. Golden: Yes, that is correct.

Robert Shapiro: In reviewing those reports, what time was Nicole
Brown Simpson pronounced dead by the Los
Angeles Fire Department Engine Squad 19?

DA Hodgman: Objection, your Honor. Calls for hearsay.

Judge Powell: Sustained.

Robert Shapiro: Your Honor, may I be heard on that? This is an official report from the Los Angeles Fire Department and part of the autopsy protocol. It is not hearsay, although State Law permits hearsay to be introduced at pretrial.

DA Hodgman: Your Honor, if I may, first of all, the People have elicited no opinion with regard to time of death, nor do we intend to. We have an independent factual basis for that. *(The time the dog started to howl).* There is no foundation; it is complete hearsay upon hearsay.

Judge Powell: At this point, the objection is sustained.

Robert Shapiro: In forming any conclusion and opinions in this case, did you at all consider the time Nicole Brown Simpson was pronounced dead?

DA Hodgman: Objection, your Honor. The question lacks foundation and is ambiguous.

Judge Powell: Sustained.

Robert Shapiro: Have you made an estimate in your official reports as to the time of death of Nicole Brown Simpson?

DA Hodgman: Objection, your Honor.

Judge Powell: Sustained.

Robert Shapiro: Would you say that it is proper procedure if a decedent was found at about 10 minutes after midnight, for the Coroner not to arrive on the scene in over 10 hours to perform an evaluation?

DA Hodgman: Objection. Vague and ambiguous as to procedures.

Judge Powell: Do you understand the question, doctor?

Dr. Golden: Yes.

Judge Powell: Okay, then I am going to go ahead and let you answer.

Dr. Golden: Measurements are more accurate the closer to the actual time of death.

Robert Shapiro: Do you have an opinion as to the time of death based on your scientific measurements?

Dr. Golden: Yeah, sometime between 9:00 p.m. and midnight.

Robert Shapiro: Now, is there something in the report that indicates that the Coroner Investigator had information from Juditha Brown, that Nicole Brown Simpson was alive at 11:00 p.m.?

DA Hodgman: I object, your Honor. Counsel is attempting to elicit inadmissible hearsay evidence.

Judge Powell: Objection sustained.

Robert Shapiro: If you had some information as to the time Nicole Brown Simpson last talked to her mother, would that be of benefit to you in estimating the time of death?

Dr. Golden: I used my scientific methods, I did not consider any phone conversation.

Robert Shapiro: Did you see any information about a phone conversation?

Dr. Golden: I heard about it.

Robert Shapiro: Who did you hear it from?

Dr. Golden: I believe I heard it on the news.

Robert Shapiro: Is that before you saw it in your report?

Dr. Golden: Yes.

Robert Shapiro: You mean the news had it before it was in your investigation report on June 13th?

Dr. Golden: I believe the news used the investigator's report.

Robert Shapiro: Are you saying the news read your investigator's report before you did?

Dr. Golden: Ah, no. No, I'm not saying that at all. All I'm saying is that I used scientific measurements and not a phone conversation.

Robert Shapiro: You arrived 10 hours after the fact and you would rather not rely on a mother's statement about their phone conversation?

DA Hodgman: Objection, your Honor. Compounded and ambiguous.

Judge Powell: Sustained.

Robert Shapiro: Doctor, did you or did you not read the official Coroner investigation report stating Nicole Brown Simpson and her mother talked by phone at 11 p.m.?

Dr. Golden: Your Honor, do I have to answer that?

DA Hodgman: Objection, your Honor.

Judge Powell: Sustained.

In retrospect, it appears as early as the preliminary hearing that O.J.'s fate would be cast in stone. Reactions to this interchange run from appalling to hilarious. Moreover, this would signal the beginning of a mass psychological experiment perpetrated on the American public, creating a system of beliefs through subliminal manipulation.

It becomes more exasperating, as cynics attempt to dismiss these events as inconsequential aberrations or nebulous issues in the face of the "mountain of evidence." Yet, with a dose of reality, that "mountain" transforms into a mirage. It then becomes clear that to conceal something, sometimes it's best to place it right out in the open. I will grant you, we have not completely described the elephant in the dark, but at least you have a feel for its trunk.

You may be flabbergasted to learn this exchange in open court took place the afternoon following an in-chamber discussion among O.J.'s lawyers, the D.A., and Judge Kennedy-Powell. Before they came out from behind closed doors, Judge Kennedy-Powell had sealed the certified phone records, and would not allow them to be introduced as evidence. We will come back to this point later, but first we must examine how we came to such divergent conclusions.

Someone once said, "The only thing God cannot change is the past." Yet, in a world where people have come to mistake freedom for apathy, do not confuse the past with "history."

There exists a media link that perpetuates the lie. Is it not obvious what most likely happened, or is it a coincidence that Dr. Golden's opinion did not support the D.A.'s suspicion? When Dr. Golden said two knives were probably used, he was replaced as a star witness by Dr. "Lucky" Lakshmanan. In the face of the probabilities, the D.A. either went on a witch hunt or they conspired to conceal a sinister plot involving the LAPD.

What was their motivation? Racism, to destroy a Black media icon by character assassination and financial ruin, for violating the unwritten code? Would such a large body of civil servants pander to such base emotions or does the truth lie in much darker dwellings? Our elected officials have been appraised of these concerns, so why does our political leadership ignore incriminations of the judicial process? Do they have something to fear? If a White man makes the same accusations that I have asserted, would he be perceived as more credible? Bereft of explanations, are we incapable of making an honest and critical deduction? If people are afraid to investigate, misunderstanding takes application. You cannot assume people will come together without effort to understand each other's position. The axiom, "we agree to disagree," does not apply in every situation. The most profound misinterpretation is that people perceive they are split along some commonalities, and they have security following this approach.

The District Attorney, along with the Los Angeles Police Department, set a case against O.J. for one of the following reasons:

(1) To get a Black man.
(2) To win a high-profile case.
(3) To solve a murder.
(4) To cover-up the real crime and conspiracy.

Which seems more probable? Would the D.A. and the Los Angeles Police Department go so far as to manufacture and plant evidence for any of the above reasons? What else can you believe if the prosecution knew the probability of a two-assailant theory was the most likely, but concluded only one man perpetrated this crime? The focus was solely on O.J. as the only killer, with no other involved, despite all of the medical evidence pointing strongly to a two-assailant theory.

Why would the findings of the pathologist be ignored or denied? To gain the greater chance of conviction against Simpson? Why does the media maintain its bias in reporting when they have been shown evidence to the contrary? Why should L.A. taxpayers sit idly while public funds are squandered in a futile contrived prosecution? Public figures enhance their images, sell commercials, generate billions in commercial media, and millions on book deals and movie deals, at the expense of L.A.'s infra-structure. The dilapidated health care system of L.A. County, along with the deplorable school district, the moribund economy with unemployment rising suffers society, pitting White against Black, the haves against the have-nots, and corporations over children. Demagogues banter race politics as if higher unemployment, higher dropout rates, higher teen pregnancy rates, higher mortality rates and higher AIDS prevalence rates are nothing more than "Race cards."

We cannot progress by sustaining a fallacy. We must be honest with each other and resolve our differences about the results of both trials. Sentiment divides people mostly along cultural experiences. Race remains a dubious factor. The media started conjuring up racial discord, focusing on Black male versus White female relationships, domestic violence sentiment, Black versus White sentiment, Black woman versus White woman sentiment and so on. The media also conjured up images of the Black male persona with various alterations: his egocentrism, his capriciousness, money and fame, all leading to Black rage.

Never did the media report that my analysis, recorded in a "Friend of the Court" brief, was served on Judge Fujisaki during the civil trial. This Amicus Curiae Brief, with my medical opinion that two assailants were involved, was immediately disallowed with hardly enough time to comprehend the contents or implications. If the deductions of our investigation are irrefutable, it raises the question of a misappropriation of government funds in a deliberate and misguided prosecutorial effort.

After the verdicts, the chasm was widened as famed Hollywood prosecutor Vincent Bugliosi alluded in his ignominious statement, "Johnnie Cochran set the civil rights movement back thirty years." To suggest that feelings would heal with time without sorting things out is disingenuous. Injustice, perceived or real, is like the scar from the lash of a bullwhip, a keloidal reminder. The distrust and the lack of faith in a system bent upon sustaining itself in place of searching for the truth remains as a festering ulcer.

Not only do the sympathizers feel victimized, but the victory seems hollow. The sympathizers are the seeds of violence because history and experience tells you that only violence or the threat of violence is a legitimate means to achieve balance; reason is no longer an option.

Is this the desired result or is this a result unanticipated? Should we work to understand the other side's point of view or should we take the risk of the mob and let that be the prevailing

24

influence? The prognosis for this course of negotiation by manipulation and intimidation forecasts impending doom.

One needs to ask one's self, "How could I get so indoctrinated to either perspective that I cannot start to comprehend another intelligent point of view?" "How did I become so easily seduced?" "How has this served me?" "Do we tolerate or compromise?" "Is there any point that we all can stand on in balance?" "Have we degenerated to the point that we are forced to accept the perspective of another without question and go along to get along?"

No understanding heightens our collective neuroses. Hysteria and anxiety are the rule. We can laugh and deride another's suffering as we become consumed with animosity. Most people that have had a negative experience with the legal system are distrustful of it. That is the main reason the trial verdicts rendered were so unacceptable.

A trial is the forum to evaluate all of the evidence. If there is no validation, then there is really no need for a trial. If the police find the evidence, go straight to jail, forget about a trial, no need for a trial in a fascist state.

If we are a free country, predicated on the tenets of democracy, then by all means evaluate all of the evidence openly. In a true democracy, racism, bigotry, fascism and discrimination are impossible. They only exist when democracy is an illusion, totally incompatible by definition, they cannot coexist. So if these conditions exist, a democracy does not. Notwithstanding, in this so-called democracy, a defined "minority" must now supplicate itself to an indignant majority for consideration of injustices and inequality.

It looks like a victory celebration after Super Bowl. The hysteria continues after the kill in a frenzy. So much exuberance and for what? Is a celebration an outward expression of relief from a profound depression? Or is this the manifestation of a deprived psychic orgasm? There has not been any recent outbursts of sentiment of this magnitude since the Lakers' last championship.

Constantly, the media reiterates that the civil trial was not a racial trial but a referendum on justice. Who actually needs to be reminded or convinced of this? Are these hollow words spoken to soothe a tormented subconscious? Is it necessary to reaffirm a conviction that your heart naturally rejects?

Think in this vein or don't think, just accept it. The communal psyche is ill at ease. This is why we see all forms of substance abuse across America and increasing crime rates in urban areas. Even the more affluent suburbs—America's showcase—experience increasing tragedies such as the Columbine massacre, the Alfred Murrah bombing, the Heaven's Gate mass suicide or the Andrea Yates' murder of her five young children.

We are spoon-fed delusions of American grandeur through the control of the airwaves, and remain ignorant of the demoralizing impact a false reality exerts. We have lost understanding on the most mundane issues and the only resolution is through force, coercion and acquiescence. What individuals hold as sacred, the masses disregard as carrion, and vultures await satiety of the jackals.

As America lurches forward and the bile churns in her soft underbelly, every step generates nausea and stagger. Where do we go from here? No brakes, tires bald, out of gas, rolling down the mountain. Why give a damn about fate? From Custer to the Titanic, must we repeat the same mistakes times a thousand? Does understanding take a back seat to expedience?

The conclusions drawn in the Amicus Curiae Brief were faxed to numerous media outlets and the silence was deafening. The conspiracy to ban this information roared like a wild fire. The D.A.'s henchmen in the Coroner's office would do the dirty work to cover the scam of the century, and like the old CIA saying goes, "He who controls the Coroner, controls the city."

Dr. "Lucky" Lakshmanan, the Chief Medical Examiner, did not actually perform the autopsies but he testified in place of Dr. Golden. In other words, he interpreted the results and reports of Dr. Golden as I have. So what does probability dictate? Ignoring the

26

actual probabilities must be done in order to maintain the integrity of the civil trial verdicts.

In post-verdict interviews, jurors said they entertained the idea of two assailants, but they were never presented concrete evidence to support the theory, so they dismissed it. Unbeknownst to them, Judge Fujisaki would not allow the Amicus Curiae to be heard in front of the jury.

Why was it so important for the LAPD, in particular Detective Vannatter, to get a sample of O.J.'s blood before all blood evidence was even collected? Since O.J. had a cut on the back of his finger, the implications were there. DNA tests on O.J.'s blood could have been collected and run after tests were performed on the evidence samples. This would only seem a prudent courtesy. Was O.J. being forthright or just naive when he voluntarily surrendered a blood sample before he was supposedly considered a suspect? Was he being foolish or did he play into a larger plot?

Chapter Two

THE CORONER'S REPORT

After the verdict of the criminal trial yet before the beginning of the civil trial, a patient of mine, who some might describe as a rather seductive piece of "trailer trash," brought me a copy of the autopsy reports of Nicole Brown and Ron Goldman. She mentioned previously she had the reports and bravely implored me to review them.

Well, of course, being a curious physician, I said, "Why not?" She brought the copy of the autopsy reports to my office and I immediately perused them for their authenticity, then settled back to read them. The reports were fascinating, the work was meticulous and the details were full.

I initially looked at Nicole's description. Obviously a beautiful woman, athletic, a Venus on paper, her descriptions came to life. Since her image was already etched into memory by the saturation of media coverage, the measurements were all the more impressive. She was approximately 5 feet 6 inches tall and 130 pounds. Her body was sculptured and there appeared to be breast implant scars. Surprisingly, her body is intact, devoid of any savage stabs. The fatal injuries were her only injuries and they were solely to her neck. Curiously, she had no defense wounds on her entire body, no indication of her having to struggle. The wounds to her neck were principally five: a laceration across her throat, which left her almost decapitated, and interestingly, four deep stab wounds clustered together on the left side of her neck. They appeared to be inflicted with a "buck knife." These stab wounds were described as flat, conforming to the shape of the penetrating knife, leaving holes through the skin of less than an inch long and penetrating about two inches deep.

This tells you the blade was less than an inch wide and at least two inches long or more. As the knife pierced the skin, it made a distinct slit-like hole. Furthermore, this hole was blunt on one side and tapered to a point on the other end, kind of like a little flat triangle or little flat wedge. The characteristics of a hole made by a stab wound from a single-edged knife. The direction the wedges point indicates the direction the sharp edge, not the point, but the cutting edge of the blade is facing: up, down, backward or frontward. Located on the **left** side of Nicole's neck, these puncture wounds were in a space the size of a silver dollar and pointing **backward,** over her left shoulder. With an assailant attacking his victim from behind, these wounds are consistent with being perpetrated by a left-hander. It is the natural left-handed pattern of destruction.

According to Dr. Lucky, who testified for the District Attorney in the criminal trial, a righty stabbed Nicole in the left side of her neck, approaching her from the front. If Nicole was initially attacked from the front by a right-handed individual, to get the proper stab wound orientation a right-hander would have to hold the knife upside down, an unnatural position. Keeping Nicole quiet

29

and restrained, the assailant somehow hit the bull's eye four times. Statistically, this is very silly. They told you that's what happened but they never demonstrated how a right-hander did it.

When I first read through the Coroner's reports, I knew immediately something else did not fit. These obvious findings were never emphasized during the trial and their significance was of great magnitude. I read it again and again, then drew it out. Sometimes it is difficult to transition from two dimensional, a flat sheet of paper to three dimensional, space occupying and real life. One has to reason abstractly to properly orientate superior from anterior and inferior from posterior. It is confusing but not irresolvable.

People have always asked me about the pictures; however, the written report is better than pictures. It is more descriptive from first-hand account and pictures can be fully deceptive. You may see a picture of a beautiful woman and when you meet her she turns out to be a man. So description by measurement and orientation is more dependable.

The path of the laceration extended across Nicole's throat. This slash killed her instantly. It was about 6 inches long, sweeping from right to left, so stated by Dr. Golden in his forensic anatomic description. This wound started superficially as it began its course under the right ear. Then it cut deeply into the vital structures of the neck, lacerating the windpipe, both carotid arteries which supply blood to the brain and her jugular veins. The blade stopped when it slammed into the cervical spine at the back of the throat, just short of cutting into the strap muscle on the left side of her neck.

If you look over your right shoulder and feel the left side of your neck, you will encounter the ropy, left strap muscle. If you place your left index finger on your right ear lobe and then slowly drag it across your Adam's apple, you approximate the stroke of the knife. The force of the sweep cut a gash into the cervical bone, an inch long and a quarter inch deep. The biomechanics of a left-handed individual attacking his victim from the rear is consistent with the described injuries. Numerous doctors have reviewed my analysis and all agree; this description has never been refuted.

The neck is a hollow structure with a wall of muscle on each side and the spine in the back. When you cut through one muscular wall, you hit the windpipe in the center of the neck which is hollow as air passes through it. It does not take much to sever the structures which bind the head to the neck and body.

It is gruesome but it's clinical, and I apologize to anyone who finds this anatomical description offensive. I am sure both victims would want the truth to be told.

Naturally, when you cut anything, you tend to be impeded by the resistance or toughness of the material that you are cutting. Furthermore, you may fatigue and stop before completing the cut. Hence, the natural path of a cut starts on the surface, or superficial, and will terminate deep, if not completed. In other words, the direction of the applied force goes from superficial to deep. Striking a tree with an ax is one example. The ax cuts through the bark (superficial) and ultimately locks in the heart of the tree (deep).

Another example might be when a chef is preparing meat in the kitchen. Sometimes when cutting a large piece of beef or chicken you are unable to make the slice through and through. Your hand fatigues and you stop deep in the flesh of the meat you are cutting which indicates the direction the knife cuts, from surface to deep. Nicole's neck laceration is superficial under her right ear and goes deeper towards her left, implying the knife moved from the right ear to left side of her neck, the natural path for a left-handed attack from the rear.

Dr. "Lucky" Lakshmanan, as Marcia Clark fondly nicknamed him, the Los Angeles County Chief Medical Examiner testified in place of Dr. Golden, the Coroner who actually performed the autopsy. Dr. Lucky described the direction of the knife slashing from left to right just the opposite of what Dr. Golden wrote and I subsequently described. Lucky said it was done by a right-handed assailant approaching from behind.

Dr. Lucky theorized Nicole was initially attacked by a righty from the front, followed by an interruption and fight with Goldman. "O.J." then returned and approached Nicole as she lay face down. From behind her, "O.J." supposedly pulled Nicole's head up by her hair, slashing her throat. Therefore, Nicole had to be approached from two different directions, according to Lucky's imagination.

My opinion in contrast, describes a left-handed attack, which took about two seconds from behind, producing all her injuries. Since the carotids feed blood to the brain, when these arteries were severed, her death was instantaneous. Her blood would forcefully shoot out of these arteries under life-sustaining pressure. You might similarly generate that kind of pressure if you took a water balloon, without tying it closed, and squeezing it forcefully. Imagine the watery mess. This would simulate the blood bath or spray from Nicole, with all due respect for the deceased.

A bruise was also described on the back and right side of Nicole's head. Initially, it went almost undetected or not described in detail. It did not bear much significance to Dr. Golden, the Coroner who performed the autopsies. The pathology of this bruise, furthermore, had marginal clinical significance (it was not the cause of death), although a great deal of controversy was generated by it. It was theorized that she was struck on the back of the head, which may have rendered her unconscious and unable to resist. However, the knife wounds still say lefty. The emphasis on the bruise was a gimmick.

I suspect that when her body dropped because her head was dangling by the vertebral column of her neck, the right side of her head swirled around and smacked the pavement, rendering essentially a peri-mortem bruise.

I am sorry if this makes you sick, queasy or squeamish. That is not my intent. You should comprehend the details and if you are reading this book, I am sure you are intelligent enough to do so.

Most of medicine we know as physicians is common sense. It accounts for only about 10% of all that is conceived of. The body is infinitely wonderful and should never be desecrated, in life or death. The more you know, the more you marvel at its fascination and complexity. The realization of how little is known propels one in a quest for the rudiments of knowledge, for our health's sake and peace of mind.

Considering Ron Goldman's fatal wounds for a moment, wedge-shaped puncture wounds were found on the **right** side of his chest. This is exactly where a lefty with a buck knife would strike his victim attacking from the front. The wedges are pointing up and forward from Goldman's perspective. In other words, the cutting edge of the knife is facing up in the direction a lefty would naturally uppercut and slash.

Goldman suffered over a dozen stab wounds to the **right** side of his face and neck along with a slit throat. Those injuries are consistent with a right-hander attacking from the rear, and consistent with two attackers simultaneously. Nicole and Ron had **mirror image** neck wounds which says again, duh, two attackers, one right and the other left-handed.

The stab wounds to the right side of Goldman's face and neck were not wedge-shaped. Most were ragged, but some wounds on Goldman's neck, face and back are tapered on both ends. These wounds are consistent with a right-hander attacking him from behind with a double-edge or dagger-type knife. This is what Dr. Golden stated at the prelim, "two morphologically different stab wounds," before he was "deep six'd" by the District Attorney. The attack looked like the victims knew their assailants and they were not surprised, but caught off guard. Goldman was restrained by a right-hander from behind as a lefty attacked him face to face.

With two assailants, there was not much time to react, compared to an attack by one assailant attacking two people. Moreover, Goldman's body was beyond the gate in the small courtyard, while

Nicole's body blocked the gate ajar. If Goldman happened upon Nicole's body at the gate opening, as the prosecution theorized, he had to levitate over her corpse and beyond to his final resting place in the courtyard.

A right-hander attacking Nicole, as described in the official version, means he had to clutch the knife upside down, approaching her face to face. Then, thrusting the knife tomahawk style into the left side of her neck while clenching the knife in an unnatural grip, he hit the bull's eye, an area the size of a silver dollar, multiple times. How do you do this? When you stabbed the victim once she would squirm, kick, strike, recoil or drop. How do you approach someone from the front, keep them quiet and hit the bull's eye four times? This is the bullshit you were led to believe, unwittingly mind you, and you swallowed it hook, line and sinker.

Getting interrupted momentarily by Goldman, according to the official mumbo-jumbo, the assailant would later return to Nicole, to finish her off. If this was the case, when going behind her, the attacker would have to flip his knife over to put the sharp edge of the blade against her flesh. After reviewing the autopsy findings, only a buffoon would assume that somehow a "soopa'nigga" could do this.

In contrast, a lefty would naturally leave these types of stab and slash wounds if he approached her from the rear. Clutching the knife in a normal grip, muffling her screams with his right hand over her mouth, he would render her unconscious in a split second. Incidentally, there would not be much contaminating of himself with a bloody mess in this classic style of execution, known from medieval times as the "garrote."

In the face of the more probable two-assailant left-handed theory, a major point that does not make any sense is the fact that O.J. cut the back of his left middle finger. It is crazy to think someone would cut the back of the knuckle that is holding the knife. If you have an accident in the kitchen, you always cut the free hand but never the back of the hand clutching the knife.

Secondly, the gloves had the victims' blood on them, implying the attacker was wearing the gloves. If your gloved left hand is holding the knife, it is preposterous to assume the victims were somehow able to wrest the glove off the hand that was clutching the knife. Lastly, the gloves have no holes in them through which a cut to the back of O.J.'s finger could have been inflicted. But I guess the "good ol' boys" figured this only a minor point. Give him a fair trial, then hang him.

Now, you have been presented two different theories: a right-handed attack versus two attackers, with one left-handed. Which theory is more plausible? Two attackers more readily describe the wounds and proposed angle of attack. Stab wounds and lacerations as mirror images imply two attackers. The attack on the left by a lefty is with a single-edged knife. Attack on the right by a righty has the markings of a dagger, a double-edge knife.

The sequence of events, according to Dr. Lucky, do not support the **lack** of a hematoma (blood bruise) on Nicole's neck. In other words, very little bleeding was noted from her left-sided neck wounds. This suggests they were not inflicted until after Nicole lost blood pressure; thus, they could not have been the first in the sequence of wounds as Dr. Lucky described.

Doctors in clinical practice, experienced doctors, are never miles apart on an obvious routine clinical presentation, only in a medical/legal context when money will change hands. Through the process of clinical investigation, most diagnoses are made through deductive reasoning. There is always a possibility, although infrequent, of a missed diagnosis. With this probability in mind, a physician must make an intelligent and learned judgment which, in general, dictates the course of treatment. This is the essence of the medical arts. You are thrown into situations where life and death are distinct realities. Measurements of uncertainty are a calculated risk. Fortunately, good clinicians tend to be right in their suspicions; notwithstanding, the degree of uncertainty. In other words your intuition, which is your best judgment comparable to a community standard, is the most respectable thing to use when no other alternatives are available. It allows you a foundation if results are adverse.

When you venture from community standards, you expose yourself to the risk of adverse outcomes ethically, medically and legally. The gold standard is based on the most likely scenarios and outcomes. As the adage goes, if you hear hoof beats outside the barn, you should think of horses instead of zebras. Or if it looks like a duck, walks like a duck, and quacks like a duck, it probably is a duck.

One usually doesn't think that a pathologist may be confronted with a differential diagnosis, because we customarily think of his findings as the final word. Sometimes the Coroner is unsure and has to make an educated guess. At times, he has the luxury of talking with other pathologists to help form an opinion. Scientific reasoning includes probabilities of occurrence which attempts to draw a predilection from randomness. It plays the hunches, betting to win. A metaphor of life experience, bringing order out of chaos, to increase the likelihood of events occurring as predicted or desired. For example, two valid options for the treatment of chest pain include (1) sublingual nitroglycerin or (2) penicillin. The appropriate choice must fit the indication to maintain community standard. If a 58 year old man with a two-pack a day smoking habit seeks medical attention, complaining of severe crushing chest pain, shortness of breath and profound weakness, if you give him a shot of penicillin and send him away, he will probably be the quietest guy in church on Saturday. The community standard would be to administer nitroglycerin, before he dies of a massive heart attack.

The justification that the victims were killed by a right-handed attack cannot be sustained by the angle of the knife blade penetrating or lancing the flesh. In order to make this type of laceration by a right-hander approaching his victim from behind, as testified by Dr."Lucky," a "righty" would have to push the knife from right to left across the throat. Any country bumpkin will tell you, it is easier to pull a cow with a rope, than to push a cow with a rope. So why ponder the inconceivable? Since there are no witnesses, deductive reasoning plays heavily.

In clinical practice, as in life, playing your hunches dictates that you have to go with the most likely diagnosis and treatment without knowing the outcome. In forensic pathology, this must be adhered to as well. If the pathologist failed to do this, then he has veered from community standard and the results are predictably adverse. If his choices are irresponsible and blatant, then they have to be considered negligent, and if they are negligent, it is either malpractice and/or malfeasance. If malfeasance is present, there's a strong suspicion cohorts exist; otherwise, what would be the personal motive for Dr. Lucky not to act in concert? Something as basic as this should show mutual corroboration between pathologists and criminal investigators. Doctors must be held to a higher standard in performance, just like certain occupations that have the welfare of peoples' lives at stake; for example, airline pilots vs. cabdrivers or civil engineers vs. piano tuners.

Left-handed sluggers hit home runs over the right field fence as right-handed sluggers hit home runs over the left field fence, just the opposite. This is based on the direction of the force and swing of the bat. The same thing can be said of the laceration made by a lefty versus a righty.

One other aspect of the autopsy reports that seemed to slip through the cracks is that Ron Goldman put up a vicious and valiant fight against his killers. All of his knuckles and fists had massive bruises and abrasions. Furthermore, he had teeth marks on his knuckles. With this much damage to his hands, you know someone's head and face was a bloody pulp. This was a violent life and death struggle. Yet O.J. returned from Chicago without a scratch, other than a small nick on the back of his left middle finger. Dr. Lucky reasoned Goldman hurt his hands striking bushes and stumps trying to get out of the way of O.J.'s knife. He testified O.J.

never received any bruises because Goldman never balled up his fists and only made flailing, sissy-like slaps at O.J.

Well if that's how it all went down, my brother, then I'll be a monkey's uncle.

Chapter Three

E.R. ROTATION

I should probably take time to accord to you why or how I'm considered an expert, in my own mind. In deference to being called obsessed or worse yet a flake, I want to share with you my humble medical background and experience. Some of the greatest lessons I learned came by way of my training at Martin Luther King General Hospital in Watts.

The center of a violent universe, this county hospital is a purgatory for patients and doctors alike. Some even tried to convince me, that when you're in a warm pile of shit and you're cozy, it's best to keep your mouth shut. Well, I wasn't going out like that. I was bound and determined to make an impression, so I would spit fire with the best of them. I take my hat off to the men and women who have and continue to dedicate themselves to serve the deluge of desperate patients.

King General is a major trauma center in Los Angeles, where even the U.S. Army sends its medical corp on a tour of duty for the purposes of encountering the type of injuries one might expect to see on a field of battle.

My first active rotation at King General Hospital during my residency was in the emergency room. I had a taste for excitement and this was the place. It was laid back, everyone dressed down and there was hustle, bustle all the time. It doesn't strike you, the seriousness of the place, until the life or death situation is staring you in the face. Watts was then and still is one of the most underserved areas in the United States. The population is generally below the poverty level, tends to be in poor health, as well as poorly educated, so the acuity level is overwhelming.

Most people that utilize the emergency room find their way there by virtue of their indiscretion. Violence and trauma, which are both commonly drug and alcohol related, represent a preponderance of E.R. patient visits. Some patients can be so obnoxious or unruly, that sometimes you say to yourself, "I can see why this guy wound up here." Then others stop or do not take their medication or have poor clinical follow-up. This is overshadowed by their lifestyles commonly of overeating, the lack of exercise, excessive drinking or smoking, drugs, the lack of understanding or difficulty with transportation. So you see a lot of people in real bad shape, many of whom are in life-threatening crises.

There is a pride which borders on arrogance amongst the E.R. staff and a sureness about oneself fostered by experience and accomplishment. So, I've got my eyes open. I came there with a feeling of confidence and inquisitiveness that I had developed through medical school. Describing the scenario in the King emergency department, putting it mildly borders on incredulous. A lobby full of angry, scared and frustrated patients who look like they were used to being there. Then in the treatment area on the inside, behind the pneumatic doors, the walls are lined with patients

40

spilling out from the treatment rooms into the corridors of the emergency department.

The more intensive and critical cases were placed in the trauma unit or the monitored area. A lot of pathology is seen but life-threatening injuries from stab wounds are very infrequent. There are the occasional stabbing and slash wounds but the majority are not critical. Of course, the majority of violent encounters necessitating an emergency room visit are caused by gunshot wounds. This is a common anecdote in a patient's past medical history when you are treating him for something entirely different, which actually caused him to seek emergency treatment.

What amazed me, although we grew accustomed to it, was the underreporting of tragic events which the people in South Central, and presenting at King General, suffered. I noted times when a dozen or more people would be treated at King General Hospital for gunshot wounds, including children and innocent bystanders, but the *L.A. Times* would not report anything. Although it seems if someone lit a fire cracker at the Santa Monica Pier, that would be considered a breaking news story. I often wonder had the *L.A. Times* reported the number of shootings that occurred in the early eighties, might it have had a positive impact on occurrences in years to come? I know at least people would have been made aware of the developing epidemic.

The Chief Resident who took me under his wing was Dr. Patrick Connell. Pat was a weird brother, but he loved his work and he loved helping people. He had more influence on me than anyone during my Internship and led me through the threshold of confidence as a professional. The guy was truly an "old hippie," which speaks volumes about Blacks. He was a "Dead-head" from Montana and did no less than two tours of duty in Vietnam. He told me he upped his age from sixteen to eighteen with the help of others and enlisted. He was basically your average Black-White guy but you knew you could count on him. He was a sarcastic cynic with a lighthearted sense of humor. We had much in common because we were both raised in predominantly White environments, which affects your personality and is distinguishable from other African Americans that hail from the teeming northern urban areas or the Deep South.

He taught me procedures on how to approach the major blood vessels we call the central circulation, using a large bore needle to start a mainline or central IV. It's a toes-curling procedure requiring you to stick a needle about the size of an ice pick right under the collarbone deep into the chest. This is commonly done with or without anesthesia. It is fraught with hazard but in competent hands is quickly facilitated. However, if you are careless or the needle hits an inappropriate mark by accident, the patient may start to hemorrhage internally or his lung may collapse, as I suspect happened to Ronald Goldman. Respiratory failure ensues because breathing is greatly impaired unless the problem is soon recognized. If recognized early, the patient has a chest tube, or just say "hose," surgically placed between his ribs to allow the trapped air to escape from the chest cavity and the collapsed lung to re-expand.

Of course, you can obviate the chance of a lung collapse, which we designate a "pneumothorax," by approaching the major vessels by way of the neck, instead of under the collarbone. The vessels approached are primarily the internal jugular veins. This is done by sticking the ice pick needle into the side of the neck behind the strap muscle, just under the ear and passing it deep into the neck towards the lower edge of the Adam's apple until blood surges into your syringe.

If it is done properly, a magenta color of blood fills the syringe and you mop your brow with your forearm, feeling relieved you are in good position. However, if it is fire engine red, you feel heat roar up your spine and hear sirens in your head. "F*** it!" You hit the artery, stupid.

Arterial bleeds can be disastrous as the blood is under life-giving pressure. If you grab your wrist and squeeze it with all your might, you generate the kind of pressure your arteries are under, so figure how far the blood would squirt if you were to cut one of these tubular vessels. Well fortunately, my teacher was very adroit and he transferred some of his techniques to me. Patients have to be in very serious condition if they need these procedures, but we were swamped with these situations most of the time and became very proficient.

Some patients were so obnoxious you had to wonder if that was what was keeping them alive. You grew more dissociated as time went on but most remained sympathetic, particularly for those simply infirmed or innocent. We had to make light of the volume of trauma to keep our sanity about the severity of the problems we faced. Then there were times like when a patient was brought into the E.R., who had been shot point-blank in the face with a shotgun. The guy's forehead was blown open, but he was still alive. He was placed on a gurney with the head elevated and he was deep breathing and hyperventilating. Part of his frontal lobes were gone along with the front of his skull.

The attending physician laid 4X4 gauze over the remainder of his exposed brain and poured saline water over them. Of course being naive and an inquisitive Intern, I asked why was that done? The attending physician said stoically, "That's all that can be done." My first experience with the senseless finality of violence. Now it is starting to take on meaning. I was amazed that the guy was still breathing and lived for about 45 minutes in this condition. Life does not want to leave a man's body. It gave me such a feeling of helplessness.

The residents in the emergency room describe themselves as members of the King General Knife and Gun Club, another example of how you have to make light of things to deal with the sea of trauma. Not a shift would hardly pass without a major and incredible incident, but the one that sticks with me most was on one

Christmas Eve.

A lady was visiting her boyfriend, who had apparently been hospitalized after being shot. She left her kids at her boyfriend's home while she came to visit her boyfriend on the surgical ward. Then came the blare of ambulance sirens, as the call came in that a child was down from a gunshot wound. She was rushed into the trauma suite. Dr. Connell and I were there waiting for the child with the rest of the emergency room team. The paramedics flung her lifeless body onto the emergency room gurney and we all went to work. I intubated her by taking an airway tube, a foot-long tube about the size of a small water hose, passing it down her throat into her windpipe. CPR was fully underway as I rhythmically squeezed the air bag, pumping air into her lungs. Here everyone sensed the urgency and desperation. The main bore IV's were started and I was relieved of the airway bag by the respiratory therapist.

The child's lips were pale and her eyes were glassy and drying as her head flopped like a rag doll. The child, an eleven year old girl, had been accidentally shot by the boyfriend's son when they happened upon a gun at the boyfriend's home. The bullet wound looked relatively innocuous as it had entered her body on the side of her left shoulder. Sometimes bullets are known to do unpredictable things, and on this occasion, it did. The bullet ricocheted through her body, which meant she possibly suffered uncontrollable internal bleeding and for this reason she was not responding to cardiopulmonary resuscitation.

The most urgent way of determining if hemorrhaging would be to visualize it directly. With twenty minutes of aggressive CPR and no response, Dr. Connell decided to crack the girl's chest open. He grabbed a scalpel and made an incision from the breast plate, between her ribs around to her side, about 6 to 8 inches long towards her back. Immediately, the blood gushed out of her opened chest and I thrust my hand into her body through the gaping incision to find this little girl's heart was not contracting. I grasped her heart in my hand and each time I squeezed her heart, blood would ooze out of the opening in her chest.

By the time you have to open up one's chest to apply intra-thoracic cardiac massage, the chances of survival border on miraculous. Once again, feeling the growth of becoming the consummate professional, I experienced the frustration of hopelessness. All the years of study, lecturing and training were useless. Most situations you are able to accept as the natural process of living and dying but it is never easy to accept the needless loss of a child's life. Here on Christmas Eve I stand with the heart of a child literally in my hand and I think about my kids and Christmas. Christmas in Babylon.

The child later underwent an autopsy and it was found that the small caliber bullet had transected or severed the aorta nearly completely as it exited the left side of the heart, causing instantaneous death. Now, that has stuck with me to this day and it makes me mad to think the *Los Angeles Times* felt the lives of children, like this one, were not newsworthy. It is a sad commentary that such stories received scant reporting. I am sure it would have made an impact on the dangers of hand guns and the level of violence we see today.

Despite the senseless tragedies I regularly saw through residency, I still love the adrenalin rush and the proficient execution of life-saving procedures in the emergency room and I will never forget the lessons I learned from Dr. Connell. Unfortunately, Pat will not read what I am writing about him. He moved to the Bay Area after finishing residency to continue the practice of emergency medicine. He was there when the Loma Prieta earthquake struck the San Francisco Bay Area during the World Series in 1989. That quake was so powerful it caused the collapse of the double-decker Nimitz Freeway onto itself, crushing numerous vehicles and their occupants.

Dr. Connell, on his stomach, crawled through the cement and rebar to help resuscitate and extricate the victims. This was the self-lessness this individual would go to great lengths and demonstrate.

Regrettably, this hero of his profession, succumbed to an asthma attack before he saw fifty—a malady so common that it is mundane. Yet again, another reminder of how infinitely insignificant our knowledge and skills are when death supervenes. Despite my extensive experiences in handling emergencies, and having seen so much pathology that I still dream about it, my training at King General Hospital/Charles Drew University in Watts prepared me well for what was to come.

Chapter Four

THE MAGGOT MAN

On another occasion during my residency, my team was summoned to the emergency room one night when I was on call. The fire department paramedics brought in a man found down, in an abandoned apartment. No history accompanied this patient and he was comatose but breathing with stable vital signs. When we got to the emergency room, we found him in an isolation room and there was a vague detachment which was out of the ordinary for the medical personnel in the E.R. No one moved forward to discuss this patient, although the M.D. working him up was with him in isolation.

As I approached the closed door to isolation, I peered through the window just as the emergency doc came busting out of the room, gasping for air. He was in a paper surgical gown with head dress, gloves, mask and booties. These were extreme measures for the routine hospital admission, but as the blast of pungent odor emitted from the quarantine, I started to understand. Never before had I been so overwhelmed by such stench.

Dr. Chiba pulled his mask down and started presenting what he knew about the patient. The paramedics did not take time to thoroughly evaluate this patient in the field. They just loaded him up in their truck and drove him to King. Dr. Chiba had the onerous task of getting an IV started and blood samples. The guy was so foul-smelling he overwhelmed everyone in the emergency room. Dr. Chiba had volunteered to tackle the dire situation.

I always looked forward to challenges, so this was just another. I had dealt with hard-working guys collapsing from massive "Q" wave heart attacks, with hysterical family members crowding around. Patients profusely bleeding, burn patients writhing in pain, along with those drowning in their own blood were routine cases. Here again, this presenting patient was a new challenge; helping someone who smelled so bad, you could hardly stay in the same room with him and breathe.

His clothes were so filthy there was no use trying to disrobe him. We just put the shears to his clothes and cut him out of them. The zipper on his fly was rusted shut and his feet were grotesquely swollen, with dirty draining sores. By now Dr. Chiba and I had both put on gowns and were working side by side. We would hold our breath for 30-45 seconds or so and then have to leave the quarantine room to take a breather. In order to expedite his care and guard against a cardiopulmonary arrest, we decided to switch off, tag-team style. Dr. Chiba would go in for thirty seconds, hold his breath and prepare the patient to have an IV started. Then it would be my turn. As Dr. Chiba tagged off, I would go in and scrub some of the dirt off his arms so that the skin site would be clean enough to penetrate the skin with an IV needle. I would put my 40-60 seconds in and switch off again. Finally, we got a good IV started and next it was time to place a Foley catheter into his urinary bladder.

We cut away the zipper and slid his pants down. To our horror and utter disgust, you could not find the patient's genitals. They were completely obliterated by maggots. It was heinous, nauseating beyond imagination. The sight was worse than the stench. The guy had literally thousands of maggots covering his groin. I had never dealt with an infestation of maggots, nor had anyone else on duty that night. I knew this patient would be coming to my service, so I would have to figure something out quick.

I had never come across in a medical text how to deal with a human maggot infestation, so I awoke my attending physician at home, and the infectious disease specialist on call. They could offer no suggestion at three in the morning, so I'm on my own. I figured a lot of water would be key and I knew of an oversized bathtub on Ward 4-C. We had to transport the patient from the emergency room to the fourth floor by elevator and then down a long hall about a city block long. I don't remember much about the elevator ride, probably because I used transcendental meditation to make it. I recall the stench lingering and wafting down the hospital corridor so that you could recognize it one hundred yards away.

Anyway, with two brave Interns and a couple of dedicated nurses, we got the guy to the bathtub. We started the water running full force and dumped about a gallon of Betadine, alcohol and antiseptic soap in the hundred gallon tub. As we lowered his body into the water, immediately we could breathe easier.

Suddenly, maggots started jumping out of the water all over the place. I swear I never believed maggots could move as fast as roaches but I was seeing it before my eyes. These slithering grubs were energized by the human flesh and blood, which could actually be seen as a red stripe down their backs. So here we are knocking maggots off ourselves, jumping up and down, doing the splits and the maggot stomp–bedlam in the bathroom. Someone shouted, "Hey, grab the guy," as he started slipping under the bubbles and water while we were momentarily distracted.

As things started to settle down, with no further excitement, we figured it was time to pull him out of the water and get him to his bed. The guy's knee was contracted and sticking out of the water, so we were not able to entirely submerge his leg. As we lifted him out, we suddenly realized that a glob of maggots had swarmed behind his knee, as it was out of the water and provided a safe haven for them. I momentarily reflected on my youth and my mother reminding us to clean behind our ears before we were done bathing. I hated that part of my bath but it meant my entire body was clean and nothing was missed. The maggots behind his knee meant we missed a spot, so we pushed that contracted leg underwater. We finally got him out of the tub, into his bed with IV running and Foley bladder catheter in place.

His vital signs stabilized, everyone took a breather and felt good about a job well executed. Suddenly, I felt nausea in the pit of my stomach and had to take a swig of Maalox. This was one of the few times in my hospital experience that I thought I would vomit. As we all kicked back and relaxed, suddenly a Code Blue alert was sounded over the hospital intercom. The location was Ward 4-C, Room 11, Bed 2. This was John Doe. What the hell could have gone wrong? Nothing in his labs nor his X-rays suggested anything life-threatening. We rushed to his bedside and went to work on John Doe for a good 45 minutes, to no avail. How frustrating to go through all this madness for three to four hours to have it all blow-up in our faces. We all had felt good about a job well done up to this point.

Before the next shift came on in the morning, our night on call in hell went for naught. "John Does" always got necropsies if they died and this time was no different. I reported during the following shift to the hospital morgue along with the pathologist and the pathology tech. I donned my surgical scrubs and gloves, and went about getting my hands bloody. I can remember reaching in through an incision into the decedent's body and grasping a cold mottled slippery organ. I would watch the electrical saw grind through the skull—opening it up like a coconut—exposing the brain. There were no obvious lesions to gross inspection. We would sign off on this case as a cardiopulmonary arrest due to an acute malignant arrhythmia. This would bother me that a scientific basis for the cause of death commonly would have to be surmised. The volume of work rendered it nearly impossible to explore all cases, in depth; we were inundated with pathology.

I spoke with my dad, Dr. Thomas Johnson, a retired general practitioner and clinical instructor with a well-established practice on the "Northside" of Minneapolis. A veteran of World War II, he would regularly impart his common sense, philosophical insight to me. He suggested that if you alter the milieu of a fragile individual abruptly, it may lead to adverse outcomes. In other words, the abrupt shock of the bath and vigorous cleansing was too much for this poor soul to take in his condition, and these events became moribund.

My department chief, Dr. Ulmer at King Hospital, would not allow us to sign a death certificate "Cardiopulmonary Arrest." He expected us to go the full nine yards with clinical insight in making intelligent, professional deductions. Notwithstanding, being very aggressive about ordering and attending autopsies as a medical resident, I always kept the decedent in the highest revere, never showing any disrespect for the dead.

All across the United States, you will find thousands of people in relatively the same condition as this John Doe. They may not be infested with maggots but their living conditions are commonly deplorable. Many suffer from chronic dementias and psychoses, dropping through the safety nets of our health, welfare and social services.

They are routinely homeless and when illness supervenes, they are commonly picked up in the street by paramedics and rushed into county hospital settings. There you may find one comatose in the emergency room, placed on a ventilator, and given life-support measures in an effort to reverse their critical condition.

51

These people usually wind up in intensive care and may have a hospital stay suffering from pneumonia, meningitis, intracranial bleeding or life-threatening abdominal conditions. They can very easily wind up in the hospital for a month or two with hospital bills exceeding a quarter million dollars then certified by the County Department of Social Services so that their hospital bills will be paid.

Now I ask you, what could you have done with over $200,000 for the same human being if you tried to reach him before he got in his present physical state? No one seems to realize investing in people is a good investment. They would rather invest in money for money's sake. But before money can be invested, it has to be labored for. Money is a representation of labor, and labor or a man's work effort in its pure form should be for the improvement of the conditions of mankind. The alchemist, or economist, has turned this into the principle of "Money begets money." It is a blight on western civilization to see homeless in the shadows of opulence, to have poverty juxtaposed against unfathomable wealth. The old tired "Preamble to the Constitution" talks about promoting the general welfare. Whatever happened to its substance?

Chapter Five

EGOS AND DISCIPLINE

My brother, Tommy, was instrumental in the development of our research and investigation. I followed the O.J. trials closely because it held a special fascination for me and I enjoyed analyzing people's reactions to how the trial unfolded. The presumptions of innocence or guilt made good cocktail talk. A fascinating aspect was that it seemed a microcosm of the world with Asians, Blacks, Hispanics and Whites indulging the system of jurisprudence. When I came to terms with my analysis of the autopsy reports, I had a chance to chat with my brother about my perceptions. We talked long-distance regularly about things happening in Minneapolis and things going on in Los Angeles.

I casually spoke about my findings and Tommy had his opinion about evidence presented. He remembered meeting O.J. on a sidewalk outside a club in Minneapolis during the sixties one cold, fall night. It snows in Minnesota in the fall, it does not wait for winter. O.J. was with Mike Berry, a footballer from Minneapolis who was his teammate at USC. The Trojans were in town to play the Minnesota Gophers and O.J. was making the rounds with a hometown hero. Tommy and Mike both played on the same high school team, Minneapolis Central, and Mike was a mentor of my brother's. O.J. was amicable and sociable but what Tommy remembered most, was that O.J. was a scholar athlete, a nice guy and his knowledge of sports was uncanny. Usually, when someone meets a famous athlete, you remember their imposing physical attributes—hands, arms, chest, shoulders, legs and feet. Tommy remembered O.J.'s stride. His footprints were visible in the snow. They showed his toes as he strode pointed inward. Tommy noted O.J. was pigeon-toed and he wondered if the footprints at the crime scene suggested someone pigeon-toed.

When I first started attempting to spread my perspective, I found it extremely difficult to explain the science and convey the abstractness by verbally communicating it. I'm better today but there are key words which elicit a three dimensional appreciation. However, it is still difficult to integrate these concepts when they become excessive. I bounced it off my brother by telephone in Minneapolis and it went over his head. Not that he could not at first conceive of it but there are initially problems with credibility. You get lost in the details because you cannot fathom that so many investigators would miss these conclusions. So, curiosity motivates you to listen intently. When Tommy came out to Los Angeles to visit me, it was then that he realized what I had attempted to convey over the phone and the gravity of these conclusions.

Tommy arrived in town with his theories on O.J.'s footprints and tracks, but as he listened to what I was telling him and I demonstrated my knife technique, he caught on and got very excited. Tommy is a guy who wears his emotions on his sleeve, so he's laughing and cursing, but I remained analytical. I told him I had gone over this—backwards, forwards, up and down, side to side. Since the first time I covered the information, my opinion has remained the same. The probabilities of any other explanation are infinitesimal. I thought to myself, things can't be this easy, there must be something I'm missing. I questioned my reasoning and I shared this with my brother. He suggested that people should be presented a visual conception to grasp these theories more readily. Well, I didn't place much weight on what he was saying because I felt the media would pick it up right away and they would provide the opportunity to present it to the public. No significant media attention ever seemed to develop, I just waited and waited.

How could everyone miss this and I interpret it so clearly? Am I missing something? Is there a conspiracy to deceive the less knowledgeable? I am not a forensic pathologist, but I can read medical reports or refer to textbooks to get a clear understanding; moreover, I have never been able to consider any other approach. I related my insecurities to my brother his last night in Los Angeles. Tommy told me before he left for Minnesota not to worry about my perceptions, they were someone else's worry. "You have no ax to grind but the record needs to be set straight."

I heeded my brother's advice and from that point forward, I never doubted myself. I know this statement seems a bit egocentric but, at this early juncture, most things I carried out as a solo warrior.

I mentioned to Tommy that I had spoken to a lawyer and friend, Bob McNeill, who also happened to be an associate of Simpson's. I went to him because Bob was a frequent commentator during Simpson's criminal trial, appearing on "Geraldo" and the "Today Show."

I had previously spoken with a number of colleagues and friends about my perceptions of the autopsy reports. One Saturday, while cruising down Sunset Blvd. heading out to Pacific Coast Highway, I got a call on my cell from McNeill. Bob and I had worked on a couple of police abuse cases and he needed some follow-up information. I casually mentioned the results of my autopsy analysis of Nicole and Ron. This was after the criminal trial but before the civil trial.

He asked if I wanted to talk with *CBS*, but I deferred, feeling uncomfortable about an immediate interview with the media. Besides, this was no more than a casual conversation. Jokingly, I invoked the attorney/client privilege and anonymity. We chuckled and got on with the next thing. I didn't think anymore about this conversation until the civil trial began heating up. As I followed the first trial closely, I felt more information would come out of the second trial. We didn't have a chance to hear from Mark Fuhrman, O.J., or Faye Resnick. As the trial started unfolding, it was obvious the bias towards the defense took center stage.

Neither during the criminal nor civil trial was the two-assailant theory elaborated. From the beginning, it looked as though O.J.'s lead civil attorney, Robert Baker, lost his direction, particularly when Fujisaki appeared to make prejudicial decisions against the defense. First, Fujisaki refused to enforce the subpoena served on Mark Fuhrman, the chief detective who found the preponderance of evidence used against O.J. Fuhrman perjured himself and took the Fifth to avoid self-incrimination during the criminal trial. Once Fuhrman was excluded as a probable witness, and Nicole's past social habits involving cocaine and fraternizing with drug dealers and hookers would not be permitted, it looked as if these rulings would have a profound impact on Baker's chosen defense.

Thinking to myself, I figured if I truly believed what I had been informally talking about, then I should commit it to writing so that I could convey this to more people. I grabbed the autopsy reports and sat down at my living room desk, sorting through what I considered the dominant wounds and fatal strikes. After three long evenings of diligent study into the early morning, I wrote a synopsis that would better explain the details to others. I took my work to the office Saturday morning and Juanita, my secretary, transcribed it while I saw patients. After a couple of proof reads, she finished towards the early afternoon. I felt proud of our accomplishment and I was so hyped that I couldn't wait to call McNeill again.

I called his office but he was not in, so I tried him at home. His mother-in-law was house sitting for him and listened to the message I left on the answering machine. She returned my call and told me Bob was at an attorney's conference in San Francisco and was staying at the Hilton. She suggested that I try him there. She didn't know the number and she didn't know the work I performed, but sensed the urgency and excitement in my voice. She encouraged me to call him. I called long-distance information and got the number to the San Francisco Hilton. Making the call, I requested to speak with McNeill. The operator patched me through to his room and now it is about 1:30 p.m., Saturday afternoon. I figure I wouldn't have much success catching him there, but surprisingly he answered the phone. I said, "Bob, it's Henry. I don't mean to disturb you, but I wanted to let you know that what I told you a few months ago about reading the autopsy reports on Nicole and Goldman—I analyzed and transcribed my findings." So Bob asked, "Do you really think you got something?" "Judge for yourself," I shot back. Then I began to read my conclusions.

As I read the first few paragraphs he became very excited. "You really have something there," he says. "You have pieced it together." He asked me what I wanted to do with it. I told him, "I don't know. This is why I came to you with it. You're my lawyer and you have been in the media as a commentator." So he asked, "Do you want to make some money with it?" I replied, "I didn't get into this to make money but I guess I could use a few bucks." "Well," he says, "let me think about it." I timidly said to Bob, "I hope O.J. isn't left-handed." Bob replies, "He's not, I just got off the golf course with him." I sighed for a moment, we bid each other adieu and I started to shut down for the day thinking about the beach.

As we were locking up, setting the alarm, the phone began to ring. I rushed to answer it and it's McNeill. Bob says he just got off the phone with O.J. and O.J. wants my information couriered to him immediately. I paused for a moment and suggested we talk on a conference call. McNeill, being in San Francisco at the Hilton was unable to set it up, so I suggested he give me the number and I would make the conference call. He said okay but to never use the number after I called it, which I have not.

I hooked up the conference call and the phone began to ring. I was anxious to see how O.J. would react to my information. The phone continued to ring but nobody answered, so we just hung up. Bob was to return the next day, Sunday, so I told him to give me a call when he got back to Los Angeles. I told him I was headed horseback riding with a couple of buddies and would be in the mountains Sunday afternoon.

We locked up the office and I heard the allure of drums beating in my head, so I took off for Venice Beach. I needed to expand my mind in the wide-open spaces on the edge of the Pacific. I'm geeked-up from the phone call and the fact that McNeill and O.J. were impressed. The sun worshippers were out crowding around the circle of drummers beating their pulsating rhythms. So much energy with water, sun and wind. Muscle guys and bare skin gals, white, red, brown and tattooed. All kinds of people mixing it up like a burrito with everything. The Mexican influence, the African drums, on the edge of the Pacific Rim. Vapor trails crisscrossing the sky and pitbulls on choke chains. Fully energized, I head to my father's house.

It's Saturday evening by now when I arrive at my dad's home in Baldwin Hills. I took my work with me and he got out of his bed in his pajamas and came and sat at the kitchen table to listen. I read it to him and he listened intently. He leaned back in his chair, took off his reading glasses, folded his hands across the top of his bald-head and said, "I don't see any other credible way you could explain these wounds." Of course, my dad being a retired physician, still maintains his love of medicine, is an avid reader and remains very sharp and analytical. He just laughed and said, "Now you're fixing to mess the game up. They don't want to let you in because they are making too much money and you're fixing to spoil it for everybody. They aren't trying to hear this. So what do you plan to do with it?" I said, "I don't know, what do you think?" Pops just started laughing at me again and said, "You're crazy for doing it but you'll go crazy if you don't do it. They're gonna kick your ass but whatever you start you got to see it through to the finish." I said to myself, cool. Just what I wanted, the green light from my dad. The whole thing is tailor-made for me, because I did my homework, I'm a fighter and I don't know how to backdown when I'm right. Besides the criminal trial had convinced me of O.J.'s innocence. The TV stayed on all day in my office and I watched it like a soap opera.

I said, "Here dad, here's your copy of my work." I wanted to spread a couple of copies around, just in case something was to happen, or come up missing, including me. That way the evidence would be protected. Laughing again he said, "I don't want that shit, take it with you. If you want, give a copy to your brother, it don't matter." He obviously thought I was making a bigger deal out of it than what it was.

Sunday, I headed out to Nine Winds Ranch. Nine Winds Ranch is located near Three Points, north of Rattle Snake Canyon at the base of the Pacific Crest Trail, near the San Andreas fault. I get with the fellas, Eddie Bernard and Glynn Turman, a couple of Black cowboys. Glynn owns Nine Winds Ranch, where he and his wife Jo Ann host about 90-100 kids each summer from all ethnic persuasions—Black, White, Asian and Hispanic—at "Camp Giddy-Up," a rodeo camp for kids.

"Giddy-Up" is one of the most positive reactions that developed in L.A., subsequent to the Rodney King-Simi Valley inspired riots. The kids bond together and there are lasting friendships formed. Some of these kids have never had the opportunity nor are they encouraged to meet and interact with kids from other cultures. Did you ever stop to think that a large percentage of adults today have never engaged in meaningful dialogue with someone of a different ethnicity, despite all of us being Americans? This is what makes "Camp Giddy-Up" so special here in segregated Southern California. Lessons are learned by the adults and counselors as well. To get out of the inner-city to the wide-open spaces has a calming effect and opens the mind to new stimuli.

Then exposure to the animals, which are an integral part of American history and development, allows these kids to gain an appreciation of what we all have in common. Our strengths, our weaknesses and how to build on them with the help of others. A good ride in the mountains is exhilarating and has you totally engrossed, so you find it mentally absorbing if not exhausting. All distractions and preoccupations melt away because you must remain entirely focused.

The heat and dust are inescapable, and the horses are always challenging. The fact is, there is always a horse that will test a man's limits and it remains humbling, but more importantly, prudent to yield not to your desires. I discovered this first-hand, being too proud to admit my riding skills did not match my cavalier bravado. As I volunteer my services as camp doctor, I think I enjoy camp more than the kids. The first summer of camp followed the week of the L.A. Riots, the great L.A. barbeque with the blackened skies and sirens, the great fire of the nineties. It was truly the funeral pyre of Latasha Harlins, a twelve year old girl, shot point-blank in the back of the head by an Asian liquor store owner.

No recent event of police brutality, by comparison, ignited the emotional fervor in the ghetto—as the camera in the convenience store rolled on the execution in Hollywood, of this South Central flower. Here another tragic event was treated as callously as cattle going to slaughter. With the media spin, it was possible for real life events to be interpreted with such contrasting views. The judge gave the shooter community service and said let the healing begin—then came Rodney King. Los Angeles burned from the Black neighborhoods in South Central, through the exclusively Hispanic neighborhoods of East L.A. and the Rampart district, in the shadows of the skyscrapers downtown, to the chic Westside. No one knew what to expect.

Now these kids are removed from the hard realities of the inner-city. The campers keep me busy as they suffer from "allergic reactions" due to the lack of electricity, to acute bouts of "home sickness." There are always the occasional bee sting, sunburn and splinters.

I was anxious to climb up in the saddle but the opportunity did not present itself until the last evening. Most of us were pretty well spent, and there was a cowboy riding a green broke stallion, trying to settle him down all day. He asked if I wanted to take over, so I volunteered, "Why not?" I came down off my perch on the bunk room banister over the stables. The scorching sun was sinking down behind the mountains, blazing up the western horizon in a burning red sunset. I figured the horse must have been mellowing out by now, just like me—big mistake. That rank pony had more fire in him than a blow torch. I figured I'd give him his head to see what he's got. He takes off down the hard-packed, dusty dirt road like he was shot out of a cannon. Before you know it, "weez' runnin' outta' road." My hips shift forward as my boots push firmly into the stirrups. My legs are locked straight out in front of me, as I lean back in the saddle and pull back hard on the reins. As the bit shank squeezes down on the horse's tongue, he shakes his head from side to side and runs faster. I shorten my grip on the reins and snatch with all my might. The horse is running full blast now and I'm looking for the brakes. Glynn and Eddie are straddling the corral as they spot me whizzing by, and Glynn spouts, *"Looks like Doc is gonna need a doc!"*

Now we're coming up on the "T" in the road, and in a death-defying act, I yanked the horse's head sharply to the right. The stud loses his balance, trips and flips over in full gallop. Instantly, everything shifted to slow-motion. The pony tumbled over head and shoulders, skyrocketing me off like Superman. I skidded along the hard dirt road just out of the way as that half-ton stallion turned a somersault, crashing down hard on his back. Out of a cloud of dust lifting skyward, the horse stood up and I jumped up just as fast. I dusted the dirt off of me and noticed blood on the ground. I felt too much like a fool to feel any pain, so I'm figuring I must have injured the horse.

I rubbed my hands over his legs and everything seemed okay. That's when I noticed my elbow throbbing. I check it, and sure enough, a nice big bloody gash filled with dirt. I played it off cool though, climbing back in the saddle. The onlookers burst into applause as I pranced back to the stable, having earned my spurs. Surprisingly, the horse is acting tamer now, realizing there's a damn fool on his back and that he'd better be careful.

Now that brush with death gave me a new perspective on my limits. Yet, as I have told Glynn, since he often warned me about what I was doing—"If I can flip a horse running full speed, hanging with the O.J. tip, ain't nuthin' but a thang."

These guys are my diversion from medicine. We bond and kick-it, riding horses, shooting pool and knocking back an occasional JD and Coke. After a hot, dusty beer-drenched Sunday afternoon, we pull the tack off the horses, spray them down with the water hose to cool them down and clean them up. I turn my horse "Blue" loose, watching him run off, lie down and roll around in the dirt. We grab a burger and a cup of coffee before heading back to L.A. on the southbound grapevine.

Riding through the Angeles National Forest on Interstate Five at night is an experience. The traffic is moving 80 miles-per-hour down the mountain, and other than stars, headlights are the only illumination you see for miles. Between the hazards of night driving and the CHP, it makes for a rigorous drive. The traffic thickens as you near the bottom of the mountain and by the time we hit the valley, we're in bumper-to-bumper sixty-mile-per-hour traffic. I arrive home after about 90 minutes and no sooner than I hit the kitchen door, before I knocked the dust off me, the phone starts ringing with McNeill on the other end. He says that he talked with Cathy Randa, O.J.'s secretary, who has arranged for us to meet for lunch.

Chapter Six

BAKER'S LUNCH

Lunch would take place the following Wednesday, at "Shutters on the Beach" in Santa Monica. Tommy was in town from Minneapolis the day of the lunch. I asked him to come with me and meet McNeill and O.J.'s people at the restaurant in Venice.

It was a cool and overcast afternoon as we grabbed a table on the patio. With a basket of bread sticks and a glass of Chardonnay, we looked forward to our quiet meeting. Here we would meet up with Robert and Phillip Baker, and Robert Blasier, O.J.'s civil attorneys. Sammy, my driver, waited in the van near the valets, to chauffeur us back to my office in Hawthorne after the meeting.

Robert Baker, O.J.'s lead attorney, was well-dressed and dapper with a bronze tan. I wondered how he managed the time to get that tan in the winter during O.J.'s trial. Robert Blasier, seemingly the more erudite of the two, was introduced to us by McNeill, and we sat down at different tables. Blasier was more inquisitive about the information I had, before joining his colleagues at their table. Maybe this was his assignment. He asked if I had seen pictures, particularly of O.J.'s hands. I told him that I had not. I was just amazed that my research had brought me so far.

When a doctor wants to express an opinion, it is better that the listener not try and control the flow of information initially, if you don't have the background to ask the right questions. Still in awe and anticipating greater interaction, I just acquiesced to Blasier's lead. Blasier said he would like for me to take a look at some pictures, then he took a copy of my manuscript and left.

We ordered the Chinese chicken salad, drank the wine, Tommy had some orange juice and we departed the beach restaurant, before the clammy ocean air grabbed us. This was the last that I would hear from O.J.'s attorneys until after his appearance on the stand. It was a working lunch for them because Allan Park, the limo driver, was on the stand testifying for the plaintiffs, and the FBI shoeprint expert would follow.

"Look at 'dem shoes," was the phrase that would echo across America. "You know he musta' did it." Damn the DNA, the cutting-edge investigation procedure of the twentieth century. All that lynch party needed in Santa Monica was some doctored-up photos of O.J. from a tabloid, which were said to match some shoeprints at the crime scene.

O.J.'s team had to get busy, and they did not know me nor my reputation. O.J. would soon follow the FBI guy on the stand as a witness of Petrocelli's, Fred Goldman's attorney. O.J.'s testimony lasted about five days. I became restless during the course of his testimony, wondering if his attorneys had studied my manuscript. When O.J. got off the stand, Attorney Blasier phoned to inform me that the legal team thought my document was very impressive but a bit technical. For this reason, he said they forwarded it on to Dr. Michael Baden.

Dr. Baden, the eminent pathologist from New York, testified

for the defense in the criminal trial and would later testify in the civil trial. I was bewildered why the defense would not interview me, if they were impressed by my research but felt my findings were too technical. I started to wonder did that old stereotype credibility issue resurface? Why not let me break it down for them? Tommy said to me, "Those guys don't seem like they got much fight in them. They look like pipe and houseshoes attorneys."

As time progressed, before the testimony of Doctor Baden which was another three weeks away, I became concerned and started to feel uncomfortable with having people aware of the work I had performed and not say anything about it openly. I did not care for my work to be out of my hands and not know how people who had received it, felt about it. Two people were already dead, and since O.J. was the only suspect being tried, I strongly believed someone else (or others) out there knew, or had something to do with the murders. I was uneasy with my work being disseminated and unaware who also may have felt uneasy about it.

I kept in touch with McNeill over the next couple of days to see if he had heard anything from O.J.'s team. I suggested that since we had not heard anything, that we should consider going public. McNeill had appeared on the *"Geraldo Show"* as a commentator and figured he would contact *CNBC*. When he reached the Geraldo crew, I was a bit nervous having my information out in a few hands and no one was making an issue out of it. I figured the sooner it was opened publicly, the sooner I would feel more secure. Bob was leaving for Thanksgiving holiday in Hawaii, but before McNeill left, he placed a conference call to the producers of Geraldo Rivera, explaining to them what we had.

McNeill's contact there said that she thought Geraldo would definitely be interested. McNeill suggested there may be a fee involved. She informed us that Geraldo would make that decision, and since he was on vacation, nothing could be confirmed. As I listened in on the conference call, Bob talked with this lady but I never said anything until McNeill asked if I wanted to leave my number. I said that they should contact him. We bid each other a nice Thanksgiving and hung up.

Bob went on to Hawaii and my paranoid/anxiety score went up a notch. I'm figuring more people will be aware of my theories and I wouldn't know who they were. I anticipated Bob's return from Hawaii over the long weekend but when I called his office Monday they told me he would be gone for ten days. At this point, I'm saying, "Aw shit!" I don't care when he's coming back, it's safer to be in the open, so I advanced the first press release:

NEWS RELEASE NO 1:   DECEMBER 2, 1996

AFTER CAREFUL REVIEW OF THE AUTOPSY REPORTS ON NICOLE BROWN-SIMPSON AND RONALD GOLDMAN, IT IS MY MEDICAL OPINION TWO PERPETRATORS (ONE LEFT-HANDED AND THE OTHER RIGHT-HANDED) COMMITTED THESE MURDERS. FURTHERMORE, TWO DISTINCT MUR-DER WEAPONS WERE USED. THE LEFT-HANDED ASSAILANT VICIOUSLY ATTACKED AND KILLED NICOLE BROWN-SIMPSON. THEREAFTER, HE TURNED TO HELP HIS ACCOMPLICE BY INFLICTING THE MORTAL WOUNDS ON RONALD GOLDMAN WHO FOUGHT DESPERATELY. THE DEATHS WERE PROBABLY FACILITATED BY THE FAMILIARITY OF THE VICTIMS WITH THEIR ATTACKERS.

THESE CONCLUSIONS ARE SUPPORTED BY THE DETAILED ANALYSES PERFORMED BY THE LOS ANGE-LES COUNTY DEPARTMENT OF THE CORONER. THE EVI-DENCE OF INJURIES SHOULD BE REVISITED TO ILLUMI-NATE WHAT HAS BEEN OVERSHADOWED. AFTER IT IS CONCEPTUALIZED, IT BECOMES OBVIOUS WHAT OCCURRED THAT FATEFUL EVENING.

HENRY S. JOHNSON, M.D., ABIM

Now I'm feeling nervous about attracting attention, as well. This was the first public disclosure released from my office. The defense team was aware of my findings and remained quiet on the issue. It made no difference to me if McNeill had taken it to the plaintiffs, defense or the court. I felt I could not trust any of them unless one of the three would embrace my opinions publicly. I drafted the news release Tuesday afternoon and started faxing it to all the major media outlets.

I got a call from Mike Carrion at *CNN*. We talked briefly, mainly about two questions: Where did I get my information and is O.J. left-handed? I informed him that I received it from a patient of mine and that I didn't believe O.J. was left-handed. That's about all that was discussed during our two minute and uneventful conversation. He deadpanned indifference and hung up the phone. He just let the whole issue die.

That same afternoon, I chatted at length with Pat Harvey, the evening anchor person at *KCAL-TV* in Los Angeles. She returned my call to my surprise and listened attentively as I elaborated. She was intrigued and we talked for about twenty minutes. I read her a portion of my synopsis, and afterward, she was thoroughly impressed. She says, "You have convinced me, now you have to convince the rest." This statement proved prophetically ironic. It is a thrill to see how convincingly easy my opinion is one-on-one, but it proves a formidable, seemingly insurmountable task, to convince "all the rest." She said she would take it to her executive producers and to the *KCAL* reporter covering the civil trial. This is the last conversation we had. Pat suggested I call her gal-pal, Starr Jones, and she gave me Starr's personal numbers. I chose to call her voice mail and left a message, instead.

I continued to work late in my office with two of my compadres, Eddy B. and Larry. Doing my research and chronically short on dollars while doctoring, has got me stretched out with late night hours. None of my friends want me to be left alone at night, so they both got my back. Starr calls late that evening from her car phone. She was hustling around as she was also covering the civil trial.

I told her who I was and that Pat Harvey had given me her numbers to call. I mentioned to her about my work and my meeting with Baker and Blasier. Starr asked if my specialty was in forensics. Before I could answer she blurted out, "Because mine is!" having some mortuary science background and being a prosecutor in New York City. She went on to say that she saw Blasier practically everyday and that she would ask him about what we talked about. Starr suggested I fax all of my work to her and after she reviewed it, she would get back to me. I informed her that I could not forward her my work but I would personally place it in her hand. Starr made it clear that she did not work that way, and that if I wanted her to look at it, to send it to her secretary, and she would arrange to get it to Starr. I told her I would send her a press release. Starr exclaimed, "I don't know if you are a flake, so I am not going to meet with you first."

She was on a speakerphone, so my dawgs could hear. Starr pressed me using her forceful barrister affects of manipulation. I could not get a word in, so I mentally dug in my heels, as she blabbed on and on. I took a piece of paper and inscribed the letters "NO," bold and large, and then held it up as a sign for the fellas to read. They started snickering with astonishment. I did not capitulate to the pressure. As she paused for a breather, I shot back, "I'm fixing to put the mustard on the hot dog." Eddy busted out laughing and I knew it was time to hang up. Other than that indulgence to deflect her assertiveness, I politely informed her that to get in-depth material from me, we had to meet in person. That was the only time we spoke until her going away party several months after the trial, at the posh hilltop home of Fred Calloway in Baldwin Hills.

The party was star-studded with a pantheon of Black celebrities. There were many wonderful, talented actors and artists there to give Starr her send off. On a bittersweet note, here was one that got through the cracks to success. Hollywood shut the gates post-O.J., as more and more talented Black actors and artists would get fewer and fewer opportunities. Chris Rock, while hosting the Emmys, noted the lack of Black faces in the audience. He caught everyone off guard when he said, "It looks like the Million White Man's March."

The March 18, 1996 edition of *People Magazine's* cover page headline read, "Hollywood Blackout"—heralding the industry's exclusion of Blacks. Ironically, a whimsical picture of Marcia Clark was also placed in the corner of this cover page.

Starr was leaving Los Angeles for New York to take on a job with Barbara Walters, and we bumped into each other at the party. As she passed me by, I nonchalantly gave her my business card before anything was said. She read the card and her eyes bugged out. Starr did a double-take, then winked and smiled. We kissed cheeks, she gave me a hug, I looked in her eyes and knew there was nothing she could do.

In retrospect, how could media personalities associated with this trial avail themselves to answer or comment on the issues I raised? First off, the claims being made were coming outside the providence of the courts. This is highly unusual, but not unheard of and certainly not inconsequential. Imagine if the murder weapon turned up. Would it be excluded from the trial and media recognition? Is the Medical Examiner a separate entity from the judicial system? Or must it get manipulated to remain in concert with the official dogma? The fact that the autopsy reports were in the public domain, and a licensed physician had stated publicly conflicting opinions to the expert witnesses, someone had to take notice of this. By the time the civil trial started, any pundits that were perceived as sympathetic towards Simpson, those with a tepid enthusiasm to discuss legal issues during the criminal trial, were banished from camera shot. Why is the maneuver to ignore, and not safeguard our right to freedom of information? Is there no watchdog in the form of the media? When communication is totalitarian, it becomes propaganda. Thinking becomes a relic, as ideas are propagated that you don't need to think about but just remember them.

The second issue that the O.J. antagonist must consider is what to do with a new challenge, a new or hidden theory. If you know the real deal, and your hater position was indefensible, how would you expect to keep that fact unrecognizable? By controlling mass communication and assuming the advocate will be overwhelmed, disinterested and just say "never mind," you grossly underestimate the willpower. If the advocate cannot be dissuaded nor dismissed, then what is the compromise, stall off the public confrontation?

Another variable is public reaction—faith shattering disgust, vindication, or abhorrence. What do you do when the mechanism to orchestrate the oversight of our legal system is involved in obstruction of justice? Public trust is the blood and foundation of our system of government. If it is eroded, the country is like a ship torn away from its mooring. Chances are good for a shipwreck. Purification is an arduous process. The public sometimes finds it too painful to know the depth of the corruption, preferring to pay heavy levies with indifference. These are the tithes paid Caesar, the proverbial "Caesar salad."

The last thing is that no one wants to believe a colored fella. It is ironic that a moratorium has been placed on the supposed purveyors of the truth. It would only serve to refute what was commonly acknowledged, that the "downtown jury" lacked the intelligence to render a just verdict, along with those people that supported the defense verdict in the criminal trial—those who supported justice.

Now comes a physician out of the wilderness, treating everything from trailer trash, the children of sharecroppers, and those desperately seeking green cards. All the expert talking heads with meaningless dialogue on bullshit. Very engrossing and believable but nothing tangible. Now which one of the experts will humble themselves and come down from in front of the cameras to South Central L.A.?

It doesn't make sense, it doesn't compute, it doesn't add up and I don't get it. Here's some jive ass doctor who's game to challenge the government's certified rhetoric. Most Black professionals, lawyers, doctors and Indian chiefs take the position that, "I can't get with this fool because I don't want to get steamrolled with him. I got to protect what I got." Some go so far as to warn me, "Boy, you need to stop meddlin' in White folks' business."

Some of those that have the insight to consider the possibility, and particularly some of you that know and ponder the implication of my opinion, masquerade as if you have never heard of it, or it simply does not exist. How often are you forced to delude yourselves and those around you this way? Is this the heart of your prejudices and insecurity? Force yourself to break out of that inner prison.

Frustrated that nobody seemed to be interested in the story, after waiting forty-eight hours to hear a response, I decided to unleash the second press release. In an attempt to gain more attention, I released it to numerous media concerns along with news shows, talk shows and commentators. The silence grew deafening.

NEWS RELEASE NO 2:   DECEMBER 4, 1996

QUESTION 1: IF YOU SNEAK UP TO A PERSON FROM BEHIND, SLIT THEIR THROAT AND STAB THEM SEVERAL TIMES IN THE **LEFT SIDE** OF THEIR NECK, WHICH HAND WOULD YOU USE?

SEE: AUTOPSY REPORT BROWN-SIMPSON, NICOLE PAGES 5-6 DEPARTMENT OF CORONER RECORD # 94-05136 JUNE 14, 1994 IRWIN L. GOLDEN, M.D., DEPUTY MEDICAL EXAMINER.

QUESTION 2: IF YOU SNEAK AND ATTACK A PERSON FROM BEHIND, SLIT THEIR THROAT AND STAB THEM SEVERAL TIMES IN THE **RIGHT SIDE** OF THEIR NECK, WHICH HAND WOULD YOU USE?

SEE: AUTOPSY REPORT GOLDMAN, RONALD PAGES 3-7 DEPARTMENT OF CORONER RECORD # 94-05135 JUNE 14, 1994 IRWIN L. GOLDEN, M.D., DEPUTY MEDICAL EXAMINER.

HENRY S. JOHNSON, M.D., ABIM

I presented this press release in a rhetorical format, attempting to reach out, after the almost complete avoidance of the issues by the media.

I pondered how is the media going to block the truth from coming to the surface? I was curious to see how long the question would go unanswered. The lack of response was not due to the lack of curiosity. Who would take the first step to investigate my claims or refute what I have stated? The mere mentioning of the doctor, decedent and the autopsy record numbers as a response, was in contrast to the rhetorical questions. I was certain that this would generate interest, but there was nothing. I wondered, did everyone fear the controversy?

People beforehand questioned, how could it happen that a conspiracy could exist in the LAPD to frame Simpson? Now I faxed out what I considered two controversial press releases, with an obvious social significance, to over fifty media outlets and I got no response. *CNN* thought that it was worthy enough to inquire, but not enough to investigate, after realizing that Simpson was not left-handed. Furthermore, one of the local news anchors was very impressed and felt it to be breaking news, but then went silent.

When more than fifty media outlets have a concerted blackout of this information immediately, it is suspiciously implicit that a larger and a much more ominous collusion exists. How was the media able to effect this overnight? It seems there is no independence in reporting and it appears that there exists a clearinghouse for all information which must approve any story or any information released. A police conspiracy seems trivial by comparison. This cannot be pure coincidence. What or who is the media protecting and does a central agency exist that censors what it does not wish the average American to hear or see?

At the very beginning of the murder investigation, everyone felt that there had to be more than one assailant. People hinted, and still do, that O.J. had help. Was it his son Jason or A.C. Cowlings? When those two turned out to have iron-clad alibis, and the D.A. stated that O.J. was the sole suspect, then everybody just went to Disneyland. With the help of the media, people started to believe that O.J. could do this by himself. While in his better days, he was known for his speed, agility and strength; post-demolition pro ball, he's just like any other retired pro who played too long. Moreover, there exists an unspoken belief that Blacks have a subliminal hatred of Whites, and that at first opportunity, Blacks would rebel, attacking their former slave masters with blades.

In American folklore, it is assumed that Blacks want to rape and pillage in revenge for what was done to Black men, women and children by that peculiar institution, which formed the basis of America's economy for over 400 years—slavery. This White folklore is couched in racial hatred which assuages the guilt repressed in the souls of Anglo-Saxons, fostered by stereotype media images. If you maintain a derogatory image of a people, and make others assume that this image is real and destructive, leading to all forms of social ills, then people will believe what they are exposed to through the media. The African American becomes the focus as the root of all American problems. In reality, this is no more than an illusion. It is based in hysteria and paranoia; nevertheless, it is well-calculated.

Black people, in general, could not accept the theory that one man could be responsible for the deaths of those two individuals, and more importantly, Black men, as a rule, do not ordinarily kill women or children. FBI statistics bear this out; however, let me qualify this assertion. Domestic violence does occasionally rear its ugly head in the Black community, and my personal feeling is that if a man should raise his hand to a woman, then an eye for an eye and a tooth for a tooth. In addition, domestic violence tends to be a phenomena attributable predominantly to illiteracy, and sisters, as a rule, won't put up with it. Besides, Black guys are good baby makers, but don't make good baby sitters. A regular brother will get mad as hell, and may even get physical, but will stop short of risking a life sentence for a booty call.

The African legacy has always revered women. More inflammatory than the term "nigger" to a Black man, is the irreverent mentioning of his mother in any sense. The mere slight of one's mother is sure to invoke the wrath of a madman. So historically, the murder of the mother of one's children is so out of character for a Black man that it is practically unfathomable. Usually, when you hear of a Black man killing his woman, it is commonly behind a depressed state related to financial stress and he will shoot her and kill himself. However, in any other instance, if you hear of a Black man who has killed a woman or a child, he usually has a history of bizarre and/or criminal behavior.

The premise that O.J. "snapped" is just as preposterous. Clinically, there is no recognized condition whereby someone just "snaps." Only on the silver screen or stage psychology do you find patients who just "snap." Then to "snap back," as Simpson would have had to do to be nonchalant, chatty and sociable on the plane, is doubly ridiculous. So, let's just avoid the armchair psychology for a moment to determine a motive for the killings. A murderer does not go to McDonald's and eat hamburgers first, as Kato testified they did. Nor would he change from tennis shoes to dress shoes afterwards, and go to do his dirty deeds.

Realizing the difficulty in admitting error or apologizing for mistakes, what other reasons would there be for failing to come to terms with the theory of two assailants? It means that the D.A.'s case starts to unravel from its inception and calls into question the entire strategy of the D.A. and the Los Angeles Police Department. The media, on the other hand, covering for these investigative bodies, are just as threatened by the truth as it seems everyone else is.

Periodically but transiently, I get the creeps; nevertheless, I am committed to see this to the end, no matter. That creepy feeling is reminiscent of days as a child coming home at night from football practice. The shadows cast by the dim streetlights and the dark foreboding trees which lined the streets, along with the dogs barking and howling, gave me the heebie-jeebies and had me on the lookout for the boogeyman. My eyes, arms and feet kept moving to get me hastily and safely home. I dreaded the walk but loved to be with my friends at practice. Despite knowing the boogeyman was out there somewhere, I always felt that I could outrun him and get home safe.

The media, during the civil trial, took a different tack from the criminal trial. In the first trial, if you were watching the trial closely, you know that pundits would commonly interpret the events exactly opposite of how you witnessed them. As the trial wound to a close, you suspected there was evidence-tampering and you rested assured of O.J.'s innocence, or at least reasonable doubt. However, during the civil trial, since cameras were shutoff, pundits did not have to rebut or interpret the events. You did not get two versions, you only got the media's version and the persuasion left you with doubts of what you had witnessed during the criminal trial.

You witnessed the testimony in the criminal trial, a Mickey Mouse "mountain of evidence," as the saying went, in comparison to the civil trial anyway. Post civil trial verdict, through the use of broadcast media, the conscience of the general public was molded into a guilt perspective. By then, you had been lulled to sleep, forgotten your previous views and stopped relying on your intuition.

With the criminal acquittal, African Americans cheered because intuitively most Black people believed O.J. was not guilty, particularly in the face of all the police misconduct exposed during the trial. On the other hand, Blacks felt dejected with the civil trial verdict, feeling in their heart of hearts that justice had been molested. Yet, with the barrage of O.J. jokes turning Simpson into a metaphor symbolizing anything negative in our courts and society, along with the yearning to feel accepted, African Americans gradually started to behave submissive. Abandoning their intuition, they acquiesced to the "belief" in O.J.'s guilt, oblivious to the fact that instinct, intuition or mother wit was relied upon by our ancestors for survival, when it was unlawful in America to teach a slave to read or write. We have come to disregard a gift from the Creator which gave us bearing and the Axis of our sphere of influence.

Mind control by coincidence or by purpose? The media proceeded to do what it tried to accomplish in the first trial. Even though Blacks initially were repulsed by the idea of a Black man killing a woman, the delusion was fostered that a White woman drove this brother insane. So maybe, just maybe, because of the circumstances, he would have or could have done it. They told you that O.J. was everything but a Black man. They promoted the idea that he had deserted the Black community, that he had left his Black wife for a White woman and that he forsook his Black family for his newly inherited White one.

Now, how all of these intimate details of Simpson's life were known is very suspicious, but before June of 1994, everyone who knew of O.J. found the guy charismatic. The moniker "the Juice" and "numero 32" were commonly bantered on the inner-city playgrounds. There was never a suggestion of selling out or being anything other than a famous brother, no matter who he slept with, as long as it was a woman. Good looks, flashy smile, heroics on the football field all made for a legend, the king of Southern California. What man would not envy living in a mansion on the hill with money, cars, pretty women, hitting golf balls all day when not making commercials and movies?

Chapter Seven

MEDIA CENSOR

    The next day, I felt the need to be more provocative as the previous two press releases had been ignored. I felt there must be someone out there willing to engage these theories in a public forum. I decided to address the hands and gloves because they were the crux of the criminal case.

NEWS RELEASE NO 3:   DECEMBER 5, 1996

A DESCRIPTION OF THE HANDS & GLOVE

AS I HAVE PREVIOUSLY ELUCIDATED, THE ASSAILANT THAT KILLED **NICOLE BROWN SIMPSON** AND INFLICTED THE MORTAL WOUNDS TO **RONALD GOLDMAN,** HELD THE KNIFE IN HIS **LEFT HAND.**

O.J. SIMPSON RECEIVED A CUT TO THE BACK OF HIS LEFT HAND. ORDINARILY A SELF-INFLICTED ACCIDENTAL CUT TO YOUR OWN HAND WOULD NOT BE FOUND ON THE BACK OF THE HAND HOLDING THE KNIFE.

RONALD GOLDMAN'S HANDS HAD FINGERNAILS TOO SHORT FOR THE CORONER TO CLIP. HE HAD NUMEROUS BRUISES ON MOST ALL OF HIS KNUCKLES, AS WELL AS TEETH MARKS, SUGGESTING HE PUNCHED SOMEONE HARD IN THE MOUTH.

NICOLE'S BLOOD WAS FOUND ON THE GLOVE. THIS IMPLIES THE ATTACKER WAS WEARING THE GLOVES WHEN HE ASSAULTED HER. COULD SHE POSSIBLY SCRATCH THROUGH THE GLOVE TO MAKE A CUT ON O.J. SIMPSON'S LEFT HAND? HER FINGERNAILS SHOWED NO SIGNS OF A STRUGGLE OR FLESH ACCORDING TO THE CORONER'S REPORT.

HENRY S. JOHNSON, M.D., ABIM

The evidence pointing to O.J. was his blood. The criminalists testified at the preliminary hearing that when they first examined the Bronco, they saw no blood. Six weeks later blood is everywhere. A left-handed attack would make it impossible for O.J. to cut a knuckle on his left hand. If O.J. killed both victims, he had to switched the knife to both hands and kept his victims silent, as well. Logistically, this becomes absurd, and from a forensic point of view, it is downright incompetent to suggest one person could do this. One point where it appeared O.J. fumbled was when the media equivocated on how O.J. cut his knuckle—what a coincidence.

O.J.'s alleged blood drops, the proverbial needle in the haystack, were collected by the rookie criminalist Andrea Mazzola. The rookie Mazzola had never been at any murder scene. In her testimony, she described how she collected blood samples at the crime scene. She stated that with a Q-tip and distilled water she scrubbed the samples from dried blood splattered on the sidewalk. She collected several samples, smeared each on a piece of cotton paper called a "swatch," labeled them with her initials, and placed them in a drying chamber (for 24 hours) at LAPD headquarters. Afterward, the cotton swatch samples were placed in small coin envelopes called "bindles" and sent to Cellmark Labs to test for DNA. Three of those swatches returned positive with O.J.'s DNA.

A funny thing was noted, however, when the world's premier criminologist and super-cop, Dr. Henry Lee, evaluated the collection procedure. Dr. Lee examined the bindle envelopes, cutting them open to look at the insides. He noted water marks on the insides of three bindles. In other words, there was a transfer of liquid, off of the cotton swatches onto the inside of the coin envelopes. Now that's a real head scratcher. How would cotton paper, after staying in a drying chamber for twenty-four hours, still be wet and with all the samples taken, why were only three wet? Yet another twist of fate, the only samples that were still wet were those with O.J.'s DNA. To add even more intrigue, the swatches containing

O.J.'s DNA no longer had Andrea Mazzola's initials written on them. Confounded, Dr. Lee was asked by Simpson's attorney Barry Scheck, "How do you explain this?" Dr. Lee replied, "Something wrong!"

Take your mouse ears off for a moment and consider that the drying chamber sat in an open atrium, where at least ninety people paraded through all day. Neither the drying chamber nor the atrium were ever locked. Reasonable doubt says bait and switch. Switch the swatches. No real need to seed the crime scene. To further the mystery, about twenty-five percent of O.J.'s test tube blood was unaccounted for. Now everybody is poker-face, from the Coroner to the LAPD, and the Scientific Investigation Division(SID).

Detective Phil Vannatter, Fuhrman's lead officer, collected the test tubes of O.J.'s blood. Instead of booking O.J.'s blood into evidence right after their interview, Vannatter took the blood with him to O.J.'s Brentwood estate. Vannatter later went to the Coroner's department and obtained samples of Nicole's and Goldman's blood. He had never requested samples of victims' blood from the Coroner on any case he had investigated in the past.

During the criminal trial, Dr. Reiters, the world's foremost expert in micro-composition analysis, would determine that all the blood specimens taken from Rockingham, the Bronco, the socks and the back gate at Bundy, contained the blood preservative EDTA, which is only found in test tubes. That implies, all blood samples taken in the investigation saw the inside of a test tube before they were placed at the scene of the crime.

According to the autopsy findings, Goldman had fingernails too short to clip, suggesting he bit his nails. The reason behind the focus on this issue is because Dr. Warner Spitz, the pathologist who testified for the plaintiffs in the civil case, deduced that the cut on the back of O.J.'s knuckle was made from a fingernail scratch. The question posed is, would a scratch bleed like that? Spitz intimated that despite Goldman's too short to clip fingernails, when an individual is threatened his fingernails would elongate, grow out like claws. This was the sci-fi theory that the "Westside" jury found believable, advanced by Petrocelli's medical expert.

During the course of the criminal trial, on direct examination under questioning by assistant D.A. Brian Kelberg, Dr. Lucky discussed all of Dr. Golden's so-called mistakes. In describing the pathology reports, Dr. Lucky mentioned the word "mistake" over fifty times. This tactic worked to discredit Dr. Golden's suggestion that two knives were used.

Dr. Golden had performed over five thousand autopsies and testified in more than seven hundred cases. He had a reputation in the legal community for being straightforward. Under blistering cross-examination during the preliminary hearing, Golden almost flipped the script given him by the D.A. After he left the stand, Dr. Golden was castigated by the media, made out to appear feebleminded and kicked to the curb by Marcia Clark.

Now enters Dr. Lucky, more hypnotic than a snake charmer. None of Dr. Golden's "myriad of mistakes" affected the actual conclusions of the reports. A national dragnet by the D.A. for a Coroner to refute Dr. Golden's findings proved futile, until Marcia Clark stumbled upon Dr. Lucky, who became the District Attorney's "Chief Medical Flunky."

Details of the nail collection process were discussed. The fingernails are cut with scissors to prevent the nail from springing off by a clipper and getting lost. The nail beds are scraped before the nails are cut. After the Coroner's team realized there were no specimens to be obtained, they ceased trying. The collection bags for nail evidence were never initialed because they were never used. Rather than comment on this as waste conscious, it was derided as a mistake. This is the flavor of how the prosecution's examination of the Medical Examiner was carried out. So much interest on the hands and none on which hand was used.

Nicole Simpson had artificial nails which were described as

perfectly intact and did not show signs of resistance or fight. She had a small cut on one finger on the palm side near the tip, which could be described as the only defensive wound on her body. Ron's hands suggested he was in a violent confrontation. He had multiple cuts and bruises; furthermore, it was rumored he was a martial artist, a Black belt.

Then there are the gloves. None of Simpson's blood was reportedly found on the gloves. Curiously, one glove was left at the site and the other one found at Rockingham. No holes were noted in the gloves. Parenthetically, O.J. stated he cut his finger on broken glass in his hotel room in Chicago. If you adhere to the theory that Simpson cut his finger in the commission of these murders, you must assume the gloves came off some time after the victims were first stabbed. The left glove would have to be pulled off because this is the hand that was cut.

You will notice the plaintiffs in the civil case went entirely away from the Coroner's office to an outside expert, to disassociate themselves away from any remnant of the Coroner's office. They brought in someone that appeared more convincing an actor than either of the two L.A. County Coroners, Dr. Golden and Dr. Lakshmanan. Curiously, Dr. Golden had a greater impression on peoples' memories than Lakshmanan, yet people forget Golden did not testify in the criminal or civil trial.

Since there were all types of rumors flying—"Were they sexually mutilated? Did he have a Colombian neck tie?" and so on, because no pictures were shown—people, with a macabre sort of curiosity, were anxious to hear what the Coroner had to say. Lakshmanan went on the stand and testified for over eight days but no one remembers a thing he said. His presentation was so boring that the commentators knocked him during commercial breaks and Judge Ito, on numerous occasions, implored him to slow down and speak more clearly.

Notwithstanding Ito's admonitions, Lakshmanan, with his distinctive Brahman accent, testified that he was selected to replace Dr. Golden on the witness stand because he could present the information more understandably. Everyone was totally exhausted and disconcerted following his testimony. If the purpose of putting him on the stand was to hide the fact that a thorough analysis would reveal two people were involved in the hit, then the prosecution succeeded in this. Not only did the jury and discerning public miss this fact but the defense allowed it to go unexplored themselves.

Doctors know I am right and it would be foolish to debate, or someone knows something I don't know and refuses to engage me in open discussion. Whichever the reason, it strengthened my resolve. I don't subscribe to any theory other than a two-assailant one and wish people would be honest about this fact.

Why would Lakshmanan go so far as to disagree with the other experts and on what account does he base his reasoning? Peculiarly, why was he testifying in the first place? This was simply queer. Who intimidated this man or coerced him into misleading the public or did he conceive of this all on his own? Will he ultimately be the fall guy when this becomes exposed? For that matter, will we ever hear of him again? As physicians have historically been perceived as bearers of goodwill, forthrightness and dependability, this trial is reminiscent of shades of Dr. Josef Mengele and his vile ethics towards his victims in Nazi Germany.

It remains a defining moment in one's educational career when people come to depend on you for your expertise and your ethic. What can you sell this intangible for? Is this a sign of the transition into the cold calculated business side of medicine and where it has come to over the years? Whenever does it occur in any science that the least probable conclusion takes precedence over the most likely scenario? Certainly not in Las Vegas. I guess everybody is entitled to an opinion but there is nothing to collect if your lotto ticket doesn't win. So don't expect to stand in line to get your money back if you haven't got the numbers.

During the first week that I started disseminating press releases, I became aggressive and put something out on an almost daily basis. I was thinking surely someone would pick this up and run with it. Aside from *CNN* and Pat Harvey, no one showed interest. The next two news releases were more provocative since the straight medical analysis was ignored by everyone. Everyone seemed caught off guard. Could it be that so many intellectuals could miss the obvious? Am I just that good or am I missing something? The media is treating me like "Casper, the Friendly Ghost." They don't see me, they don't hear me.

NEWS RELEASE NO 4:   DECEMBER 6, 1996

THE RECAPITULATION & PRONOUNCEMENT

BASED ON THE CONCLUSIONS I HAVE DRAWN FROM THE AUTOPSY REPORTS OF NICOLE BROWN SIMPSON AND RONALD GOLDMAN, IF O.J. SIMPSON COMMITTED THESE CRIMES HE HAD TO USE HIS LEFT HAND TO KILL NICOLE AND THEN SWITCHED THE KNIFE TO HIS RIGHT HAND TO DO IN GOLDMAN, OR IS IT MORE PROBABLE THAT TWO ATTACKERS WERE INVOLVED?

SOMETIMES IT IS A DIFFICULT TRANSITION, FROM TWO DIMENSION (WRITTEN WORDS) TO THREE DIMENSION (VISUAL CONCEPTION) IN THE ANALYSIS OF THE AUTOPSY FINDINGS BUT I ASSURE YOU THE CONCLUSIONS I REACHED ARE UNDENIABLE.

NOTWITHSTANDING, THE IMPECCABLE CREDENTIALS OF THE PATHOLOGIST, SCIENTISTS, INVESTIGATORS AND JURISTS INVOLVED IN THIS CASE, I DEFY ANYONE TO REFUTE MY DEDUCTIONS. I MYSELF BEING AN AFRICAN AMERICAN PHYSICIAN, BOARD CERTIFIED IN INTERNAL MEDICINE, TRAINED AT KING GENERAL IN SOUTH CENTRAL LOS ANGELES AND HAVING SERVED ON THE BOARD OF DIRECTORS OF CHARLES DREW MEDICAL SCHOOL, ALONG WITH DR. KEN SHINES, DEAN OF U.C.L.A. MEDICAL SCHOOL, DR. LEROY WEEKS, EMERITUS, DR. ROBERT TRANQUATA, DEAN OF U.S.C. MEDICAL SCHOOL AND DR. BENTON BOONE, BOARD CHAIRMAN, CAN ATTEST TO A REWARDING ACADEMIC AND CLINICAL EXPERIENCE WHICH PROVIDED ME THE INSIGHT TO

ARRIVE AT THESE CONCLUSIONS.

HENRY S. JOHNSON, M.D., ABIM.

Adequate attention has been drawn to my findings, but still no one cares to engage me, so I set about to provoke a response by issuing a challenge. I defined my position based on conclusions drawn from the autopsy reports. While analyzing the results, one quickly comes to the point. Common sense tells you they were both grabbed from behind. If not, how do you subdue someone from the front and keep them quiet? I guess you have to use your imagination and qualify your reasoning for it numerous times.

It is difficult to communicate a picture of how the wounds looked according to the pathology reports, but this should not be difficult to see if a doctor routinely reviews pathology reports. Now since two teams of pathologists were involved in the testimony at both trials, I figure if they missed it, no one wants to acknowledge this. Of course, no one dares to respond because doctors would have to agree or look stupid.

When I stated I defy anyone to refute my deductions, I knew they couldn't make chicken salad out of chicken shit, and that's all they had. Simpson paid all that money and I never heard blip. I don't figure Simpson is in a position to say much; besides, I did my work at no charge, so I'm throwing down from all different angles.

After I challenged everyone, I gave a bit of information about my background. I remained ignored and no one solicited my input. Who the hell wants to admit they missed something anyway? The "Dream Team," I assume, felt they could not afford to venture from their game plan for some ill-designed theory that relies on abstract reasoning. No one usually knows how to deal with something coming out of left field. I was sure to be perceived as strange. Why would a licensed professional come forward with such a bizarre assertion, particularly a doctor, who you know is bound to be conservative and not want to get involved at any level and at any rate? Why doesn't he have legal representation?

I have had problems trying to explain my findings by describing space orientation. Imagining puncture wounds or stabs, their shape and their orientation on the body, is perplexing. I have remained observant of how people respond to certain phrases and wording which seems to create images. The key to understanding is the ability to visualize what the wound looks like and appreciating how a weapon would naturally be held as it makes contact with the flesh. I wanted to describe this in the simplest terms without resorting to a thousand words to generate this picture. Finding the easy way is difficult. It is like breaking through a communication barrier. It is further encumbered by the difficulty of maintaining the images in mind's eye, which may lead to frustration, disorientation and ultimately disinterest.

When people cannot retain information and integrate it into their memory, their ego shuts down their ability to process information. The recipient becomes dissuaded. He gives up and doesn't try to comprehend because it is frustrating to realize and push your limits to concentrate. It also handicaps my ability to get my message across because people just don't get it commonly, when you force them to use their imagination. Looking at the shape of the puncture wound and figuring out the orientation of the knife is like looking into a mirror and identifying the position of things as they are reflected from another mirror. It becomes awkward and the more complex, the more confusing.

Now, either this information has to embarrass a few, or they all knew this, both the defense and plaintiffs, but for some obscure reason decided not to expose this. Nevertheless, I continued to put it out there. The abstraction of spacial orientation is unlocked but not so readily by the spoken description. Where did all the scientists, investigators, doctors and lawyers take a detour? When did reasoning turn into crude speculation?

Now, if you see a fax coming across an editorial desk on a doctor's letterhead, making a statement regarding some new and critical revelations about the medical evidence, and then defies all those involved to prove him wrong, why would these attestations fall on deaf ears? Ignoring the truth, whether it is obvious or obscure, when it has been brought to your attention, means either you are not interested in knowing the truth or you have something to hide.

Why would one not want to know or acknowledge the validity of my claims? Prejudice has a great deal to do with it. Some people want Simpson to be held accountable for this tragedy, in part, because of their angst towards interracial relationships and that a White man was killed. The fact that O.J. is Black had guilt aspersions from the very beginning.

Secondly, to admit that one has overlooked something so fundamental or made a gross error in judgment has to generate anxieties of public humiliation. Is it so improbable that I might be touted as extremely perceptive or is the current attitude to factor a Black man into the defining equation too earth-shattering? Whatever the reason for hiding the truth, I am sure it has something to do with the actual murders.

NEWS RELEASE NO 5:   DECEMBER 11, 1996

I HAVE DELIVERED TO YOU PROOF BASED ON THE AUTOPSY REPORTS OF NICOLE BROWN SIMPSON AND RONALD GOLDMAN, PERFORMED BY THE LOS ANGELES COUNTY DEPARTMENT OF THE CORONER, THAT AT LEAST TWO ATTACKERS TOOK PART IN THE EXECUTION OF THESE TWO INDIVIDUALS AND THE MAIN PERPETRA-TOR WAS LEFT-HANDED. THIS INFORMATION ALL BUT EXONERATES O.J. SIMPSON. I HAVE FAXED THIS INFOR-MATION TO ALL THE MAJOR MEDIA OUTLETS INCLUD-ING RADIO, TELEVISION, NEWSPAPERS ETC., YOU ARE ALL AWARE OF IT. NO ONE HAS ENDEAVORED TO INQUIRE OR MEET THE CHALLENGE. THIS ISSUE WILL NOT FADE AWAY. IT IS PRESENTLY ON THE INTERNET AND RECEIVING A VIGOROUS RESPONSE. I WAGER IT IS THE HOTTEST COMMENTARY ON THE INTERNET; OVER 1000 INQUIRIES IN THE PAST 48 HOURS. WE HAVE ENCOUNTERED SOME VEILED OBSTRUCTION FROM THIS MEDIA OUTLET AS WELL. WHY DOES MASS MEDIA REFUSE TO RECOGNIZE THE STORY? IS THERE AN ORGA-NIZED MOVEMENT TO DENY FIRST AMENDMENT RIGHTS? IF THE MURDER WEAPON WAS DISCOVERED WOULD YOU TREAT IT THE SAME WAY? LET US NOT MAKE MOCKERY OUT OF OUR DEMOCRACY. YOU ARE USING MASS MEDIA AS A DIVISIVE TOOL BETWEEN ETH-NIC GROUPS IN AMERICA. THIS DOES NOTHING TO ENHANCE RACIAL HARMONY AND UNDERSTANDING. BOTH WHITES AND BLACKS ARE TIRED OF THE DIS-TRUST AND THE WIDENING SCHISM BETWEEN FELLOW AMERICANS. IF THIS INFORMATION HELPS TO VINDI-

CATE O.J. SIMPSON IN THE EYES OF WHITE AMERICANS OR HELPS CLEAR UP ANY MISCONCEPTION IN THE HEARTS OF AFRICAN AMERICANS THIS WOULD HAVE HEALING AFFECTS ON THE SHATTERED AMERICAN PSY- CHE. WE ALL HAVE TO LIVE TOGETHER. IT BEHOOVES US TO HAVE GREATER COMPASSION FOR EACH OTHER.

RESPECTFULLY,

HENRY S. JOHNSON, M.D., ABIM.

By now, almost a week had passed since my last attempt at making a media splash. It's obvious that I am purposely being ignored and I figured I'd moderate my efforts because it was not going to be broadcast. Despite the media's unwillingness to expose this material, I figure someone is looking at these media advisories and that it has an impact at some level. Confidently, I advanced my position again and again with no rebuttal, not even an enunciation to the accuracies of my statements. I'm sure in some circles these accusations elicit anxiety, if not downright panic. Once again, it points out the fallacy of the argument that one assailant could have perpetuated these sadistic crimes.

I have long realized the depth and implications of my state- ments and feel that I would experience the wrath of those responsi- ble for obviating this evidence. Still determined, I feel I have come too far to be dissuaded by the pretense of a lack of public interest, the intimidating legal structure, or worse, the perpetrators themselves. To show presence and a conviction to bring understanding to the people remains my objective.

I would go a step further by suggesting O.J. appears exonerated by these conclusions. It's obviously supportive of his claim of innocence. My tactics, which aim to be provocative, are deflected and avoided. You sense there are people in the media aware of these claims and are biting at the bit to analyze them, but remain hobbled, unable to practice their vocation. Some have probably come to experience, for the first time, constraints placed upon everything they were taught to believe in.

I assume it must be discouraging to a few involved, having first-hand knowledge of this media conspiracy to suppress this information. Particularly, when questions are posed of such magnitude, they could be career-threatening, or worse.

"Keep your nose clean. This guy is eccentric and inconsequential. Give him time and he will run up against too much resistance to persevere," is the operative philosophy. If you ignore it, it doesn't exist. What is paramount is to avoid giving it recognition; then it bears no credibility.

Everybody around me figured the Internet was the ticket. A Web page was created and references were made to this subject in the chat rooms. A counter was also put in place to measure the interest level. My son Jesse, a computer whiz kid, monitored the Web page he created but his motivation was for young ladies and his buddies. I did not personally have the expertise or affinity for computer action. The immediate response in the O.J. Simpson debate in computer chat rooms was an immediate dissipation in argument. The antagonists on the Internet were disconcerted and made no attempt to refute anything objectively. The pro-O.J. advocates were suddenly buoyed.

The inquisitiveness was brisk, then suddenly the Web started to flash a warning across my son's computer screen. It stated in part, *"this controversial subject should not be posted in certain chat rooms or bulletin boards. There is a service agreement when you sign on, between the World Wide Web and Earth Link, that the user must adhere to; otherwise, all service will be terminated immediately.*" A veiled threat to impede the spread of the real facts. The ongoing rhetoric both misinforms and engenders strong emotional reactions. The more you scratch the better it feels and the more it itches. Why stop scratching?

I can't place all the blame on my ignorance on the working of the Web; however, the Web has been highly exaggerated in its ability to freely disseminate information. There is no guarantee that this vehicle would catapult this topic into the forefront of breaking news. It reinforces the cognizance that I have for an arduous task of bringing the facts to public awareness. It also points out how fatalistic people are, that things cannot change once impressions evoke a negative emotional reaction. Like the saying goes, "You can't fight city hall."

I am sure, based on the efficiency of their effort to keep this information sequestered, that this is not the first time the media has acted in concert to block important facts from ever being considered in an open forum. Mass media, which is the trustee of the First Amendment rights for Americans, has reduced the Bill of Rights to a weapon to be used exclusively by megalomaniacs and not as a check and balance for citizens against tyranny. It should be at all times a pillar of liberty in a free society. More and more, I start to feel less and less inhibited about making accusations against those I perceive as obstructionists to free communication.

As you watch people squirm and rationalize why this information should be considered irrelevant, you realize how fragile is their self-esteem. In reality it seems more innocuous, never having to face the real issues, just continuing to live a facade. Even a hamster is content on a treadmill; as long as he thinks he is getting somewhere, it occasionally stops, rests, eats and drinks. His confinement is no longer relevant because he is absorbed in his routine, with no desire to consider his predicament.

Now the complexities which exacerbate the agitation and tension between racial groups has remained a fixed element in the score of arguments surrounding O.J. Simpson. Here is a golden opportunity to expunge dissension, yet it can only be effected through a thorough examination of all relevant factors.

We as citizens have the rights and privileges to manage our affairs. There exists a usurpation, an abuse of authority, to our collective disadvantage. It is analogous to Princess Diana's chauffeur-driven car. While traveling at dangerous speeds on a collision course, no one has the controls. Racial harmony becomes a fleeting illusion circumscribed by tolerance, glossed over with a bit of paternalism. Whites and Blacks grow weary of the malcontent and adversity as we grope in the dark for answers. After a point, it becomes easier to acquiesce to the bombastic propaganda, because up to now, there has been no basis on which you could intelligently reason.

The collective consciousness suffers from a panic disorder, basing decisions and social interaction in this framework, a formula for disaster. It leads to the perverse idea that safety can only be achieved through division and domination. People at a glance become faceless. Empathy dries up and now you can justify negative outcomes of social interactions. Due to the perceived incorrigible nature of poor people and dark skin, police brutality can be tacitly accepted as a necessary evil. As indications have it from a skewed perspective, the streets are safer at the expense of this form of corruption. Now passively justified because these are "animals"—less than human—that we are dealing with.

As quiet as it is kept, Black and White Americans have more in common with each other than they like to admit. Culturally, we have shared experiences, the nuances of which have a bonding effect. We have similar physical attributes, we like the same foods, drinks, clothing, music, sports and styles. We basically want the same things as well—a safe environment in which to live and raise our families, a chance to make a good salary and feel secure from outside threats. These commonalties would crystallize if something did not foster antagonism between people. Understanding and accountability will lead to greater compassion. Compassion will guarantee we can achieve our goals, while minimizing dissatisfaction.

American race relations are a stage for the world to see. They act as a bellwether to conflict in the free world. There is a direct correlation between internal hypocrisy and American conflicts around the world. There are people around the world evaluating American style and look to us for direction and influence. So if mixed signals are projected, as we feign democratic ideals, and at the same time demonstrate a covertly oppressive system, then we set a pattern for the developing world to emulate.

We promote this unhealthy development of consciousness in our youth. This is similar to the conditions and protests in the '60s during the civil rights movement and the anti-Vietnam war protests. We seem not to learn from past mistakes and are bound and determined to repeat them. I don't know if it is just me but when I look into peoples' eyes today, I feel a sense of distance and unresponsiveness. People seem detached and immutable. What breeds this is misinformation. It's like a curse has befallen us and will maintain a perilous state of confusion only to climax in disaster. This is one reason to bring forth the truth, that it may in itself nurture a more compassionate future.

Bob McNeill called me from Hawaii and we agreed to talk when he got back to Los Angeles. When he returned he subsequently got busy and we didn't talk for sometime. Now, I truly can't blame him, though. He's really no different from the majority of lawyers and commentators. Everyone agrees with my findings but no one wants to stand behind them. Or everyone prefers to stand apart from them. I interface with quite a few lawyers, doctors and other professionals who are influential in their own right. Everyone ducks these issues. People are curious and very supportive until they get the hard core evidence in their hand. Then they suddenly remember they have prior engagements, commitments—"conflicts of interest" is the operative phrase—they are unable to get involved. A lot of guys, when they realize the gravity, tell me their firms represent county contracts and they can't get involved. One attorney advised me that he would not get involved even with a fifty thousand dollar retainer. So I started trolling for an agent but kept coming topside down.

In the meantime, I'm putting out all these press releases about my theories, waiting to see who or what would grab hold of it and run with it. I feel like I'm giving them all a swift hard kick in the ass and they act like they don't feel a thing.

One morning, I'm lying in bed with my wife waking up to the *"Today Show."* Bryant Gumbel and Katie Couric were probably the least biased pundits I saw as I checked accounts of the trial, surfing different networks by remote. I watched to see what issue would make the news of the day. In the opening segment, Gumbel announced that Dr. Michael Baden, the forensic medical expert for O.J. Simpson, testified he believes two killers were involved in the murders of Nicole Brown Simpson and Ronald Goldman.

I sat straight up in bed. No need for "Starbucks." I was thoroughly awakened. My wife was excited by the news and I thought to myself, finally someone has publicly agreed with what I have been touting. Gumbel even sounded excited.

I remembered O.J.'s attorney Blasier told me he sent my work to Dr. Baden, and I was overjoyed with the fact that a renowned pathologist was boasting my two-assailant theory. It felt like a major breakthrough in this corrupt and illegal trial, I was on cloud nine. Not much came out in the media reporting throughout the day as to why Dr. Baden felt this way, yet no mention was made of the southpaw theory. Dr. Baden never discussed the pattern of tissue damage in his reasoning to suggest a two killer theory, only that he never heard of one guy subduing two people, keeping them quiet at the same time.

The following day, the *L.A. Times* reported that Dr. Baden was made to retreat from his position under a withering cross-examination by Attorney Ed Medvene, Petrocelli's go to man, the mastermind and brains behind the civil case against O.J. Simpson.

Now deflation sets in again. Dr. Baden testified as a highly paid defense witness recruited by Robert Shapiro during the criminal prosecution. During the criminal trial, Dr. Baden's testimony was relatively inert. No mention was ever made of a two-assailant theory, until after he reviewed my material sent to him by Blasier during the civil trial. I will never believe I was the first to realize these findings from the Coroner's report; nonetheless, it never became an issue during the criminal proceedings.

Dr. Henry Lee, despite testifying in both trials, failed to advocate a two-assailant theory until he published his book. Intimidation was palpable during the criminal prosecution, as every stodgy witness and attorney played to the camera. Only until I started to rattle the cage did someone go out front and make the call. All these forensic experts: Dr. Baden, Dr. Spitz, Dr. Golden, Dr. Lakshmanan and Dr. Lee have far more forensic experience than I, nor do I pretend to have the pathology expertise of any of these professionals. Yet, you don't need a doctor to tell you that your nose is bleeding. I'm a bloodhound for simplicity. There is nothing complicated about Dr. Golden's autopsy reports, and I believe what I know.

There's something rotten in Denmark. Why these doctors failed to express in lay terms what is obvious in the autopsy reports beats me; I can only speculate.

I could have demonstrated my conclusions to any officer of the court, from O.J.'s lawyers to Judge Fujisaki. Not one of those doctors can honestly say I am wrong. Furthermore, there was never any mentioning of a left-handed assailant. I'll give all of these super-experts the benefit of the doubt and say they did not recognize this fact. Otherwise, you can bet your last dollar, not one of them will step forward and refute anything I'm saying—not for blood or money.

Rather than focus on the mortal wounds and how they were inflicted, Dr. Baden and Medvene got into a pissing contest about how much blood was spilled on the ground. After two days on the stand, Dr. Baden's testimony went off like a premature ejaculation. Dr. Baden could have put the nail in the coffin of the money-grabbing civil prosecution of O.J.; instead, Medvene twisted him like a pretzel and left the jury thoroughly befuddled.

Nevertheless, for his antics and blustery delivery, Baden was rewarded with his own *HBO* series after the verdict was in. These doctors could have set the record straight, but they either lacked the courage, the ethics, the insight or flat out took the thirty pieces of silver and high-tailed it. I was totally appalled and leery with this blown opportunity. I started to wonder what was up with the new "Dream Team." My wife realized how big of a letdown it was for me and suggested we take time out and go down to Tijuana for a Mexican reprieve.

Chapter Eight

AFFIRMATIVE ACTION IN MEXICO

We take off for a Rosarito Beach condo in Baja California, Mexico—about three hours south of Los Angeles. We make a pit stop, exiting off the San Diego Freeway at Dana Point, home of the Browns'. We've been on the road for about two hours already. I look over at my wife and tell her, "I gotta make water, Ms. Daisy." We water down, gas up and head out for the border. Finally, we arrive at our destination, a charming villa on the playa. The roar of the Pacific, with the tranquil ebbing tides, made the frustration melt away. You can't help but relax. Sipping on a cold beer, I find myself drifting into reflections of successes past. I have a strong affinity for Mexico and its people. Mexico gave me an opportunity that was not afforded me in my own country, the chance to start medical school.

I left Minnesota heading for Mexico in the summer of 1976. I really didn't know what to expect, having heard horror stories of Americans' experiences abroad. The rap from the Association of American Medical Schools and the A.M.A. was that only one out of five who sought education outside the country would ever return to the United States as a physician. I thought to myself, stuff your statistics, I have every plan of returning to the States and I'm all packed up and ready to go.

I make my connection, after leaving Minneapolis, in Chicago. I spent the weekend with my Uncle Arnim and Aunt Mary, who gave me their encouragement, before boarding Mexicana Flight 206 direct to Mexico City. The flight was good with plenty of hot food, fruit, pastries and drinks. The foreign air carrier service made my flight memorable and there was no first class. I made my connection in *Districto Federal* and then on to Tampico, on the Gulf of Mexico. About eight hours south of Brownsville, just below the Tropic of Cancer, Tampico was Mexico's original tourist resort, with the likes of Waldo Pepper flying in and Douglas Fairbanks hanging out. I first discovered Tampico through the want ads in my college newspaper.

The seventies was a time where thousands of Americans were going abroad to medical school. As a matter of fact, the University at Guadalajara was considered the largest "American" medical school in the world, with over 4,000 Americans attending. I did not want a school this big, so I chose UNE-UNAM at Tampico, the National Autonomous University of Mexico. There was a stigma that existed with going to school in Mexico, which I felt was ill-founded. There were many capable students as Mexico's emphasis is on producing doctors, in contrast to that of the U.S. where our system acts to weed people out. Going abroad to unfamiliar surroundings, without any previous knowledge, was a big step for me.

I arrived in Tampico and went to the *Posada Motel,* a quaint, tropical abode in the middle of nowhere. It's June of the bicentennial year and the night is hot and muggy. A Brazilian band played in the night club, with the windows sweating with condensation from the air conditioner, that peered out to a garden patio, surrounding a swimming pool. I left the frigid, smoke-filled bar and went out by the pool for a breather in the warm, humid night.

A gardener tidied up the patio, after putting chemicals in the pool. I spoke in my limited Spanish, figuring if I was to learn the language, I would have to engage everyone often in conversation. Furthermore, I wanted to get a sense of the affability of the people and their political consciousness.

A couple of "Gringos" appeared on the scene in bathing suits—loud, brash, big square bellies, fresh sun-baked skin, with towels draped around their necks. The gardener tells them it's after swimming hours and the pool is closed. The night was warm and a refreshing swim after a day of traveling seemed just what the doctor ordered. These guys were bent on diving into the cool waters of the pool.

The gardener stood aghast when the two guys cracked, "It's okay, we're Americans." I felt embarrassed these clowns were so arrogant. They cannonballed and belly-flopped into the pool before the gardener could tell them, in broken English, he had just put powerful chemicals into the pool. Apparently these guys weren't affected by the chemicals; their tequila-soaked brains could not detect anything. I thought to myself, how could they leave their country and not show any regards for the etiquette of their foreign neighbors? I was bored and tired, and figured I would go to bed.

The morning woke me, the side of my face sweating from the hot sizzling sun beating down on my head, through the motel window. I showered up and dressed, heading for the dining room. Grabbing a cup of coffee, some pastry and melon, I decided I would take a look at the school. I got a taxi and asked the cabbie to take me to University Medical School, but he knew nothing about it. That's peculiar, I thought. How could one not know where the medical school was, the town wasn't that big? I figured what the hell, I arrived late last night and hadn't seen anything, so I didn't mind going for a ride. I hopped in the cab and we drove down the main drag to town. There's just one main road through town and I figured probability has it, the school would be on the main drag.

We boogied ten miles on down the road to the center of town without seeing anything. We ultimately stopped by the main library to see if someone knew something, and soon discovered the school was back in the opposite direction. The problem was there were not many street signs, so when we headed back up the road, we had to feel our way around. Up Avenida Hidalgo, past the Posada Inn and out towards the airport, we approached a "T" in the road intersecting the major highway, defined as such only because it was paved. We veer to the right and the cabbie spotted the school sign, pointing it out to me. A plaque about three feet by five feet, with the letters U.N.E. splashed across it, resting on the ground, leaning against an old dilapidated house. The sight was like a pie in the face. Speechless, I thought, *"Aye-yie-yie-yie-yie,* what have I gotten myself into?" I wanted badly to go to medical school, and I knew I'd be in for an experience, but not the shock of my life.

I remembered one of my main criteria for choosing a school abroad was that the school was recognized by the World Health Organization. Since this criteria had been met, I told myself it couldn't be all bad, so I would roll with it and not panic.

I tell the driver to take me back to the motel. We make a U-turn, drive back past the airport, swerve back onto the main drag, heading for the tropical ambience of the motel. I needed to chill-out and regroup. We pass by some new buildings with construction in-progress. The craftsmanship and artistry in Mexican architecture is very unique and charming. As I admired the archways, stucco, rock and tile, I spotted another sign with the letters UNE. This time, however, the letters were styled in the masonry on the top floor of this new building.

"Hold it!" I shouted to the cabdriver, but he kept going. Then

I thought, how do you say stop in Spanish? *"No mas, no mas."* He slowed down and looked over his shoulder. *"Escuela aqui,"* I said, pointing at the building. The cabbie made an abrupt U-turn in his '56 Chevy, driving across the grassy meridian, heading back up the road. The motel was in sight and walking distance, so I grabbed some dollars out of my pocket and gave him a couple which was plenty. I got out to inspect the school.

The Mexican students were out for summer break, and the thirty-or-so Americans that would attend, had arrived early for pre-med Spanish classes. The main building was completed and the hospital was under construction. I headed up to the second floor to the admissions office and found the reception very warm and friendly. I introduced myself, feeling more at ease; they were expecting me, since I had phoned a couple of days ahead. I met the admission's secretary and she introduced me to the chairman of the school. Afterward, I was taken on a tour.

The classrooms were new stucco, with a scent of fresh mortar, equipped with ceiling fans and large open-air windows. There were thick green vegetation, palm trees, vines and bushes surrounding the school, a clearing carved out of a jungle.

They took me to see the anatomy department in the back of the school, overlooking a steep dense overgrowth in a water runoff. Adjacent to the main classroom was the anatomy vat, a square pool about two feet deep and eight feet wide. It was filled with a murky, inky, glistening liquid. In it was the body of a man floating face up with what appeared to be other body parts submerged or floating, used as specimens for anatomy dissection. Now I'm thinking, I probably won't enjoy anatomy lab very much. I've had my mind blown enough for the day, so I figured I'd head back to the hotel.

I take off, walking down the highway. There's not much traffic, it's hot and humid. A few shabby structures built of tin and plywood dotted the landscape, with weeds, trees and brush along the dusty road. I spotted a flock of buzzards looming overhead and picked up my pace because I didn't know if they sensed I'm on their menu. My eyes were suddenly pulled down towards a pile of sand the rain had washed onto the walkway in my path. Before my foot touched the ground to complete my next step, I just about jumped out of my skin. There was a partially exposed skull of something with real big teeth. I made one of those quick, slick, sideways jukes off the sidewalk into the street. "Geez, what the hell was that?" I thought. Then I could make out the bones of its ribcage drying in the sun. This was the biggest, meanest, most ferocious looking dead dog I have ever seen. That's what the buzzards were snacking on. The Tampico Humane Society with their wings fanning out, flying in a big circle, and it isn't even noon yet.

I get back to the hotel where I see some familiar faces, some White folks. Some other students had arrived a day or two earlier, and were relaxing in the hotel lobby. I'm tired and thirsty from the walk down the desolate highway, so I sack out on a plastic-covered loveseat in the lobby. The plastic was sweating more than me, and stuck to my shirt like flypaper. I immediately sit up and think, this place is going to take some getting used to.

A couple approaches and sits down to start up a conversation with me. It doesn't occur to me that they might be here for the same reason that I'm here because, momentarily, I forgot what I'm in Tampico for. They introduce themselves and ask if I'm a medical student. Now reality sets in again. I say, "Yeah...Yeah, that's right." It all came back to me now. "I just got here and I keep getting my mind blown." They start laughing and Pam, the student from Berkeley, says, "Isn't it great?" Well, it's different. They said they were going to the beach and asked if I wanted to go along. I looked at the slowly whirling ceiling fan, the bellhop talking in Spanish with the concierge girls, the damp Spanish newspapers and magazines on the coffee table, and felt a drop of sweat rolling down the back of my neck. "As long as there ain't no sharks," I replied. She says, "Come on, we were there yesterday and the water's great." I tell them to hold on while I go to my room. I grab my trunks, a towel, and head back to the lobby where I find my new friends and take off for the beach.

Mexico is an intriguing country and the tropical beauty is astounding, but contrasts with the abject poverty. Once you leave the main thoroughfare, you are off to ill-repaired byways, with detours and craters. Some holes are so deep, cars have to come to a dead stop and let one wheel go into the hole at a time. It takes half an hour to drive three miles. We arrive at the warm, and most of the time, pristine Gulf of Mexico. The white, sandy beaches with jungle that comes to the edge was deserted most of the week, so your only company would be the colorful parrots, macaws, monkeys and the ever present schools of dolphins.

We would spend countless monotonous days on the sun-drenched beaches, bored cuckoo between study breaks. It makes you realize how much you take for granted, the small things back at home. You could easily go nuts from the sun and culture shock if you let your mind wander. So you had to get busy and learn to appreciate your surroundings to make the best of it. If you wanted to achieve your goals in the shortest time with the least amount of anxiety, you didn't dwell on what you didn't have—you took advantage of what was in front of you. This required you to stay focused. It was expensive, and fortunately the Feds insured student loans for study abroad which enabled me to go to Mexico. I could ill-afford to blow my stay because a second chance would not be readily available.

Now, having left a highly competitive and academic climate—the University of Minnesota—Mexico became my Affirmative Action. I was a fair student in Minnesota, notwithstanding the anti-war movement and starting an early family, which I had to leave behind to pursue my education. My MCAT admission tests were competitive and I felt I had a pretty good shot at getting into an American medical school because of Affirmative Action. These programs grew out of the riots of the Civil Rights Movement in the sixties, but three strikes (three attempts) and I'm out, that is, out of the U.S.A. This was the year of the bicentennial and I got to celebrate it in Mexico because I figure it would take another bicentennial before Affirmative Action gets me into an American medical school. I figured I would do like the White boys do, like my father advised me three years before, go to Mexico.

Now other Americans are starting to come in and there are about forty Americans in all. Jews, Italians, Germans and Anglos from the East Coast and good ol' boys from the South. I'm the only Black, and guess what, nobody wants to room with me. All the folks coming into the hotel had their set agendas, or so they said, so I was on the outs. Most of the newly arriving medical students maintained a perpetual look of disgust on their faces. Now I'm getting concerned because everyone has moved into their new abodes and the hotel is starting to eat up my allowance.

I had been off exploring the city on my own for the first couple of weeks, while most others did not care to venture out. By now, I'm sure you figured I'm the only Black man in Tampico. More like, probably the only man who knew he was Black. There are a lot of Mexicans that look like we're cousins but they don't seem to comprehend that.

During a break from lecture, I met Howie, a Jewish kid from New York. Howie's from Brooklyn, and he isn't clicking with the other hicks. He's feeling alone and he sees me minding my own business, so he strikes up a conversation. Howie asks if I want to make a beach run. Since I'm frustrated with my attempts at seeking adequate housing, I'm game. Well, it turns out we have the same sense of humor. I tell Howie I'm looking for a place to stay and I'm getting low on money, so he says, "Why don't you move in temporarily with me?" Howie says he's house sitting until the rest of his group arrives from New York and I could stay there until they get there. He's got a big house and he is there by himself, so I could take him up on it. Me and Howie started hanging out and getting to know each other better. By the time the others got in from New York and realized an "N"-man was staying at the house, they wanted nothing to do with the place. So they leave Howie high and dry, and I got a nice house de facto.

By now, all the wholesome gringos are grouped up and that leaves the skags. We wind up with seven misfits as roommates. We occupy a spacious bungalow with an enormous veranda on the second floor. Nestled on a garden acre manicured with a grove of mango, avocado, coconut and banana trees, we somehow make it work. Our motley crew included Bones, an older brother from Halifax, Nova Scotia, two Jews from Brooklyn, two Texas rednecks, a "Nazi" as Howie nick-named him, and myself.

Roy, the "Nazi," a "motor-head," was a gun enthusiast from Connecticut, a blue-blood, ex-Marine from the Nam era. He gave everybody the creeps. Since I was the only one out of the crowd he couldn't intimidate, we became chums as I saw he was having the same problems I did trying to locate some place to stay. I talked Howie into letting Roy move in, and now some of the slack was being taken up by more people and more money.

Now Roy is panicky and overreacts to the slightest provocation. His books are slow coming from the States so I tell him don't worry, I can't read two books at a time and I will share mine. No one wanted to see Roy go off because you didn't know if he was capable of "flashing back," so everyone was glad I could allay his anxiety by loaning him some books. Things start settling down and we are all going to our Spanish classes. We even got a couple of Dobie pups and a kid goat for the home front.

Soon we would face our first med-school exam in Spanish. Everyone was shaky because no one wanted to blow anything. We were caught with a shortage of books before the test, and it just so happened Roy had a copy of notes that I needed, to bone up for the test. I went to ask him to borrow his notes, and when I did, Roy went ballistic. He started yelling and ranting, startling everybody in the house with his tirade. I stood my ground and reminded him how I lent him some texts when his books didn't arrive on time. So he begrudgingly says, "Okay, I'll let you look at my notes, a page at a time. Sit your ass on the floor right next to my desk. When I'm done reviewing each page, I'll pass it down to you."

I figure what the hell, I'll placate him so I can go over the notes. Everyone in the house hears what's going on and they were thoroughly disgusted. I figure the floor is clean and I ain't trippin', I'm just focused on passing the test. I sit down on the floor next to Roy's chair, and he reads and passes a sheet of notes down to me, one at a time.

It's early in the morning, as we are cramming before the test, and one of the pups comes into the room, seeing me sitting on the floor. The cute little frisky pup scampers over to me wagging his tail, and cuddles up close. He was so excited, he started peeing, pissing all over the notes. Roy blew a gasket, freaks out, upsetting the entire household. When everybody realized what happened, they were howling. We could not study any more that morning. We all took the test and did well. Roy was pissed off that he did not do any better than the rest of us. He knew more because he studied more intensely than any of us. We really didn't know what to emphasize so we just read the books, cover to cover.

Medicine and science are universal languages. Although the dialects of languages are different, the language of science is readily identifiable. Medical texts are translated and written in several languages, so you can study in English, but you take the test in Spanish. About six weeks pass before we get a break. Most of us decide on seeing America so we head for the border. Rusty from Long Island, the good ol' boys from Texas, our flaming Spanish instructor, and I travel back to the border in Rusty's jeep. I couldn't wait to get out. I drank some water on the border and it went to work on me right away.

We rode to Corpus Christi and Carlos and I continued by bus. We arrived in Houston about 10:00 a.m. Saturday morning and by now I'm totally wasted. I'm headed for my uncle's house in the Third Ward. I got to use the bathroom bad, because my gut's about to explode. I get to my uncle's house, drop my bag, rush to the bathroom and drop my pants. I wiped out the entire front side of the house. I thought the fumes pervaded the entire neighborhood and Hazmat might get a call. I got myself together and I went to stretch out on the bed. I closed my eyes and that's all I remember.

I woke up Sunday about 10:00 p.m., having been in a coma for about thirty hours. Now I'm worried about missing class on Monday and there's one bus left heading back to the border, an express leaving at midnight. I'm running late, the last to get on the bus and there's people seated in the stairwells and aisles. I squeeze into a very uncomfortable spot on the back stairwell, but at least I made it. I'm feeling good now because I should make my Brownsville connection with the guys heading back to Tampico.

The express, an old Trailways bus, is hot and crowded. I couldn't take it being cramped up for a twelve-hour ride, so I had to search for a better spot. I made my way to the back in complete darkness, except for the light of the countryside night. Now I'm stuck in the back by the bathroom with the odor and there was nowhere to go. I leaned momentarily against a door in the back and the door pushed open to a dark, windowless walk-in space. I groped in the darkness along the creaking wooden floors, and figured I might be in the luggage compartment, now I got plenty of space. I lay my duffle bag under my head, stretch out on the floor and make myself comfortable, although I can't see anything in the pitch black and heat. There was no way I would miss returning to Tampico for my afternoon class, so I had to make the best of a bad situation, I had come too far to quit.

Soon a couple of girls and a guy came back to investigate for themselves, found the luggage compartment accommodating, and

111

decided to join me. Someone had a transistor radio and dialed in some Conway Twitty. Now we're honky tonkin' on down to Mexico in the luggage compartment of a Trailways bus. Someone lit up a joint to mask the fumes, but I held my breath.

During my first year in Mexico, I truly learned how to study. I felt a degree of trepidation competing against White kids in high school and college. Very few classes did I excel in, it did not matter if they were pre-med courses or liberal arts. I knew that the pre-med curriculum at Minnesota was very competitive. Large classes at the beginning of the quarter would be narrowed down at the end to less than a third. Strangely, I understood what I studied in the book but I scored poorly on the tests, affecting my confidence more than my self-esteem. I felt I could compete with the White students, but I seldom proved it on tests.

Thus, I practiced self-ridicule and felt discouraged a lot of the time. To a large extent, we were on equal footing, in Mexico. There were times when we would discuss what we had read and inevitably it would get competitive. Soon sides were drawn and there would always be ten against me. I held my own, although there were several guys that were very sharp and most of us passed the National Medical Boards the first time we took it. The ambience change shattered a facade for me in what seemed an impenetrable wall of "White male-dominance."

These are some of the feelings I experienced when coming up in a predominantly White educational environment. Here down Mexico way these things were held constant, so that imposition was relegated to insignificance. It gave me a boost in confidence which now started to parallel my self-esteem. I taught myself and studied my ass off at my desk made of orange crates and plywood.

My stay in Mexico was a very rewarding experience. I cannot remember a negative experience except flying back to Dallas and a customs officer wanting to know where I had been. I told her I was attending medical school in Mexico, then she asked me, "Why did you come back?" Dismayed, I replied, "I don't understand your question. Is there a reason Americans have to explain why they would like to return home to their country?" She grumbled something unintelligible, motioned to me and with body language, indicated she wasn't interested in explaining herself and to shove off. I figured another classic example of American double-entendre. Most times White folks ask me a loaded question, there is a deflating punchline to it. Why they seem to do it, I don't know. Sometimes I wonder, do they treat each other like that? Other ethnic groups do not routinely show this condescension. The Mexican people were warm and friendly. I was accepted openly among all classes of people. There is obvious class distinction in Mexico with the upper class Caucasoid appearing, and the laborers, dark-skinned or indigenous appearing. Yet, despite class separation, they're all proud to be Mexican.

Most Mexican middle class were infatuated with the blue-eyed blonde mystique. They found me intriguing, almost novel, but remained distant. They were very fond of me and showed an outward affection, although barren of any amorous attraction. There is a distinction between "Old Mexico" Mexicans and Mexican Americans. Some of the more backward thinking ones assume that Black people are just carefree and happy-go-lucky. Commonly, while walking through "El Centro," in the parks, on the streets, or even riding a bus, some ignoramus might approach me smiling and childishly ask me to dance.

Initially I was offended by it, but I held my contempt. You could tell these people were given false impressions of Black people through media images, so they could not be entirely faulted and I didn't hold it against them. They actually wanted to see me break out in a little diddy, so I would make a game of it. I'd tell them, "Okay, I'll dance for you if you would sing while I dance." I would start clapping my hands and say, *"Canta me, canta!"* Now they realize how silly it sounds and become embarrassed. We would laugh it off with a clearer appreciation.

Mexico allowed me to gain much needed confidence. It gave me the discipline to pass the medical boards and I felt like nothing could stop me now. I will always have a love and a great deal of gratitude towards Mexico, as all Americans should. They are our back to Latin America. They provide us with fuel oil, as well as fresh vegetables to feed us in the winter, not to mention a resource for labor in jobs that most Americans would not do. How could it be that the President-Elect of this border country of over 100 million people could be assassinated within 20 minutes of the San Diego urban sprawl and none of us have a clue? Whereas, a case of spousal abuse in Northeastern Pennsylvania grabs national headlines in Southern California. Not to underemphasize the consequences of domestic violence, but we seem to have displaced our order of importance to issues that have taken on international consequences.

While studying abroad I received passing grades on the National Medical Boards. That paved the way to transfer back to an American medical school. A percentage of all medical students have difficulty and may not pass the first time they take board examinations, but I had the good fortune to score a passing grade. There was a push by the Federal Government that year to allow more Americans who attended medical school abroad to re-enter stateside.

I applied back to my home State, the University of Minnesota, and found that door still rusted shut. I corresponded with over eighty medical schools and got the "regrettably we are unable..." line. The Association of American Medical Schools was against any transfers. I decided to pass through Nashville to personally check out Meharry Medical College, one of the four historically Black medical schools in America. I spoke with the Dean of Admissions at an impromptu meeting, and he told me if Meharry accepted me, they would lose their accreditation. "No sirre! We ain't gwin' mess 'round wit' dat. Boy, you muss be crazy!" There was no chance for me to matriculate. I was downhearted, but I knew I had to continue my search. A fellow medical student who was attending Meharry suggested I talk with Dr. Carruthers, the deputy for admissions. Dr. Carruthers was gracious, considerate and intrigued by the fire in my eyes, to gain a medical education outside of the country. I told him that I wanted to send him a copy of my board scores along with my grades, and that I had already spoken with the Dean. He said he would look forward to receiving my scores. I thanked him and left Nashville, feeling that door was closed as well.

As the summer came to an end in 1978, I started to pack my bags, heading back to Mexico. The weekend before Labor Day, I received a letter from the Medical College of Pennsylvania, formerly known as Women's Medical College. "Congratulations, you have been accepted into the second year class." I changed my flight and scurried off to Philadelphia, "City of Brotherly Love."

Chapter Nine

BACK TO AMERICA

Philadelphia was still tense from the "MOVE" bombing, the fire that consumed a city block, when the Philly police dropped a bomb on a row house. Occupied by a perceived radical group of African Americans, this event stood out as the beginning of modern-day tactics of urban warfare, *a la* Branch-Davidians at Waco. Since I was a late arrival, I had difficulty locating a place to live. The school let me temporarily camp out in an abandoned section of a dormitory no longer in use. Philadelphia proved troublesome to find a spot to stay near school. For example, I would see posted on the school bulletin board, "Houses for Rent" or "Apartments for Rent." Time and time again, I would make a phone call to inquire and be invited right over. I'd grab a bus or cab and show up in the tree-lined neighborhoods, not far from the banks of the Schuylkill River. Owners would peer out their doors, and ask me, "What do you

116

want?" When I told them, "I'm the student that just called from the medical school to ask about the apartment," they would say, "No vacancy," and slam the door in my face.

It was humiliating and I was resigned to the solitude of the desolate abandoned dormitory for almost a month. Living out of vending machines, spending most of my time in the library, it was a lonely time, but I was happy to be in an American medical school.

A White kid named "Charlie," a classmate of mine, said he just moved out of an apartment, and it was vacant, real nice and close to school. He took me over to meet the landlord and look at the apartment which was great—spacious with sky lights, close and affordable.

The landlord told me she had to think about it when I asked her if I could get the place right away. By now, I was getting a little stir crazy at the dorm, and feasting on vending machine soup with the four pack "Oreos" every evening was playing out. I anxiously called her later that evening, to plead with her my urgency and she replied, "No vacancy." I was devastated.

The following day, Friday afternoon, a couple of Black female students invited me to their home away from campus to have dinner. They felt sorry for me because everyone knew how I was living. I was walking around with a lump in my throat, feeling hassled by the school to hurry up and move. Trying to study in the face of housing discrimination was really getting me down.

As we were leaving, I spotted Charlie. I told the ladies to hold on for a moment, because I needed to speak with him. I walked over to Charlie, who was very excited for me, then he realized I wasn't smiling. Charlie said, "What's up, don't you like your new apartment?" I said, "She turned me down, and it felt like a knife piercing my heart. I don't feel I should have to bear this pain by myself. It's not your fault, Charlie, but you set me up for this letdown and I wished somebody White could experience the torment of doors slamming in their face. I thought I would share with you some of the disappointment I suffer because of my black skin. For this ungodly reason, I'm still living out of vending machines in an abandoned dormitory." Although no one should have to endure the shame and rejection, I wanted a White person to appreciate the agony. "I'm strong and I'll get by, but this is a cold, cruel world you people control." I did not have the luxury to wallow in self-pity, just had to stay focused and hang tough.

So it happened over the weekend, Tommy called the school and left a message with the Dean's secretary for me to call home immediately, it's urgent. Thinking the worst, my heart felt like a ton of bricks. I'm dragging around a pretty rugged cross by now and I don't need anymore to bear. I called home to Minneapolis, and Tommy tells me, "You received an acceptance letter from Meharry Medical School. They gave you a spot in the third year class." I thought to myself, just like God planned it. Once again, I get strength from my enemies. Meharry offered me a seat in the third year, and I would not lose any time in the transfer back to the USA, as most foreign students did. I let the school administration know and they said they would hold my spot while I went to Nashville to check. I sent a telegram back to Philly with best regards. I stayed down in Nashville and accepted my seat.

Meharry was a new and interesting experience, because this was the first time that I had actually been surrounded predominantly by Black people while going to school. From elementary school, through high school and college, I was educated in a sea of White faces. Now I'm going to class with a majority of people who have always been in predominantly Black educational environments. From pre-school to medical school, most of these students experienced quasi-segregation. A lot of them were in the same fraternities and sororities, and some even knew each other back in kindergarten.

Meharry is a family of trained medical professionals, with a core group of medical students. It has educated more than forty percent of America's Black doctors, and a good number of physicians around the world. Ironically, the students looked upon me as an outsider coming in from Mexico.

I was so excited about going to an American medical school, I could hardly wait to sit in the lectures and take part in the discussions. Seemingly aggressive in class, to most students I appeared an oddball, subsequently I was ostracized, by and large. Coming from a social climate surrounded by White folks, I don't maintain the same social nuances of Black people who hail from predominantly Black social environments, so I knew I came off weird. A lot of kids were there on a social service program that took a lot of them out of the economic market of the health care industry. When they graduated, they had to commit to providing four to six years of social service in underserved areas, such as Indian reservations, before they could return to do a residency or start a private practice. The benefit of this program was that it paid their tuition and provided students a monthly stipend.

A lot of kids bought new clothes and cars, so they were well-dressed and had wheels. I showed up in jeans, T-shirts, cowboy boots and walking. I would go to the library while the gang fraternized, concerning themselves with girl watching, and where the party would be that weekend. In class, I was perceived as arrogant and a show-off, because when a question was asked, I would answer it immediately. I didn't mean to be showing off, I just didn't want to waste much time scratching my head, pondering the answer. I wanted to hear more from the teacher, and if you knew it, say it. Since I was an outsider, this only fostered more resentment.

Pretty soon blatant animosity developed and I was impelled to take a defensive posture. Most kids were happy to see me guess the wrong answer so they could heehaw in my face, but my habits had already been set in Mexico. I had no problem with studying eight hours or more a day, as a matter of fact, I rather enjoyed it. I loved sitting in the library for hours on end just reading all the latest medical journals and textbooks.

Things reached such a feverish pitch, that whenever I opened my mouth, I was commonly ridiculed. It got to the point where I was perceived as obnoxious for the slightest response. My professors seemed to enjoy my commenting though, and they liked the interaction of an inquisitive and aggressive student, but of course this created more and more antagonism. One day we were all sitting in the school auditorium for a class meeting, and I noticed that every time I would offer a suggestion, it would be put down or ignored.

There was a Mexican American student in my class and he turned around and told me, "Henry, you got some good ideas but we don't want to hear them." Then I looked up and realized that everybody was listening to one of the only White students in the class. He was the only one saying anything and they all seemed to be captivated by him. I had visions of a shepherd leading his flock. Back then, just like now, nobody cares to hear what I'm saying.

Most of the friendships I developed while at Meharry were with students from Third World nations, as I guess I was perceived as someone from a third or different world. I did not gain the respect from the student body until I got out of my jeans and boots, and threw silk shirts and shark skin suits on my back.

Growing up around my father, a positive role model and a sharply-dressed man, along with watching the players and hustlers in the neighborhood, who were impeccably dressed—and sometimes the only role models for the less fortunate—I knew how to dress. Having traveled to Africa, Europe and across America, I had a flair for style, so it was time to get clean again.

Since I was ostracized, appearing like a know-it-all hick, wearing jeans and cowboy boots, I might as well get into my 'gators and silks. It immediately set a new tone for me at school. Sometimes not only do you have to play the game, you have to be the best at the game, because Black people understand the "Mac," and the "Mac" is what Black people seem to directly relate to the most.

I never lost my zest for study and my time at Meharry was

short and sweet. I tried to learn everything I could and stay aggressive. I hung around the hospital when there was no reason for me to be there. I followed the surgeons into the O.R. for emergency surgery, to absorb anything to give me an edge. My determination paid off, putting what I learned to my advantage when I came to Los Angeles to do my Internship at Martin Luther King Jr. General Hospital in South Central L.A.

Chapter Ten

KILLER KING

Martin Luther King, Jr./Charles R. Drew Medical Center gets its reputation hammered in the media. The *L.A. Times* newspaper constantly points out the hospital's flaws but never reports on any success stories. People that utilize the hospital commonly have a discouraging experience, not unlike dealing with any other governmental bureaucracy, but the blame seems to fall directly on the medical center's structure. The administration has not applied itself, nor does it have the where-with-all to combat the negative images used to portray the hospital. King General, built about twenty-five years too late, and born out of the Watts Riots, is administrated by L.A. County. There is a general misperception that inefficiency is prevalent because African Americans run the medical center. Those that are in the administration at King are so overwhelmed by the task of managing a critically-intense facility, while at the same time answering directly to the county health department, that intransigence is the order of the day. People working in the hospital become disillusioned with the policies and the workload, as well as with the expectations of the patients and their families. This sets up a critical and destructive cycle. One must repel feelings of despondency and frustration in order not to impart them to the patients. The doctor, however, is presumed to be the reason that King is perceived as repulsive or dreadful, when in fact it is not the fault of the doctors, the nurses, the administrators or any singular group. The tone was set into motion at the hospital's inception. Destabilizing factors were put into place to undermine everyone's confidence, creating disorder. No one knows how to undo the damage to King's image that survives to this day and is projected out of proportion to the realities within its walls.

People in the street taunt King General Hospital as being "Killer King, Public Enemy Number One." Every horror story has been embellished, rumors fly everywhere. As an employee, depending on your mind-set, you might feel insulted or find some demented humor in the sarcasm. It hurts too when someone catches you off guard with one of their demeaning comments. I did not care to be painted by these pseudo-comedians, foolish men and women, and I became very impudent with slackness in the hospital.

Most people are hard working and end up overworked. This problem seems irresolvable using the present formulas. I did learn to better cope with people and their sickening comments. Guys, donkey laughing at my affiliation with King, would abruptly sober when I informed them, "Yeah, I work at Killer King, in fact, I'm the Chief Assassin." Then the jerks wouldn't be laughing any longer as they felt a cold chill, the response I wanted to evoke in them, as I snickered grimly and snickered the best.

Some people show up to King E.R. in such a critical mess, it is nothing short of one miracle after another that people are snatched from the jaws of death; yet, there are no complimentary public relations and nothing good ever seems newsworthy. I remember one Saturday evening around midnight, the emergency lobby was in its usual chaotic state of flux, with the triage desk swamped and the TV lounge with standing-room only. Babies running around in diapers, mothers chasing them in slippers yelling and screaming. Disgruntled drunks may stagger around waiting to get stitched up or a shot of penicillin, under the watchful eye of the "old pros," the hospital security.

As we sat at the nursing station beyond the trauma unit, suddenly we heard a loud prolonged crashing sound that scared the daylights out of me. It came from the lobby and my first guess was that a hospital gurney may have overturned, but it was just too prolonged. I could not imagine what it was, so I had to get a look. I left the E.R. nursing station running out through the power doors, past the triage desk in the lobby, to find a car had crashed through the E.R. and slammed into a wall.

I thought to myself, this is crazy. People in the crowded emergency room lobby were staring wide-eyed, mouths agape in a state of shock, lined up against the walls. That's when I realized the car was still running and smoking, amid the twisted steel beams, plaster and shattered glass. Everyone was scared, screaming and dazed. I shouted to the security guards to clear the kids out of the back seat of the car, as I dove into the driver's side to shut the engine off.

It was smoking bad, smashed into a wall, and I thought it might start a fire or worse, blow-up. The toddlers in the back seat were so frightened they were frozen stiff. There was broken glass and steel all over the waiting room floor. The mother had driven her car one city block off the main street onto the hospital property, turned right, drove another sixty feet, turned left, and floored it, smashing through a wall of sliding glass doors and steel frames. She continued to drive through the entire emergency room lobby before slamming into a wall as the patients scrambled out of the way.

I don't know what the lady or her girl friend, who rode in the front seat were thinking, but the driver was "wired and gone." I looked into her glassy, wide-eyed gaze as we started to move towards her. The woman panicked and began to run around like a chicken with her head cut off. As we closed the circle around her, she hit the deck and started writhing around in the broken glass like a snake. The guards grabbed her in a headlock, took her by her ankles like a log, and wrestled her into the security station. I just thanked God that I did not come out to the waiting room to face a bloody disaster.

The following morning, my wife waited for my report when I came home from call. There was always some shit to talk about. I told her a patient thought she could get faster service if she used the E.R. drive-thru. My wife couldn't believe her ears, yet more incredulous, again the *L.A. Times* refused to report anything.

A short time later, a couple of guys came through the emergency room and said they were screenwriters. This was all new to me, but the senior residents said screenwriters came through periodically. They asked if I knew of any story that might be of interest and I recounted what had happened. They implied that they would donate something to the hospital or give me credit or money for the story, but this was more talk than substance, I never saw them again.

About three months later my wife points out a trailer on television, advertising the evening show and says, "Hey, there's your story." Sure enough, the commercial for the series episode from *"St. Elsewhere,"* was previewing a car crashing through an emergency room. How ironic, old man legacy good enough for primetime, but real life drama not newsworthy. The pattern is starting to develop.

Chapter Eleven

SERVING THE JUDGE

I regularly bounced ideas off my brother Tommy back in Minneapolis, who is an aficionado for constitutional arguments. Since no one was being open about the obvious autopsy findings, Tommy runs past me the idea of something called an Amicus Curiae. "Well, what the hell is it?" I asked. He breaks out a legal description and explains to me it is a vehicle by which an expert who has information that has been overlooked or undiscovered, but yet has high probability of influence on the court, can bring this evidence to the attention of the court through what is generally termed a "Friend of the Court" brief.

Tommy faxes me a legal definition and an academic description of an Amicus Curiae. I share the concept with another attorney, Larry Brooks, a patient and friend. Brooks suggested that I practice medicine and let him practice law, a very practical admonition. He

126

advises me the Amicus Curiae is only used in appellate cases and this was not the place to advance the brief.

With my naive view of the court system, and by definition, Brooks not technically correct, I had a gut feeling, and being mule-headed, I wouldn't listen to him. I spoke with my brother again and asked if he could forward me a copy or boiler plate and theory, along with an example of a format. When I got a chance to review them, I called Attorney Brooks and said, "I am bound and determined to see this thing through." Again he asserted himself, but I pointed out to him my understanding of the legal description—anyone could file this motion at a jury trial—so in the most basic terms I feel justified.

Brooks throws up his hands and yells, "Okay, I'll have to put my people on it to research, but it's going to cost you about five hundred dollars." I said, "Wait a minute, just tell me what I need to get started. I got an outline and I know what I want to stress, I just need the format." So he instructs me to get a copy of the complaint that was filed against Simpson in the civil trial by Goldman and follow its cover page.

I set about sending one of my road dogs to get a copy of the complaint. When I mentioned to him what the task was, he became very apprehensive. The thought of it obviously had him spooked. The guy intimidates most people he meets but faced with what seemed daunting and precarious, he did not relish the idea. He intimated the improbability of accomplishing this goal without alarming others and bringing unwarranted attention. Obviously, he wasn't looking forward to getting a copy, and after two half-hearted attempts, he inferred that there was no access to these records.

In the meantime, Sammy, my "go to" guy, has a "whatever" sort of attitude, and the request to go to Santa Monica Courthouse didn't faze him. Sammy was dispatched to the file room of the courthouse, where an array of people stood in the two-hour-long line, with Sammy camping out at the tail-end. He finally reached the file clerk, a baldheaded, arrogant Black man. Sammy requested a copy of the front page to Fred Goldman's complaint. Now everybody's head turns and all eyes are on Sammy. A curious look envelops the face of the clerk as he pauses for a moment before he goes off to process Sammy's request.

The clerk asked Sammy, "What do you want it for?" Sammy tells him, "I'm just a courier, man, my boss wants it, so how much money do you need?" Now the guy's face turns to a look of anguish with his eyes talking. Sammy, completely flustered, after spending two long hot hours in line, exerts himself to get what he requested. The clerk hesitantly gets the document together and gives the document to Sammy and says, "Fifty-seven cents." Sammy comes back to the office with the cover sheet and when we see the document its like, "Wow," a very impressive moment.

Now, Tommy has sent the layout for the Amicus Curiae. I impress my theories on the boiler plate and immediately fax the cover sheet, boiler plate, and embellishments to Attorney Brooks' office. Brooks drafts up the Amicus Curiae document in presentable legal format, and Juanita's son, Paul, acts as a courier between Brooks' office in Long Beach and Juanita's home in Downey, up the road 10 miles. Juanita got her hands on the document when she went home that evening and brought it to work the following morning. Our next problem was to figure out how to serve it. We contacted another law firm the following morning and sought advice on how to prepare the proof of service. It would ultimately be addressed to Judge Hiroshi Fujisaki, in Department Q, Superior Court, Santa Monica.

With some creativity, we prepared the document and I selected Juanita to serve it. The sense of urgency seemed perpetual. Juanita was all shook up by my request but she gussied herself up and off she went to the Santa Monica Courthouse. She was nervous but Juanita is the kind of person that is compelled by challenge. She is very captivating and has the qualities of a fine actress. Juanita

128

bulldogged her way right up to the metal detector before entering the courtroom and was met by security. Juanita informed the marshal she was there to serve Judge Fujisaki. The marshal told her to take the document to the file room. She followed the marshal's directions and went downstairs to wait in the two-hour line.

When Juanita finally reached the file window, she encountered the cantankerous old bald guy, who took a look at the document. Again, he becomes alarmed and edgy. His voice cracked as he anxiously spoke up, "Miss, please take this back to the courthouse, I mean the courtroom. We don't handle any O.J. mess in this department." His voice went up a pitch as his palms began to sweat. The paper rattled as his hands trembled, passing the document back to Juanita. He urged her to take it directly to the court, that he could not accept it. In frustration, Juanita marched back up the stairs and headed for the courtroom.

Again, she was confronted by the marshal who reiterated to follow his directions and take it to the file room. Annoyed, Juanita took the document out of the envelope and sternly replied, "I'm tired of the run around, I'm here to serve the judge." Now the media hounds start to converge on Juanita and the marshal. Another officer approached to see what all the commotion was about. He pulled the document from Juanita and quickly scanned it, astounded. He put it back in the envelope and immediately escorted Juanita through the metal detector and out of the throngs of media mongers into the courtroom. Juanita was led to a seat at the lawyers' table in front of the judge's bench. All eyes in the courtroom were transfixed on her now and Juanita acts as if it is her duty to serve the judge.

The documents were taken to the judge's secretary and she huddled with other courtroom personnel before she approached Juanita. She says to Juanita, "Please return to the file room and I will see that matters are taken care of." Juanita was then escorted by deputies to an elevator.

As the three got on the elevator and the doors closed, the ride to the basement was unnerving. The elevator jolted and started descending slowly. Juanita had to concentrate to keep her legs straight. The ride seemed like an eternity, claustrophobia mixed with butterflies and a sense of urinary urgency. The elevator jolted to a stop, the door slid open and Juanita stepped out into a gauntlet of police. She aggressively stepped forward to the file room window.

She was again confronted by the same character who at this moment was accompanied by another file manager. He started rapidly shaking his head from side to side, stuttering and complaining, not wanting to get involved with something this explosive. As the clerk balked and stalled, the judge's secretary appeared and informed them that they should accept the document. The old guy was so jittery he turned to ask Juanita, "What do you want me to do with it?" Juanita told him, "Stamp it received and give me a copy." The guy stamped both copies and the judge's secretary snatched the judge's copy out of his hand. Juanita reminded ol' baldy that she needed her correct change and a receipt.

We had accomplished a milestone. Juanita was a bundle of nerves and she is a panicky senorita, but she maintained her composure and should be nominated for an Oscar. When she returned to the office, we were tickled to death and got a bang out of the entire ordeal. As we laughed and joked, the phone began to ring, it's Tommy calling from Minneapolis. "Congratulations," he says, "Geraldo just read your Amicus Brief on his evening program." We were all excited and anxious to see his commentary. We wondered how he got it so fast, we had just served it.

Well, no sooner had we served it, a *CNBC* field reporter got access to a copy and faxed it to Geraldo Rivera. We checked the local listing to see when Geraldo's talk show would appear on the West Coast and headed home to watch the show. Then there he goes presenting the document:

PETITION TO FILE AN AMICUS CURIAE BRIEF

RECEIVED

JAN 0 6 1997

SUPERIOR COURT
WEST DISTRICT
SANTA MONICA

Petition For Amicus Curiae Brief

SUPERIOR COURT FOR THE STATE OF CALIFORNIA
COUNTY OF LOS ANGELES

FREDRIC GOLDMAN, an individual, and KIMBERLY Erin Goldman, and individual, Plaintiff, vs. ORENTHAL JAMES SIMPSON, an individual, and DOES 1 through 5 inclusive,	) CASE NO. SC036340)) PETITION TO FILE AN AMICUS CURIAE) BRIEF AS TO CAUSE OF DEATH OF) DECEDENTS NICOLE S. BROWN AND) RONALD R. GOLDMAN; AND REQUEST) FOR LEAVE TO APPEAR AND TESTIFY) THERETO)))))

To the Honorable Hiroshi Fujasaki, Presiding Judge in the above entitled matter. I Henry S. Johnson, am a medical doctor duly licensed by the California Medical Board as a practicing physician within the County of Los Angeles, in the City of Hawthorne and State of California.

I respectfully request permission to appear in the above entitled matter and testify as a friend of the court as to my medical findings in respect to the events leading up to and resulting in the deaths of the decedents Nicole S. Brown (hereinafter referred to as "Brown") and Ronald R. Goldman (hereinafter referred to as "Goldman").

I believe that information and analysis would assist the trier of fact in understanding and resolving the complex issues before them. After, an independent medical review of Los Angeles County Department of Coroner's autopsy reports number 94-05136 (re' Brown), and 94-05135 (re' Goldman) I am under the opinion that the following points should brought to the attention of the fact finding body:

1. It appears most likely that Brown was attacked and killed by an assailant wielding a knife in his left hand.

2. It appears highly probable that Goldman was attacked by two assailants wielding two distinguishable knives.

3. It appears that Goldman fought a prolonged fight and took several minutes to succumb to his injuries.

It is my respected opinion that a visualization as to the orientation of the knife wounds would add credibility to these points and should be promulgated to the jury to improve their insight, please see attachment "1."

If called as a witness I could competently testify as an expert witness to my medical review and findings.

Dated: January 8, 1997

Respectfully Submitted

Henry S. Johnson, M.D.

Upon receiving the Amicus Curiae Brief that afternoon, Fujisaki excused the jury. While he examined the petition, a very succinct two page document, he grew agitated by its implications. The guilt of O.J., concluded long before the start of the trial, would not be derailed by exposing the truth in Santa Monica. Fujisaki could almost taste the glory as he orchestrated the pomp and pageantry. He was the Asian apology for the humiliation perceived by the Japanese American Community when Ito supposedly lost control of his courtroom, permitting an injustice to prevail. In defiance of the medical analysis attached as an exhibit, for which the judge had no expertise and could not have possibly formed an objective opinion, Fujisaki's last official act of the day, the denial of the "Friend of the Court" brief, would return to haunt him like a Phoenix rising.

I deemed it more appropriate for the judge to hold off any decision until after he was able to thoroughly examine the material which was submitted. Yet, an Amicus Curiae is at the discretion of the court and it is the judge's prerogative whether to admit the brief.

A number of people who saw the program called to let me know. It was thrilling to see the brief with my signature flashing, which had been faxed to Geraldo no sooner than he went on-the-air. In his ingratiating style and his contrived intellectual grasp of the subject matter, Geraldo purposely butchered my name, cowardly avoiding the mentioning of the three main points of the brief.

I requested a copy of his show from Burrell's Taping Service, then isolated the sound bite to study it. It is still funny to watch, because Geraldo makes such an outrageous fool of himself. Most people never realized this without seeing it in context. So after contemplating my response, I figured I should write Geraldo to share my thoughts and feelings with him.

I routinely followed the *"Today Show"* for trial commentary, appreciating Bryant Gumbel's slant. I felt after he left the program, the reporting seemed to transform into a cheap rehash of monolithic rhetoric. Matt Lauer had Geraldo Rivera on a morning interview and I believe Tavis Smiley was on the same show. I don't really remember what they discussed other than to say it was condescending and patronizing. It reeked and I was moved to comment, sending a certified letter to Geraldo.

Geraldo Rivera   January 21, 1997
C/O CNBC
Fort Lee, New Jersey 07024

Dear Mr. Rivera:

Your disparaging acknowledgment of the Amicus Curiae Brief (Case SCO36340; Rufo, et. al. vs. Orenthal James Simpson) served on Judge Hiroshi Fujisaki, on January 8, 1997, showed contempt for a constitutional process and serves to subvert the truth. Whatever Judge Fujisaki's motivation to disallow the Amicus Curiae, does nothing to diminish the validity of the facts therein. The points raised:

1. It appears most likely that Brown was attacked and killed by an assailant wielding a knife in his left hand.

2. It appears highly probable that Goldman was attacked by two assailants wielding two distinguishable knives.

3. It appears that Goldman fought a prolonged fight and

(continued)

134

took several minutes to succumb to his injuries. are the most crucial pieces of evidence to surface during the entire trial. Suppressing evidence to maintain the status quo of the legal system makes a farce of freedom of speech. Do American values only mean something to the powerless?

After watching you being interviewed by Matt Lauer on the Today Show and avoiding the issues I brought to the court, brings into question the moral ethics of American Journalism. I am sure you are aware if the jury renders a plaintiff verdict, what I have divulged will become paramount.

Respectfully, Henry S. Johnson, M.D.

Geraldo was well aware of who I was, although he feigned ignorance. He used my document during his national broadcast but avoided any contact with me. On the other hand, local media never mentioned zippo, nada, zilch. What Geraldo inadvertently demonstrated was how the most significant party in the entire investigation was neutralized. The fact that a doctor determines the cause of death was taken completely for granted.

Chapter Twelve

DEATH CERTIFICATES

At face value, it would seem absurd to assume the killings were not a double-murder, but technically all you have are two dead bodies until the cause of death is officially determined by a doctor. Before you get a ton of dirt on your chest, a doctor would have officiated your death certificate.

There are several ways to die: double-murder, murder-suicide, double-suicide, voluntary manslaughter (mortal combat), and lastly, suicide in conjunction with accidental death. The autopsy report, along with the death certificate, gives the official cause of death, and a doctor makes the call based on his findings. So before you determine that a crime has been committed, a doctor must certify what has happened. You will never find a cop, a lawyer, a judge or a news reporter's signature on a death certificate; only a doctor's.

The death certificate, in certain respects, is analogous to the birth certificate. It is the official announcement that you no longer exist in vital form. Most people think in terms of birth certificates, because they have personal use for them during their active lives, and birth is usually a more popular event than death. A death certificate is the center of a bureaucratic process and its importance to physicians, or significance, gets lost in the ritual of filling it out. The death certificate's importance in this case, as with any other, gives the legal description of one's departure. In other words, the cause of death is outlined and certified by a doctor's signature and license.

Now, I don't like signing death certificates because they represent the loss of a human being and are a poignant reminder of the fallibility of my profession. It can be, and is, a solemn experience. Aside from the philosophical considerations, there exists a protocol which at times can be stinging. I have signed countless death certificates, and had a few unpleasant experiences with some that have formed an indelible impression on me. I got sued once because the cause of death, stated on a death certificate, did not match the pathological description at autopsy.

An elderly lady was transported by paramedics to Robert F. Kennedy Hospital Emergency Room, in a coma. Being the Internist on call that night, I received a page concerning her. She had an electrolyte imbalance which we term hyponatremia. In essence, the natural salt concentration in her blood was so low that it became life-threatening, and plunged her into a comatose state. She was transferred to the Intensive Care Unit (ICU), treated with fluids and salts, and responded appropriately based on blood analysis; however, she remained delirious.

The nurses in the Intensive Care Unit felt the patient was stable enough to be transferred, as her care was becoming custodial and there was a pressing need for acute-care beds. By evening, I ordered to transfer the patient to a monitored bed on the Direct Observation Unit (DOU). Early the following morning, the patient suffered a cardiac arrest. Sudden death is always a potential outcome but seldom anticipated.

The patient's elderly husband had expectations which exceeded reality. He came apart when he learned of his wife's death. To make matters worse, no one was able to contact him before he arrived at the hospital. He worked as a cabbie during the graveyard shift, and arrived at the hospital before visiting hours Saturday morning. To further aggravate matters, he glided unnoticed past the nursing station as the nurses were changing shifts. He walked straight into his wife's room to discover her draped and prepped for viewing.

The guy wigged out, sobbing hysterically. Enroute to the hospital, I learned of all the confusion. I placed my car phone back on the stand and put the pedal to the metal. Exiting the freeway, I rushed into the hospital through an unlocked door on the loading dock, a short-cut to the DOU. There I found my patient's husband supported by a wall, weeping and wailing. He was an old, Portuguese man and very suspicious of everyone. I tried my level best to console him and convey our deepest condolences. Some life crises are beyond a physician's control. I had been taught to always make sure relatives of critical patients are not overly optimistic, leaving a ray of hope. Yet sudden death will always catch you off guard. I had prepared him for the worst, but not for a surprise. His sadness turned to anger.

I gently prodded him for an autopsy, a delicate subject during troubled times. He said he could not make that decision at the moment, but would consider it over the weekend. I remained empathetic, but I had to get on with my job, so I hoped we could revisit the subject Monday morning when the pathologist would be on duty.

When Monday rolled around, I telephoned the pathology department in the morning about an autopsy. I just needed to confirm it with my patient's husband. I went to my office to start my day, when an undertaker showed up with a partially completed death certificate. I assumed that Mr. Maderas, the patient's husband, decided to forego an autopsy and contacted a mortuary. I knew from past experience that undertakers are pushy to get a death certificate completed. It allows them to move along post-haste in their funeral preparations. I have to fill out the Doctor's section that includes a space which details the cause of death.

Without an autopsy, the cause of death is an educated guess. Through training and experience with the end results of disease processes, you get a pretty good feel as to why someone died. At times it becomes routine to describe the cause of death and you don't need an autopsy. I ran through my mind the differential diagnosis for sudden death, which has very few causes. Most commonly it is an arrhythmia, an irregular heartbeat, which fails to sustain blood pressure with cardiovascular shock supervening. Another cause may be a disruption of blood flow to the heart or brain, for example, from a massive heart attack, stroke or bleeding to death.

I put my most likely assumption on the death certificate, signed it and the undertaker was happy as he gleefully skipped out of my office. Little did I know, that afternoon the decedent underwent an autopsy which surprised and upset me. I always like to pay respect to the dead by attending their autopsy.

Mr. Maderas was still very hostile and pissed off about his wife's death. Then the pathology reports come back and their results differed from my diagnoses on the death certificate.

Mr. Maderas became consumed with anger and melancholy. He remained unreasonable and felt vindictive. He sought legal advice, found an attorney to represent him and served me with a summons. Shaken, I immediately phoned his attorney, Mr. DeMarcos, and explained to him my version of events. I pointed out that initially I met the decedent, Mrs. Maderas, in the emergency room in a comatose state. She had a life-threatening sodium concentration disorder so severe, I had never encountered a level that low in all my training at Los Angeles County Hospital. Her sodium concentration was 106, with one hundred and forty being normal; no salt in the soup.

The patient was 75 years old but looked like she was in her

nineties, and the only medication she was taking at home was thorazine, a major tranquilizer which could have led to the electrolyte imbalance. I explained to Attorney DeMarcos that the patient was managed in the Intensive Care Unit, and although debilitated in a very precarious state, her death was sudden and unanticipated. Her outlook was critical from her initial presentation, the reason she was placed in the I.C.U. This is the last place anyone would want to wind up in a hospital because, by definition, you are as close to death as you are to life.

Attorney DeMarcos said he understood and that he would talk to his client and resolve the problem. I felt comfortable after talking with the attorney, only to be surprised about six weeks later, when I was served with a Motion for Default judgment against me. My first encounter with a condescending, conniving attorney. Since I had not responded to the summons in writing within thirty days, this attorney moved ahead after telling me he would take care of it, by filing a Motion for Default. I had to quickly consult with an attorney. I turned to my friend and neighbor, Attorney Phillips.

Contrary to public perception of doctors, things had been shaky for me financially since medical school, and my malpractice insurance had just lapsed. It is very dangerous to practice in an emergency room without malpractice coverage. Everyone that comes through the emergency room and gets admitted to the hospital is very sick, worried and excited, and accompanied by very disgruntled and anxious family members; therefore, malpractice insurance coverage is imperative.

Often, grieving family members tend to transfer the blame for their loved one's sickness onto the doctor that is caring for the patient, or onto the nursing staff or hospital. No one cares to take responsibility upon themselves. I felt I had done nothing wrong, the patient presented in very bad shape. This would be a costly defense, but I was in no position to settle, and the attorney for the plaintiff was pushing for maximum compensation. This case was ultimately headed for trial.

There were a number of doctors involved in the lawsuit, which also included the hospital. Whenever I admitted a patient to the hospital, I routinely had two or three doctors evaluate the patient for complications in specific organ systems. The doctors who helped to co-manage the patient ultimately concurred with the pathologist, but parenthetically advanced that because of the patient's mental status, it obscured the possibility of diagnosing what was wrong. The pathological diagnoses included: (1)Acute peritonitis, (2) Perforating duodenal ulcer, and (3) Cirrhosis. Curiously, the patient's hospital chart disappeared and it did not resurface for over a year.

When I finally got the opportunity to review the medical records, I questioned whether there was variance in the nurses' charting. Their notes were substantial enough to suggest that there was oversight on the part of the physicians, which ultimately led to the patient's demise. This was very perplexing to me. There had been four very meticulous physicians that had consulted and co-managed this patient's condition, yet none of us had a recollection of ever seeing what now appeared in the nurses' charting. Furthermore, no one remembered any nurses telling us or advising us that they spotted occult GI bleeding found in the feces and had made notes to reflect that. Their notes now charted early signs of occult GI bleeding. All of these inconsistencies led the plaintiff's attorney to become very suspicious. He also had professional consultants, or should I say hired guns, review the records and they concurred with the pathological diagnoses.

I finally got a copy of the patient's records and went over and over it in my spare moments, practically on a daily basis. The patient's chart was the size of a telephone book and with the doctors' and the nurses' "hen scratch" writing, it was difficult to decipher. I must have read over the patient's medical reports at least a dozen times. Finally, after three weeks of testimony in Superior

Court, it was my turn to take the stand.

The night before I would be sworn to tell the truth, I looked deeper into the details of the pathological description. I knew that acute peritonitis was not a cause of sudden death. Acute peritonitis, which is an infection of the abdominal cavity, can be insidious, painful and fatal; still, I had a problem with this diagnosis.

I went back to the bibles of medical school: Robbins' Textbook of Pathology, Cecil and Lobe's Textbook of Internal Medicine, Utterman and Sodeman's Textbook of Pathophysiology and the Textbook of Surgery. I looked up the classical description of acute peritonitis. The diagnosis is made when you crack open the abdominal cavity. You will either see a putrid, foul-smelling pus which is obvious to gross inspection, or failing to see such an appearance, you must take a specimen of the peritoneal fluid, culture it, and review it under a microscope. When I compared it to what the pathologist had described in his autopsy findings, this was not done. He described his findings solely as a brown, watery fluid.

Since the autopsy found the patient to have cirrhosis and she was obviously malnourished, she could have multiple reasons for brown, watery fluid, which is better described as ascites. This opened up a broad differential for the abdominal findings of the pathologist, and de-emphasized the diagnosis of acute peritonitis as the cause of sudden death. My expert witness, Dr. Bishop, a UCLA Gerontologist, agreed.

What mostly startled the court was the fact that I would challenge the doctor who everybody felt had the final word, the pathologist. When I presented these details to the jury with my white shirt sleeves rolled up to the elbows and my tie loosely knotted around my neck, carrying a half dozen ten-pound textbooks into the courtroom, the judge told me I looked like I was either going to paint the courtroom or start a fist fight.

I took the witness stand and my lawyer began my direct examination. The plaintiff's Attorney DeMarcos was leaning back in his chair at the table in front of the judge's bench, chewing on the eraser of a pencil. The legs of his gray pin-striped suit were pulled up so you could see his low cut socks and his bare ankles. He was anticipating the *coup-de-grace*, but felt a jolt when I said the pathologist's diagnosis was wrong.

DeMarcos immediately sat straight up and furrowed his brow, almost biting the eraser off his pencil. He could not believe what he had just heard. He never subpoenaed the pathologist, and had already gambled with his expert witnesses. DeMarcos ran into my attorney in the men's room, side by side at the urinals, turns to him and says, "I wish I never got involved with this case."

As I looked across the room at DeMarcos, I thought to myself, "You son of a bitch. I trusted you to resolve things, and now you have cost me all this money in your greedy pursuits." I wished we could've taken that courtroom out to the parking lot where I could render to him what he was begging for, an "old fashion ass kicking." But God is good, I'm all forgiving, and I was blessed by a jury that came in with a not guilty verdict. Nevertheless, the hospital received a judgment against them for allowing Mr. Maderas to slip past the nursing station before visiting hours and was slapped with a $75,000 judgment.

The second time a death certificate became a major issue for me was when a patient died, and the mortuary service was pressing to get a completed DC in 24 hours. At the time I had two offices, one in Century City and the other in Hawthorne, and I would spend half a day in each. The mortician contacted my Hawthorne office and pressed them to locate me immediately to get my signature. My staff informed him that I would be in the Hawthorne office that afternoon, and that's where he should bring the death certificate. He demanded that they page me urgently to get my signature. Since they did not strictly obey his orders, he hung up the phone and called the Medical Board of California. The office staff paged me to let me know how obstinate the mortuary director was, that I should be prepared.

When I came to Hawthorne that afternoon, not far from LAX, a secretary from the Medical Board called me. She asked me, "What's the hold up on signing the death certificate?" I told her I was waiting to see the mortician, and 24 hours had not expired since the patient's death. I would sign the certificate as soon as the undertaker brought it to my office. She sarcastically asks, "Are you sure?" I told her, "I'm about as sure as I want to be." She says, "What do you mean by that?" I told her, "It means whatever you want it to mean. I've already stated, and my staff has informed the mortician, that my signature would be placed on the death certificate today." She told me, "You'd better make sure you complete it." I replied, "Have a nice life."

The guy shows up, straight anal retentive, and throws a hissy-fit about how unprofessional my staff is. He gives me a two page, single-spaced letter, detailing how I should improve my business and that I should immediately terminate staff. I tell myself, in the future, if I'm ever unfamiliar with a patient, having just encountered them on an emergency room call panel, I will refer any such patient if they expire to the Coroner's office for autopsy and signature on the death certificate. Unfortunately, the need arose before the week was out.

A patient in bad shape came through the emergency room, expired, and I deferred to the Medical Examiner for completion of the death certificate. The Coroner's office contacted me and told me to forget about an autopsy on this patient, that I was obligated to sign the death certificate myself or else. So I figure I don't need the hassle, I should just get busy, acquiesce, play like a soccer ball, getting kicked by one bureaucrat to the next.

I don't like to sign death certificates but on this occasion I was forced to do it, and as it turns out it is a fundamental part of my bailiwick and not many doctors sign them. For the most part, psychiatrists don't, pediatricians don't ordinarily sign them, obstetrician gynecologists don't ordinarily sign them, nor do surgeons care to sign them. They tend to fall predominantly on the Internist, and since we represent a minority, this tends to make us experts at it. As an Internist, I commonly see life fade into death, so I feel I have the expertise and competence to discuss the cause of death with anyone, including a Coroner.

Just like the Heaven's Gate case, when the Sheriff arrived, he stated it looked like mass suicide; however, this assumption was not officiated for 72 hours. You didn't know if 37 poisoned two, or two poisoned 37 until the Coroner officially said mass suicide.

In the Bundy case, we had two dead people without an official cause of death. It was ultimately certified as a homicide by the Coroner, and he based his conclusions on how the wounds were inflicted. Before you get absorbed in the blood, the DNA, the Bruno Magli's, the hat, the gloves, the time-lines, the love, the allegations, spousal abuse or anything else circumstantial, you must consider the cuts first. The cuts detail the crime, and without cuts, you have no blood and you have no DNA.

Dr. Lakshmanan testified he felt most likely that one man using his right hand murdered these people with one knife. If this opinion is what influenced the D.A.'s investigation, it was totally misleading, a probability less than finding a match to O.J.'s DNA in the general population and lacking one scintilla of common sense.

Probabilities play a very important role in our daily lives. Most of us don't have to consider the odds because we have been accustomed to someone else calculating them for us. In medicine, we have probabilities or predictions of outcomes. If you choose the most probable treatment course based on the prevalence of a condition, along with the signs and symptoms following the course of predilection; that is considered community standard. Any variance is most commonly indefensible, especially if the outcomes are adverse.

A non-unanimous jury pool is a probability. Reasonable doubt is a probability. Going from the sublime to the mundane, obeying traffic signals takes into account probabilities. If a traffic signal turns from yellow to red, it is more prudent if you would yield and stop, rather than attempt running a red light. Chances are you can make it through a busy intersection without causing a major mishap or getting cited by the local long arm of the law; however, is it worth the chance? Buying Lotto tickets is playing probabilities and probability dictates one man did not commit this crime.

Chapter Thirteen

ZIONISM AND BLACK WOMEN

Since I never received any response to my first letter to Geraldo, and he continued his campaign of disinformation, several months later 1 sent him another certified letter. This time I detailed the factual basis that obliterates the conventional rhetoric and raised the spectrum of an F.C.C. code of ethics violation. In theory, the Federal Communication Commission should enforce First Amendment freedom of speech rights; however, in this case the F.C.C. would choose not to buck Wall Street.

O.J. was deemed a pariah and a Black one at that. The fact that his adversaries employed subversive tactics to persecute him was considered inconsequential, by-and-large. Any law in California would be subordinated, making O.J. an example to Black people. Rather than Geraldo or his producers contacting me, I received correspondence from the head honcho of *NBC's* in-house legal counsel, Howard Homonoff:

NBC CABLE NETWORKS LETTER FROM HOWARD HOMONOFF

 **NBC Cable Networks**

CNBC NBC

HOWARD B. HOMONOFF
General Counsel

Fort Lee, NJ 07024

Homonoff@cnbc.nbc.com

November 3, 1997

Re: _Rivera Live_ Telecast of January 8, 1997

Dear Dr. Johnson:

We are in receipt of your letter of September 23, 1997 concerning the above referenced Rivera episode and have discussed your concerns with the show's producer. While CNBC appreciates your interest in its programming as well as your desire to contribute your thoughts to the discussion of the O.J. Simpson civil trial, we do not believe that it would be appropriate to revisit the subject at this time. In addition, a great deal of time has passed since the telecast last January and the trial has long since concluded. At this time, _Rivera Live_ has no plans to explore the civil trial further.

Of course, if circumstances change, the show may consider a follow-up program and may at that time review your request to share your opinions with our viewers. We thank you for your support of CNBC and appreciate your efforts in bringing your concerns to our attention. If you have any further questions about this matter, please feel free to contact me.

Sincerely,

Howard B. Homonoff
General Counsel

Why would some hot airbag of an attorney send this bullshit letter and tell me that *CNBC* had no interest in exploring the civil trial any longer, despite O.J.'s appeal having yet to be decided? Weekly, it seemed, for any trivial thing, the media was all over O.J. like a cheap suit.

Now, I start to tally up our small victories. All the big shots that I'd had contact with found a way to weasel out of confronting the truth. Geraldo was O.J.'s most boisterous antagonist among the bevy of pundits. His nightly commentary about the trial was the substance of his talk show format, and his abject disgust of Simpson tainted his reasoning. At the same time, aspersions were cast on African Americans for their failure, in part, to buy into the rhetoric and misinformation broadcast non-stop.

The spectacle of a Black defendant who matched dollar for dollar the expense waged by the state prosecution—demonstrating that money buys justice—proved a major embarrassment to the criminal justice system. Furthermore, this served to intensify the animosity towards O.J. and his supporters from what was euphemistically described as the "angry White male," combined with a virulent Jewish antipathy. During a conference of lawyers and media about the O.J. trial held at Loyola Marymount University, one legal analyst poignantly conveyed this wretched resentment blurting out, "When Jewish blood is spilled, someone has to pay!" Jewish contempt towards the African American community was palpable.

African Americans in the entertainment and telecommunications industry, those in front of the camera and those working for the studios, took the heaviest hit, part and parcel, to the virtual Jewish grip on that market. Shapiro, derided in his synagogue for defending Simpson, was induced to surrender the profits from his "O.J. book" as a peace offering to the temple—a gesture seeking forgiveness. Gerald Uelmen, Dean of Santa Clara Law School and legal counsel for Simpson in both trials, stated during an interview with me on *Pacifica Radio,* Berkeley, that all members of the "Dream Team" have encountered repercussions in the aftermath of the not guilty verdict.

This apparent Zionist influence on the media has functioned to foment hostilities against Black people, just as D.W. Griffith, the Jewish patriarch of Hollywood, did with his epic film *"The Birth of a Nation."* Black people over the past century, and still to this day, are seemingly used as a buttress and decoy against anti-Semitism. African American images in the media tend to evoke distaste or apprehension, serving as a diversion or distraction from anti-Jewish sentiment. Zionism then becomes an afterthought.

These media pundits made the Simpson trial a race issue long before Johnnie Cochran stepped on the scene. There were so-called opinion polls which projected the percentages of White folks that thought like this, and Black folks that thought like that, how women felt versus how men felt. These "opinion polls" served to form opinions rather than measure them. Their ulterior motive, as Caesar succinctly put it, to "Divide and conquer."

The outcry reached a crescendo when Cochran compared Mark Fuhrman to Adolf Hitler. Every Rabbi in Southern California had his two cents worth in the *L.A. Times;* the front page looked like the editorial section. Cochran never obtained permission to invoke the name of this arch-nemesis, and they responded like Johnnie desecrated an icon. Cochran further inflamed the zealots by employing the Nation of Islam's security force as his personal bodyguards during the trial. Lastly, two weeks after O.J. was acquitted, Minister Farrakhan would take a million Black men to the White House.

To be sure, these incidents started the venom to churn. The next thing we would witness was a spate of church bombings, a mushrooming of hate crimes against Black people, and a deluge of hate sites on the Internet. The loss of Affirmative Action affecting Black children's enrollment into colleges, and a proliferation of three strikes, twenty-five years to life sentences—for everything from drug abuse to minor offenses, with Blacks and Mexicans representing ninety percent of the convictions—seemed politically motivated at the same time, coincidently. America's prison population escalated 200% between 1995 and 2000, surpassing Russia, inheriting the dubious distinction of being the incarceration capital of the world.

People are intimidated by what appears to be a Zionist undercurrent and will immediately disavow any recognition of a schism in Black and Jewish relations, or the fact that the "Trial of the Century" had any impact on them. The average fool will tell you that any drama across ethnic lines will produce a thirst for blood or retaliation. It would be naive to assume that hostilities spawned were not somehow intensified by ethnic influence.

Moreover, some Jews, along with some Black intellectuals, as well as a percentage of Whites, who were uncomfortable with the media presentation and the guilty verdict, feared retribution if they spoke their minds. In other words, they preferred to swallow their freedom of speech rights and keep their mouths shut, in order to avoid the threat of being blackballed.

Colleagues, intellectuals and friends have pleaded with me, "Henry, don't mess with the Jews. It's too dangerous and you can't win." Eldridge Cleaver once said, *"There's two kinds of people in the world; you're either the problem or the answer to the problem, and if you keep your mouth shut, you're part of the problem."* It's okay to openly discuss drug abuse of Blacks and Hispanics, the rate of unwed mothers and teen pregnancy among the low income, the high school drop-out rate and the rate of incarceration of Blacks, Latinos and poor Whites. Yet, if one mentions the slightest critical remark towards Jews, immediately people start to hyperventilate, you're branded anti-Semitic for telling the truth.

Not to appear apologetic, having dated Jewish girls in high school and college, Jews have educated me, have come to my rescue both financially and legally in the past. Notwithstanding, some of my colleagues are Jews, for whom I have the utmost regards. Nonetheless, as an ethnic group, they have targeted Blacks for ridicule and it has only acted to demonize the Black male in society.

I know there are boat loads of obsequious Black intellectuals that will start to clamor that, "You shouldn't oughta' say these kinds of things; that Jews have been good to us and don't bite the hand that feeds you." There he is, the so-called Black man with his hat in his hand and a shit eating grin on his face. Disgusted with the White man, worried about the Mexican, mad at the Asian, and scared of them Jews. He'd rather *kowtow* than tell it like it is. Let me remind you, an "Uncle Tom" is the most despised person. His own people hate him and those that use him pretend to have respect for him. Who would ever trust a man that would turn his back on his own people?

Black people need to solve their own problems, but we don't need to be patronized or saddled with the negative media images we have no input in creating. And yes, at times I have felt scared, it's a normal human emotion. Yet despite feeling that way, I know it will not last and I have the courage to see my way through, sustained by the words of Emiliano Zapata, *"It is better to die on your feet, than to live on your knees."*

A lot of Black people, particularly women between the ages of twenty-five and fifty-five, have an aversion to the mentioning of O.J. One Black patient of mine offered me some advice to live by, "Learn how to stay out of White folks' way. Ya' see, it's better for you to be watchin' them, than for them to be watchin' you!" Somehow, some Black people believe that certain issues which affect White folks, don't affect them in their isolated little minority world. That's one reason so many are often heard moaning, "I'm so tired of 'dis, we need to move on. I heard 'nuff bout O.J., he ain't never done nuthin' fo' me."

Still my most staunch support has come from senior Black women. Strong, proud, intuitive and Christian principled, they are old enough to remember the likes of Emmit Till, Medgar Evers, the four Black girls killed when the Sixteenth Street Baptist Church was bombed, or the gunning down of Dr. King. Some even grieve their own personal tragedies having seen their fathers, brothers and sons brutalized and devoured by the dragon of America's legacy.

This generational detachment has acted to cripple Black social progress. We have become our own worst enemy. It underscores the fact that Black society as a whole does not control the dissemination of meaningful information in it's community. Beholden to commercial dollars, and subject to the devices of the perceived Zionist influence on telecommunications, along with the bias and distorting effects, results in distrust and dissension among Americans.

The fact that a lot of Jews as power brokers in the media know the truth, but remain silent, can only be defined as un-American. America will only remain strong and unified through forgiveness; however, honesty always comes first. If I'm wrong, forgive me, as I have forgiven you.

The ostensibly Jewish polemic projected in the media, which expresses the deepest conviction in O.J.'s guilt, was exemplified by Fred Goldman's mass appeal via the U.S. mail to households having surnames of Jewish ethnicity. I appreciate the fervor which stems from their background and experiences; however, everything that is not pro-Zionist is not anti-Semitic.

The tea leaves did not bode well for O.J. with Shapiro at the helm. The sun was sinking rapidly on O.J.'s prospects to extricate himself from a Damoclean fate. O.J. would have to recruit his ace-reliever, Johnnie Cochran early, and Shapiro begrudgingly poisoned the water proclaiming, *"Johnnie played the Race card."*

Did it ever occur to anyone, why a key member of the "Dream Team" would coin this jaded phase? Neither the prosecution or the court ever raised the issue. Like a subliminal stimulus, this triggered an intensely visceral reaction for White folks in particular—their reasoning obscured by emotion. An apocalypse which would portend a widening gulf among Americans. Every time I hear the phrase "Race card," I cringe as though I just heard an utterance from the devil. Yet O.J., like Trotsky, would have to watch his allies like he watched his enemies.

Realizing the difficulties with gaining exposure remains a very frustrating and humbling experience. Analyzing White Americans who believed the media accounts of what took place, one draws the conclusion that on an emotional level, their instincts impel them to feel threatened by any non-White. Basic instinct, coupled with emotional momentum, set the stage for reaction; in other words, it is more comfortable to believe "he did it" than to consider the opposite. Symbolically, mass media defers acknowledgement of my protest. Who has come forth so forcefully? Not even O.J., himself.

You are judged by your actions and not by what you say. Simpson's actions are on public display because his persona was sold to us. Most have the opinion that O.J.'s media image belies an aloofness, an abyss of apathy, which is perceived as insensitivity or inappropriateness. What we fail to appreciate is that there exists a mind and will unique to O.J. Simpson, which has not been communicated since the murders, and is lost in the barrage of media projections.

Why is it that groups or Black organizations are unwilling to openly respond to my assertions? It is singularly so influential that anyone becoming informed of these conclusions is captivated, more to a gut felt response. It is not a question of believability, it is a process of conviction.

In the beginning, the media coverage would reiterate frequently that O.J. was not a suspect, but the intimations were he was guilty. The parade on the freeways of L.A. seemed preconceived. It would generate an outpouring of sympathy for O.J. Up to the point of the "chase," O.J. was being hammered by the media, all but convicted. Where was this guy going, heading north towards Brentwood on the San Diego Freeway, driving 45 miles-per-hour?

In California, we're used to high-speed chases, reaching speeds of 90 to 100 miles-per-hour on surface streets. With sirens blaring and automobiles crashing, suspects drive through yards, jumping out of cars while still rolling. Darting in between backyards and garages, soon police dogs are brought in to sniff them out, with SWAT teams in tow. That "chase" looked more like a funeral procession.

I was standing in a marina sports bar on Lake Minnetonka, watching the NBA championship play-off. Suddenly, the game was interrupted by the breaking news coverage of the freeway chase. The atmosphere in the restaurant seemed surreal, filled with gaiety and tainted by vengeance, as if the crowd was laughing at someone suffering.

I felt shattered, having always visualized O.J. as an icon, he now appeared to be a fallen one. Sympathetic, yet feeling hurt and disgraced for Simpson, he seemed like a wounded animal. Then as I looked around this affluent suburb of Minneapolis, where a Black man feels like he is at a remote outpost, these people in my surroundings showed no remorse, giving me an eerie uneasiness. My wife and in-laws were with me but I was oblivious to everyone, thoughts racing through my mind as people celebrated the stalking of O.J. on national television.

I knew there were problems with the D.A.'s case and I thought they were sweating Simpson too much, too soon. The irony was the outpouring of support shown along the freeway overpasses. As the investigation and trial progressed, the feelings towards O.J.'s guilt or innocence were gut wrenching and there are still those that remain on the fence. The evidence pointing to guilt was overwhelming, yet even more perplexing, were questions about results found in the lab, which supported the theory of a conspiracy. There exists a burning desire to believe in Simpson's guilt, which had more of an emotional impact than a Black man beating the system—although some people were elated to see that.

The African American community was riveted to the televising of the criminal trial because one of her sons, a sports hero and legend, was in a predicament and it weighed heavily on our communal conscience. The superstars in the more mundane vocations of society, particularly African Americans, are not readily identified or distinguished by media attention. Athletes are the ones that garner the accolades. They are part of a profit-generating sports enterprise and historically disenfranchised. However, after their stardom fades, their glory still lingers. The athlete returns to a more routine lifestyle, although the superstar tends to elude the public. It remains a small world and no decent human being would wish for a murderer to be in their midst.

I occasionally heard, during the lengthy trial, from a few Black people and some women in particular, that, "I know O.J.'s guilty but I hope he beats the case, it's payback time." Transiently disheartened by such comments, fortunately this view was not heartfelt nor the most prevalent point of view, but a reaction to the bitter sarcasm against O.J. in particular, and Black Americans in general, through media saturation.

Nevertheless, one must ask, what compels a person to consider it payback time? Is it the granite mind-set that seems to permeate all cultures and turns empathy inward? Nothing is truly gained by becoming introverted, which should be replaced with introspection.

The conspiracy to destroy O.J. is part of a larger phenomenon in America, that has a propensity to demolish the image, and assassinate the character of successful Black men, such as: Dr. Martin Luther King, Malcolm X, Paul Robeson, Muhammad Ali, Marcus Garvey, W.E.B. Dubois, Mike Tyson, Michael Jackson, Jesse Jackson, Elijah Muhammad, James Brown, Marvin Gaye, Jimi Hendrix, Bob Marley, Don King, Louis Farrakhan, Ron Brown,

Huey Newton, Adam Clayton Powell, Mumia Abu Jamal, Rubin "Hurricane" Carter, Geronimo Pratt, Nelson Mandela—just to name a few, and countless other outspoken Black men willing to challenge the status quo.

Meanwhile, we don't want to offend anyone, so as Black folks, we avoid talking about this sensitive topic openly—however, O.J. still draws national attention.

All the talking heads, legions of stooges find it beyond their ethical threshold to admit they are possibly mistaken. Incest and child pornography are more popular topics on the Internet than the reality of a prosecutorial cover-up and collusion with an unethical Medical Examiner. The planting of evidence to convict O.J., by a couple of crooked cops with Nazi tendencies, ironically combined with a Zionist bias, among all the media hypes, seemed to form an unholy alliance to destroy a Black man.

Emotions turn to shear rage. That which is irrational becomes rational, and that which was rational became perfunctory. Black and Jewish dialogue at best, has remained apologetic, if not superficial. Some Black folks have come to feel that if we could only get back to business as usual, we would gladly carry O.J. to the altar. Others were so thrilled justice prevailed, that in our jubilation and exaltation of Johnnie Cochran, we exposed some deep inner feelings.

None of our leaders would make a peep, as our mothers, sisters, daughters and wives were castigated, proclaimed the dumbest jury ever impaneled. Hold your tongue, swallow your pride, look and act confused so that you may be dismissed as unaccountable. This will give an explanation for your inappropriate behavior, and definitely don't put your faith in another brother.

Ask yourself, why haven't you heard what Dr. Johnson is saying from a White man? A Black female journalist from New York once told me, "I've got to hear this from somebody higher up." Yes, it's risky business to put your faith in something you hear from a Black man. Just remember, his color causes him to be perceived as

157

lacking credibility.

Not a single politician, Black or White, would come to the defense of this jury. We all knew and sympathized with their onerous task of jury sequestration. Never in our history have we seen that process last that long—you must commend their sacrifice. Instead, criticism was heaped on them as they were, and still are, scorned.

Rodney King's all-White jury in Simi Valley, which has the blood of the fifty-seven deaths on their hands—riot casualties—did not receive the same enduring criticism as O.J.'s "downtown jury."

The criminal trial jury was largely made up of single Black females. Initially, it appeared that this jury was impaneled with this composition in mind, so if O.J. was found guilty, no one could criticize their decision. If you look at the background of these women, they were predominantly middle-aged government employees, single or divorced Black women. Your suspicions may tell you that maybe these women would feel annoyed by the image of a highly successful Black man with a White wife—that emotions might tip the scale of justice.

Early on, public sentiment was incited by focusing on the irresponsibility of interracial relationships and how Simpson turned his back on the Black women in his life. When this tactic proved impotent, a new persuasion was advanced. That is to say, the scope was broadened to focus on racism rather than on the interracial taboo.

In the initial phase of the investigative reporting, popular opinion was split along the lines of guilty and not guilty. It was only after the focus went off the interracial relationship aspect that a diversion of opinion started to develop more along racial lines. More than his guilt or innocence, Black people questioned whether O.J. would get a fair trial. Others felt the converse, however, that Simpson was guilty but would be able to finesse his acquittal. We were constantly reminded that race was not an issue when the civil trial began. In spite of a jury pool in Santa Monica exceeding forty percent African

American, somehow an all-White jury was impaneled.

Race consciousness has always been a part of the American landscape. Article I, Section 2, of the United States Constitution described Black people as *three-fifths of a person* for purposes of taxation and representation. Since that still did not satisfy the balance of power for the Northern States, which had smaller populations of Blacks, and imperiled the Union, a bicameral Congress was created. Each State would have two elected delegates to the Senate where the ultimate power of Congress would rest. Thus, America moved away from the idea of becoming a democratic republic—taking the power away from the people—and embodied the mantle of a plutocratic confederacy. The document which ordained America as the United States defined America's racist philosophy at its inception. You must be able to act in spite of racial issues or in concert with racial issues, because they are unavoidable.

Black media outlets and organizations pretend to ignore this work. It remains peculiar that Whites have O.J. forums on television and radio, but Black people never do. This subject obviously intrigues people. *The Los Angeles Sentinel, The Final Call, Jet, Ebony, The Jamaican Gleaner* and a number of African American newspaper publishers across the country—I have kept all of them informed, but I could never seem to motivate any of them.

The subject has generated such comments as Supreme Court Justice Sandra Day O'Connor suggested, to consider a change in the jury system, and raised debate on the constitutionality of key issues. Then it seems Black people have no meaningful comments worth airing on radio or television. Most middle class Blacks wish it would all just go away. The problem is Black people do not control their means of communication, which is so vital to self-determination. Without control, we do not define who we are or what we stand for, and the images created are of a six foot eleven, slam dunkin', saggin', rappin' gangster.

Most likely, if I could be proven wrong, I would be tarred and feathered, on a rail and on my way to Phoenix. Medical malpractice, and more probable, malfeasance occurred, at our expense as citizens. Our criminal justice system lurches along as it swells like a parasite on society. It burdens the taxpayer, and disrupts and destabilizes the family structure of the convicted. The reality of its debilitating effects on society is not readily apparent. There are more Black men behind bars than in college or the military which has effectively decreased the birthrate of African Americans by over thirty percent. New age slavery and genocide rolled up into a nice, neat package.

The system must serve the people and not vice versa. It must be the guardian of human rights and not destroyer of the rights of humans.

Chapter Fourteen
THE VIDEO

In the early stages of our research, Tommy was on one of his monthly sojourns to L.A. following our phone discussion regarding the autopsy reports. The implausibility of what was testified to by the Coroner did not register with him until he was able to visualize what I described. When he attempted to simulate the attack using his right hand, he realized how ridiculous it was to suggest that a right-hander killed them. Tommy concluded this fact would best be conveyed by a video.

The video was born out of the desire to bring this information to public awareness and to facilitate understanding. When I first attempted to spread this information, I found it extremely difficult to explain the science and convey the abstractness by verbally communicating it. When Tommy suggested that people should be presented a visual conception to grasp these theories more readily, I didn't place much weight on what he was saying. I felt the media would pick my information up right away and they would provide the opportunity to present it to the public.

No significant media attention ever seemed to develop, I just waited and waited. Then a street soldier, a brother named "Jazzy," came into my office in need of some medical treatment. As usual, the standard conversation in my office was about O.J., so we kicked the discussion of O.J. around and Jazz suggested I hook up with his cousin, Lenora, a cable TV producer. The problem with public access cable is that no one seems to be tuned into it. Normally, you pick it up by accident as you scan the channels. I reluctantly agreed to go on Lenora's show after some time had passed, because a clown can't be choosey who his audience is. I never wanted to give up on the broader commercial market, despite up to now being completely shutout. No one was beating down my door, so this prompted me to get busy with public access television.

I spoke with Jazz's cousin Lenora, and she hooked me up with Michael G., a cable access personality with a show airing in South Central L.A. It's on in the afternoon and shows music videos, debuting local talent. I went to the small cable studio on Manchester Boulevard not far from the Reginald Denny flashpoint of the Rodney King riots. It was my first time in a studio, with amateurs operating the cameras. They had the unusual task of filming a serious interview on a dance video format.

I had recently done my first live interview with John Kushner at *KOGO* Radio out of San Diego. The interview went off so well, the station replayed it at least a half dozen times over Christmas holiday week. A lot of my patients told me that they heard me on the radio. In that interview I sounded too academic and technical. I know people understood and there were a lot of call-ins, but I needed to improve my delivery because I did not want to lose any listeners. I just wanted to float my mind and let things develop on their own, not wanting to bore anyone with the details.

So here we go, the music is dope and the beat's got us rockin', but I had no idea Michael G., the host of the show, would superimpose me on this medium. Michael introduced me and I came on to start my delivery. I just couldn't jettison the baggage and the first segment dragged. I needed to get more energy into the presentation, having a strong urge to bring the audience in close to have a heart-to-heart talk.

When we returned to the air live, Michael G. started to explain what I was trying to get across. This was a wake-up call. Michael could not explain anything for me because he did not understand it himself. He had been interjecting bits of commentary and humor during the first segment to stimulate things. If I was going to intrigue anyone, I needed to take a deep breath and take it to the street. Just free flow like dancing, like boxing in the ring and not get absorbed in academic perfection. I remembered what a mentor of mine, Larry Wilson, a motivational speaker at the *Pecos River Conference Center,* once described as the perfect communicator. Talk straight from the heart, free and captivating while unrehearsed, spontaneous and inspiring; so I went for it. Sure enough, this time I had impact.

I took on a new aura and everyone in the studio was awestruck. Even Michael G. was calling me the good doctor instead of Hennnrrry, as he initially opened.

I reached into my coat and pulled out a sinister looking dagger, which I described as the weapon used on Goldman. When Michael G. looked at the knife, his eyes popped out and instinctively he said, "Ooh!" I knew I was back in control and finished strong, daring anyone to discount what I said. We went out on a song and the engineers in the recording booth came out to shake my hand. It was the first time I had experienced such an outpouring of enthusiasm.

The show plays in a circumscribed area of South Central Los Angeles, appealing to the music video crowd. I had to take what I could get at this stage. An old acquaintance of mine told me that he had seen the show and said he was very impressed. I was surprised an adult had watched the show and found it captivating. I spoke with Lenora a day later to get a feel for what the call-in response was. Two calls came in, one complimentary and the other very derogatory. She said that the second caller sounded like the voice of a White man and she did not want to tell me what was actually said. It was surprising to me that a White guy could be watching this cable show when its broadcast area is limited to the ghetto, South Central L.A., and this has remained a curiosity.

Another patient of mine, a budding actress who was familiar with my work, wanted to put me in touch with someone in the business that could arrange a television interview. Cruising down the Marina Freeway, she noticed Randell Briggs, her friend and producer. She got his attention and exited off the freeway. Briggs, a local cable producer, had a program a lot of people were familiar with, *"Urban Survival Techniques."* He had just arrived in Los Angeles after driving across country from Washington, D.C. She told Randell how excited my information made her and that she thought it would highlight his program. They immediately went to a phone booth and placed a call to me. She put Briggs on the phone and we started rapping.

Randell was skeptical and had a similar perspective about Simpson, as most people did following the civil verdict media spin, but I straightened him right around. I said, "Randy, everyone has their opinion, but I have a medical expert opinion. If you have not seen nor understood the autopsy reports, then you would be wise to be quiet and listen," and so he did. As a matter of fact, he got twisted. Randell decided we should immediately go on-the-air. He came to my office the day of the taping and Tommy was in town, so we all piled into the van, with Sammy driving, and took off for Continental Cable Studios. There was no planning, Randell just introduced me and we both ad-libbed.

Briggs was my ghetto Cecil B. DeMille. If you go to the dic-

164

tionary and look up the word cantankerous, you would probably find definition numero uno, Randell Briggs. He's your typical dark-skinned, nappy-headed brother-man. Raised in Charleston, S.C., Briggs did a stint in the Navy riding both diesel and nuclear submarines. Sometimes he made you think he left his mind about 40 fathoms deep. He received his early training as a cameraman in the military and you have to give the guy credit, when he works he's a professional. The first video we produced had good timing and energy, but the second feature was a monster, ask Petrocelli. When he first saw it, he said, "Oh, my God, this is amazing!"

I had even passed off a copy of the video to Phil Baker, one of O.J.'s civil attorneys before the $33.5 million dollar judgment was awarded. Phil knew of me before we did lunch in Venice. A mutual friend, Jeff Gutierrez, my kids' Dean of students at St. Bernard's High School, who occasionally joined me at LAX Firing Range where we'd shoot off a couple dozen clips, invited us both to his wedding in La Paz, Baja California. Phil went, but my time, like my dough, was chronically tight, so I laid low in L.A.

Phil was happy to hear from me, and I told him, "Phil, you gotta see this video, it knocks 'um to their knees. If it gets out, it will shake everybody up before the judgment award comes in." He told me to get it to him right away. I hand-carried it to his office in Santa Monica and we talked about Jeff's wedding party. He was anxious to see the video and told me he'd get right back to me over the weekend. Right back never came.

We produced the second video by accessing a video library of the first trial. One of Tommy's friends in Minneapolis, Prince's surrogate father Mr. Anderson, made recordings and kept a very meticulous inventory during the trial. We made it a family affair, utilizing the fastidious and compulsive tendencies of my sister Linda. She had a little lag time making the transition to L.A. after leaving Booz-Allen in D.C., so we figured why not throw her a bone.

Linda is a research specialist, being one of the first women to ever graduate from Princeton University. She's so loyal to her alma mater that if she were cut, she would probably bleed orange. Her persnickety character traits, along with the arrogance bestowed on her through her Ivy League education, turned Linda into the ultimate ball buster. I couldn't have asked for a better pitbull. Linda's tenacious propensity drove me and my brothers nuts as kids, but now we could put it to our advantage.

Linda pulled the trial transcripts on cue off the Internet. Tommy secured about forty hours of video of the testimony the Coroners gave during the preliminary hearing and the criminal trial. He sent it to Linda and she analyzed it for pertinent statements made by the doctors so we could compare them to the results of my analysis. Our finished product, based on the actual autopsy findings, in contrast to the contradictions made by the Medical Examiners, convinces everyone that the doctors were part of a larger cover-up and that O.J. was most likely set up. The video was entitled, appropriately, *"Suppression of Evidence"* because it spoke for itself.

The outtakes from the forty hours of testimony were juxtaposed against me describing the actual findings in the autopsy reports. Briggs pulled a studio camera and one of his students, and came out to my office. We utilized my staff, Sammy, Juanita and Irene to demonstrate how the wounds had been inflicted. In the criminal trial, they never wanted to show you the details of a re-enactment because they knew it would raise suspicion; furthermore, it would have looked silly the way they described it. Briggs is so good, we only had to shoot one take, and *voilà*, a low budget ghetto masterpiece.

In the meantime, I continued my media bombardment, yet still remained censored. My fax machine was smoking, routinely sending out editorial commentaries to dozens of media outlets and organizations, with no takers.

Here is a partial list of distinguished people and organizations who received copies of our information and video production

"Suppression of Evidence," but chose to remain silent:
FRED GOLDMAN, JOHNNIE COCHRAN, GERALDO
RIVERA, LARRY TAFT, MERRITT MCKEON, CHIP MURRAY,
L.A. SENTINEL, OPRAH WINFREY, TAVIS SMILEY, JANET
RENO, *L.A. TIMES, THE TODAY SHOW*, LARRY KING,
YVONNE BURKE, JACK KEMP, PETE WILSON, *ESPN, CNN,
NBC*, MICHAEL JACKSON, *KABC*, ROBERT BAKER, GIL
GARCETTI-LOS ANGELES COUNTY DISTRICT ATTORNEY,
DR. LAKSHMANAN-LOS ANGELES COUNTY CORONER,
JUDGE H. FUJISAKI, ROBERT MCNEILL, LEO TERRELL,
NAACP, THE RAINBOW COALITION, THE BROTHERHOOD
CRUSADE, ACLU, *KJLH, "THE BEAT,"* HOWARD STERN,
PAT HARVEY, STARR JONES, TED KOPPEL, *BET,* MILTON
GRIMES, MAXINE WATERS, *THE GLOBE, THE STAR,
REUTERS, AP, "HARD COPY," KMEX*, BARBARA WALTERS,
KTLA, ETC.

I assumed a few of those shared their opinions. Everybody in
the ghetto that saw the video production gave it a four-star rating.
Another of my cowboy buddies, ex-LAPD Sergeant Clay Tave—a
mentor to Bill Pavelic, Cochran's P.I., and also ex-LAPD—slyly
grinned when I asked him what he thought about the video. Clay
said, "That video is all over Brentwood."

Over twenty doctors have described it as flawless. Dr.
Lakshmanan testified he would not stake his reputation on his testimony in the criminal trial, ironically in contrast to myself. In no
unequivocal terms, I staked my reputation on my findings. I figured
this would add some fresh material for the O.J.-bashing comedians.
It is funny how things happen, we got a new addition to my neigh-

borhood. Tody Smith, a retired pro ballplayer, moved in across the street. Tody was instrumental in encouraging our pursuits. A motor mouth, Tody could give O.J. a run for his money. Tody played on the 1970 USC Rose Bowl Championship Team. Known as the "Wild Bunch," they included Jimmy Gunn, Charlie Weaver, Bubba Scott and Al Cowlings. Tody had signed an affidavit, among twenty-five others, attesting that A.C. was with them at a party at the time of the murders.

These guys still hung out together after their professional careers ended, and they looked like the walking wounded. I watched Tody die from the ravages of professional football. He was on the 1982 Dallas Cowboys Super Bowl Championship Team, and if the Tobacco Companies are liable, then the NFL should be liable too.

Tody often recounted that the Trojans' victory over Bear Bryant's Crimson Tide in 1970 cracked the dam of segregation in southern universities. Bear would never again allow local talent to leave Alabama only to come back and beat the pants off of him. That game ushered in college integration in the South.

Tody was so impressed with the video, he turned his brother, Bubba Smith, on to it. Brother Bub, another controversial figure in the annals of pro football, never made the Hall of Fame, but grabbed notoriety in the *"Police Academy"* sequel. Bubba had exposed the video to a lot of people across the country from John Madden to Bryant Gumbel but it seemed like talking underwater. Tody, on the other hand, was friends from USC with Leroy 'Skip' Taft, O.J.'s mentor and financial advisor. Tody arranged to get a copy of the video to Skip.

Tody got back to me a few days afterwards and told me, "Great news, Doc. Skip Taft loved your video and was impressed by your honesty and professionalism." Tody encouraged me to contact Taft right away and gave me Skip's phone number. I called Skip Taft immediately. This was during the time that O.J.'s appeal was being considered by the California Appellate Court.

Skip was very candid about the financial situation and was not optimistic, feeling the appeal was not very strong. I asked Skip what he thought about the video we produced, and he told me, "I haven't seen it yet." I said to myself, "Here we go again." I got back to Tody and let him know I spoke to Skip. I said, "Tody, either Skip is bullshittin' me or you are!" Tody got mad and said, "I don't have any reason to bullshit you, Judge." Well, I figure I'm not in with the SC crowd anyway, I just wondered if someone from USC had the guts to face a "trial by fire," and resurrect their once most admired Alumnus. Tody said, "Johnson, one thing no one will ever be able to deny, whether you're right or wrong—at least you have always been sincere."

Our ghetto juggernaut continued to rumble with patriotism as its fuel. Thomas Jefferson would be rolling in his grave knowing how the Constitution had been perverted to destroy O.J. Moreover, if a man who has fortune and fame could be framed and indicted, along with laws violated in a pogrom to persecute him, then the average working stiff does not have a chance, no matter what color he is. Notwithstanding, the obstruction of justice by the prosecution of Simpson, with the D.A. and the LAPD knowing full well Nicole and Goldman were alive as O.J. rode to LAX by limo, the civil trial decimated the "Bill of Rights" to the U.S. Constitution. In Santa Monica, that body of laws was abolished and never fulfilled.

The Constitution represents a contract amongst all citizens in America. If the contract is breached for one citizen, it means that it is null and void for each and every one of us. Desperate to bring these issues to public awareness and not knowing how to break through the White code of silence—the media censoring of this vital information—I shot off a letter to the U.S. Justice Department addressed to Janet Reno, along with a "Who's who" cc list. I asked in the interest of taxpayers, for the Department of Justice to examine the implied improprieties of the California Superior Court:

February 25, 1997

HONORABLE JANET RENO, ATTORNEY GENERAL
OF UNITED STATES DEPARTMENT OF JUSTICE
WASHINGTON, DC 20530-0001

DEAR JANET RENO:

I AM WRITING YOU AS A CONCERNED <u>TAXPAYER</u> IN LOS ANGELES COUNTY THAT YOU MAY OFFER SOME INSIGHT AND RESOLVE OVER WHAT I FEEL IS A SUPPRESSION OF EVIDENCE IN THE O.J. SIMPSON CIVIL CASE, A DENIAL OF MY FIRST AMENDMENT RIGHTS, POSSIBLE MALFEASANCE AND COLLUSION TO CONVICT O.J. SIMPSON, WITH A MISAPPROPRIATION OF PUBLIC FUNDS.

AFTER REVIEWING THE LOS ANGELES COUNTY DEPARTMENT OF THE CORONER AUTOPSY REPORTS ON BROWN-SIMPSON, NICOLE; LOS ANGELES COUNTY CORONER RECORD #94-05136; AND GOLDMAN, RONALD; LOS ANGELES COUNTY RECORD #94-05135; IT IS MY MEDICAL OPINION AT LEAST TWO ASSAILANTS WERE INVOLVED IN THE CAUSE OF DEATHS. THE AUTOPSY REPORTS AND THE PUBLIC PERCEPTION DEMAND AN INDEPENDENT ANALYSIS OF THESE RECORDS. PLEASE TAKE TIME TO REVIEW THE ENCLOSED VIDEO INTERVIEW.

Respectfully,

Henry S. Johnson, M.D.

cc: Honorable Maxine Waters   Mayor Willie Brown
     Governor Pete Wilson   Oprah Winfrey
     Ted Koppel   Pat Harvey
     Diane Sawyer   Starr Jones
     Yvonne Brathwaite-Burke   Larry King
     Rolanda Watts   Oliver Stone
     Matt Lauer   Tony Brown
     Tavis Smiley

The letter was sent to everyone on the list along with a copy of the video production. Attorney General Reno received a copy of the autopsy synopsis I prepared as well. The response from the media and the cc list was, "Who cares?" I did receive a postcard from Tavis Smiley at *BET, Black Entertainment Television*. He took time out to jot me a short "thank you" note for sending him a copy of the letter I had sent to Janet Reno. Tavis wrote that I'd probably hear directly from the Justice Department, he never mentioned anything about the video, but he wished me all the best. That's it and that's all. Just as Tavis predicted I did hear from the Justice Department, a few months later, but it seemed they completely missed the point:

HENRY S. JOHNSON, M.D.

U.S. DEPARTMENT OF JUSTICE

U. S. Department of Justice

Criminal Division

Washington, D.C. 20530

JUN 1 1 1997

Dear Dr. Johnson:

Your letter to the Attorney General, in which you offer your medical opinion on the slayings of Nicole Brown Simpson and Ron Goldman, has been forwarded to the Criminal Division for response.

The jurisdiction of the federal government over murder and other violent crimes is limited to categories of crime which have a relationship to U.S. governmental functions, interstate commerce, or other recognized areas of federal responsibility. Under the United States Constitution, the remainder of the criminal justice jurisdiction is specifically reserved to the states. The federal government has no authority to intervene in the matter concerning O.J. Simpson since this case falls under the jurisdiction of the state of California. We are therefore returning the enclosed video to you.

We regret that we cannot be of further assistance to you in this matter.

Sincerely,

Ronnie L. Edelman
Principal Deputy Chief
Terrorism and Violent Crime Section

172

When the second video was ready for screening, it had to be bicycled around to different studios around L.A. to broaden our viewing audience. Since Dr. Golden and Dr. Lakshmanan were included in this video production, we made a general announcement that they were debating me that night on cable TV. We got busy and faxed the announcement to all the media outlets.

Now, this advisory did not go unnoticed. Immediately, the media flooded the Coroner's office with calls asking if it was really true that the Medical Examiners were going to debate Dr. Johnson. No one from the media ever called us. Briggs didn't even know that we were sending the announcement out until he received a call from Continental Cable's Crenshaw studio.

The secretary whispered to Briggs, "Ooooooo, you' in trouble!" Briggs said, "Girl, what you talkin' 'bout?" She replied, "The big boss called down here from Orange County headquarters because the Coroners called them, wondering what in the world was going on." Scott Carrier, the spokesperson for the Coroner's office, left a message and wanted Briggs to call him. Briggs took the number and got Carrier, the Coroner's spokesman on the line.

"Good afternoon, Mr. Briggs. I understand you are the producer of the cable TV show *"Urban Survival Techniques"* and will be airing a debate between some Dr. Johnson and the Coroners tonight. Well, the Coroners know nothing about a debate and we would like to know what is this all about?" Briggs replied, "No big deal, just some video clips from the O.J. trial, with Dr. Johnson narrating."

Carrier sighed and stated, "Well, that's a relief. The media has been flooding our office with calls all day and the Coroners are shittin' bricks." Briggs asked the spokesman if he could see the advisory that got everyone so worked up. Carrier told him, "Sure, just give me your fax number." When Briggs recited my fax number, Carrier immediately realized he was actually talking to Briggs at my office and dummied up, abruptly ending the phone conversation.

Yet such a small world, I would indirectly hear from Mr. Carrier a few years later. While attending a retirement reunion for the Los Angeles Rams Alumni hosted by Deacon Dan Towler at Hollywood Park Racetrack, I chatted with retired pro Bob Schremp, Vice-President National Football League Alumni. Somebody started chiding me about O.J. when Bob asked me if I ever heard of Scott Carrier. He said Carrier, the Coroner's spokesman, is his friend and neighbor. Then things got serious and Schremp let me in on a little secret, Carrier had confided in him that, *"O.J. did not murder Nicole or Goldman."* That's when I realized not everybody in the Coroner's office was full of shit.

Briggs proceeded to wear the cable system out from Inglewood to Hollywood, with our *"Suppression of Evidence"* video interview; however, we didn't see fire nor smoke. No one in the media asked me anything or said "diddley" but you knew they watched the cable show that night. Mysteriously, the three sets of submasters of that show were somehow erased by someone at the cable studios, despite the fact that the tabs were broken on the "three quarter inch" made for television cassettes that would have prevented them from being mistakenly copied over.

The Black managers over at the Crenshaw studio felt it was time for a change from Briggs' weekly format and decided to "can" his informative show and replace it with a husband and wife tele-vangelist prayer and healing broadcast. Talk about someone getting pissed off, Briggs was beside himself. All you would hear from him was "MF" this and "MF" that, every other word, and the guy is always loud and don't give a damn. Chronic CO2 narcosis, I figured. Briggs had trained most of the people working at the studio and won "Director of the Year" awards, but his proteges would stab him in the back. He went out the door warning them, "The writing is on the wall for all ya'll. You'll be cutting each other's throats if you are afraid to address the real issues." I told Briggs to come on down to my office where he could work part-time for me.

Tommy concludes everybody that gravitates towards me is dysfunctional, but they're good people. He wasn't telling me something I didn't already know. Briggs lost his job for the work that we were doing, and I wouldn't leave him high and dry. I knew his dedication and discipline, he doesn't mind strappin' up if necessary and Briggs has zero understanding for bullshit. He's a soldier and takes very seriously the purpose of our mission, as everybody else around me does. While some colleagues of mine started distancing themselves from me and others who knew me, belly whooped and snickered, calling me obsessed, believe me, none of them were missed. I have never been surrounded by a more sincere, dedicated, rag tag group of people than these guys who are pledged to death to see the truth come to light.

Grandma "Sweet" Minnie, a supporter of mine, once told me, "You don't worry, Doc. If someone tries to take a shot at you, I'll take the bullet 'cause I got your back."

These are my people and there is nothing phony about any of them. They wouldn't let me quit if I wanted to. My only problem is having to deal with their egos, like a lion tamer.

On a philosophical note, O.J. once told me that people's egos are what first attracts you to them. Despite the fact that at times it drives you insane, it's what you find exciting about them. The guy without an ego goes by dull and unrecognized. This gave me a new appreciation of O.J., because who knows more about egos, confidence and winning than ballplayers? Now I got a better grip on things and it's more like controlled agitation.

Chapter Fifteen
BACK TO COURT

At the behest of the little guys, my supporters and compatriots, we devised a strategy to bring public attention to the exposing of taxpayers to liability, caused by suppressing evidence and obstructing justice in the O.J. prosecution. The problem was finding a lawyer who was brazen enough to represent our cause. Everyone I talked to was either way too busy and didn't have time or they had a conflict of interest. One attorney was honest enough to say he wouldn't get involved with this project, even with a fifty thousand dollar retainer.

I knew if we ever hit pay dirt, long lost friends would be suddenly showing their faces, and lawyers would be thick as flies on a turd. Tommy says, "If nobody out in California will stand with you, then stand alone. Remember, you'll never taste the ham if you're scared to look the wild boar in the face." I continued to beat the bushes until I was directed to an industrious paralegal named Ruben.

Ruben is a classic. I was referred to him by another lawyer who was interested in reviewing my documents, but could not represent me. I was happy to get help with drafting a complaint. I go to see Ruben at the Santa Barbara Plaza in the Crenshaw District. His office sits in a complex of rubble that withstood riots, earthquakes and gang bangers. It stands across the street from the projects mockingly called "the Jungle." It sticks out as a monument to the dismal plight of a Black business district abandoned for urban development and Mega Malls. A tall, rusted chain link fence leans over weeds and plywood surrounding the office building. When you drive through the parking lot, negotiating the pot holes, you get out watching your back all day. Night time is out of the question. These are modern-day ruins of functional embarrassment.

You enter his office through a reception area, chronically absent of a secretary, and pass down a common hall with shared offices. The old building, with old carpet musk, is very imposing. Finally, you locate Ruben's cubicle, a cramped space which he calls his office. Ruben is a jovial, imposing dark-skinned fella, dressed in coat and slacks from near matching suits. An old radio is permanently tuned to *88.1 KLON Jazz* for background music and a disgusting chair awaits his clients.

He sits behind his desk on a chair obviously much too short, balancing on three legs, with one leg missing. Pecking away at his Smith & Corona, he's got plenty of "Wite-Out," but needs a new typing ribbon. Ruben's documents are printed with lettering which may be bold or faint, making them difficult to concentrate on. They give off a strobe light effect which might elicit a seizure if read too intently. He produced a brief for me full of typos that might be better described as malaprops. Ruben functions by hopping from one deadline to the next, and ordinarily cannot be found apart from twenty-three hours before cutoff.

He jumps on a bus and rides it across town to my office to get paid before he starts to work. So there's Ruben, sitting in my waiting room with his legs crossed, kicked back, with a mouth full of chips, resting his feet on the coffee table watching a football game. The soles on his patent leather loafers have seen better days, but he's cool. You gotta like the guy and I don't mean to be supercilious, but the guy is a real character. He takes my ideas and puts them in a framework which is presentable to the courts. Out of all the legal minds and professionals I have dealt with, Ruben is the guy that had the courage to produce the documentation after he rides the bus from the 'hood to the USC Law Library.

Ruben understood what we were trying to do. He saw clearly the racist machinations underlying the media cover-up of the corruption at the hands of the D.A. Through his efforts, he sought closure to a painful incident that took place years before in Tulsa, Oklahoma; the site of America's largest mass burial, over 300 Black men, women and children brutalized by the police and White southerners, in the name of good ol' White Christianity in 1921.

Ruben grew up in Tulsa, and one afternoon as an eight year old, he and a friend thought that they would play a little prank and slip into better seats in the "Whites Only" section at a movie matinee. Unfortunately, they got caught. The manager, a White fella with tobacco dripping from his jaw, escorted them out through the back door and kicked Ruben so hard, he felt his tailbone crack. You don't forget these kinds of things, but maybe setting the truth in the open was Ruben's way of dealing with the past. He is a symbol of the principles we all hold so dearly, but most are afraid to stand up for.

After I filed a complaint with L.A. County, I waited for the county's response. I figured I'd rather negotiate a settlement with the county rather than engage them in a prolonged legal battle, which could prove expensive and embarrassing. The complaint was forwarded to the county's general counsel who replied to my complaint via postcard. Taking an arrogant posture, they suggested that I waited too long to file a complaint, and what I should do is seek legal representation.

I presented my argument to numerous attorneys and most took the position that the feasibility was bleak. It is too incredible to back-up a lone, half-cocked Black doctor, when all experts had failed to identify the same findings. After the complaint was drafted, I decided to use my office address in Hawthorne, California, not far from LAX, the San Diego Freeway, and the Pacific. The municipality of Hawthorne falls under the jurisdiction of Torrance Superior Court, known for its conservative decision making, as well as its bias towards its police who have their share of civil rights complaints. I figured I'd give them the opportunity to redeem themselves.

I took the complaint to the Torrance Courthouse and waited in line in the file room. The file clerk took my complaint and became curious as she stamped the date on the complaint for Status Conference. The problem I had with the date was that I was filing June 20th and the First Status Conference would not take place until December of 1997. The sheriffs were impounding Simpson's assets and my complaint was not receiving any attention. I did not want to work in the dark—susceptible to covert or overt attack—and the stage not set until December.

My strategy was to protect the taxpayers of L.A. against government waste. If O.J.'s case was overturned after his assets were confiscated, taxpayers would be on the hook to reimburse his losses. In order to block this police action, I filed a Motion for Injunction to stay the execution of the $33.5 million dollar judgment against Simpson until my complaint was heard. If I could get the Injunction, then the date in December would not make any difference. It would bring about public awareness and I would feel safer being high profile than low.

I posed the question to the file clerk, "How could we get this motion put in front of the courts as soon as possible?" She advised me of a procedure called an Ex Parte Hearing. I had to file notice of an Ex Parte Hearing and serve the defendants within 72 hours prior to the hearing, including Fred Goldman, Sharon Rufo, the Browns, the Medical Examiner and the District Attorney.

I gave Sammy and Don, my runners, the Proof of Service and a copy of the Injunction and dispatched them to the Coroner's office and the District Attorney's office. Sammy had previously served the Coroner with a Complaint for Medical Malpractice at the county hospital. He went to the reception area where the Coroner's secretary received all mail. When the receptionist, a young arrogant Hispanic lady, saw the subpoena, she became nervous.

After making Sammy wait for about 30 minutes, she contacted the inner office and told Dr. Lucky's personal secretary, "There's a Black man in the reception area waiting for Dr. Lakshmanan." A White lady came out to see what was all the fuss. When she realized Sammy was there to serve the complaint, she told Sammy, "I don't know why anybody wants to serve the Coroner. The taxpayers got their money's worth."

So now, Sammy was back on his way to serve the Coroner again. When he walked into the office, he announced in his booming voice he's got more papers for the Coroner. Immediately, the Hispanic receptionist started scrambling for the White lady. Once again, the old blonde reappeared with a look of disgust on her face, asking Sammy, "Are you back? What is it now?" Sammy told her, "Don't get upset with me, I didn't do nothin' wrong, y'all's the one that did somethin' wrong." She snatched the complaint from Sammy and disappeared again into the bowels of the Coroner's department. Then it was time to serve Fred Goldman.

There were hearings going on in Santa Monica regarding O.J.'s assets and the whereabouts of the Heisman Trophy. The media, although toned down, was still camped out at the courthouse. Juanita had her assignment. With the Proof of Service, the Motion for Injunction, and notice of Ex Parte Hearing, I drove her to Santa Monica and kicked back on the lawn with the media. Several of them wondered and looked perplexed why a brother was hanging out on the lawn outside the courthouse.

Juanita took the documents inside and it was about 45 minutes before she reappeared. O.J., Skip Taft and Fred Goldman were there in an inner-sanctum of the courthouse. Juanita waited for her break, then Fred Goldman came out. He looked like he appears on television: a tall, broad shouldered guy, big bushy mustache, kind of a serious appearing "Rip Torn." He did not want to accept the documents but Juanita appeared innocuous enough, he was curious and was served.

We left the courthouse and headed for the parking lot as some media crew looked on wondering what this Black man and Hispanic woman were up to. Monday rolled around and it was time for the hearing. My crew got it together, Randy, Sam, Juanita, Irene and a group of supporters. I would represent myself. We went down to Torrance, arriving there around a quarter after one. The Ex Parte Hearing was scheduled to be heard in Commissioner Thomas Parrott's chambers.

Parrott was the only Black Commissioner in L.A. County, if not the first. I had met him previously and recognized his name on the door to his courtroom. McNeill had invited me to a fundraiser for Commissioner Parrott at the home of retired NFL Running Back, Jim Brown. Overlooking the Hollywood Hills, there was a modest group of supporters, a friendly crowd jamming to the DJ along with some Smoky Joe's Barbecue. Around the pool, with our plates filled on a warm California evening, the view down from the Hills at the lights of West Hollywood was spectacular. I wondered if Commissioner Parrott would remember me and my political donation I made with the tacit expectation of a political favor. Just being facetious, I didn't really expect any favors, I just hoped to be treated fairly and given a chance to air my grievance.

We congregated at the end of the hall next to a makeshift office, used for domestic disputes and family matters. Most of the people going in and out of the little cubicle were young Black adults. Guys with pants sagging off their butts and little mommas chasing their "youngins" up and down the halls, unable to keep pace running in house slippers. About the best they could do was yell threats at their rambunctious kids, who seemed to enjoy creating havoc.

My eyes scanned the hall for whom we would be opposing. After lunch, the 4th floor was empty. I noticed a couple of young Black attorneys approaching, with the demeanor of county employees, lacking the swagger of attorneys in private practice. One of them started to converge on a Hispanic female, dressed in business attire, seated on a bench.

A White fella with a thick head of shocking white wavy locks appeared, pacing the hall, wearing a tight suit. He seemed frustrated as he walked right past me, glancing at me. I nodded and he threw his head back, making the profile of his nose parallel the ground. With his face towards the ceiling and his eyes shut as he walked, I thought he would trip. I looked down at his worn brown pointed shoes and up at his olive plaid double-vented sports jacket buttoned snugly around his belly, and sensed he must be my adversary.

The bailiff unlocked the courtroom and we all entered the gallery. I had no idea what I was doing, but I remained cool and collected. The Hispanic lady that was seated on the bench in the hall also entered the courtroom. The lawyers pushed through the swinging gate and went to the podium in front of the court secretary to sign in, and I followed their lead. We all took our seats, anxiously awaiting my day in court. It's a quarter past two and the courtroom starts buzzing with whispers, impatient for cases to be heard.

Sam sat near the bailiffs, a male and a female deputy. He overheard one ask the other, "What is taking so long?" "The judge is in his chambers reading the Johnson information," the bailiff replied. Shortly the judge's secretary walked out into the courtroom and announced, "All parties here for the Johnson complaint are summoned to the judge's chamber." The three of us filed in, the young lady turned out to be county counsel and the white-haired guy was representing Goldman. Judge Parrott, sitting there in a casual shirt with his shirt sleeves rolled up, asked us to be seated and made us all feel comfortable.

Commissioner Parrott turned to me and asked, "So tell me, Dr. Johnson, what are you trying to do, overturn the verdict?" I said, "No, I'm not. I have filed a complaint against the county for malpractice to bring public awareness to mitigate a potential liability for the taxpayers of L.A. County." He said, "What do you mean?" I told him that I performed an independent review of the autopsy reports on Nicole Simpson and Ron Goldman, and reached a different conclusion—that two perpetrators were involved in the slayings with the principal killer left-handed. I told him there were indications that the Coroner and D.A. were aware of these facts and they have potentially committed malfeasance, exposing the taxpayers of L.A. County to litigation. Attorney Lambert, Goldman's attorney, blurted out, "Johnson's case does not have any merit." I retorted, "Rather then see my taxes spent on fraudulent litigation, I would prefer to spend them on the floundering L.A. Unified School District and the county hospitals. I shouldn't be taxed to help underwrite politicians' political agendas and help them make book deals and movie deals. It's an imposition on my due process, so don't tell me that my case does not have merit."

Commissioner Parrott asked, "Why is county representation here, they're not involved in the asset seizure?" I said, "If it wasn't for the conspiracy involving the D.A. and the Coroner, we would not be here in the first place." The young lady looked at the floor, she had no comments. Now, I'm sitting on the edge of my chair with my chest sticking out, expecting to hear a rebuttal from the attorneys, when Commissioner Parrott says, "Why would you file your case here? We don't need this here in Torrance." I told him, "I filed it here because my office is in Hawthorne and that's in the Torrance jurisdiction." Parrott says, "Well, you have an L.A. residence, you could file this case anywhere." I told the commissioner, "If that's the case, I'm in the right place." So he asked, "Why don't you have legal representation?" I replied, "The lawyers I have talked to shy away from this, they're concerned about political repercussions." Parrott looks at me, chuckles nervously and says, "I don't see any political repercussions. This is going to bring a lot of media attention, I think you need to serve this in Santa Monica."

The Commissioner looks at me beseechingly and says, "Please take your case to Santa Monica. Tell you what I'm gonna' do, I'm going to dismiss your motion without prejudice. Just withdraw it and take it to Santa Monica."

Now, I felt prepared to deal with the oral arguments from the attorneys, but I did not expect the judge to throw me a curve. I looked at Commissioner Parrott and thought about the few Black men that were in his position. I knew he was under some pressure and wanted to evade the issue, so I decided not to press it, even though I knew I had the right to be in Torrance. Besides, what kind of ruling would I get if I went against the Commissioner's recommendations?

So I figured I'd let the brother off the hook. I said, "Okay, your Honor." The judge excused Lambert and the county counsel and asked me to remain in his chambers. When they left, the judge wanted to hear more of my arguments. The court secretary stood there in amazement as I elaborated my findings. I mentioned my meeting with Baker and Blasier and the use of my information before Dr. Michael Baden testified in the civil trial. Since the *L.A. Times* never emphasized a two-assailant theory and there was no discussion of the left-handed involvement, I was compelled to file an Amicus Curiae Brief, which Judge Fujisaki denied.

Commissioner Parrott was intrigued and seemed pleasantly surprised. He was interested to see more of my arguments and findings, but suggested that I get legal counsel. I gave him a copy of the video, told him I appreciated his advice and left his chambers.

Walking back out to the courtroom, sensing we had attained a degree of success, at the same time I felt disconcerted. We left the courthouse and returned to the office to pow-wow.

I tabled the idea of a Motion for Injunction, while I let the complaint stand for the December hearing date. Thirty days elapsed before I heard anything from the county. Since the county counsel never responded to my complaint, I went back to the courthouse and filed a Motion for Default. The file clerk checked the docket and told us there was no recorded response from the county within the thirty day cutoff. Great news, I thought. I went to lunch and returned to my office to see some patients, when I received a fax. It was an answer to the complaint, along with a court order to deny my Motion for Default. It had all been back-dated. A hearing for a Motion to Demurrer was set for thirty days.

The media remained oblivious and the file clerk gave me one of those "Don't ask me, I don't know nothing" looks. In the meantime, still notifying the press on every move we made and scanning the paper daily to see who would engage these issues, I noted an article about a lawsuit filed against Marcia Clark.

Merritt McKeon, an author, a battered women's activist and attorney, filed a complaint against Marcia Clark for violating a court order by publishing crime scene photos of Nicole Brown Simpson.

Merritt was a friend of the Browns' and co-authored the book Stop Domestic Violence, with Louis Brown, Nicole's father. I traced her down in Laguna Beach and commended her on her aggressive stance against public officials exploiting victims for their personal profit, and mentioned the results of my work. She seemed interested to see what I had, so I invited her to my office since she taught part-time at West Los Angeles Law School, nearby.

I also invited a friend of mine who knew O.J. from college and played professional football as well, Reggie Berry. Reggie played with the San Diego Chargers and the Denver Broncos in the seventies, and was also the President of the NFL Retired Players

Association in Los Angeles. A number of retired players are patients of mine because they placed their confidence in Reggie recommending me to them. I have seen a lot of guys banged up without health or disability benefits. By comparison to O.J., with their degree of disability, most of these retired players knew, "No way, Jose" could O.J. physically do what he was accused of.

Merritt initially was hostile towards O.J., but mystified watching the video. She looked over at Reggie and said, "Oh my God, the son of a gun didn't do it!" She took a copy of the Amicus Curiae Brief with her to review. Merritt now found herself doubting her beliefs she held so confident, and could not reconcile the facts with the media accounts. You could sense Merritt's sincerity and she did not relish the idea of being duped into believing O.J. guilty. She wanted some answers and we encouraged her to join us. I advised her of my upcoming hearing, although the Ex Parte Motion had been denied.

Chapter Sixteen

THE COURTHOUSE CAT FIGHT

I spoke to Merritt a few days later, she was very busy trying to set up her new law office. She had toned down her vitriol against O.J., and was now more benign. She made comments about the misgivings in the D.A.'s office, and about the evidence which supported the theory that O.J. was not guilty. She was prepared to join our crusade.

We decided to get together on the night before the Demurrer Hearing. The gang met in the conference room in my office. Merritt came up from Laguna Beach, as I had promised to cover her hotel expenses so she would be ready to show up in court with us. She was initially timid but with time she became gung ho. She presented the idea to combine our lawsuits, her *Qui Tem* suit—a case she had against Marcia Clark—and my suit against the Coroner and District Attorney.

Merritt exerted herself and domineered the discussion. Here we all sat watching in amazement as Merritt challenged my motive for debate. She accused me of attempting to control, for control's sake, and then asked sarcastically if I wanted to be the lawyer. Totally disrupting the flow of the discussion, we all sat back in disbelief.

The prior evening I had read her Motion to Consolidate to Tommy in Minneapolis and he said it sounded good, but I did not have a chance to give it a thorough going over. I knew my complaint had broader social implications than Merritt's, which should not be minimized in place of her suit against Marcia Clark. I knew that Merritt had something more tangible and greater public exposure; she would be recognized for her association with Louis Brown. A milestone for me would be to gain more significant exposure, and I figured this would be more important than guiding our team through the legal maze, knowing a tuna doesn't swim with sharks.

Now, I didn't want to destroy the momentum by forcing my hand, and my staff was embarrassed but sympathetic towards Merritt, so I made an attempt at spontaneous peacemaking. Cooler heads supervened, and I felt I should acquiesce since my fundamental goal stood a chance to be realized.

At this point the debate stopped, not for resolution sake, but for expediency. The bone of contention was should the attack be directed at the system, or should it be more focused? I felt that every division of the criminal justice system would support each other, including the Superior Court bench. It would be futile not to remain circumspect and on guard for a flank attack.

Merritt seemed to disregard this perspective, and her gestures and comments were cynical. We remained focused for the greater part of the evening, but I sensed that Merritt was not fully grasping the subtleties that would result in failure.

After our conference was over, I took Merritt to the Best Western Hotel up the street. I paid for her evening stay and walked her to her room. She unlocked the door, pushing it open, with the stale odor of the musty hotel room greeting us. She flipped the light switch on, and I went for the air-conditioner and curtains on the windows. I peered out on Hawthorne Boulevard into the darkness, across the parking lot, and started to feel the weight of what we would embark on. By the window sat a crummy little table, waddling on uneven legs, as we set our soda cans and elbows on it. The dim low watt bulb cast obscure shadows across the well worn carpeting. The minutes seemed to tick off slowly now. I knew Merritt was tired, but the room made you feel that you would not sleep well.

I wanted to emphasize again my concerns about the trickery and treachery, notwithstanding the game plan. Merritt would represent me and we would move for consolidation. I told her I was prepared to argue my motion, if hers was denied, and that I felt strongly in a taxpayer's lawsuit, despite its history of denials. I also reiterated the philosophical points and their social implications. I perceived that now she started grasping the passion in my argument. Finally convinced that she submitted to my viewpoint, I was comfortable with her pressing me to leave her room.

In the morning, I went to the "Jungle" to pick up "Sweet" Minnie. She was up at the crack of dawn, cleaning and chain smoking. Minnie's enthusiastic and makes you feel inspired, having the wisdom to listen. I opened up to her, as my emotional state of mind was to talk with someone about my anxiety about the way the discussion had ended the previous evening. Minnie was sympathetic, as she naturally is, and it felt good just to vent.

We arrived at the office at 7:30 a.m. where we had agreed to meet so we could all ride together in the van. Randell was the last to arrive. We climb into the van, Sammy cranks it up and we're off. Looking out the windows, cruising down the side streets, the van wobbles from side to side, swishing the coffee around in my stomach. The radio is tuned to 94.7 FM, "The Wave," but my mind was alternating between nervous boredom and anxious anticipation. Everyone is quiet and pensive.

We arrived at the Torrance Courthouse ready for our day in court. Randy, with video camera in hand, cajoles his way past security, and we are off to Department M. We get on a crowded elevator, all six of us, and push the fourth floor button. As our eyes wandered from stare to stare, ceiling and walls, Merritt turns to me with a worried look and asks with a sense of urgency, "Why are we late?" Now it's a couple minutes after 8:30 a.m. I don't like it but I figure I have never seen court start on time. The last time I was in court, in Torrance a month ago, it started an hour after schedule, so I had a gambler's comfort. It's stupid, this sentiment, it mollifies your nervous agitation of being late.

When we get to the end of the hall, I was so confident about our arrival time, that when Randell reached for the courtroom door, he would snatch on it and find it locked. To my disillusion the door leaped open. I swallowed the frog in my throat and took three steps through the door as it closed behind me. We crept into a semi-filled courtroom, and scooted past people who were already seated. I felt like a spotlight was on me and that my britches were split.

Case number one was beginning, as we sat down in the gallery. I felt a bit relieved as our entrance went rather unceremonious, and the court's attention was engaged in the first case.

Merritt, looking a bit disconcerted, was prompted to approach the court clerk and sign in. I intimated that I should go up to the clerk and advise her of my presence as well, but Merritt cut her eyes at me, so I just sat back and exhaled. She checked in and returned to sit next to me, as we listened to the proceedings. I got lost in the vernacular, but I picked up on the nuances.

Judge Lois Anderson-Smaltz seemed like someone longing for recognition. She surveyed the courtroom like a chicken watching a farmer with his hatchet. Wanting to impress everyone that she was in charge of her courtroom, she was rude and capricious. She did not tolerate what she perceived as jawboning, although a lawyer may have had a good point. On one occasion, after being snappy and stubborn, she suddenly realized she had made a mistake. Discombobulated, she finally regained her composure with all the aplomb of someone who had just farted in a crowded elevator. She went through cases 1, 2 and 3 with the precision of a neurosurgeon with Parkinson's.

Now our moment had finally arrived. As Case 3 wound to a close, Merritt and I glanced at each other. We raised up on our haunches, pushing the side rails of our seats to stand up and heard, "case number five" called out. My first reaction was, huh? Oh well, we'll just sit here and she will come back to us next. Now as case five wound to a close, I looked around the courtroom to get a feeling of where everyone's emotional level was. There were about twenty-five supporters and several onlookers in the gallery. I looked back at Merritt and then started to raise up again to let her pass me. That's when I realized the judge was no longer in the courtroom. Smaltz must have dropped through a trap door behind the judge's bench.

Merritt got up and immediately approached the clerk. The courtroom sat patiently, totally bewildered. I looked at the expression on the clerk's face and could tell that something was not good. My vision focused next on Merritt, who appeared now almost stricken with panic. The court clerk took delight in antagonizing Merritt, informing her, "Sorry, your case was dismissed, too bad." Merritt grew pale with dejection. Outraged, she turned from the clerk with utter disbelief and seemed to stagger back to her seat.

I felt like someone thumped me on the head so hard, it made me smile. I was stupefied, feeling somewhere between a day late and a date rape. For the third time, I had been out-maneuvered, not by the opposing counsel but by the judge. Most of us assembled outside the courtroom, completely baffled. Then I thought to myself, I have to get more of an answer than just turning around and silently leave the courtroom without ever opening my mouth. I did an about face and marched back into the courtroom with

Merritt and Randell following. I went straight to the clerk, who was an attractive middle-aged blonde, with her hair ratted and sprayed stiff. She wiggled in her chair as she spoke.

Merritt joined me at the clerk's desk, and before I could say anything, Merritt spoke up saying, "I'm here to represent Dr. Johnson, with moving papers for consolidation of our complaints." As the clerk raised her face up from her feigned work, she stared at Merritt with such a scowl, it looked like something out of *"The Exorcist."* Merritt handed the clerk her substitution motion, and said that she wanted to be heard. The clerk's eyes said, "What are you doing with the enemy, bitch?" She took a look at Merritt's pleading, and said, "This is the weirdest motion I have ever seen, take your papers and get outta here!" throwing Merritt's papers back to her.

Astounded, Merritt stepped back and exclaimed, "What kind of procedures are these?" The clerk shot back, "You're being argumentative." Now with Merritt's intelligence thoroughly insulted, she rhetorically asked, "Do you call this justice?" The clerk turned caustic, started batting her eyes, wiggling violently, and snapping her head from side to side. She shot her arm straight up in the air, which looked about five feet long, and started popping her fingers like a bullwhip, yelling, "Bailiff, clear the courtroom!" Totally mystified, this was one of the most bizarre days of my life, a reality more freaky than the imagination. Two White women squaring off behind O.J., in public, with everyone in the courtroom watching, as they snarled and screamed at each other.

I walked over to the bailiff who was still seated and he calmly asked me what was going on. I explained that we came for a hearing today and that we were told our case was dismissed. He said, "I never heard that any case was dismissed, since calling the court to order."

I get on my soapbox, proclaiming our videotape shows a conspiracy to suppress evidence that clears O.J., and that certain people are afraid of its exposure. This is the reason the judge shamefully vanished from the courtroom. It is a disgrace to the judicial system and the American Flag as it stands on its platform behind the judge's bench. "Remove the flag from the courtroom!" I demanded.

The bailiff looked like he was thrown for a loop. Suddenly, a big, burly Black woman deputy barreled out of the judge's chambers and started shouting, "Everyone, get out of the courtroom!" She was frightening and aggressive, without provocation. Mostly elderly people and clergy were there supporting me and I felt responsible for this deranged intimidation, and the humiliation of seeing a Black woman deputy sheriff behaving this way. She barked at Randell to shut his camera off, and then shot over to the other side of the courtroom and got right up in Reggie's face. Reggie, a big guy and ex-pro ballplayer, never flinched as she stared menacingly, ranting and slobbering, bad breath and all.

Reggie was not attracting attention, he was just a quiet observer. She was bent on sweating a big guy and questioned why he had a book in his hand. She then turned her attention to a White lawyer standing next to Reggie, paused for a moment, and looked him up and down. The lawyer spoke up, asking the deputy, "Is something wrong?" She grimaced with contempt and said "No," then abruptly turned and headed back into the judge's chambers, hot under the collar, grumbling to herself.

We all cleared the courtroom and I apologized to my supporters for what had happened. It scared the hell out of them, but I felt the experience was worthwhile. Everyone had direct exposure to some of the frustration I had dealt with for the past several months.

Most of these folks were seated before the judge entered the courtroom and no one heard or saw anything that remotely resembled a hearing. People were shocked and disappointed to see our system at its worst. We went down and gathered outside in the front of the courthouse pondering what had just happened. As the hot sun beat down on us, Merritt seemed as though she experienced a transformation. She saw the genuine goodwill of our supporters, and I doubt if she had ever been around a group of Black people who were so personally touched. It was a powerful moment.

I introduced Merritt to our supporters, and she spoke some words which the crowd warmly embraced. Then I shared some of my reflections. "I know we are only a spark, but if we gently take care and fan it, it will grow. There can never be complete darkness as long as there is a spark, and presently we are the dedicated keepers."

Randell roamed about, panning the entire gathering with his home video camera when a security guard approached, and told us we had to move. He stated we were blocking the visibility of the parking lot, as terrorist threats were ever present. He's got no gun, but he's got a uniform and he's got orders.

Randy, on the other hand, is doing what he came to court to do. So now, one guy with a job is intruding on another guy working. Randell became agitated by the interference. He spoke up and asked the guard if he would stop obstructing him as he filmed. Randell showed no restraint as he displayed his disdain. He told this security guard, who coincidentally was also a Black man, that he would never speak to a White cameraman with WKKK call letters on the side of his camera. I turned around to see what all the jibber-jabbering was about, and realized we were not wanted here. We needed to beat it before some lackeys started to get pushy.

We went back to the office to lick our wounds and regroup. I knew we would be back another day to fight, and stronger; but everyone seemed to take it rough. Minnie went into Juanita's office, closed the door and just sobbed. Merritt, on the other hand, was dazed and could not believe a White woman would be treated just like a nigga'. I didn't mind telling her, "I told you so." We got the ruling in the mail a few days later, "Motion for Demurrer sustained without leave to amend." In other words, my complaint was denied with prejudice.

Of all the lawyers I spoke with following the judge's ruling, not one could believe that the judge actually sustained the demurrer without leave to amend. The judge effectively cancelled our legal claims in the Torrance Court. We followed up by tracking down a transcript of the minutes from the hearing and it took us a week to finally corner the judge's court reporter, Lisa Guerrero. Lisa told Juanita, "Let me tell you something, so you'll stop buggin' me. Judge Lois Anderson-Smaltz instructed me not to *record any minutes* of the hearing, so you've got none."

Trying to get a judge to do the right thing is like trying to catch a catfish with your bare hands.

Merritt had her confidence thoroughly rattled. I suggested since she had co-authored a book with Louis Brown, that she talk with him about her feelings and doubts; however, she just could not muster the chutzpah. Merritt called my office later in the week and spoke with Juanita, saying she could no longer represent us, that it was a "conflict of interest," but she was willing to write a book with Dr. Johnson. Juanita told Merritt, "Why don't you tell Doc yourself? He's in his office. I'll get him for you." "That's all right, don't bother," she replied, "I'll talk to him later..." click.

I said, "Whoa!" She left me standing at the altar. It sent me into a tailspin. Usually, when I experience a spectacular letdown, as a reaction my day-dreaming increases exponentially and I commonly find myself drifting back to more tranquil times, to my childhood.

Chapter Seventeen
COMING UP IN MINNESOTA

Born in Minneapolis in the summer of 1951; our family's beginnings were in the "projects." Phyllis Wheatley Settlement House, around the block, provided hot lunches and childcare for me and my older brother, Thomas the Third. My mother cared for my younger brother and sister, while my dad attended the University of Minnesota Medical School. Mom had Tommy first, when she was thirty years old and then had five more babies in a row. She was a "late starter," having dropped out of college when her father died. She joined the Women's Army Corps in 1942 during the War, so her younger sisters could go to college. "Hen'retta" as she was called was strong yet genteel, born in middle Georgia. The granddaughter of an ex-slave, Henry Stewart—my namesake—she was forthright and independent.

Her father dropped out of the University of Chicago Medical School in 1908 to return to middle Georgia, tending the homestead of his recently deceased father. He was best friends with Elijah Poole, who would later change his name to Muhammad. They were raised in the African Methodist Episcopal Church. In the military, mom met my father, Tom Johnson, Second Lieutenant in the U.S. Army. They married and were sent to West Africa on a tour of duty. Dad worked with the U.S. Public Health Service based in Liberia to control malaria during World War II.

Liberia was founded by ex-slaves who left America and returned to Africa. In 1847, Liberia became the first nation in Africa to gain independence. It remained a satellite of the U.S., until the recent wars and AIDS epidemic that has enveloped most English speaking countries in Africa.

Dad rode a Harley-Davidson, with two Colt 45s strapped to his waist, up and down the dirt roads of Monrovia. He hailed from East Texas, the grandson of a mulatto ex-slave, with a proud heritage of those collaborating with the underground railroad that headed to Mexico.

There were slaves that could not follow Harriet Tubman because they were considered desperados. These men and their families stood up in defiance to the cruelties of slavery. Most slaves were cooperative and labored in the fields; however, some did not submit to the cruelties and humiliation inflicted by that evil institution. Some who felt threatened would not allow their loved ones to be brutalized. To stand up to a ruthless slave master meant capital insubordination and was dealt with severely and harshly. Rather than suffer, they would fight to the death of themselves or their master. If the master was injured or killed, the slaves were put to death or became fugitives. Heading north was out of the question. They took to the swamps and the dry river beds, heading southwest through Louisiana and Texas to Mexico.

There were hideouts along the way where runaways could find rest during daylight, and provisions, for they traveled by night. They sojourned in the dry river bottoms and followed the fork west to make it to Mexico. Vigilantes didn't care to search the river bottoms in the moonlight because those heading south had nothing to lose and would not return, dead or alive. History seldom captures the defiance of the underdog, only the victor's story is told. Dad was precocious, and entered Wiley College in Marshall, Texas, when he was fourteen. Graduating at eighteen, this was generally the end of the road for the educational pursuits of Blacks in Dixie, post-graduate schools were segregated. After you graduated from a Black College, your choices were few. Janitorial jobs for college grads were plenty or possibly a shot at getting into grad school at Tuskegee, Meharry or Howard—if you knew somebody. In those days, these were the only post-graduate schools Blacks could attend in the South. If you were determined to further your education, you would have to somehow find your way up north.

The African community in Texas had remote ties to Minnesota. The Twenty-Fifth Infantry of Buffalo Soldiers transferred there to Fort Snelling. This Black Infantry left Texas on detail to capture Sitting Bull, following his defeat of Custer at Little Big Horn. Ironically, Custer wanted nothing to do with the Black troops, feeling they were inferior and untrustworthy. Notwithstanding Custer's delusions, the Buffalo Soldiers were able to negotiate the surrender of Sitting Bull and his people. So much for Custer's indiscretion; obviously, remnants of that same tunnel vision still exist today.

Dad's Uncle Teddy used to play in the fast lane and hustled as far as the Twin Cities during the prohibition years, making contacts for Canadian Whiskey and bringing it back to Oklahoma and Texas. Uncle Ted recounted stories about how pretty the country was and how friendly the Scandinavians were in Minnesota. With canvas painted and the need to go north, my father traveled to Minnesota to start post-graduate school, prior to the war breaking out. He was drafted but set his mind on returning to Minneapolis after the war, and this is where my parents settled.

Mom, a trojan by nature, took no prisoners. She was a Staff

Sergeant for the Women's Army Corps after attending Spellman Finishing School in Atlanta. She was God-fearing and very respectful, but would not backdown from anyone when she knew she was in the right. She kept us clean, well-fed and well-behaved. Even when my brother convinced me to break out of daycare at Wheatley, by crawling into a hole dug under our playground fence, she made us clean up and walk back to school.

Dad spent from sun-up to sun-down at medical school. He would come home, have dinner, then go to work in construction during the graveyard shift. My father, as well as other Black men from the "Northside Projects," worked on the cold, steep, muddy banks next to the swirling murky waters of the mighty Mississippi. Lifting wheelbarrows of sand and pouring concrete, they helped build the bridges across the river in the early fifties.

When the other guys learned that my dad was a medical student, they would later recount that they forced my father to sit on the cold damp banks of the river and study his lessons by kerosene lamp. They would carry his load to help feed his family because they wanted to see to it that this African American became a doctor. Thanks to those guys, Dad graduated in 1954.

Mom knew it was very difficult and if you allowed your dedication to falter, it was over. Dad, along with his study partner, Abrams, the only other brother in medical school at Minnesota, were so fearful of blowing their anatomy lab and flunking out of school, they kidnapped a cadaver from the pathology department and took it to Abram's apartment in the projects. There they would dissect the body and study it, risking the consequences of finding a couple of Black guys dissecting a White man in the "projects." My mother, to her dying day, swore she could still smell the formaldehyde reeking from their clothes when they came to our apartment for lunch breaks. They put the guy back together, stuffed him in a croker sack and into the trunk of dad's '49 Chevy. They drove back to the University morgue and no one could quite figure out how these "colored boys" knew their anatomy so well. They passed with flying colors.

I can remember spending Saturday nights, at least I think they were Saturdays, in the dark smoke-filled living room, leaning against my father's and my uncle's knees as they sat swigging Pabst's Blue Ribbon and Hamm's beer in front of the flickering black and white television. Their eyes were transfixed on the Gillette-sponsored prize fights. Sugar Ray Robinson was the Saturday night favorite and sometimes my uncle would sneak me a tasty sip of beer, when my mother wasn't looking.

We always had three square meals: eggs, bacon, sausage, grits, biscuits, pancakes, syrup and molasses in the morning. Greens, beans, salads, potatoes, rice, pork chops, chicken and roast in the evenings. Food was abundant and there weren't any Mickey D's or Kentucky Fried. My uncle and my dad's friends commonly stopped by to eat Mom's good soul food cooking.

Despite the abundance of good food, I preferred what my friends in the projects had to eat, mayonnaise sandwiches and meatless spaghetti with Kool-Aid. I know this was vexing to mother, as she often reminded us of all the hunger in the world, and that it was sinful to waste food, besides being disrespectful to those struggling to provide you with this blessing.

What stands out most in my childhood is that my parents never argued in front of us kids and I attribute that to the respect my mother showed her family.

My formative years were a microcosm of Black kids. I met my first White friend when my dad took a job as the prison physician at Stillwater State Penitentiary, the final home of Coleman Younger of the James Gang. Positions for young Black doctors graduating medical school in those days were scarce. We moved out of the projects to a little old town on the St. Croix River at the Wisconsin border. We lived in a wooden bungalow which looked like a turn-of-the-century mansion. We lived in the shadow of the penitentiary and had trustees, both Black and White, providing service to us. I would run past the wrought iron spear-picketed gates and into the barren halls of the penitentiary, skipping through the corridors. These were halcyon days and it was here that I met the Warden's daughter, Christine, and we became playmates. We had a ball playing together and I had a crush on her. I knew she was different but it bore no significance to me at this tender age. The most indelible memory of her was when she left me hanging in the air on the teeter-totter as she dismounted. I crashed to the ground so hard, my teeth clattered and I bit my knuckle, causing it to bleed. I still have that small gash on my finger. Kids played innocent tricks on me in the projects, and I regularly got jacked up. I never took it real personal, but I learned to be more observant. I learned that people could hurt you and not know the extent of how much or have mal-intent.

Despite being swallowed up in a new all-White environment short of the prison trustees, I was never truly aware of any malice in my surroundings. My mother kept the family in touch with what was the extent of the Black society of Minneapolis by weekend visits back to the projects, fifty miles away from Stillwater. We periodically vacationed back to the South. I can honestly say I had no social compunction about my skin color or heritage. This was the purity of my early childhood experiences.

My first lesson in racial distinction came when I was eight years old, traveling to Georgia by train in 1959. I loved traveling by rail across country. There was almost never a dull moment. The roar of the train, the noise, the smells, the power, the vibration and jostling, and then the dizziness and vomiting. It didn't matter, I never stopped running and exploring the entire train. The conductor went nuts as he side-stepped and hopped over the puke and other mess I had created throughout the train. I didn't care, it was my world.

We arrived in Memphis where we had to change trains. We all

picked up our belongings, and headed across the station. All of us hungry, all five little ones and my mom. In the lobby was a wonderful bright and shiny restaurant. Stainless steel, white tile, beautiful picture windows, with the smell of burgers, french fries and ice cream emanating from the door. The place was bustling and we could not help but get excited. We rushed the door to sit down at a table. A waitress came over, and before I could say "hamburger," the waitress told us, "Sorry, we don't serve Negroes here." She was polite but I didn't understand. She informed us, "Colored folks are served across the lobby." No big deal, I was too hyped to get upset. I was looking forward to my next adventure.

We all picked up our belongings and headed across the station. Suddenly, a stark contrast ensued. We abruptly went from the modern, high gloss tile and stainless motif, to the down home spring-slamming, wooden-framed screen door facade, complete with interior flies, dust-swirling ceiling fans, and creaky wooden floors. An empty, dark, dingy cafe with an old fat sister, greasy apron and spatula in hand. "May I see a menu?" my mother asked. "No need," said the lady, "We only got bacon sandwiches." I had no real sense of disappointment, just bewilderment. Mom prodded on, "Where do colored people eat in a nice place?" "Y'all should get a cab and go 'cross town." Mom handed the lady a dollar, and we picked up again. This time, though, things turned out swell. Fried chicken, mashed potatoes, chocolate cake, and all the red soda I could drink. Man, I like traveling like this, but I don't know what sticks with me more, the good time or the rejection.

We were on our way again as we boarded the "Dixie Flyer," destined for the Deep South. Plenty of cotton gins, magnolia trees, and "Whites Only" signs; nothing more than a peculiarity to me. As a child, I never truly understood the menace behind the symbols.

We had a great summer at Grandma Flagg's. Innocence was the sign of the time. My worst enemies were the spiders and the bees and the nights were so very dark. We chased chickens around the pecan trees in grandma's backyard and dashed away from the grumpy, old, muddy hogs. Life was grand. Walking barefoot through the watermelon patches, chasing the cows back to the barn. No running water, but who cared? We got away without taking a bath. I must admit, I preferred my cold glass of homogenized milk back in Minneapolis to the warm stuff only my uncle could seem to get out of the cow's udder. I never got the hang of it, and the milk skeeting against the side of the pail did not look like it went well with my "Rice Krispies."

After saying good-bye to my cousins, half cousins, second and third cousins, we packed up our grandma-made quilts, boxes of pecans and canned peaches. Mamma' Flagg gave each of us a big hug, and I just hoped she wouldn't get any of that "Dixie Peach" snuff in the corners of her smile on me when she kissed me good-bye. A summer with the kinfolks down South. Surrounded by people who looked like me, I never thought about the contrast of my home up North. My upbringing remained idyllic.

As I matured, I became more knowledgeable of my heritage and the greatness in the people of color. I gradually started to develop pride, notwithstanding, the fact that I almost never saw, or seldom heard, Blacks on television or radio. College Bowl games in those days were all-White and boring. I appreciated the accomplishment of Black cross-over artists, like Nat King Cole and Rochester, because they were the only ones you would commonly see. Still, they weren't my heroes. My heroes were Hoppalong Cassidy, Tarzan, Wild Bill Hickock and Rin-Tin-Tin. My first true Black hero was Floyd Patterson, as I listened to his knockout of Ingamar Johanson on the radio. Then it shifted to Cassius Clay, whom I could watch on TV. Now I'm starting to connect with something on a more conscious level.

James Brown, "the hardest working man in show business," started making things funky, but I never figured how other people viewed these two men until I was a teenager. By now, we had moved to the southside of Minneapolis, away from Stillwater, as my dad started to build his medical practice. Dad is a strong, masculine figure. To me, I thought that the world revolved around him. He was always impeccably dressed, had a beautiful smile, gorgeous cars, and was always reading or listening to jazz. His friends would come by the house on the weekends and evenings, and they would talk for hours about civil rights. To me, they seemed loud and boring. It intrigued me, the tidbits of Black history, but I did not understand the social commentary and its implications. These people seemed to venerate my dad who belonged to everything from Prince Hall, thirty-third degree Mason, Potentate and Commander of Johnny Baker VFW.

My dad's accomplishments I never entertained an idea to match, but I always wanted to impress him. There was no more fulfilling reward than to see my dad smiling at me, beautiful wide grin, strong white teeth and reassuring eyes. I never heard one person utter a scornful word against my father. Everyone seemed proud of this strong, intelligent, Black trailblazer. He was my balance against the distracting images on TV back then, which still affects my reality today. Still, media images distort perceptions, yet what seems apparent readily dissolves in the crucible of time. Time, as a measurement of reality, will ultimately prove to be the undoing of the "Trial of the Century."

Chapter Eighteen

GOD IS WATCHING

It is remarkable how many people comment to me about God. This entire tragedy has had religious undertones, beliefs and references to the Bible dispersed throughout it. Johnnie Cochran and Denise Brown were known to prominently wear their crosses, and Cochran made numerous references to biblical passages and moral arguments. O.J.'s mother, Eunice Simpson, kept a Bible on her lap on several occasions and there were references to O.J. relying on Bible study, as he whiled away his time in his cell.

Most Black people that are staunch supporters of O.J. are very spiritual and voice some aspects about biblical parables themselves. I also find that my most ardent supporters have a strong religious conviction. A friend of mine pressed me, asking what was my motive for doing what I am doing? I thought long and hard about what actually motivated me. I always wanted to be able to say, in the briefest terms, what compelled me to stay the course, but I

205

could never come up with one single profound statement to sum up my feelings. I just flat out told her, "I don't really know why I am doing what I am doing." I am admonished as much as I am encouraged. Some of my purpose has been shrouded in my zeal to give the perspective of a Black man, in an interracial relationship. Interracial marriages at times are perhaps more stable than some same-race marriages ironically, because there are forces that wish to disrupt them. Most experts attempt to explain the psychodynamics of an interracial relationship, in other words, why these people are attracted to each other.

My wife and I, as well as our kids, find ourselves in situations as simple as going to the neighborhood supermarket can be a real adventure. It seems at times that people intend to make you feel uncomfortable, and you find them staring, with their imagination going a hundred miles-per-hour. Based on people's facial expressions, you figure most do not have positive thoughts in their minds. So many things are taken for granted and so much is sacrificed, then again I start to think about how so-called Christians behave until they have their conditioned emotions triggered. I can remember going to my AME church with my Caucasian wife, having brown-skinned women rolling their eyes at me, and then wondering if church was a game to them or if Jesus himself might be prejudiced. Then I snap out of the delusion to focus on the teachings of Jesus, the common denominator of which is love. I still can't say clearly why I pursued this, so my friend told me, "If you can't say why you're doing this, then it must have been a mission given to you." My religious patients explain that God is working through me and guiding me, and that they are praying for me.

One sweet, elderly lady told me that my fight has already been won, yet another reassured me that the victory comes not on your time, but on God's time, so breathe easy. I always hear the familiar phrase, "God bless you and the work you are doing." Never have I heard or received so many blessings from people I hardly know or even have ever met. It is quite moving and inspiring. Interestingly, people become very spiritual when they appreciate a burden, or have it lifted. In contrast to the churches that act as community focal points, I believe the power of faith is my main motivation for speaking openly against tyranny and injustice. The truth is spiritual and the truth does set you free. If you are honest, then the truth makes your heart strong and you feel the power when you hear it. On the other hand, if you are dishonest, the truth creates anxiety, anger, and nervous depression; indeed, it's a formidable task to hide an elephant in a closet.

Chapter Nineteen

TWO BIRTHDAY PARTIES

I got a call from Irma Reed, R.N., a retired nursing supervisor from King Hospital. Everybody surrounding the "Trial of the Century" knew Irma. She was O.J.'s chief supporter in the mean streets of L.A. When at King, Irma fought for the residents that caught hell during training, and she adopts what she calls her "boys" like a protecting she lion. She won't tolerate one sarcastic remark about O.J. in her presence. Irma is sweet as banana cream pie but if you piss her off, she's bold enough to spit in your eye and dare you to wipe it off of your face. I had to deal with her occasionally at King, but grew fonder of her after residency. Irma supported O.J. in both trials, and on more than one occasion, she and my sister Sharon ran into each other, because Sharon was my biggest street advocate and inevitably their paths crossed. Both of them are the same, very disarming, but if rubbed the wrong way they will get in your face like a bad case of acne. Irma and Sharon became acquainted among the protestors and the media circus out-side the Santa Monica Courthouse.

Whenever we had a general announcement that we expressed as an editorial release, aside from flooding numerous media fax lines, Sharon and Juanita would go to the lawn outside the court-house and saturate those covering the trial with this provocative information. Predictably the releases amazed the camera crews and reporters but the only question most people wanted to know was, "Is Dr. Johnson Black?" Irma told me she was arranging a birthday party for O.J. at Gagne's Restaurant in the Crenshaw Plaza and wanted to invite me and my staff to the party back in July 1998.

Despite all the work that we had put out, this was the first for-mal introduction that I would have to O.J. Simpson.

I popped for six guests and we all dressed to kill, heading to this private set at the Creole restaurant. My wife Andrea and I, Sharon, Juanita and her husband John, and Larry, my backup. I needed extra eyes and ears, because I had no idea of what I was walking into.

The previous night, I had offered to take O.J.'s sister Shirley and husband Ben out to dinner at "Harold & Belle's" Restaurant located in a blue collar neighborhood of West Jefferson in Los Angeles, for some southern dining. I shared a bit of my background, the work my staff performed and talked about the autopsy findings. You could sense that suddenly a weight was lifted off Shirley as her chin raised and her eyes brightened. Shirley's spirits seemed forlorn as she fought to maintain a sense of pride. It was at the height of the fury heaped on O.J., and his family were outcasts. Shirley, a nurse in the Bay Area, was ostracized from her job when it was learned that she was O.J.'s sister. The entire family was feeling oppressed, in a state of gloom.

While chomping down on some appetizers, I told her that the phone records of the Browns' would clear O.J. but were never shown to the jury. Shirley grabbed her chest, it hit her like a freight train. I explained to them about the Field Investigator's Report for the L.A. Coroner, dated June 13, 1994. The Investigator's report, based on the statements made by Louis Brown, related that Nicole spoke with Juditha Brown about 11:00 p.m., the night she was killed. The Coroner's Investigator, Claudine Ratcliff, was given that information from Louis Brown, the morning after the bodies were discovered. Yet this statement was subsequently retracted a week later on June 20th, when Louis Brown found his way to a remote, graffiti-covered, industrial section of East L.A. where the Coroner's office is located. He pushed the time they were on the phone back from 11:00 p.m. to sometime earlier between 9:30 p.m. and 10:00 p.m. Judge Kennedy-Powell would not allow the Coroner's Investigator's official report to be submitted as evidence.

If the statement of 11:00 p.m. for the time of the phone conversation was certain, it would coincide with the same time that O.J. was in the back of a chauffeur-driven limousine, on his way to the airport. I informed Shirley that during the preliminary hearing, the phone records of the Browns' and Nicole's were sealed by Judge Kennedy-Powell, during a closed session in the judge's chambers, on July 8, 1994. Robert Shapiro, in the same meeting, offered to stipulate that 10:17 p.m. was the time that Nicole spoke to her mother by phone.

Marcia Clark refused to accept Shapiro's stipulation, stating that she could not remember what the phone record said, although she had subpoenaed the records to see for herself. Despite Marcia Clark having produced the records in open court the previous week and having provided Shapiro with a copy, Clark explained to Judge Kennedy-Powell that she somehow had misplaced the records. Clark stated she needed time to locate them, prompting Judge Kennedy-Powell to make the ruling that, "Until we have a stipulation, the phone records are sealed, and I don't want the transcripts of this chamber meeting released."

Shapiro and Clark returned to open court for closing arguments, when Shapiro opted to stipulate, once again—the time of the phone call. Marcia Clark said, "There's no evidence to support your stipulation, there'll be none," and Judge Kennedy-Powell bound O.J. over for trial. Shirley clicked her tongue and said, "Uhm, uhm, uhm!"

I said, "That ain't the half of it. Six months later, Marcia Clark offered People's Exhibit #35, a graphics art depiction of the phone records, which stated the Browns were on the phone at 9:37 p.m. speaking with Nicole from their home in Dana Point. Shapiro then pompously stood up and stipulated that Marcia Clark's Exhibit #35 was accurate and depicted the actual time that the telephone calls came in. The official copy of the phone records was never shown to the jury."

The Browns had stated previously that they left the Mezzaluna restaurant some time between 8:30 p.m. and 9:00 p.m. At least a half dozen employees from the Mezzaluna stated the same thing. In order for the Browns to have driven home to Dana Point—75 miles south of L.A.—in less than one hour, meant that they averaged 100 mph. Somehow the Browns' family, including Nicole's parents, two of her sisters along with their two small children, who were lying without seatbelts in the back of their jeep, "managed" to drive the distance in record time, lickety-split.

Leaving the trendy section of Brentwood, driving down Wilshire Boulevard onto the San Diego Freeway, they headed south past the San Diego/Santa Monica Freeway Interchange. Past peak traffic converging on LAX Airport they continued on their way through Long Beach and Irvine. Exiting the I-5 freeway, they continued on a ten-mile stretch of dark winding road, until they arrived at their beachside house. The trip was 75 miles, down the busiest freeway in the United States.

Marcia Clark's exhibit was proof that the Browns did it in about 45 minutes. Not only that, but Shapiro now had just stipulated <u>twice</u> to two <u>different times</u> for the same phone call. Shirley, looking as if she was holding back tears, said, "I feel like someone just kicked me in the stomach." So I replied, "Let's eat."

The food was just as good as the conversation, and by the time we were done eating, Ben and Shirley said they were one hundred percent in my corner. They would be more than willing to do whatever they could do to help. They could see the end in sight to their family's suffering. I pulled out a credit card to pay for dinner, and I passed it across the aisle where Larry was seated. He was sitting there, eating catfish by himself, minding his business. Ben was surprised, not knowing Larry was quietly observing. I told him, "I've got no idea what I'm into or where I'm going, so I always use an extra set of eyes." Ben starting smiling, and said, "I like how you operate." We left the restaurant too stuffed for dessert. It was real upbeat, and we would see each other at the birthday party.

At the party were O.J. and his staff, along with Shirley, Ben and O.J.'s daughter, Arnelle. Other guests included his vocal advocates throughout the Black community and friends of Irma Reed. The party was real cool, good food and drinks with some live, light jazz for background. Everybody was having fun, and O.J.'s staff specifically came to my table and congratulated me, like I was the guest of honor. I practically upstaged O.J. at his own birthday party, and I had never met or talked to any of these people. It was like a receiving line at my booth in the corner. O.J. even came down and sat with us. It was awesome to see how charismatic and engaging that O.J. is in person. The guy is totally engrossing and when he is at his best, he keeps you hanging on every word. The guy exudes confidence, as well as admiration for the little guy. He's got schmoozing down to a science.

Before the night was over, after we sang "Happy Birthday," I was invited to make a toast to O.J. They brought me up to the head table, then someone started tapping a spoon on a champagne glass. I'm still reminded by friends of the words I spoke during the toast. "Here's to O.J., a man of the century, and a man that will lead us into the new millennium. Everything is all right, and everything is gonna be all right." Before I could finish my words, the crowd jumped to their feet and started cheering. The band started up among the hip-hip hoorays, and I turned to O.J. and said, "God bless you, son. Your strength will come through forgiveness." O.J. said, "I know." Then he picked up the butcher knife they brought him to cut the cake and made kind of a hacking slice, getting frosting on all of his big fingers and knuckles. I thought to myself, this guy don't know what he's doing with a knife, he's a klutz.

O.J. suggested that we get together for a quiet meeting with our ladies over dinner. He wanted to hear more about our research efforts. Shirley and Ben would be heading back to San Francisco the next day, but by now they were two happy campers, and there was Irma—75 years old—out on the dance floor leading everybody, doing the electric slide.

After the birthday party, a week had passed and I never heard anything from O.J., despite the fact that he had invited me to dinner. I don't know if there was a clash of egos, but I started to sense something that still puzzles me; O.J. remains distant, yet close. I had O.J.'s phone number and since he was the one traumatized, saturated with theories and evidence, I figured I would initiate the contact.

I was chilling out in my office following a hectic afternoon seeing patients, when I took a shot at calling him and got him on the line. From the first time I talked to O.J. on the phone to the last time, his phone demeanor pretty much stayed the same. He showed some interest but sounded bored, apathetic or depressed.

The conversation was awkward at first, getting past the usual salutations, then O.J.'s tone suddenly changed and he says, "Hold on Doc, hold it! They're about to tear down my house!" I said, "What do you mean, O.J.?" O.J. replied, "Turn to Geraldo." I hit the remote, surfing the channels, stopping at *CNBC,* and sure enough Geraldo was flaunting the national countdown to the destruction of Rockingham. The bulldozer rumbled into the wall of the mansion, its plow became a battering ram. The treads dug in, crushing everything in its path. Another diabolical debut to boost Geraldo's ratings and feed America's addiction to violence.

I could hear O.J. breathing over the phone, watching this senseless travesty, so I asked him how it made him feel? O.J. somberly replied, "I raised my kids in that house, my dog is buried in the garden."

I knew the bank owned the property and they could do whatever they wanted with it. I just remembered how beautiful his home was, when I attended the gala O.J. hosted in his yard after he was set free—a fundraiser to stop gang violence in L.A. I thought to myself, I never saw a hearse pulling a U-Haul. I saw plenty of men in the past generation lose all of their assets to the IRS, and plenty of the present generation lose everything to cocaine. You can't take anything with you.

I told O.J. better the house than you. You got your health, your sanity and your kids, and whatever the Creator wants for you, don't worry, you'll have it. O.J. kind of laughed and said, "You got that right," and asked me to call him back later that evening. He said he tees off early in the morning and drives his kids to practice after school, so try him in the evening after dinner.

I was in my office after hours fielding phone calls on the back line. I decided to place a call to O.J. and no sooner than he answered, Tommy called me long-distance. I told O.J. to hold on for a moment while I clicked in a conference call. Since Tommy was calling from Minnesota, it gave him a chance to meet O.J. and we could both go at him simultaneously. We tell O.J. that we believe we have something that will completely exonerate him. I told him about the lunch that we had with his attorneys, and that Dr. Michael Baden was given information that I had uncovered for review, before he testified in front of the jury in Santa Monica.

O.J. was unaware of my two-assailant lefty theory and I told him that there were other issues that tended to support my theories as well. The fact that the Browns' telephone records were never admitted as evidence, and what was substituted in place of them was clearly an impossibility. It somehow went undetected that exhibits submitted in both trials indicated that his in-laws were able to drive what normally takes 90 minutes to two hours, in less than an hour.

O.J. said, "I don't think my guys would have missed that. I believe I saw the phone records." I told him, "They either missed it, or they hid it." O.J. responded saying, "I'm sure I saw the phone records, and I believe they said 10:37 p.m." I told him, "I know they did," and he shouted back, "No, I mean 9:37 p.m." I said, "Bet, O.J. You will never see a copy of the Browns' phone records that say 9:37 p.m. It was impossible for them to have made it home by that time." I told him, "As a matter of fact, put a grand on it." He said, "O.K." So I told him, "Get the records then."

I called O.J. again about three weeks later. I asked him, "Have you got the records yet, because I want my money?" He laughed it off, and I told him to stop stalling. The implications were he'd been sold out. He told me to give him a week, and he'd put me in touch with his secretary, Cathy Randa.

About a week later, I called him again. This time, he told me, "Give Cathy a call. She's gonna handle it." So I dialed Cathy Randa, and I explained to her what we were looking for. Cathy told me she talked to Attorney Robert Baker, and Baker told her not to give me anything. O.J. had previously mentioned that he needed a place to store all these records, which were consuming the space of a friend. I told him that I had enough office space to store all of his records, so it was all right with me if he wanted me to pick his records up.

I told Cathy Randa that I didn't need all of O.J.'s records, particularly in the face of Baker telling her not to give me anything. I told her all I needed was access to find a copy of the phone records.

Cathy referred me to her sister-in-law Carolyn, who stored the records in her garage. When I spoke to Carolyn, she told me she had to get back to me. I phoned her again about a week later and Carolyn told me that she could not release the records because she did not know who the records belonged to. She elaborated that she had picked up the records from Baker's office after signing an invoice. She stated that Bill Pavelic, Cochran's Private Investigator, had amassed all the records, so she didn't feel comfortable releasing the records to me.

Well, I reported back to O.J. and told him his custodian of records did not know who the records belonged to. O.J., perturbed, exclaimed he would contact his people and take care of it. A few days later, I contacted Carolyn once again. This time, she told me that she had spoken with Pavelic, and he told her, "Anyone working as hard as Johnson deserves the records, so turn them over to him. Just let Johnson know the phone records aren't there."

By now, O.J. had moved out of Rockingham and relocated on top of Palisades Hills, above Sunset Boulevard. Football season was starting, which worked nicely towards an opportunity for a group of guys to sit down and have something in common while building a rapport. O.J.'s pad in the sky was beautiful. There was a 270 degree panorama of Los Angeles, looking down on Dodger Stadium to the east beyond the new Getty Castle. One could scan an arc looking at the downtown skyline, around through Long Beach Harbor, the Vincent Thomas Bridge, Palos Verdes, and watch as the 747s touched down at LAX. Continuing to pan to the west, there was a view of the sailboats leaving Marina Del Rey where the ocean meets the Pacific horizon.

Reggie would usually accompany me when Tommy was not in L.A. We would all go up on the hill and kick back, chowin' down on some chicken wings, and O.J. would dominate the conversation. His phone demeanor is just the opposite of meeting him in person. He is totally unassuming and gregarious. Everyone visiting seemed a little tense and suspicious, yet O.J. is stretched out on the couch, laughing.

Ike Turner stopped by, played the piano for us and thanked O.J. for taking the heat off of him. Ike laid claim to the fame of being "The Most Hated Man in America." Ike said, "They had me mashed down flatter than a pancake and I couldn't do nothin' 'til they got O.J."

O.J.'s focus on points in his trials at times becomes subjective and it was obvious he did not have a grasp of the objective details of our research. He would talk for hours, we just listened, and he never wanted you to leave. When he paused only to take a breath, I would shoot him a question to get at some meat on the bone. It made him slow his roll and boxed him in to deal with the issues that I raised. O.J.'s entourage of golf buddies and memorabilia vendors, along with domino friends, would occupy his interest. Any women that were around were fiercely loyal to O.J., and there weren't any trollops or airheads. Wading through most everybody's opinion took up most of the time, before they realized the difference between what they believed and what I had uncovered. You see, an autopsy report is a pretty concrete document. There is some abstractness but my interpretation is a medical expert opinion. Without having the luxury of talking to the pathologist who performed the actual autopsies, any ambivalence becomes an educated guess which may or may not diminish credibility. However, Einstein would find my conclusions difficult to challenge, because it's a no-brainer.

So I finally got O.J. cornered, where all his rhetoric played out, and I confronted him with the actual autopsy findings. When he began to realize the actuality or the degree of violence, he was aghast—a look of panic overcame him. Everyone in the room was quiet while I talked, and O.J. listened. Then O.J. blurted out, "Dr. Baden promised me Nicole died quickly and never felt any pain." He seemed fearful that Dr. Baden may have covered up the way she died. I immediately sensed O.J. was not ready to hear any specific details, based on the look in his eyes, so I said, "Dr. Baden told you the truth, Nicole's death was instantaneous." As I described the mechanism of how she died, it was too difficult for O.J. for me to continue. Finally, I hit him with the news that Pavelic told Carolyn, the phone records were not in the piles of documents. O.J. looked dumbfounded, and I quipped, "The thousand dollars you owe me, put it in your kids' trust fund."

O.J. was further in the dark that I had filed an Amicus Curiae Brief in conjunction with his petition to the California Appeals Court. I did some research, and received copies of an Amicus Curiae Brief filed on another case by a law firm that specializes in such briefs. Very few lawyers have ever filed an Amicus Curiae, and I figure most attorneys only remember the theory behind the brief, which they were exposed to in law school. The samples of the brief which I reviewed had been accepted by the California Supreme Court. I felt if I was going to have any chance of my brief being accepted, I needed to follow the format of a previously accepted brief. The document I filed was an inch thick, complete with exhibits, and very impressive by anyone's standard. We notified the media immediately by flooding media fax lines with press releases, yet still no acknowledgement. Within a week of being filed, the Amicus Curiae Brief was denied, with the following order faxed to me:

AMICUS CURIAE BRIEF DENIED

IN THE COURT OF APPEAL OF THE STATE OF CALIFORNIA

SECOND APPELLATE DISTRICT

COURT OF APPEAL · SECOND DIST.

FILED

DIVISION FOUR

JUN 2 4 1998

JOSEPH A. LANE   Clerk

V. GUZMAN   Deputy Clerk

SHARON RUFO, FREDRIC GOLDMAN and LOUIS H. BROWN, et al, Plaintiffs, v. ORENTHAL JAMES SIMPSON, Respondent and Appellant.	B112612 (Super. Ct. No. SC 031947) (H. Fujisaki, Judge) ORDER

THE COURT:*

    The application of Henry S. Johnson, M.D., for leave to file an Amicus Curiae brief has been read, considered, and is denied. The brief seeks to inject into the appeal evidence independent of that which was received in the trial court. "[W]e are confronted by the rule that an amicus curiae must accept the case as it finds it and that a 'friend of the court' cannot 'launch out upon a juridical expedition of its own unrelated to the actual appellate record.'" (*Pratt v. Coast Trucking, Inc.* (1964) 223 Cal.App.2d 139, 143.) While there are exceptions to this rule (*E.L. White, Inc. v. City of Huntington Beach* (1978) 21 Cal.3d 497, 510-511), the current application falls within the general rule.

*VOGEL (C.S.), P.J.   EPSTEIN, J.   HASTINGS, J.

When I received the Appellate Court ruling, I immediately went to the law library to research the cases the court had relied on to deny admitting my brief. The case law which supported the opinion of the Appellate Court only acted as a subterfuge. I saw through it and followed up, detailing the flaws in the case law they referred to, by filing a Petition to Reconsider the Amicus Brief and served the petition immediately on the Appeals Court.

PETITION TO RECONSIDER AMICUS CURIAE BRIEF

IN THE COURT OF APPEAL OF THE STATE OF CALIFORNIA

SECOND APPELLATE DISTRICT

DIVISON FOUR

SHARON RUFO, FREDRIC GOLDMAN and LOUIS H. BROWN, et al,	B112612
Plaintiffs,	(Super.Ct. No. SC 031947 (H. Fujisaki, Judge)
v.	**PETITION TO RECONSIDER**
ORENTHAL JAMES SIMPSON,	**AMICUS CURIAE BRIEF OF**
Respondent and Appellant.	**HENRY S. JOHNSON, M.D.**

TO THE HONORABLE APPEALS COURT:

I, Henry S. Johnson, M.D., acting in pro per as Amicus Curiae request the court to reconsider the decision to deny the *amicus curiae* brief filed in support of tax-payers and appellant. The denial is based on the erroneous conclusion that the brief seeks to inject into the appeal evidence independent of that which was received in the trial court. Contrary to this opinion; **(1)** Exhibit no.1 page 1 of the *amicus* curiae brief shows that this evidence, submitted in the form of an

221

1   amicus curiae brief was stamped received by the Santa Monica trial court,

2   January 8, 1997. **(2)** The factual evidence found in Los Angeles County Coroner

3   autopsy report no. 94-05136 q.v. Nicole Brown Simpson and autopsy report no.

4
    94-05135 q.v. Ronald Goldman, for which the *Amicus Curiae* bases his
5
6   conclusions, is the same evidence relied upon for testimony in the trial court

7   case no. SC031947 by Warner Spitz, M.D., expert witness for plaintiff and

8   Michael Baden, M.D., expert witness for the defense. **(3)** The analysis of said

9   autopsy reports by *Amicus Curiae* was received and reviewed by Robert Blaiser,

10
    appellant's civil attorney and later forwarded to Michael Baden, M.D. prior to his
11
12 civil trial testimony. **(4)** For these three reasons the rule cited (Pratt v. Coast

13 Trucking, Inc. (1964) 223 Cal. App. 2d 139, 143) does not apply.

14

15 The medical opinions of both medical experts were at variance, and Dr. Spitz'

16 testimony that the *cause of death* of Ronald Goldman being a loss of liters of

17 blood from a stab wound to the aorta, is not substantiated by Ronald

18
    Goldman's official autopsy report. Secondly, although Dr. Baden testified that
19
20 more than one perpetrator was involved in the murders, he failed to

21 demonstrate any scientific basis for drawing that conclusion.

22

23 The more clinically and forensically accurate assessment by a consensus of

24 twenty physician-specialists is in concordance with the opinion of *Amicus Curiae*
25
26
                                        (2)
27
28

1 as detailed in the *amicus curiae* brief, section II, <u>Statement of Facts;</u> that there

2 was at least two assailants involved, and the more lethal perpetrator was left-

3 handed. This theory, when compared to a single right-handed perpetrator

4 theory, has a probability of greater than a *trillion* to one.

5

6

7 By all indications it appears that the Los Angeles County Coroner was well

8 aware of these facts, and brings on a strong suspicion of malpractice and/or

9 malfeasance on the part of the Los Angeles County Medical Examiner as well as

10 the District Attorney. This is further exemplified by Marcia Clark's submission of

11 the *People's Exhibit no. 35* in the criminal trial case no. BA097211. The *exhibit,*

12 a reproduction of Juditha Brown's phone record, dated June 12, 1994,

13 purportedly demonstrates that the Brown family allegedly drove from

14 Brentwood to Dana Point, eighty (80) miles away in *less* than *one* hour prior to

16 speaking with Nicole by phone. Conventional wisdom suggests this exhibit is

17 fraudulent, which patently contradicts Lou Brown's account in the *coroner*

18 *investigator's report* that his daughter was alive at 11:00 p.m. speaking to his

19 wife by phone. This increases the likelihood of malfeasance and exposes the

21 taxpayers of Los Angeles County to over one hundred million dollars

22 ($100,000,000) in liability to indemnify the civil servants of Los Angeles County

23 against claims made by appellant, Orenthal James Simpson.

24

25

26

27 (3)

28

223

Furthermore, evidence introduced in the civil proceedings being the same evidence submitted in the criminal trial in which the investigation was paid for by tax revenues creates a proprietary interest for taxpayers. The judgment for the plaintiffs should be arrested on the grounds that there is error appearing on the fact of the record which vitiates the appeal proceedings.

It cannot be over emphasized the need for the Appeals Court to consider this argument made *viva voce*. This question of violations is presently most appropriately handled in the California Superior Court to obviate the need to apply for relief in the federal courts.

The court should grant the application for leave to file an amicus curiae brief. I declare under penalty of perjury under the laws of the state of California that the foregoing is true and correct.

Respectfully submitted,

Henry S. Johnson, M.D.
Medical expert/Amicus Curiae

Date: July 16, 1998

(4)

224

As you can see, the petition draws reference to implications of obstruction of justice by concealing the Browns' telephone records. When the court received the petition, as was our policy, we again notified numerous media outlets; but the pattern continued, no mention was made. This time, however, the court would take at least three weeks before they tendered a response. Then, I received notification from the Appellate Court, a document with one line on it:

CASE NUMBER: SC 031947
PETITION TO RECONSIDER A.C. BRIEF OF DR. JOHNSON IS DENIED

The word denied was misspelled, and someone used a pen to correct it; moreover, no one signed it. I figured another example of judges protecting judges, and just like "Pops" said, "They are not going to let me into the game." Notwithstanding the court's rebuke, and the media's censorship, I secured an interview on *Pacifica Radio* by serendipity. A maverick radio commentator, Wendell Harper at *Pacifica Radio* in Berkeley, invited me on his weekly talk show.

Wendell heard about me through a group of people I met at Representative Diane Watson's birthday party. One of my mentors and friends, Dr. Randall Maxey, held a surprise birthday party for Diane at his home in Ladera Heights—the upscale, Black, middle class neighborhood in Baldwin Hills. I had received an invitation previously; however, a conflict developed in my schedule, which all but precluded me from attending.

A week prior to the party, I spoke at the L.A. Chapter of the Black Panther Party headquarters, and was subsequently implored to address *Mother R.O.C.*, a support group of women whose sons had either suffered from police brutality, died while in custody, or were killed by police under questionable circumstances. Since I had this conflict in my schedule and having to make a choice of caviar and champagne versus the support group, *Mother R.O.C.* took precedence over Representative Watson's birthday party.

I was warmly received at their monthly meeting held in a small church in South Central Los Angeles. The group was moved by the talk I gave and the video presentation, yet seeing what this group of women had suffered, I was humbled, but encouraged by their reception.

I left the church impassioned, and still had time to make it to the birthday party. There was a receiving line, waiting to congratulate Diane, when one of the hosts questioned me about our work. She insisted that I should present it to Diane, and exhorted that I produce a copy. I knew the rumblings in the community were that I was obsessed with O.J. Simpson, so when I went to the party, I didn't want to sweat anybody and I chose to leave my material in the trunk of my car and give people a break. The guests and host would not leave it alone, insisting that I indulge them in our efforts.

Diane was intrigued by my grasp of the evidence that had thus far been suppressed by the courts and the media. She intimated that Gil Garcetti, then District Attorney of Los Angeles County, shot his mouth off too early and too much. She sensed something was wrong with the criminal investigation, but she is a politician. Yet, by going to the party, it led to me doing numerous interviews on *Pacifica Radio.*

On one occasion, Wendell Harper arranged an interview that included Gerald Uelmen, Professor and Dean at Santa Clara Law School and co-counsel on the "Dream Team," along with myself. It was a very enlightening experience. Initially, it seemed that Dr. Uelmen swashbuckled with each and every legal argument I raised, which included numerous constitutional violations. Besides the professor's scholarly remarks seemed detached.

Then, a caller preferred that I respond to a question, and asked, "If O.J. did it, wouldn't he have been covered in blood?" I answered, "If O.J. did it, he had to be in two places at the same time, because Nicole and her mother were on the phone at 11:00 p.m., as O.J. rode in a limo."

It came out in trial, the Brown family left the Mezzaluna restaurant in Brentwood, close to 9:00 p.m. It takes almost two hours on a Sunday evening to drive from there to Dana Point, at the southern end of Orange County, practically on the border of San Diego County. I recounted, "The actual phone records were never admitted into evidence, and no one wants to presently deal with this issue." Suddenly, Wendell caught the professor off guard when he asked, "Dr. Uelmen, do you care to make a comment?" The silence was deafening. Dr. Uelmen was speechless for about five seconds and then started to chuckle. He spoke tongue-tied until he could regain his composure, saying, "I'm sure the evidence offered in the civil trial was the same as the evidence offered in the criminal trial." Then, he abruptly changed the subject entirely.

For the rest of the interview, however, Dr. Uelmen was one hundred percent in my corner. Wendell Harper stated that Dr. Uelmen was doing some good work for the Oakland Cannabis Club to help patients suffering from terminal illnesses exercise their right approved in Proposition 215—the legal consumption of marijuana for medicinal purposes. I told Dr. Uelmen on-the-air, that I would send him a copy of the video and my work, which changed the opinions of any doubters. He said he looked forward to receiving it.

After the show, I overnighted Dr. Uelmen the video, along with the Amicus Curiae Brief, and wrote him a thank you note for appearing on-the-air with me. Dr. Uelmen proved either too busy or inconsiderate, because I haven't heard a reply from him yet. Subsequently, I learned Dr. Uelmen was in Judge Kennedy-Powell's chambers, along with Marcia Clark, Bill Hodgman, as well as Robert Shapiro, when the judge sealed the phone records. So maybe he just wants to distance himself from the fallout.

Since we had proved to O.J. that he was not in possession of a certified copy of the telephone records, he reluctantly signed on with us so that my team, now dubbed, "Ocean Medicolegal Investigators," could go after the phone records. O.J. was still in disbelief. If you drive a four hundred thousand dollar Bentley, you don't care to see a used Chevy station wagon race past you on the open road. O.J. had invested his life savings into a multi-million dollar legal "Dream Team" which spared him from doing life without parole. Now here we come with solid theories held together with spit and bubblegum, and never asked for a penny.

O.J. was racked with ambivalence, seemingly suffering from the "Black Man Credibility Syndrome." Some people have it worse than others. San Francisco Mayor and former Speaker of the California Assembly, the Honorable Willie Brown, once said when he gets on a commercial jetliner, flying with a Black captain made him nervous. At times, when I'm talking with people, and their deep-seated beliefs are challenged, they become catatonic, you may actually see their eyes roll back in their heads, momentarily.

I run into credibility issues when I least expect to. On one occasion, I went to a San Diego Chargers' game, which honored their Alumni, as a guest of Reggie Berry's. Reggie, a defensive back on special teams played along with Johnny Unitas, Deacon Jones, Dan Fouts and Mike Garrett. When we arrived at the stadium we'd have brunch with some old pros, like Paul Lowe, Sid Gillman, Don Coryell and Kellen Winslow to name a few. After we ate it was time to head out through the tunnels and onto the field. It was incredible for me, standing at midfield on the fifty yard line with those legends in front of one hundred thousand fans.

Retired pro ballplayers are a unique crew. A set of individuals totally consumed by past glory, they imbibe the drink of fame. They are gregarious and the rehashing of old tales heightens their euphoria. There is an undercurrent of frustration, however, of feeling left out of a successful enterprise; in other words, professional football as we know it today, which they were fundamental in creating.

They are left out in the cold in terms of benefits, and they were the foundation of its present popularity.

Football seems to be a healthier business annually, but the retired players seem to be worse off. They perseverate as much as or more than any retired professional I have met. How many times can you recount a great hit, play or touchdown? There is a festive camaraderie which glazes over the sadness and frustration.

Fan Appreciation Day should be a time when legends, large or small, should be honored. This stage is in front of fifty to one hundred thousand people, fans not in touch with those that propagated the hometown sentiment. These guys are the flesh and bone that this industry was built on. Most are no more than shells of their past selves, but who cares? They are lost souls, cripples who have come to be appreciated by none other than themselves, if even that. They have given so much of their bodies and psyches to entertain us, and it is for the most part forgotten.

So here I am, fortunate enough to vicariously share reflections of memories of glory days past. We go to celebrate at the after-game tailgate parties. Curiously, in the face of the camaraderie and fond reflections, the tailgaters appear segregated. Now here is a crew that has given its better days—sweated, bled, cried, moaned, cheered and celebrated together. Times that the regular working stiff only vicariously enjoys, but after the game, the sports heroes go in their separate groups.

Since me and my homie, Reggie, are comfortable around all segments of society, we can schmooze with the White boys. Chatting with us about past exploits, we all rehash and relive past times. Inevitably, we reflect back on our boyhood days, then we realize three of the four of us in conversation are from Minnesota. The fourth guy is from Madison, Wisconsin. Jokingly, Reggie makes a comment about all the strip joints in Madison. Doug from St. Cloud wryly inquires, "How do you know?" Reggie replies, "O.K., if I gotta tell ya', my cousin was a stripper." Billy, the guy from Wisconsin, starts touting the achievements of Doug, the fella' from Minnesota. He tells us Doug is a fighter pilot, has worked with the Secret Service in the military, and advised the producers and Tom Cruise during the filming of *"Top Gun."* Doug flashes a military I.D. at Reggie, and immediately Reggie starts ribbing him about killing folks. Billy, on the other hand, went to get us some beer and pistachios.

We had a good time, on another balmy Southern California day after a great football game. Joking in the stadium parking lot, while guzzling beer and popping pistachios, we swapped "fish stories."

The guys knew Reggie had played defensive back and on special teams in the seventies, but they were curious about my connection with the San Diego Chargers. Reggie informed Billy and Doug that I was a doctor, and a little one-upmanship started developing as Reggie also informed them that I was a pilot as well.

The chit chat continued, until we all ran out of jokes and the evening started to set in. We parted ways and Reggie and I went back to our truck. It was a great afternoon, and it was time for us to head back to L.A.

We drove towards the freeway and took a look at the freeway onramp, then reality sets in. We both figure we ain't ready for this, so we bypass the freeway and drive into an upscale neighborhood just past the stadium. Reggie wants some candy and I want to use the restroom before we hit the road. We see a shopping center and recognize a crowded sports bar. You could tell from the parking lot that everyone was having a good time inside. We got out and strutted towards the bar.

Reggie looks at me and notes that we are going into an exclusively White sports bar. The same would not happen if we were White and the bar patrons were predominantly Black. We know what each other is thinking and we started laughing again. I say to Reggie, "I know a lot of Black guys that would not feel comfortable going into an all-White bar either."

We bop into the bar, grinning and gazing, to set the tone. No sooner than we walked past the bouncers, who are eyeing us along with what seemed everyone else in the place, someone calls out to us. It's Doug and Billy—the Minnesota/Wisconsin tandem. I guess jocks think alike as it seems we all had the same idea.

Now these guys are the center of attention, standing with a group of people at a table, and they call us over. They want to buy us a couple of beers and meet the gang. Billy introduced us and then makes a humorous comment about my business card. I doubt if Billy had ever met a Black physician, and my parchment card added to his curiosity, chiding me about how flimsy it was. He had asked me for my card, back at the tailgate party to see if I was real. My card has a distinctive quality to it, and was obviously something that Billy found novel. By now, he has bent the card's corners and folded it through the middle. He was a little tipsy and on a roll as an impromptu stand-up comedian. He spins off from there and starts a tirade of sarcasm, talking about me being a pilot, as well as a doctor.

As he chatters on incessantly, entertaining the group, I nonchalantly pulled my pilot's license out of my wallet, as he was thoroughly indulged in himself. He was caught off guard as I casually passed it to him and stops in mid-sentence. As he is holding my license out at arm's length to read it, he pauses for a moment, looks up to the crowd and announces surprisingly, "He ain't lying, he really is a pilot." His eyes reverted back to the lamenated card, and with a flick of the wrist, I snatched my license out of his hand so fast that it shocked him and the crowd. Not only was he flabbergasted to see my license, but me suddenly grabbing my ID after he made such a condescending remark took him totally by surprise, and startled everyone around the table. He suddenly grew red with embarrassment as he said, "Hey, let me have that back." I knew I had him upstaged and my insides were busting, as I spoke up, "You need to learn how to read faster, shorty," sliding my ID back into my wallet. The crowd busted out laughing as his face turned even redder with a smile plastered from ear to ear.

This is a classic encounter sometimes experienced with White guys. A genuflect response or lack of faith in what a Black person tells them. People have a problem with black credibility—not unlike the criminal trial jury—never considering their personal shortsightedness. I have also experienced this with some Black middle class folks who refuse to accept my theories or at best are fatalistic about its influence. Others do not care to explore any options other than what is presented in the media. Those that prove the most difficult to convince about the credibility and worth of my postulates are the conservative, upwardly mobile Blacks.

To set an example, one afternoon when I was working at a small community hospital in Watts, nicknamed "Baby King," a 55 year old Black woman came into the emergency room with her husband. She was suffering from diabetes out of control, severe hypertension, pulmonary edema and dangerous cardiac arrhythmias. All laboratory results suggested an acute heart attack. An E.R. physician, an older White fellow, was treating her and I stood at the work station in my starched white coat, white shirt and tie, jotting down notes and studying the patient's X-rays. The E.R. physician was in scruffy attire, working the patient up before he transferred the patient to my care. The patient's husband was going from the work station, where I was standing, to the bedside where the E.R. physician was working, and talking between me and the White doctor.

This Black man was very apprehensive and nervous about his wife's condition and appeared confused. The three of us gathered at the doctors' work station, and after everyone's formal introductions, the emergency room doctor reported to me the findings and treatment plan, and asked for my opinion. I looked at the patient's husband and I informed him that his wife was gravely ill and that the condition could get worse. She was critical and could possibly die, and needed to be managed in the Intensive Care Unit.

The brother turned to the emergency room doctor and questioned what I told him. I sensed a degree of insecurity in the emergency room doctor, and myself being trained in the county hospital and Board Certified in Internal Medicine, I exuded confidence which allayed some of the anxieties of the emergency room doctor. He would confide in me and ask questions, and I would help to direct his medical management. However, the patient's husband felt more comfortable receiving an answer to his questions from the White physician. Everything that I would say to this Black fellow, he would cross-check it with the White doctor.

So now here we go, a real roundtable discussion. The White doctor asks me a question, I give him the answer. The Black man asks me a question, I answer his question, then he confirms it with the White doctor. The White doctor asks me another question, I give him the answer. The Black fellow standing next to us asks me another question, I give him his answer and he confirms it with the White doctor again.

There is a real confidence problem amongst Black people and Black professionals. As a doctor, however, I cannot allow this sort of denigrating interaction to affect my judgment, most people cannot help themselves. This is the extent of their reality testing. When a guy's in pain he wants relief, whatever works best to allay his anxiety he will revert to it every time, whether it's right or wrong. As Black folks, we have a long way to go. Even my colleagues at times have a perception block and it can work to a patient's detriment.

One night, I was passing through the emergency room to the parking lot at "Baby King." Century Community Hospital, as it is really known, was located in a front line neighborhood of South Central. A place that if you don't know where you are, you got no business where you are. Through the emergency room entrance, came a Black guy leaning on a White guy dragging him in. The brother had been shot while sitting in a car when someone standing next to the window fired point-blank. Striking him in the head, miraculously it didn't put him down.

His friend helped him to the emergency room onto a gurney in the trauma unit. The nurses surrounded him and helped to position him better as they fought to pull his jacket and shirt off. The patient was resistive and combative, and needed restraining by shackles on his wrists and ankles as a protective measure. As these leather bracelets were fastened, the patient felt threatened which made him more belligerent. He was lying prone when he immediately raised up, and started to violently shake the gurney, screaming and shouting. The explosive impact of the gunshot wound to the temple had caused his eyes to swell shut and blood to trickle from his nose. He was a muscular guy who wore a Hero's jacket, but his hairstyle suggested he was a player.

I followed into the trauma unit to offer any assistance, trying to calm the guy down. He abruptly sat up and told me he would kick my ass. The nurses took his clothing into the nurse's station, and I was called in to verify the patient's belongings. The male nurse reached into the patient's jacket and pulled out a wad of cash. He was surprised and so was I, but we had to take inventory. He started to count the money, so many twenties, fifties and hundreds amounting to over five thousand bucks. The nurse looked at me confused and asked me if I remembered the last number he said. I wasn't really paying attention, being preoccupied with the gunshot wound. I said to count it over again, but the nurse was too "nervous" to keep count.

I went back to assess the patient who was relaxing, but who immediately sat up again in a rage. He had an entrance wound in one temple with an exit wound out the other. Some brain matter came out of the exit wound and lay up on his cheekbone. We knew we could not manage this patient in this small hospital; there was no active neurosurgeon. We would have to transfer the patient to a Trauma Center. The nursing staff contacted the county, and informed them of the patient's condition. The county dispatched helicopter transport from UCLA to take the patient to King-Drew Medical Center.

I contacted King Emergency Room and waited on hold. The patient remained pretty calm while we anticipated the arrival of the helicopter team. We positioned our cars with headlights on and flashing lights, to direct the helicopter to the impromptu landing pad we made in the parking lot. When the helicopter finally touched down, a medical team from UCLA Medical Center filed out.

We were glad to see "Life Flight" finally arrive. They were professional and impressive in their sleek, black jumpsuits with gold studs, buttons and epaulettes. Their new uniforms projected authority, confidence and organization. They took control of the patient and we stood back. They came off somewhat arrogant, representing an elite crew from UCLA. They hardly said anything to me, apparently they felt better to assess the patient themselves.

The health officer in charge of the patient prepared the patient for transport, obtaining a copy of the patient's records. As they aroused the patient, he became defiant. The doors to the trauma room were partially closed, but you could plainly hear the commotion. A few moments later, the doctor came out and flatly refused to take the patient in transport. "The patient is too agitated and uncontrollable," she elaborated, as they kept up their pompous and arrogant posture. She explained, "It would be too hazardous to transport such an unruly patient in a small helicopter. In a fit, he could possibly topple the aircraft."

At this point, knowing there was no hope for the patient at the community hospital, I spoke up and declared, "I will control and restrain the patient." Then I asked the charge nurse for a safety pin. The flight doctor turned to me and sarcastically asked, "What are you going to do, stick him?" I asked her to hold her comments and watch what happens. When I approached the patient's gurney as he lay flat on his back, I rolled a bed sheet and used it as a tie down. I

235

draped it across his chest and through the rails of the gurney. Then I went under the gurney, up behind his neck, and looped the sheet around his neck, tied it, and pinned it to the pad on the gurney.

Now the patient is resting comfortably with this sheet across his chest, his ankles and wrists restrained. The sheet, configured around his neck, protected him from the cool, night air; however, if he attempted to raise up, the wrap around his neck would tighten and discourage him from getting up. The more he fought the tighter the wrap became.

I ordered a 10 milligram (mg) shot of Haldol (a liquid straight-jacket) in the hip and a 5 mg. bolus of Valium, intravenously. I then ordered the nurse to fill a syringe with 100 mg. of morphine. The flight doctor and charge nurse exclaimed, "That dose of morphine would kill the patient." I told them, "I know, but better he goes than we go." I was determined to render the patient unconscious if he became unruly. I continued preparing him for transport.

I maintained a soft-spoken reassuring conversation with the patient. The conversation was between me and the patient, and no one in the emergency department was aware of what I was telling him. I informed the patient, "You will surely die if you don't behave. I am your only chance for survival, and there is nothing we can do for you at this small hospital." I told him that the Emergency Flight Team refused to transport him because of his unruly behavior, and the extensiveness of his wounds would lead to a brain infection and death. "I will take care of you if you will cooperate," I promised, and reminded him that, "I'm holding an overdose of morphine and the nursing staff has warned that it would kill you. I will guarantee your safe arrival at a Trauma Center, but the helicopter is small, and I do not intend to lose my life trying to save yours. If you are uncooperative, I can no longer guarantee your safety." Although his eyes were swollen shut and his face was a bloody mess, the patient managed to smile and said, "Please help me, Doc."

I took the syringe filled with morphine and stuck it into the IV tubing that was flowing into his vein. Everyone paused breathlessly as I bolused the patient, with only 4 mg. of morphine. I wanted my patient to feel comfortable. I taped the syringe to the IV tubing and stated, "We're ready for transport, take the patient to the helicopter." I asked the charge nurse for three ampules of Narcan in case I needed to reverse a morphine overdose and I grabbed an airway kit with an intubation tray for precautions. We took the patient to the helicopter and loaded him in the cabin, which seemed like the inside of a Volkswagen. We laid the patient down next to the pilot and I positioned myself behind the patient's head. We all strapped in, the pilot revved up the helicopter, and it's lift off.

Just before we were airborne, I notified King Hospital that we were transporting a trauma patient to their hospital. The resident in charge refused the patient, stating the emergency room was too congested. I told them that King was the nearest Trauma Center and this patient's condition becomes a priority. I said I would take full responsibility for overruling his authority and that I will continue as planned and bring the patient to King. The doctor said they didn't have ambulance transport from the heliport to the hospital. Knowing the campus layout, I suggested they bring an emergency room gurney to the heliport, with six runners. We could hustle the patient the quarter mile from the heliport to the emergency room. We were on our way.

Cruising through the night skies of South Central L.A. at a low altitude, the homes, yards, cars and people in the street seemed surreal, with the street lights dazzling. When we swept over the King-Drew Complex, it was an impressive sight. A massive island of industry in neglected South Central Los Angeles. Very few people get a view of it from this vantage point and it makes you proud of your affiliation. As we alighted on the heliport, we were greeted by six guys and a gurney. We transferred the patient to the E.R. gurney, and then went double-time down the straightaway through

237

the parking lot to the emergency room entrance.

We rolled the patient into the trauma room and hung his IV up. The attending staff was peeved because I had overruled them, as they started conducting the management of the patient. The patient was very calm, and immediately an endotracheal set was ordered, as the staff rushed to attempt intubation. The patient had been mildly sedated resting comfortably and the procedure was not explained to him what these doctors were about to perform. The doctors attempted endotracheal intubation using a blade resembling a shoehorn attached to a handle, shoving it down the patient's throat. This would be followed by placing a small hose down into his voice box.

Now, to approach a person with the idea of inserting something down their throat, when they are fully conscious without adequate sedation, is ridiculous. Despite the patient's eyes being closed, he was alert to his surroundings, so predictably he starts to fight. Chaos breaks out in the Trauma suite.

After two unsuccessful attempts at this, with the patient clenching his teeth, the young residents figured they would attempt a nasal approach. They lubricated the breathing tube, then attempted to insert it through the patient's nostril, then passing it down his throat. Again, the patient starts thrashing wildly. He sneezes, causing his nose to bleed, and his face swells up as big as a balloon, like a monster—with subcutaneous emphysema. The emergency room personnel became more and more frustrated with each attempt.

I spoke up and suggested that they let the patient take it easy for a moment. I recommended someone should check his level of consciousness and cooperation, order a CT scan, contact the neurosurgeon, get an X-ray and give him some oxygen. The residents relaxed, thinking that maybe this wasn't such a bad idea. Suddenly, the attending physician started barking out orders. He was upset that his residents were listening to an outside doctor. He told them that he had not given the order to stop the intubation attempt, and to get back and finish the procedure.

Now, this could have been any doctor, but he happened to be White. The flight doctor, on the other hand, was an attractive blonde. I don't know if she induced him to go off on this power trip, but he went on ranting orders as he imposed his will on the entire emergency room staff. The doctor was totally obnoxious. In the midst of all this confusion, I announced who I was and my affiliation with King Hospital. The E.R. attending physician cut me a nasty glare as I was introducing myself. "I don't give a crap," he piped up. "No one pulls my chain."

Such irony, a White guy initially helping the injured Black man, and now, because of credibility, a White guy potentially made matters worse. I looked at the flight doctor and she shrugged her shoulders, so I signaled that we should leave. We walked back to the helicopter in the starry night, feeling content with what we had accomplished. We reached the chopper and climbed in for a lift back to my car at the Century Community Hospital parking lot.

The patient survived the ordeal but there was some criticism from the neurosurgical staff about his emergency room management. The patient came back to Century Community Hospital six weeks later and collected his $5,200. I never received any compensation for my services, my only consolation was that the patient survived and I got an adrenalin rush.

Chapter Twenty
A POOLSIDE MEETING

O.J. told me he would set up a meeting with Dan Leonard, his attorney who had drafted the appeal of the $33.5 million dollar verdict. This commitment I placed a lot of importance on, after being patient for almost ten months. To put it in perspective, from the time we first met and made our friendly wager, up to the point of this meeting with O.J.'s Attorney Leonard, just about a year had elapsed.

O.J.'s attention was all over the place and it seemed to most of my supporters and antagonists that the phone records were a non-issue for O.J. It appeared to some as if we were more intent on clearing O.J.'s name, than he was. To me, someone going through all the changes that O.J. went through, his behavior could easily be explained by a term that gained prominence after Vietnam—Post Traumatic Stress Disorder. It would never fail almost daily, some screwball would tell me what he would do if he was in O.J.'s shoes, another hypothetical almost comic-book response. If you've never been there, you can't say truly how you would react.

Whatever you figure O.J. should have done or be doing, one thing remained clear, the guy maintained his composure through his trials in the face of the media barrage. About the only other person that possibly came close to his self-control, composure and discipline was Hilary Clinton. O.J. never got a chance to grieve in private. He maintained a public persona while the camera stalked him to titillate America's TV addiction.

It seemed about the only thing O.J. could concentrate on, aside from his responsibilities, was golf and dominoes. Whatever was going through O.J.'s mind left everyone guessing because O.J.'s attention span accordioned on us. Every move we made needed perfect timing and cohesion, which always seemed a struggle. So finally, a meeting would take place the morning after tax day, 1999.

The first news I got that morning was that my mother had died. She had been bedridden from a stroke for over five years and her speech was markedly slowed, but she always smiled when you came into her room. I'm just so grateful to my sisters for taking such good care of her at home. My eyes still well up with tears of pride and joy, when I think of her. That day, I never heard anything from O.J. Disheartened, I concluded my work must go on with or without Simpson.

I did not speak with O.J. for almost a month, until Tommy interceded. Despite Tommy's hard-biting brashness, he can be just as diplomatic. Whatever was said, he got O.J.'s attention, and so the meeting was set again. We went to the house on the hill and O.J. graciously apologized, knowing we were in his corner.

We sat out on the pool deck, a California perfect, shining Friday afternoon, enjoying the majestic panoramic view. Dan Leonard was seated in a lounge chair, tie loosened, jacket off, wearing dark glasses and sipping Merlot.

We all were introduced and shook hands, yet Leonard never stood up or removed his shades. O.J. poured me a glass of vino, but Tommy refused, as usual. Then, O.J. demonstrated his gift for gab. The conversation was lighthearted until Tommy cut O.J. off and said, "Dan, you know why we're here?" Leonard said, "Yeah, you're here to discuss the administrative gaff." "Administrative gaff," I thought—I really don't need anyone to define anything for me right now. I spoke up and said, "Dan, we believe we have something here that will completely exonerate O.J." Leonard shot back, "Aw, that will never happen!"

To hear him say that startled us all, including O.J. Tommy had a look of disbelief on his face. Leonard realizing that he was about to bite down on his toes, tempered his remarks by saying, "I mean, it would take too much time and money, and would have to be tried all over again."

I replied, "First, exonerate him in the court of public opinion, and then move on from there." Dan says, "Oh, okay, now I see." Then O.J. exclaimed, "Dan, you know we took the stipulation for the phone records." Leonard, still kicking back with his shades on, flinched when I responded, "O.J., you didn't take anything. Shapiro took the stipulation in the criminal trial and Dan, you took the stipulation in the civil trial." Leonard replied, "Ah, I don't know about that, I don't remember." I said, "Yeah, you took it. I got the transcripts right here in my briefcase. I'm here to find out why you took the stipulation." Tommy jumped in saying, "Henry, Henry, don't go there," causing me to snap back, "Stay out of it!" reflexively raising my voice. Once again everyone paused startled, shifting our gazes back and forth.

Then Tommy opened up, "Dan, the phone records are a monumental point in the entire trial." We had already laid the ground work after pressing O.J.'s custodian of records to admit she did not possess a copy of the telephone statements. Furthermore, Tommy had taken it upon himself to audit the District Attorney's files.

242

Tommy had called me from Minneapolis and announced that he needed to speak with the D.A. Now, to most all of us lay people, you get cold feet and break out in a cold sweat thinking about talking to the District Attorney, but Tommy's the man. He flies in from Minneapolis and he's all business; blue pin-strip suit, Wing Tips, white shirt and tie, he heads down to the 19th floor of the Los Angeles Hall of Administration. Tommy had an appointment with District Attorney Hodgman, but Hodgman conveniently played phone tag. Not to waste any time, Tommy headed for the file room and archives, where he met with the custodian of records for the L.A. District Attorney, Corrine Mposi. After the ice was broken, Tommy informed her what we were looking for and why we were looking. The custodian found it inconceivable for the Browns to arrive home in the time Marcia Clark and Dan Petrocelli had stated, because she occasionally enjoyed spending weekends in San Juan Capistrano and knew the travel times.

Ms. Mposi went to check O.J.'s criminal file, and returned to inform Tommy that the files were still sealed. She could not understand why Judge Ito maintained a seal on the files after the case was closed. She said she would do what she could, but she could not permit Tommy to peruse the files.

After a couple of weeks had passed, we received correspondence on Los Angeles County Superior Court letterhead, that read:

Dear Mr. Johnson,

After reviewing the 23 volumes of sealed criminal files of O.J. Simpson, I was unable to find any telephone records, nor subpoena, or minute orders regarding the open court discussion of the phone records dated 6/30/94.

Sincerely, Custodian of Records.

243

Tommy returned to the Hall of Administration and was advised that he should go to check for the records in the evidence department. When Tommy went to the exhibit custodian, he learned that the District Attorney had received an unprecedented order signed by Judge John Reid. The order granted the D.A. permission to remove all the evidence used to prosecute O.J. Simpson, from the custody of the Los Angeles Superior Court. This order was given in the face of O.J.'s pending court appeal, as well as O.J.'s custody battle for his children. All the evidence became D.A. Hodgman's personal property. Moreover, the evidence was illegally removed because O.J. was never notified. When we told O.J. what had happened, he asked where were all his personal items they had confiscated from his home.

Tommy went back to the D.A.'s office a day later to talk with Hodgman about the removal of the evidence, but still could not locate him. This line of investigation quickly turned into a cul-de-sac. Frustrated, Tommy got on the elevator to leave the 19th floor, and pushed the lobby button. The door shut and the elevator plummeted to the 10th floor, bouncing up and down, getting stuck between floors.

Tommy momentarily rattled, immediately called me from the elevator to let me know what was going on. He said, "I don't know if this is just a strange coincidence, I just wanted to alert you to where I'm stuck, if anything should happen." Tommy pulled the alarm, which sounded all over the building and deputies were yelling to cut it off. Tommy yelled back, "Get me out of here first." He let the alarm ring for almost half an hour. Finally, a maintenance worker and deputy forced the door open, but it was stuck between floors. Tommy bent down in his suit and told them he would jump out the five feet to the floor, but they advised him not to do it. If he missed, he might drop another ten stories down the elevator shaft.

They finally got him out, hoisting a ladder into the opening, and when Tommy returned to Hawthorne, he said the experience was an omen. He would not be going back to the D.A.'s office.

So, here we sat at poolside, and the cat's got O.J.'s tongue. Dan Leonard intimated that he thought he could get the phone records, but the California Appeals Court had jurisdiction and he didn't want to rock the boat. Dan said, "O.J., we got three good judges here, we don't want to ruffle them. We think we can get them to lower the judgment." Tommy said, "Lower the judgment? Man, how long is it going to take for you to get the phone records?" Leonard said, "Give me three weeks, I can do it in three weeks."

Suddenly, we were distracted because someone had contacted the Department of Children's Protective Services. Social workers appeared at the door to investigate whether O.J.'s kids were in danger living with their father. O.J. and Dan went inside to see what it was all about, and Leonard returned to the pool deck pissed off, huffin' and puffin' about these County Inspectors coming to O.J.'s home.

I went inside and O.J. introduced me to the social workers. I told the Inspectors that I had been around the family for almost a year, through the Christmas holidays. The children were well-adjusted, there was no danger, no problem. The ladies were very friendly and apologized.

I went back out to the pool deck where Dan and Tommy were quietly talking. Tommy said, "Dan, when we turn this around, you know there is a lot of money that could be made." Leonard took a drag off his cigarette and said, "I already got paid." I shot back, "Don't say another goddamn word to me about money!" Looking out over the L.A. Basin, I continued, "If the D.A. framed O.J., then they have framed thousands of other people out there, so don't say shit to me about money!" Dan lit another cigarette and walked away.

Tommy turns to me and replied, "I'm glad you said that, let's get out of here." O.J. was talking on the phone as we were leaving and Leonard went out on the driveway, talking on his cell phone. O.J. says, "Wait a minute, fellas. Where are you going?" Tommy says, "We gotta go, O.J., just remember, Leonard said three weeks." Well, three weeks never came.

The table was already set for a preemptive strike, after the meeting with Leonard proved fruitless. We had already contacted the Legal Compliance Department, at what was then GTE, to request reproduction of a certified copy of the Browns' and Nicole's phone records. The same records previously subpoenaed and acquired by the criminal court.

On December 30, 1998, we received a Compliance Status Report from GTE's security operations in San Angelo, Texas. They stated that our request could not be honored because the records had been destroyed when the three-year limitation had expired. I wasn't surprised that we did not immediately receive a copy of the phone records, just mystified why they would give me such a lame excuse. I knew the FBI could get copies of records over 10 years old, and since the records had been previously subpoenaed by the court, they were obliged to maintain a legal file for at least seven years, anyway.

We figured we would raise the stakes and make them respond to a subpoena again. We contacted the Sheriff of Tom Greene County, Texas, to serve GTE with a subpoena for the production of records. GTE had shifted their archives out of California to their headquarters in San Angelo, which led to our interstate correspondence.

When the custodian of records at GTE received the subpoena, she called our office immediately. She explained that California Public Utility Code prevented GTE from releasing the records without the customer's permission or a court order. We told her the L.A. County Superior Court subpoena she had been served supersedes the California Public Utilities Code. Besides, we only wanted a reproduction of records previously delivered to the court.

Since GTE's headquarters was in Texas, the California subpoena was not binding on them. Yet, the custodian of records attempted to hide behind California Public Utility Code to avert performing her duties to produce the records. She did not want to accept the subpoena, but told us with a court order, GTE would produce the phone records. When asked why did GTE initially tell us they destroyed the records, she said she couldn't answer that. She was instructed to refer us to GTE's legal counsel, maybe he could sort out the double-talk.

An attorney for GTE then called from Ventura, California, and asked that all correspondence be sent there. He refused to answer whether the phone records were destroyed or could be reproduced. In the meantime, I was introduced to an outspoken advocate of O.J.'s from Washington D.C., Attorney Mary Cox. Mary was brought to my office as a departure from visiting her relatives in California. She was eager to see what we had to present.

We went to lunch, and I elaborated on the improbability of the drive times which Marcia Clark and Petrocelli introduced as evidence against O.J. We got into a philosophical debate over the double jeopardy issue, and that the spirit of double jeopardy had been violated as a recourse to hold O.J. liable for the deaths of two White people. Most people felt that if O.J. was accused of killing a couple of Black folks, say for instance, his ex-wife, it would have remained back page news and never garnered the worldwide media attention.

I told Mary that my brother, Tommy, had an idea which could possibly be used to force GTE's hand to produce the phone records. The proposition was to file a Federal Rules of Civil Procedure, Motion 27, that would protect any evidence from destruction. We felt it best to file in the State of Texas, since GTE ignored the California subpoena, and get litigation out of California. Mary intimated that she wished to discuss the concept with some legal minds that she often went to for advice, including her brother and attorney, Cliff Blevins, in San Diego.

The FRCP 27 Motion is a very infrequently filed petition to

protect evidence that may either be destroyed before trial or rendered useless relative to time. For example, preserving testimony from a witness that might have a terminal illness could be obtained through a court order, if perhaps the witness might die before trial testimony is received. O.J.'s lawyers had already submitted his Appellate Brief in Los Angeles, and there was no going back to the well, as far as that was concerned.

It would be extraordinary at this time to petition the Appeals Courts to order the release of the phone records. A Rule 27 Motion, on the other hand, could be filed without a complaint pending. We were unsure of the condition of the phone records having been told the records were already destroyed. Furthermore, being unfamiliar with GTE's policies in terms of archiving records, we sought the court's jurisdiction to protect this crucial piece of evidence.

We held long evening discussions, long-distance phone calls, and my sister Linda suggested that we share this concept with a legal consultant and friend of hers, Dr. Quijano. They were working along with Irv Rubin of the Anti-Deflamation League (ADL), on the death of Sherice Iverson. Sherice, an 8-year-old girl, had been found raped and murdered in a Nevada casino. Linda formed a support group, *Voices of The Innocent*, that worked with the parents of Sherice, and Winnie Strohmeyer, the mother of the young man who was accused and had confessed to the murder.

The *L.A. Times* reported the young Strohmeyer murdered Sherice, out of anger that Johnnie Cochran got O.J. acquitted.

On several occasions, Winnie Strohmeyer, along with Leroy Iverson or Shiela Immanuel—the parents of the young murdered child—would meet with Linda and Dr. Quijano in our office to sort out questionable aspects of the murder investigation.

They came to understand that if more light could be shed upon what investigation we pursued, it could potentially shed light on the murder investigation of Sherice's murder. Unlike Polly Ann Klaas, the little white child and rape-murder victim that became a cause celebre and a crusade for Polly's father and Fred Goldman, this black child's death faded into darkness as quickly as folding a newspaper. Her parents were made scapegoats, just like most Black people caught in the wrong place at the wrong time—forced to apologize after being victimized.

Dr. Quijano decided to help study the case law that would go into the draft of the Rule 27 Motion, with Attorney Cox overseeing the work to completion.

On August 31, 1999, we served the Federal Court in San Angelo. We contacted the Texas Secretary of State to find the registered agent for GTE that would accept service, and located them in Dallas. The petition asked the court to issue an order compelling the GTE Corporation to avail themselves immediately for deposition, and to produce for inspection, all telephone statements terminating at the residence of the Browns and Nicole for June 12, 1994, between the hours of 8:00 p.m. and midnight. We also asked the court to protect all telephone statements produced by GTE, in regard to the case of the People of the State of California versus Orenthal James Simpson, case number BA097211.

It was explained to the Federal Court that the certified phone records were received in the Superior Court of Los Angeles, but sealed and never entered as evidence. The records were surreptitiously removed from O.J.'s sealed criminal file, and no one has been able to produce a copy. The depiction of the record, submitted as evidence to the jury in both trials, was never certified. It was a replica of the so-called phone record and the juries never saw a true copy.

Communication we received from the California Highway Patrol, the California Department of Transportation, and the Automobile Association of America (AAA), supported our contention. To travel the seventy-five miles from Brentwood to Dana Point in the time reflected on Marcia Clark's and Dan Petrocelli's exhibits, was impossible. All three agencies concurred, the travel time for that trip on Sunday evening in less than 90 minutes, impractical. Most assuredly, it would have entailed high rates of speed and recklessness, stupid crazy.

Now we've got more brains on the case, but no one's got the ticket—the bar card—that commands attention. Attorney Mary Cox was game to play ball and it was refreshing to find an attorney that was willing to practice law, instead of trying like "Monty Hall" to just "Let's Make A Deal."

Every improvement on a rough draft had to pass the mettle of Mary's scrutiny and she put both feet in the mix without getting paid a nickel. We were so proud to have Mary out front—a principled, Black female attorney in the trenches. Eccentric, yet like the salt of the Earth, dedicated to fight in the cause of justice.

Since there was no money, the only recourse that could be utilized to format a legal brief proved to be untiring amateurs. Mary maintained a cat-o-nine-tails, whirling over our shoulders, until a document was forged to which she felt confident to affix her name.

The document was served in San Angelo, Texas, a one-horse town with no freeways, yet the seat of a Federal Jurisdiction. A circuit judge covering the Federal District, stretching from Dallas to El Paso, would rule on the motion. He would pass through San Angelo maybe twice a year, and the nearest courtroom he would frequent most often was Abilene. Our petition was forwarded by FedEx to San Angelo, then driven from San Angelo to Abilene, about three hours away.

From the time we filed it by courier, with the Federal District in San Angelo, it only took 23 hours to get a ruling. It came back before Attorney Cox received *Pro hac vice*, court permission to practice in the Texas Federal Court. The answer we received from USDC Judge Sam Cummings to our motion to protect the record was, REQUEST DENIED.

Judge Cummings reasoned that we did not conclude why GTE, based in San Angelo and a major employer in West Texas, should be considered an adversary—notwithstanding the fact that

GTE refused to honor a California subpoena. The judge obviously made our motion a priority in the West Texas Federal District. His decision shot back so fast it gave me a whiplash, too fast for the media to take notice as well.

We went back to the drawing board. Within ten days of the denial, we filed a Petition to Reconsider the brief, based on two pages of California, Texas, and Federal case law. This time, it took Judge Cummings four days to render a decision. The media had always been appraised, but O.J, cited for making a rolling stop, grabbed more headlines. For the second time the motion would be denied, again. The judge was not going to bear this monkey on his back. He advised in his ruling that we needed to take our motion out of Texas.

It was obvious from the facts in the petition, the accusations could not be taken lightly. Yet, judges have wide discretion, and they don't necessarily have to rule in your favor, even if you are right. We would have to fight our battle on another turf.

Chapter Twenty-One
I'M COMING ELIZABETH

Back in L.A., we decided to put plan "B" into action. A Motion for Declaratory Relief (FRCP 45) would take center stage, to deal with civil rights violations—rights guaranteed by the U.S. Constitution. For example, O.J.'s Sixth Amendment right to confront witnesses and evidence used against him. As Americans, these rights we often take for granted, yet if they are abused for one, they are meaningless for all citizens. We're not talking about racial profiling, but an abuse of judicial discretion. The team went to school once again.

In the meantime, Tommy contacted Lou Brown to seek his cooperation. Lou Brown seemed like a guy that needed to bond with someone and vent, particularly with another man. His only son appeared to be O.J., and the rumblings from people in Lou's community were more critical about his loss of control over his daughter. He was held partially responsible for his daughter's lifestyle and the fact that she married a Black man.

It is difficult for a man to keep all of his thoughts to himself and not confide in another man, so Tommy seemed to fit the bill. Lou would talk with Tommy for an hour or more on several occasions, and ultimately told Tommy, "I have found God and I wish to clear me and my wife's name."

In retrospect, it appeared the Brown family was pained to accept whatever was to develop at pretrial. Once Tommy and Lou had their initial phone conversation, Tommy reported the specifics to me. We thought it best to confirm, in writing, what they discussed. Hence, I faxed Lou the following:

Dear Louis H. Brown: *Nov. 11, 1999*

I was asked to send a letter by fax to your attention following the discussion you had this morning with our field liaison, Thomas Johnson. Tom informs me after speaking with you, that you would be kind enough to help our research team resolve an issue which has a direct bearing on the integrity of the investigation of your family's tragic loss and to prevent a failure of justice. Our organization represents the interests of taxpayers against violence, judicial indiscretion and fiscal irresponsibility.

As you may be aware, the fruits of our research support a theory that invalidates evidence submitted by M. Clark and Petrocelli, regarding certain phone calls made from your home on the evening of June 12, 1994.

This issue remains unresolved because no one has been able to produce any phone statements and all phone records and exhibits have been removed or are missing from O.J. Simpson's sealed criminal files. Our hope is that you will give us written permission to obtain a copy of your authentic phone records from GTE, for June 12, 1994.

Please bear in mind that neither you nor your family are a target of our investigation. We sincerely need your help. You have our deepest condolences and you also hold a key to mitigate an American tragedy.

With kind regards,

HENRY S. JOHNSON, M.D., CEO

Lou mentioned to Tommy he felt something was wrong with the criminal investigation. When he learned the D.A. had removed all the evidence used against O.J., Lou confided that he thought they were scoundrels. Lou said to Tommy, "I feel I'm finally talking to a man I can trust." Lou was willing to cooperate and sign the consent, he just needed to talk it over with his wife, Juditha.

About a week later, Tommy contacted Lou Brown once again, and Lou said, "I talked to the D.A." They told him not to sign any consent. D.A. Hodgman informed Lou he would send him a copy of the phone records. Lou said to Tommy, "Wait for Hodgman to fulfill the request; otherwise, you should get the records anyway you know how, without my signature."

Tommy told Lou he doubted the veracity of Hodgman's guarantee, but he would be willing to wait. About three weeks would pass before we received any correspondence from Lou. Then to our astonishment we received a note from Lou with a fax copy of the phone record and Exhibit #35, which Hodgman had forwarded to Lou.

LOU'S LETTER

Louis H. Brown
Monarch Bay Dr., Dana Point CA 92629-3435

Mr. Thomas Johnson —
Mission accomplished —
Enjoy your holidays —
Respectfully.

Louis Brown

1:05 hrs —

THE BROWNS' PHONE EXHIBIT #35

Juditha Brown
Phone Records - June 12, 1994

Date	Time	Place called	Number ca
6 Jun 12	9:37 pm	W Angeles CA	310 447-86
7 Jun 12	9:40 pm	W Angeles CA	310 826-04

NOTE: PAY ATTENTION TO LINES 6 & 7

PHONE RECORD ENLARGEMENT

ime   **Place called**

:37 pm   **W Angeles CA**

:40 pm   **W Angeles CA**

GTE

PAGE 6 OF 17

TELEPHONE NUMBER: 716 499-3262
BILL DATE: July 4, 1994

GTE REGIONAL CALLS (continued)

Calls billed to
716 499-3262

Direct Dialed Calls (continued)

	Date	Time	Place called	Number call
1	Jun 9	3:53 pm	W Angeles CA	310 826-041
2	Jun 10	4:03 pm	W Angeles CA	310 826-044
3	Jun 21	10:19 pm	W Angeles CA	310 826-044
4	Jun 12	12:20 pm	W Angeles CA	310 825-041
5	Jun 12	12:53 pm	W Angeles CA	310 836-041
6	Jun 12	4:37 pm	W Angeles CA	310 441-241
7	Jun 12	4:40 pm	W Angeles CA	310 826-041
8	Jun 13	6:30 am	W Angeles CA	310 826-040
9	Jun 13	4:52 pm	W Angeles CA	310 826-040
10	Jun 13	7:15 am	W Angeles CA	310 636-161
11	Jun 13	7:58 am	W Angeles CA	310 826-040
12	Jun 13	3:58 am	Los Angeles CA	213 485-233
13	Jun 13	3:06 am	W Angeles CA	310 476-841
14	Jun 13	10:09 am	Los Angeles CA	213 363-871
15	Jun 13	10:33 am	Beverly Hls CA	310 278-651
16	Jun 13	10:41 am	W Angeles CA	310 431-512
17	Jun 13	10:39 am	W Angeles CA	310 826-269
18	Jun 13	11:18 am	W Angeles CA	310 476-993

NOTE: PAY ATTENTION TO LINES 6 & 7

Upon inspection of the document, I found too many problems with that piece of garbage. Hodgman sent a copy of Exhibit #35 along with a facsimile of the Browns' phone record superimposed, but refused to certify its authenticity.

The time of the phone calls Juditha made to the Mezzaluna and Nicole were indicated on lines 6 and 7 of the phone record. These two lines on the statement were the only phone calls shown to the jury. Lines 6 and 7 on the copy of the statement sent to Lou Brown by Hodgman appeared blotted or smudged, yet clearly highlighted on the graphic art exhibit that was shown to the jury.

Karen Crawford, the evening manager of the Mezzaluna, testifying on direct examination was asked, "What time did Juditha Brown call the Mezzaluna?" Crawford answered, "About 9:30 or 9:35 p.m." After Ms. Crawford established who Juditha was, and that the Browns' party of 10 was at the restaurant earlier that evening, she said Juditha asked her if someone found her glasses. Karen stated she put Juditha on hold, checked the seating area and asked the busboys if they saw any glasses.

Crawford then checked with the other waiters and managers, and looked in the Lost & Found, but nothing turned up. Crawford testified she remembered where the Browns had parked, out in front of the Mezzaluna on the street. Crawford recounted that she went outside and looked around on the sidewalk, and then spotted some glasses in the street. She wiped the mud off the glasses and returned inside to the phone, to describe what she found.

Juditha identified the glasses and told Ms. Crawford she would contact her daughter and have Nicole pick the glasses up. They hung up at that point and Juditha then called Nicole. I only go into detail about this portion of Crawford's testimony because, according to the copy of the phone record Lou sent, all of what I just described took place in less than two minutes.

People moved at warp speed that night, including:

Crawford's search for the glasses, Juditha dialing and placing two phone calls in less than two minutes, the Browns' seventy-five mile drive home in less than an hour, and O.J.'s ability to stalk, murder, clean-up, shower and catch his flight on time.

The toll charges for those two phone calls were also concealed on the copy of the phone bill sent by Hodgman and forwarded to us. This is probably one of the reasons Hodgman had one of those "Fred Sanford's, 'I'm coming to join you, Elizabeth'" attacks during the trial. Crawford, along with six other people including the Browns, testified that the Browns left the restaurant between 8:30 p.m. and 9:00 p.m. The exhibit entitled, "Juditha Brown's Phone Record, June 12, 1994"—submitted as evidence in both trials—had the time of 9:37 p.m. adjacent to the Mezzaluna phone number. Marcia Clark and Dan Petrocelli thus presented evidence to show that the Browns were able to travel seventy-five miles through Los Angeles in less than an hour; that's 75 miles from point A to point B, with ten of those miles on surface streets.

If the Browns actually made a 9:37 p.m. phone call from their home, they had to leave the Mezzaluna before they ate. Yet, their bill at the restaurant was over $200 dollars.

Robert Shapiro and Dan Leonard stood up in court and stipulated that the time of the phone calls depicted on the exhibit were accurate. Thus, Shapiro stipulated twice to essentially two different times—which were almost forty-five minutes apart—for the same phone call.

When questioned about the time stamped on the American Express receipt, to establish the approximate time that the Browns were still in the restaurant, Karen Crawford testified that the clock on the American Express Card voucher machine was not working nor was the NCR cash register clock.

On the other hand, Ron Goldman's time card demonstrated that he punched out at 9:50 p.m., and the time clock was presumed by everyone to be accurate. Yet, another employee, Tia Gavin, the only waitress that served the Brown party of ten that night, alluded that the time clock had never been set to daylight savings time. That would mean the time Goldman punched out was actually 10:50 p.m., but why nit-pick? Nine Fifty or Ten Fifty, what's an hour among "friends?"

The 10:50 p.m. punch-out time for Goldman is more consistent with the normal time frame for real world events that night. It would mean that after 10:50 p.m., Goldman subsequently left the restaurant. He then walked two blocks home, took a shower and changed clothes before he started his neighbor's car and drove to Bundy. What time was it now? O.J., according to Allan Park, his chauffeur, was entering his limousine at 11:00 p.m., late for his 11:40 p.m. departure. I wrote Lou Brown again as follows:

Dear Louis,   *Dec. 30, 1999*

I hope this Holiday season has found you in good health and spirits. I am exceedingly gratified by the rapport developed between you and Tom. I was genuinely surprised by the expedience with which you were able to retrieve and forward a copy of the phone statement sent to you by D.A. Hodgman. It is an objective measure towards accomplishing our mission, but to paraphrase an axiom of Ronald Reagan, "Trust but verify." To be explicit, our position at Ocean Medicolegal Investigations is that the 9:37 p.m. phone call allegedly made by your wife to the Mezzaluna is a mistake, and that your family arrived home on Sunday evening, June 12, 1994 at a much later time. This point can only be validated by the authentic phone statements certified by GTE. Therefore, will you please help facilitate this by signing the consent (it does not require notarizing) and forward it to my office? Louis, with your cooperation, your integrity will pave the way for understanding and harmony for all involved.

Sincerely,

Henry S. Johnson, M.D.

Lou never responded to our plea, so I told Tommy to call him one more time. Tommy was reluctant to contact Lou again, because there was an obvious change in Lou's demeanor from the initial "I found God" conversation, and the subsequent "I talked to the D.A." conversation. Everything seemed to have turned from sugar to shit.

On the other hand, there was one more thing that needed to be clarified. Lou Brown wrote on the bottom of his correspondence in his own handwriting—1:05 hours. I told Tommy to press him on the consent, and inquire if he was saying he drove home in an hour and five minutes. Thereafter, Tommy contacted Lou Brown for the last time and Lou told him, "I'm not going to sign any consent. Whatever Hodgman sent is good enough." So Tommy asked him one last question, "Lou, what did you mean by this 1:05 hrs? Are you saying you drove home in 65 minutes?" Lou Brown answered, "Indeed!" Well, that was all we needed to know.

Mr. Brown followed up with a brief note to me which seemed almost cryptic, and thus I responded in closing...

(Sent Via Certified Mail)

Dear Mr. Louis Brown   *January 14, 2000*

I received your correspondence dated January 7, 2000, concerning our request that you authorize the release via consumer consent of certified copies of your phone statement for June 12, 1994 from GTE, to verify the authenticity of exhibits submitted as evidence of your wife's and Nicole's last conversation. We regret that you elect to disregard our appeal for your cooperation. Your reply to me seems ambiguous at best and I least of all care to assume you are being evasive or not acting of your own volition.

I wish to share with you some perspectives; that fact that you state you drove home from Brentwood to Dana Point in 1:05 hours is very troubling. Louis, you and I being residents of Southern California both know, you would have to drive with utter reckless abandon with your grandchildren in the car and you still would most likely fail to arrive home in this amount of time. Secondly, as you now claim you arrived home in about an hour it seems incredulous that within eight hours following your daughter's death your estimation stated to the Coroner's Investigator was closer to two and a half hours. Lastly, a statement attributed to you reported in the LA Times June 1994, read that Nicole called you in Dana Point that Sunday night after you all arrived home, and spoke with your wife.

Conclusions of our research show that at minimum there were two assailants involved in the double-murder of your daughter and that a left-hander was the more lethal assailant. Furthermore, the attack occurred after 11:00 p.m. while O.J. was being transported to LAX via limousine. Any allegations contrary to these deductions are purely speculative and/or deceptive. By all appearances there is a suggestion of collusion and a conspiracy to obstruct justice; however, we are more aggrieved by the derision in racial tolerance these events have fostered.

Louis, we have all felt you are a God-fearing man with integrity and would do the right thing; therefore, we again implore you to sign and return the consumer consent.

Sincerely,

Henry S. Johnson, M.D.
CEO, Ocean Medicolegal Investigations

This letter went by certified mail and though it was accepted, there was again no response. I showed O.J. Lou's reply to our request, and his chin and shoulders slumped. Shaking his head with a look of disappointment, I could sense his hurt and frustration. I thought to myself, "That's really messed up." At that point I felt the Browns were so rotten, I didn't know how they could stand the taste in their mouths. I said, "O.J., why don't you just ask Lou for the phone records?" O.J. replied, "I'm not asking Lou for shit!"

Our next move would be to take the advice of USDC Judge Cummings, and file in another Federal Jurisdiction. My man Larry thought he knew of a lawyer that might be game to file the motion, Doug McCann. Attorney McCann initially showed interest in our theories but told us we had to prove to him O.J. didn't do it. Tommy said, "McCann, you miss the point!"

We were in the conference room in my office, Doug, Tommy and myself. McCann absorbed information quickly and while speed-reading our documents, came off arrogant. Understandably, on the average, an attorney may have problems accepting legal theory from a lay person.

McCann was sitting there perched on a chair, leaning back, cocky, taking it all in. Suddenly, as O.J.'s guilt, which he had taken for granted, seemed to legitimately be questioned, McCann's facial expressions started changing. The facts which proved O.J.'s innocence—the suppressed evidence—overwhelmed him and momentarily shorted out his mind. You could see him calculating travel times in his head and when presented with the collection of documents, he lost his cockiness at the same time he lost his balance. The chair he was leaning in flipped over backwards, tossing McCann over in a somersault. He picked up his chair, and sat down again with a different look on his face. I looked at Tommy, and without missing a beat, we continued the dialogue.

When we were finished, Tommy asked Doug, "Man, you all right?" Doug played it off like nothing ever happened; however, the gauntlet was cast to the floor, his integrity challenged. When Tommy brought up the idea of a Motion for Declaratory Relief, Doug jumped at the opportunity to show he was bold enough to stand shoulder to shoulder with two Black men. Doug is deceivingly aggressive, but at times appears timid and confused. He was so impressed with the information presented him, he relied on us to draft the Federal Action. We filed a complaint in the United States District Court in Los Angeles, and no longer could the media avoid the topic.

Chapter Twenty-Two
TERRORISTIC DOLLARS

We received a degree of coverage on the news wire service, when Christian Boone of *APB News* and Linda Deutsch of the *AP News* service picked the story up. We began to engender a critical analysis by the commercial media; nonetheless, the story was still-born. It never saw daylight in the national media networks. A local provocateur chose to challenge the merits of our claims, Gloria Allred. An attorney, radio personality, women's advocate, and probably O.J.'s biggest female antagonist, Gloria represented the Browns for a time during the civil trial.

Domestic violence became the *cause du jour*, compliments of O.J. Simpson. Yet, any legal purist would tell you, domestic violence should have had nothing to do with the prosecution of Simpson on a murder rap.

This golden opportunity, however, would not be missed. The issue of domestic violence would be elevated to a status as the greatest anathema affecting American society. It would transform into a cottage industry for law enforcement, trial attorneys, the courts, and all the counseling services trying to make a buck, intervening on domestic affairs. County jails would swell with arrests when 911 calls brought police into domestic disputes, thanks to O.J. Thereafter, we would see a new term applied to an age-old problem; domestic disputes would be redefined as terroristic threats.

The toll of the legal turmoil created by aggressive law enforcement intervention, both dehumanizes and destabilizes the fundamental family structure. Rather than placing all emphasis on police intervention, the problems of domestic abuse, violence, and disputes should be addressed by social intervention, prevention, and counseling. The cost emotionally and financially is overwhelming for those affected, and the end results effected by the courts can be even more destructive.

All violence should be abhorred and with appropriate deterrence. There is no justification for obnoxious behavior, but the focus should be on aggressive prevention in place of over-zealous prosecution. Statistics show the cost of litigating restitution or resolution does nothing to mitigate the atmosphere conducive to domestic violence.

From a psychological standpoint, a subset of people that have the most difficult time realizing the phone records are proof of O.J.'s factual innocence, are those people that have suffered from or had experience with domestic violence themselves. Difficult memories are rekindled in the debate over spousal abuse, and all of their negative feelings tend to be projected onto Simpson. Therefore, this emotional barrier often impedes any rational assessment of all the evidence. Unfortunately this group was pandered to, in particular, by the media pundits and women's rights crusaders, with O.J. the sacrificial lamb on the altar.

Gloria invited me on her radio show—after we both appeared on *Court TV*—to discuss the Federal filing and the phone records.

Gloria had seen the same phone record exhibit that had been submitted by the D.A. in the criminal trial and Dan Petrocelli during the civil trial. Yet she wanted to know if I had seen any other phone records.

Early on during the murder investigation, there were about a half dozen women employees of GTE who had pulled up the phone records because of the contention of Lou Brown's initial statement that the call was made at 11:00 p.m., which he subsequently changed to 9:30 p.m. Those women were immediately terminated from their jobs at GTE, so no one really knew what was out there, and what might be hidden.

Gloria said, "There's no need to look at any phone records, because O.J.'s attorneys already agreed to the replicas." She accused me of pulling a publicity stunt. Up to this point I never had any antagonistic interview and I didn't know where she would take me. It proved to be a good exercise for me, however. I have to say thanks to Gloria, she opened up the L.A. market to a new perspective, and she has more temerity than a gaggle of your male pundits.

Gloria proved to be a bluff, however, when I joined her for an in-studio interview, but she continued to prevaricate about how fast she could drive the distance to Dana Point. When I challenged her on that point, she changed the subject. It was obvious, she did not sincerely believe what she preached. All the gall, fire, and brimstone she espoused against O.J., was for ratings. You could sense that when faced with reality, despite all her hyperbole, she did not really believe O.J. was guilty. She remained rhetorical for most of her interview, and when she could not shake me, she brought Denise Brown on-the-air, just by coincidence.

Denise called the radio station during our interview. Her public persona vacillates between abrasive and contrived, and on this occasion, Denise was in rare form. She started out by saying, "I don't know what is going on," but then lashed into me about bringing the issue up. She seemed to protest too much, like she had something to hide, and behaved like a scorned woman.

She persisted, asking, "Why do you want to bring this up?" When I said, "To bring closure," again she asked like a parrot, "Why would you bring it up?" Denise continued, "You're just hurting my parents." I replied, "Maybe the grandchildren would want the truth to be known." Denise responded, "My family could have arrived home in that amount of time, to place a call by 9:37 p.m., that it was entirely possible," but she never said what time they actually arrived.

When Denise testified in the civil trial about the time the family arrived home, she failed to give a straight answer. She suggested, "8:30, no 9:30, figure around 10 o'clock. Wait a minute, 9:30, no. I think a quarter to 10:00, yeah that's right."

On the radio her voice continued to project her anger and resentment. Then suddenly she screamed out over the airwaves, "My sister was laying with her throat cut open, covered in her own blood! Goddamnit, why don't you just leave it alone?"

Several people have asked, "Why won't the Browns just release the phone records?" By the time the Browns pursued the child custody battle with O.J., a lot of people felt that the Browns grieved the loss of their meal ticket, more than the loss of their daughter. At *KABC* Radio, the number one talk station in Los Angeles, Attorney Allred's shtick was to squabble and haggle over non-issues, and did nothing to diffuse my allegations. She challenged O.J., on-the-air, to put up a million dollars to prove our point about the phone records. It was obviously a roust, particularly if what the media was displaying publicly was the authentic record. If the phone record exhibit wasn't a fake, what would be Gloria's reason to challenge O.J. to put up a cool million dollars to actually see the real record?

This supported our contention that the D.A. and Petrocelli played fast and loose with the phone records—like a game of Three Card Molly. O.J. rightfully should have had access to the phone records to completely vindicate himself. I decided to take Gloria where no one had yet met the challenge. That is, the key points raised, in effect the two-assailant theory, the drive times, and the fact that Nicole was alive as O.J. departed LAX. *"Publicly disprove my allegations by risking the loss of your bar card, license or badge because I stake my reputation and medical license behind my declaration."* I suggested, *"Whoever is wrong, should surrender their license or capitulate."* Gloria refused my wager, nor did any other professional care to step up to the plate.

It is sad to see a prominent figure choose to embrace notoriety and monetary gain over ethics. Gloria did a series of interviews with me on *KABC*. I only wished I could speak with the African American community on the local L.A. stations, which attracted a Black listening audience. I felt the ratings that I generated for Gloria at *KABC* helped to catapult her into her nationally syndicated *"Power of Attorney"* television show, along with her co-host, my boy, Christopher Darden.

Darden seemed perpetually tormented by internal demons. He's really no different than most brothers that practice law, defrocked probably describes them best.

Chris moved into my neighborhood shortly after the criminal case, and as fate would have it, we became personally acquainted. The story of how we met is convoluted, but it turns out that Chris and I have a liking for expensive tequilas, and before he knew my avocation, we developed a rapport. We'd have dinner together, or I'd stop by his home, smoke a cigar, and sip one hundred percent Agave.

One day, I'm at O.J.'s sipping *Belvedere*, and the next day sipping *Patron* with Darden, not breathing a word about either to neither. Not that I cared, but I didn't want to disturb their habitat. I doubt if Chris ever knew anything about the phone records during the trial. I just think he was a brother caught up in the system, and used like most of us. He autographed his book for me, which I read, and I really don't think he's that bad of a guy. Both he and Gloria showed me their personal side, but sometimes commitment overshadows your personal qualities. As time progressed, Chris grew leery of our relationship, and I can't say I blame him. He's got book deals and fame—I've got ideals and faith. Chris could not afford to maintain our friendship and chose to unceremoniously break it.

It happened at "La Louisiane Bar Restaurant" in View Park, a ghetto-fabulous section of L.A. Irma Reed stopped by my office and since my jalopy stalled out on me, she gave me a ride home. She was hungry, so I suggested we stop by the "La La" and check out the Monday Night Football chicken special. Darden was there, surrounded by a flock of groupies, when I recognized him and pointed him out to Irma. I told her I knew him and she wanted to meet him, so I made their acquaintance.

She was thrilled, took his hand and held on. The next thing I know, Irma has adopted Chris as one of her "boys," and they're swinging their hands together. Then Irma acknowledges to Chris that she's O.J.'s biggest advocate, and Chris says, "I thought Johnson was." Their new-found affection seemed to falter, then Chris became surly for no reason.

By now, well aware of the work I was doing, Chris tried to avoid me, but I wouldn't let him. Darden says, "O.J.'s a murderer, and we didn't need any phone records to prove his guilt," betraying his ignorance. He continued, "And Johnson, you look crazy trying to defend O.J. Anyone who believes O.J. is innocent, worships the devil."

I said, "Chris, you were played by the devil, so be a man and come clean. Where's your self-respect?" Darden backed down and started brooding. We had apparently drawn the crowd's attention, and people that knew us both suggested it's better that I leave.

I have no animosity towards the brother, despite our ghetto confrontation, and life's too short to harbor a grudge. Gloria, on the other hand, has more clout. She used Denise as other people have, and it's unfortunate the Browns got played like a baby grand. They would better honor their flesh and blood, Nicole and grandchildren by telling the truth and releasing the phone records.

We finally completed the Motion for Declaratory Relief with McCann as the advocate. Filed in Los Angeles, our showdown would soon approach. GTE, still named as a defendant, retained representation by *O'Melveny and Myers* Law Firm, a behemoth among legal professionals in the west. Why GTE (Verizon) would select a B2 bomber to defend against a flea, I don't know, but I was honored. *"The Big O,"* as they are known in legal circles, has been implicated in the greatest boondoggle to surface in Los Angeles since the Rodney King riots.

This firm performed the due diligence on the L.A. Unified School District's Belmont High School—a quarter billion dollar bust. This prototypic high school was built on a shallow oil field exuding toxic fumes, as well as explosive gases, that seeped into the newly constructed school building. These conditions at this newly built, yet uncompleted, high school would have put 3,000 mostly Hispanic kids at risk annually.

At the same time that *"The Big O"* took up GTE's cause to withhold the phone records—which threatened to expose a massive conspiracy—the Los Angeles District Attorney concluded concurrently that O'Melveny would not face prosecution related to this toxic waste high school, a virtual *quid pro quo*. Fortunately, the IRS has cut through L.A. corruption and started its own investigation, considering fraud and malfeasance charges against the Big "Zero."

When notice of our Complaint for Declaratory Relief hit the media, O.J.'s attorneys started calling him. He hadn't heard from any of them for months, but suddenly O.J. was getting a barrage of phone calls, asking O.J. what did he call himself doing? I went to see O.J. in his new pad back on Bundy, and he seemed panicky about all the responses that he was getting from his attorneys. Then O.J. tells me, "I believe you now, since all these guys have been calling me. I just wish you'd allowed my attorneys to see what you did before you filed it."

I said, "O.J., I have always been open to your attorneys, but no one seemed interested in talking to me." O.J. said, "Well, at least you should have run it past Skip Taft, I trust Skip. He might not be the sharpest guy on the planet, but he pays attention to detail. I can always count on him [sic] to cross his i's and dot his t's."

Well, the first thing O'Melveny did when they were served the complaint was to threaten us with a contemptuous letter, demanding that we withdraw our complaint. Their attempt to bully us didn't work, although they had McCann's knees knocking as fast as his teeth were chattering. However, by the day of reckoning, McCann was able to steady his knees. He went into the Los Angeles Federal Courthouse in front of United States District Court Judge Dean Pregerson. O'Melveny sent three cookie-cutter attorneys but McCann, hair still wet, suit too big, and boots needing a shine, took over the courtroom. His delivery was that of a back water, holy roller. He pleaded for decency, fidelity, and mercy. O'Melveny pleaded for sanctions.

Judge Pregerson read the complaint and realized the implications were devastating. Yet, knowing that we were tap dancing on a high wire, he stopped short of throwing us out of court. He would not ignore the contents of the brief. Judge Pregerson directed us to return to the Los Angeles Superior Court and file a Motion to Compel the District Attorney and GTE to produce the phone records. He ruled that until this was done, our case was not ripe for Federal Court. He dismissed our complaint with leave to amend, only to admonish us not to return unprepared. His spin was that the context of the complaint bordered on being frivolous, yet the contents had substance. We left the court relatively unscathed, but knew the real fight was in front of us.

Chapter Twenty-Three

HUMILITY COMPLEX

In the morning, I got three calls from *FOX News Channel*. One from Shepard Smith's *Hot Button Topic* producers, one from the producers of Paula Zahn, and the third from the producers of *The O'Reilly Factor*. I agreed to do *The O'Reilly Factor* interview, and figured one news presentation for the day was enough. I did not want to over-saturate the public, presenting my argument in a day. Tommy suggested at the insistence of the *Hot Button Topic* producers that I do both shows.

Actually, the producers of the *Hot Button Topic*, while pleading their case, warned me against doing the Bill O'Reilly interview. They said O'Reilly would make me look bad, he's really tough. Bill O'Reilly is very dogmatic and sometimes ultraconservative. What most conservatives fail to realize is that most of the Black working class is conservative as well, but Republican rhetoric turns

Black people off.

Bill O'Reilly would routinely interview the conservative leadership in the country, and at the same time his news commentary was considered the leading topic on cable, exceeding Larry King as well as Geraldo. O'Reilly had the number one cable broadcast. Most Democrats of any stature avoided his talk show format, from Jesse Jackson to Bill Clinton. So when they told me Bill O'Reilly was tough and would make me look bad, I said, "Swell," just what I was looking for. Someone to actually challenge what I advocated. I agreed to do both shows.

The *Hot Button Topic Show* went so well, the initial antagonizing condescension seemed to implode on itself after I peppered the hosts with all the excessive discrepancies in the so-called "mountain of evidence." They could only gasp and stammer wanting to hear more of the evidence that I had to offer. No longer did they challenge anything I said, but still let my theories drop like a hot potato.

Unlike Jon Benet Ramsey's case—where the pundits espoused multiple theories on her inscrutable murder investigation—here was a golden opportunity for *FOX News* to deliver a bolo to the general public, a credible analysis of a more convincing argument. Realizing our theories exposed the entire fraud surrounding O.J. Simpson's prosecution, they'd rather shadow box than fight.

FOX sent a limo to my office and carried me to the studio to get ready for my interview with Bill O'Reilly. A bi-coastal studio interview is an unusual experience. Aside from the production crew that's in another location, and the camera technician, you are the only person in the studio. You look into the lens of a camera, and if your gaze shifts, no longer do you appear to be making eye contact with the audience. You appear to be fudging around, as the camera watches your profile, you look like you're talking to a curtain.

You have to concentrate on staring at the lens, and you can't see whom you're talking with. This is a handicap for anyone that is not familiar with how images are projected to the public. So here I am, getting ready for my biggest live on-air interview with Cable TV's number one host, a set up. The crew in the studio made me feel comfortable as they wired me up. The mini-mike was fastened to my lapel, and the earpiece positioned in my ear. We do a sound check and suddenly I hear Bill O'Reilly talking to me, but I can't see him.

I'm trying to get used to everything, wanting to appear credible and convincing, but without cues and coaching, there is so much for a novice to be distracted by. O'Reilly says, "Hello, Dr. Johnson. Welcome to *The O'Reilly Factor.* Before we get started, I just wanted to tell you that I'm not interested in discussing any unproven theories, I want to stick straight to the facts." I thought to myself, "Damn, this guy's trying to muscle me even before we go on-the-air." So I tell him, "Bill, I'm glad you said that, because facts are all I'm gonna give you and it should be a pretty lively discussion." O'Reilly never said anything to me for the next 10 minutes, until we started the live taping.

The first thing he opens with is questioning me about O.J.'s Web site. O'Reilly starts out by saying that he is disgusted with the fact that O.J. would set up a Web site, finding it ridiculous, a total waste of time, and wanted my opinion. I thought to myself, is this guy really gonna' take me here? He just told me he wanted to discuss facts. I replied, "A lot of people think the Web is a lot of hype. O.J. wants to do what all entrepreneurs want to do on the Internet, make some money the American way." I continued, "But you know, Bill, I did not come on your show to talk about O.J.'s Web site. I came to talk about the phone records and the suppression of evidence in O.J.'s prosecution."

My approach is the antithesis of the legal profession's. Making an accusation or asking a question without knowing the actual conclusion is a no-no for lawyers. However, a doctor in a medical practice always has to make decisions and judgments without knowing outcomes. By making assumptions based on probability, I'm used to guessing right. So I figure Bill O'Reilly is in unchartered waters, attempting to refute anything I say because it all has a degree of subjectivity.

He flashes the exhibit of the phone records to refute my allegations, and I replied, "My friend, this is no more than a pipe dream." I explained to him what he supposedly demonstrated to the viewers was a phony record. Then O'Reilly says, "Dr. Johnson, now this is becoming very confusing to me." I shot back, "Then I'll straighten you out." By then, I knew I struck a vein. Any time you can take someone away from their sustained security and pulverize their beliefs, kind of like when Columbus proved the world wasn't flat when everyone believed you would fall off the edge, reasonable people capitulate. It is only the paid antagonist that keeps up the front. You could sense at this point, they don't truly believe O.J. guilty—they just _want_ to believe he's guilty.

After we returned from a commercial, I chased O'Reilly around his own studio, but could not pin him down to any serious challenge. So much for the tough guy making me look bad. I never let up on him, and the producers shut my mike off so Bill could get the last word, demonstrating the crux of White America's superiority complex. They seemed to forget that humility is a virtue, and it makes you a better person when you can admit when you are wrong. I appreciated the opportunity to debate O'Reilly during the live on-air taping, I just regretted the fact that a guy that purportedly could deal openly with an issue, made excuses while he smiled like the Cheshire cat.

Chapter Twenty-Four
THE GHOST TO COMPEL

Back in court, we would follow the advice given to us by USDC Judge Pregerson. We would return to the scene of the crime, where they hid the phone records—the Los Angeles Superior Court. When we filed a Motion to Compel the D.A. and GTE to produce the phone records, it was done in Los Angeles Criminal Courts Division 101, the same courtroom where O.J.'s criminal trial was held. Superior Court Presiding Judge Larry Fidler calendared the hearing, ironically, on the anniversary of the deaths, June 12, 2000. This time, McCann decided he would get a friend of his, Tony Zinnanti, to draft the motion. It was a motion that created a lot of anxiety, as the implications would suggest.

On the day we entered court, the media was in full force, and there was a host of supporters which accompanied us to the Los

Angeles Criminal Courts Building. The Rampart Police corruption scandal was under full investigation, and all timing seemed to converge. Attorney Zinnanti wrote a marvelous brief, for which there could be no rebuttal, yet you could sense the trepidation as he was not ready for primetime. We were challenging the Cyclops—the L.A. Criminal Justice System—patriot missiles vs. pea-shooters. When we walked into the courtroom, I smelled trouble. The bailiffs and courtroom personnel knew the judge would fake a Hail Mary, and run the Statue of Liberty from his old play book.

We took our seats in the gallery behind McCann and Zinnanti, the "Daydream Team." Judge Ito's wife, Captain Margaret York, head of LAPD Internal Affairs, who almost caused the Mistrial of The Century, was sitting incognito in plain clothes in the courtroom. After Mark Fuhrman and the Rampart Police corruption scandal, I was bewildered why she made her presence, she's already got plenty on her plate.

Before the judge came to the bench, the court clerk asked all attorneys to come to the judge's chambers. Hodgman was there representing Los Angeles County, and O'Melveny's lawyers were there fighting to keep the phone records sealed, along with McCann and Zinnanti. When the judge called the lawyers into his chambers, the courtroom took on a new complexion. My sympathizers and I remained in the gallery as the lawyers went into the back room. Suddenly the courtroom resembled Soweto; all the White fellas leave the courtroom, leaving only Blacks and Mexicans. When the lawyers returned, the D.A. and O'Melveny had smirks on their faces, McCann was red as a fire truck and Zinnanti looked like he had just seen a ghost.

The court was called to order and McCann argued first. There was no change in our position, O.J. had a right to review evidence used against him. However, just like past courtroom conduct, the opposing attorneys had no rebuttal because the judge argued their case for them. Judge Fidler's position was that it was too late for

O.J. to clear his name. Attorney Zinnanti argued that since DNA was now clearing men of crimes they were falsely convicted of—some that were sometimes ten or more years old—O.J. had every right to see records which may completely exonerate him.

Judge Fidler asked the District Attorney, "Hodgman, what happened to the phone records?" Hodgman answered, "They were sealed, your Honor." Then Judge Fidler asked, "Did the Dream Team get a chance to look at them?" Hodgman replied, "I guess so—as far as I know." Fidler responded, "Well, that's all there is to it. This case is closed. There's no need to mandate any phone records."

O'Melveny's attorney looked like Monica Lewinsky standing in front of the judge, begging the judge to sanction us for asking to protect O.J.'s constitutional rights. The judge ignored O'Melveny's overtures, and we escaped another bullet—no phone records, no catfish.

We went out to the 13th floor lobby, where the media was setting up for an impromptu press conference. *"The Big O"* and the District Attorney ducked the media, but my team showed up. McCann and Zinnanti spoke words in defiance of the judge's rulings, and then it was my turn at the mike. I was so proud of these men, two White guys in L.A. that stood up for honesty and integrity, and I let them know how honored I felt to see them willing to fight for justice. It is the American people that were **DOUBLE-CROSSED** in a scandal that has shaken the foundations of judicial democracy in the free world. The media erupted in applause. They knew we were right, but they couldn't print it. Whatever was said in the chambers impacted McCann and Zinnanti. After the hearing, they floated away from us, but before departing they told me, "We can never go back to court." Yet, they were completely unabashed now about their beliefs in O.J.'s innocence.

We went back to the court a week later to seek a copy of the in-chamber transcripts, only to learn that Judge Fidler had sealed them as well. So much secrecy and for what? The great American

DOUBLE-CROSS—"Above the Law" is an understatement. USDC Judge Pregerson left the door open for us but no one dared to walk through it, and the media was silent as the lambs.

O.J. says, "I appreciate what you guys tried to do, but we'll never get our hands on the phone records." He also appreciated the fact that of all the innuendos cast, O.J. was glad we never mentioned Johnnie Cochran. "Don't say anything bad about Johnnie," O.J. says, "because Johnnie Cochran had nothing to do with it." I told him, "I know, O.J., Shapiro handled the phone record issue before Johnnie joined the Dream Team."

All my investigative group could do at that point was wait. Then something came to me on my e-mail. O.J. was packing up, moving to Florida, so he could protect his few remaining assets, when my team discerned something quite interesting. Always searching for clues, we came across some transcripts of the District Attorney resting their case in July of 1995.

The Dream Team would take over to present O.J.'s defense. While the jury was excused from the courtroom and everyone was bored to death, falling asleep from procedural issues, Marcia Clark was arguing for certain pieces of evidence to be included in the jury deliberation. She explicitly wanted the jury to view the gory pictures, taken by the Coroner, of the victims' mutilated bodies before autopsy. Johnnie countered her arguments, saying the pictures were too gruesome, and were more prejudicial than probative.

Marcia continued to press her case, that the jury needed to see just how brutal O.J. actually was. Johnnie again says, "The jury saw the pictures already, and they don't prove anything, they only made the jury very sick." The jury needed a recess to recompose themselves. The pictures did not tell you who did the crime, but were very inflammatory. Johnnie continued, "Ms. Clark, you have not proven your case, and we have not had an opportunity to present ours. The jury should not be influenced by those horrible pictures." Marcia would not give in and responded, "The jury needs to see just how violent and sadistic O.J. really was."

Johnnie, completely flustered and angered, exclaimed, "Look, Marcia, the jury doesn't need to see everything, **WE AGREED NOT TO SHOW THEM THE PHONE RECORDS.**" Momentary silence came over the courtroom.

Now Johnnie's got Marcia eating out of his palm. Johnnie straightened his tie, and started his charming eloquence again, but body language was stronger than words. Nobody had much more to say, yet Ito silently ruled in Marcia Clark's favor.

When I finished telling O.J. this story, his heart dropped into his jock strap. Appearing dejected, O.J. suddenly seemed relieved. Then he got angry. O.J. says, "I need proof of that, can you back up what you say?" I said, "O.J., I have never brought you any bullshit, and I'm not bullshittin' you now. Tommy's got the proof, but he couldn't pull you off the golf course for a moment before he had to leave for Minneapolis."

What else could be said? The D.A. showed an exhibit of the phone records in February; then in July, five months later, Johnnie is still trying to leverage the phone records. So what could be hiding?

Chapter Twenty-Five

OLD BOYS' RULES

O.J.'s appeal was now calendared for oral arguments to be presented. I received notice by mail from the California Appellate Court, along with an application to present oral argument. The application had my office address on it, but in place of my name was the word, "Unknown." I filled the application out and sent it back to the court. A week later, I got a call from the Deputy Clerk of the Appellate Court. Deputy Guzman informed me an Amicus Curiae is not permitted to give oral argument in this Appellate Court. I asked, "Why is that? Is that a written rule of the court?" He tells me, "No," so I asked, "Then why would I be sent an application?" Guzman replied, "You were on a list to be served." So I inquired, "Is it the policy of the court to serve the 'Unknown', because that is who it was addressed to?" I had already spent hours preparing for oral presentation and he tells me, "You should write to the court for clarification."

I took his advice and wrote to the court:

December 13, 2000
Court of Appeal
State of California
Second Appellate District

Re: **Request to Present Oral Argument**
RUFO, SHARON et al., V. SIMPSON, ORENTHAL JAMES
Case No. **B112612/SC031947**

To the Honorable Appeals' Court:

On November 28, 2000, I received a call from the Clerk of the Court who informed me that my application was denied to give oral argument in the above referenced case calendared for Dec. 14, 2000, in support of the Amicus Brief Filed June 18, 1998. As unwritten policy of the Second Appellate Court, he stated in part, "an Amicus Curiae is not allowed to give oral argument in this court." After I learned of the denial subsequent to returning the application which was sent to me from the Second Appellate Court, I inquired why an application was directed to my office in the first place. He explained that I was on a list to be notified although he was not sure why the application I received was addressed to **"Unknown."**

As my brief states and my oral argument expounds, evidence suppressed in both criminal and civil trials verify that two killers perpetrated the crimes Mr. Simpson was accused of. The one killer theory fostered in both trials is not grounded in reality. The phone records admitted in both trials were fraudulent for which the true and certified copies would prove that Nicole and her mother talked *by phone at the same time Mr. Simpson departed to LAX via limousine. The only conclusion one can draw is that the indictment of O.J. Simpson was an obstruction of justice and a conspiracy of the DA office in collusion with the LAPD. The Santa Monica verdict of $33.5 million is cloaked in double jeopardy and a gross violation of constitutional principles. If it pleases the court I can substantiate these declarations; notwithstanding, the court must not condone the corruption in a fraudulent prosecution and allow the integrity of our judicial system to degenerate by ignoring the truth. The citizens of this State and Nation deserve more.*

Respectfully,

Henry S. Johnson, M.D., Amicus Curiae

I received a reply from the court a week later. PETITION TO GRANT ORAL ARGUMENT BY DR. JOHNSON DENIED. I was informed that I could attend the hearing, but I could say nothing.

I went to the California Appellate Court and the courtroom was heavily stacked against O.J. Simpson. Dan Leonard was there to present oral argument for the appeal he had written. Petrocelli was there for rebuttal, as well as Attorney Horowitz representing the Browns, and Sharon Rufo's attorney.

Leonard argued that the Santa Monica verdict should be reversed, because the court erred by precluding Fuhrman's testimony. Furthermore, the crystal ball punitive damage award of $33.5 million was excessive and should be set aside.

I'm the only Black guy in a filled courtroom, listening to the fate of another Black man being decided. Dan Leonard looks over his shoulder and sees me. I had not seen Leonard in over a year, since our poolside chat. He looked ready to admit defeat, but I nodded to show my support, feeling it all a sham anyway.

The court recessed for ten minutes before oral presentation in O.J. Simpson's appeal would start. I went to the men's room to get myself straightened out and I ran into Leonard. You could sense he wasn't very optimistic, but I shook his hand firmly, patted him on the shoulder and told him to give it his best shot. We went back to the courtroom and the judges called the next case, Rufo and others vs. O.J. Simpson. Judge Hastings, one of the three Appellate judges hearing oral argument, spoke informally stating, "In face of the LAPD's Rampart Police investigation, people could easily take another perspective on the O.J. Simpson prosecution."

Attorney Leonard presented a solid oral argument, and Petrocelli came along with his rebuttal, touting the "mountain of evidence." When the hearing ended, we went down to the street entrance in front of the Ronald Reagan State Courthouse. The plaintiffs' attorneys were there and received kudos along with some imbecilic questions from the media. Some of the media retinue recognized me in their presence, however, and associated the issue of the phone records which was already haunting O.J.'s antagonists.

Dan Leonard failed to show up to the press conference, but Petrocelli was there stating the Appeals Court should uphold the will of the people. I remained poised to ask Petrocelli, in front of the media, if he thought the certified phone records would prove O.J. could be in two places at the same time. Petrocelli glanced at me out of the corner of his eye as he stood in front of the mike.

Standing next to the reporters and cameras with the press, I yelled "Dan!" to grab his attention. Petrocelli abruptly ended his statement to the press and quickly walked away from the microphones. At that point, I walked up to the mikes and stated to the media gathering that O.J. never should have been indicted. The "Trial Of The Century" was the "Scam of the Century." The phone records would prove it, but the records were suppressed, sealed and stolen. Thus far, no judge nor lawyer has the courage to produce an official copy of them.

The American people deserve to hear the truth and nothing less. We will never give up exposing this fraud. We will be back in Federal Court. No one was there to back O.J., so I figured I'd let them have both barrels. When I finished speaking, a flurry of questions started coming at me from the media, but once again nothing would be mentioned in broadcast or print.

A few weeks later, I would receive a copy of the Appellate Courts Ruling. The verdict of the Santa Monica jury was upheld, including the $33.5 million dollar judgment. I immediately contacted Simpson, and FedEx'd him a copy of the ruling. After he got a chance to ponder the results and conferred with his attorneys, they indicated that they thought his chances for any legal victory was bleak. They suggested that he should stop wasting his money—stop fighting because he would never win anything. Just go on and live out his life with his pension and kids.

O.J. asked me, "What do you think, Doc?" I said, "O.J., it behooves you to continue to fight to clear your name, and expose the corruption in the criminal justice system. You could potentially help other men that were falsely convicted and whose lives have been destroyed." O.J. said, "I want to fight but I can't afford to continue." So I told him, "Well, let me see what I could do."

O.J. says, "My lawyers tell me the Appellate ruling is worded too slick. They don't see no way around it." Everyone felt outsnookered. To throw in the towel and cut his losses was not real comforting advice to O.J. One thing for sure, if the Appellate ruling was not appealed to the California Supreme Court, that would essentially cancel any chance to raise any constitutional issues in Federal Court. O.J.'s legal recourse would be dead and gone. All State remedies had to be exhausted. In effect, he must appeal at every level before any Federal Court would consider any pleading.

The Appellate ruling would be certified, effectively 30 days after notification of their decision was received.

When I received the 65-page Opinion of the Appeals Court, I sent O.J. a copy and started to dissect the Opinion. It was not going to be easy, getting a brief in front of the Supreme Court. There was a 10-day deadline to appeal to the California Supreme Court after the Appellate ruling was certified. Getting an appeal in front of the Supreme Court requires that certain guidelines are met. Most lawyers will admit it is a formidable task, and other than your jail-house lawyers who have nothing but time to think legal strategies through, in most cases, one must petition the Appellate Court to reconsider their ruling before making an appeal to the Supreme Court. Since it took over two years for the California Appeals Court to make a ruling, a second petition to that court seemed like an exercise in futility. O.J.'s only option was to appeal directly to the Supreme Court.

I sought out an argument for the California Supreme Court based on a contention in the Appellate Court opinion. The appeals court addressed the concerns raised by Dan Leonard, yet found that Judge Fujisaki followed the letter of the law. Therefore, the court upheld all findings of the lower court, including the amount of the judgment.

Before I began to dissect the Appellate opinion, I thought to myself—"What's the best way to grab a catfish?" I reminisced about all those orange crates and plywood I used as a desk I made to study by in Mexico. I could still hear my father's echo, "Finish what you start." I thought about all the good men that go unrecognized for their efforts and about the little guy who longs for a fair shake. I thought, this ain't gonna be easy. I took my shoes off so I could think more clearly.

As I read through the brief, I slid right past a paragraph that I didn't comprehend. It seemed as though the wording propelled me on to the next page. Something in the back of my mind told me to just skip over it and keep on reading. I suddenly came to a halt about two pages beyond this paragraph, realizing what I had just done. I said to myself, "Wait a minute, I can't gloss over something I don't clearly understand." I backed up and read it a second time. Then I read it a third time, a fourth time and still didn't get it. I read it again and again with the same results. So I decided to separate it and write it on a flashcard. I could refer back to it after I finished reading the document.

The paragraph remained perplexing to me, so when I was through, I just tucked the flashcard into my back pocket and walked around with it. At any spare moment, I would pull the flashcard out of my pocket, read and ponder its meaning. About a week later, I'm soaking in my bathtub around midnight, staring at my flashcard. Suddenly, a light came on. It finally sank in what the "code" really meant.

I jumped out of the tub and went to my desk. I grabbed a pen and it would not stop writing until I slammed it down about a quarter to four in the morning. What I discerned was that California Evidence Code inadvertently protects a snitch or a crooked cop. This obscure concept, incorporated as the State's Evidence Code, would be the essence of a Supreme Court Appeal.

According to the California Rules of Court, Evidence Code 1292 reads as follows: *"hearsay testimony is made admissible if the issue is such that the party to the action or proceeding in which the former testimony was given, had the right and opportunity to cross examine the declarant with an interest and motive similar to that which the party against whom the testimony is offered has at the hearing."* This is the proverbial camel through the eye of the needle. This part of the California Evidence Code is bad law passed by the State legislature. This definition of an exception to the hearsay rule, a rule that only applies in California, is not recognized in any other State in the Union or Federal Court. The unconstitutionality of the hearsay rule impedes a defendant's right to examine all the evidence against him.

In a nutshell, in accordance with Rule 29 of the California Rules of Court, an appeal should be made directly to the California Supreme Court to clarify a question of law. The question is, does the strict criteria to meet California Evidence Code 1292, Exception to the Hearsay Rule, violate O.J. Simpson's Sixth Amendment right—guaranteed by the United States Constitution—to confront witnesses and evidence against him? Just in the nick of time, a petition to the California Supreme Court was filed with O.J. acting in *pro se*, without legal counsel going it alone. A few pundits in the media attempted to make some dimwitted commentary about Simpson representing himself, yet none of these glib "intellectuals" cared to address the issues at hand.

Here's what happened. The plaintiffs—Fred Goldman, Sharon Rufo and the Browns—were able to use all the evidence which Detective Mark Fuhrman uncovered against O.J., but O.J. was not allowed to question how Fuhrman discovered it. Mark Fuhrman was protected by Ito and Fujisaki from potential criminal exposure—an abuse of discretion by the courts in both trials.

Mark Fuhrman found the preponderance of physical evidence; including the bloody glove at Rockingham, the blood in the Bronco, the blood in the driveway, and the bloody sock. He also testified as a witness for the prosecution against O.J. in the criminal trial. Subsequently found guilty of committing perjury, Fuhrman denied ever using the term "nigger" while under color of authority, a uniformed officer.

An abuse of discretion became an element in the State's case against Simpson, when Ito allowed Fuhrman to take the Fifth on cross-examination to avoid self-incrimination. President Clinton was impeached for his little imbroglio, yet Mark Fuhrman was allowed to go fishing. Legal theory has it, that when a prosecution witness gives testimony against a defendant, he in essence waives his Fifth Amendment protection. He must continue his testimony, or be remanded to confinement—a contempt of court, for refusing to testify. In other words, you can't testify for one side and refuse to be examined by the other.

It was a mistrial when Ito allowed Mark Fuhrman to meander out of the courtroom, concealing the fact that O.J. was framed. Secondly, Ito effectively violated the Sixth Amendment, rendering O.J. ineffective assistance of counsel, when Ito's wife Captain Margaret York, head of LAPD Internal Affairs, was subpoenaed but ultimately excluded as a witness. She had previously reprimanded Mark Fuhrman for improprieties under the color of authority.

So Mark Fuhrman, the LAPD's and the D.A.'s "Golden Boy," rode into court on a white horse with bouquets of roses thrown at his feet; however, F. Lee Bailey ran Fuhrman out of court riding a white rat.

In the civil trial, all the evidence which the disgraced Detective Fuhrman had uncovered was sanitized by virtue of a flaw in the California Evidence Code. This evidence could be used against O.J. and validated as material; yet O.J. was denied the opportunity to examine the witness who "uncovered" this incriminating evidence. A witness who previously lied under oath, planted evidence on people he routinely arrested, and whose testimony was proven to be false during O.J.'s criminal trial, subsequently leading to O.J.'s acquittal.

Fujisaki allowed all the evidence uncovered by Mark Fuhrman, but refused to enforce the subpoena served on Fuhrman by the defense. Fujisaki ruled that if O.J. could not prove that Fuhrman tried to frame him, Fuhrman did not have to testify—a lousy ruling that protected a crooked cop.

The California Appeals Court ruled that other plaintiff witnesses "established" how all the evidence was discovered at Rockingham, independent of Mark Fuhrman. The fact that Detective Fuhrman testified he was alone when he discovered the glove was immaterial. Since Fuhrman made that statement on direct examination, the hearsay rule made it inadmissible because that statement was not made during <u>cross-examination</u>. How those witnesses were able to "prove" that the glove was discovered at Rockingham was never challenged. The evidence code reads only cross-examination testimony is admissible. Since Fuhrman took the Fifth on cross-examination, meant there wasn't any testimony received on cross. The code thus shielded Mark Fuhrman from committing perjury a second time, and potentially exposing the conspiracy to obstruct justice.

In contrast, Federal Law, along with the laws in the rest of the 49 States, adheres to a Uniform Evidence Code which allows all testimony given under oath to be examined. Not in California, though. The strict criteria applied in this instance has a propensity to protect a bogus prosecutorial witness, sublime "old-boyism." The plaintiffs got a shot at O.J. with his wrists handcuffed behind his back. Compared to the Uniform Evidence Code practiced by any other State, or the Federal Court for that matter, this peculiarity in California's Rules of Court is even in conflict with the Magna Carta from the Middle Ages in England.

To bolster the fact that evidence against O.J. could be proven fraudulent, the issue of the phone records reinforced the assertions made in O.J.'s petition.

It was explained to the California Supreme Court that an abuse of judicial discretion occurred at the preliminary hearing when Judge Kathleen Kennedy-Powell sealed the Browns' and Nicole's phone records. O.J. should have never been charged based purely on the fact that Nicole Brown Simpson was still alive at the same time O.J. departed for LAX, but the "Trial of the Century" had to go on.

Since the jury was never shown the authentic phone records, they were nullified as Triers of Fact by the court. In the 11th hour, all of the plaintiffs' attorneys—Petrocelli, Gelbum and Horowitz—jointly filed an answer to the petition. They rested on their laurels that the "mountain of evidence" proved beyond a shadow of a doubt that O J. was guilty. Furthermore, they begged the court to refuse O.J. access to the phone records despite the fact that the plaintiffs had used a replica as evidence against him. They wrote that O.J. should be denied the right to this evidence, even if his claim was legally valid.

No laws applied to this case, other than "Old Boys' Rules." If fraudulent evidence convicted an "N"–man, so what? This trio of impresarios neglected to address the issue of whether the evidence code violated the Sixth Amendment of the U.S. Constitution.

Ironically, another Amicus Brief was filed by *Haight, Brown and Bonesteel. LLP,* Certified Appellate Specialists in conjunction with O.J.'s Supreme Court appeal. It stated that the method to calculate the judgment against O.J. was a violation of the Eighth Amendment, and a form of indentured servitude. Furthermore, this crystal ball formula, deemed cruel and unusual punishment, had been struck down by the U.S. Supreme Court in a previous case.

The *"Rufo Formula,"* as it has come to be known, has been used against other California residents as well, based on its publication in the Simpson matter. It prophesies your potential future income, using this as a basis to decide the amount of compensatory and punitive damages you must pay.

The California Supreme Court denied the Amicus Curiae Brief of this prestigious law firm as well.

Within ten days of Petrocelli and Horowitz's pleading to the court, we filed a reply to their answer which stated in part, although the Court of Appeal record reflects "that petitioner Simpson does not contend, that the evidence is legally insufficient to show he is the person who committed the murders, it is not O.J.'s responsibility to go on a 'wild goose chase' in an effort to discredit the supposed 'mountain of incriminating evidence'." Petitioner Simpson maintains that his right to constitutional protection can not be abridged by State Law.

This single most important issue has the clear and potential effect to right an injustice, sustain the integrity of the California Criminal Court's jury verdict, and to reverse the civil court findings against the petitioner.

This is a constitutional question that should be addressed by the California Supreme Court. In paraphrasing Article VI, Section 2 of the U.S. Constitution: *this Constitution and the laws of the United States which shall be made in Pursuance thereof; shall be the supreme law of the land, and the judges in every State shall be bound thereby, anything in the Constitution or laws of any State to the contrary not withstanding.*

The plaintiffs' motivation to fight exposing the certified telephone records was seemingly to avoid potential self-incrimination and indictment. Petitioner believes all evidence should be presented without tampering to the jury. Moreover, petitioner believes the court, the plaintiffs, their attorneys, along with the petitioner's ineffective assistance of counsel, have acted to conceal the certified telephone records which would prove Nicole Brown Simpson was alive at the <u>same time</u> O.J. departed for Los Angeles International Airport in the company of his chauffeur. *Lastly, O.J. attests that he has never been in two places at the same time.*

Petitioner Simpson believes the continued concealment of the certified telephone records, which were subpoenaed and belong to the citizens of California, perpetuates an obstruction of justice, and aids and abets the true murderers.

What is more ironic and a conflict of interest is the fact that Attorney Petrocelli, who seeks to collect the $33.5 million dollar award against O.J., is associated with the same law firm, *O'Melveny & Myers,* which has acted willfully to block O.J.'s access to the Browns' GTE phone records.

The California Supreme Court has an <u>obligation</u> based on Article VI, Section 2 of the United States Constitution to uphold the *Supremacy Clause*, the law of the land.

The California Supreme Court needed to take an extension—an extra thirty days to make its ruling. In closed session without recording or stenography, the Supreme Court held their noses, turned thumbs down and unanimously agreed to deny O.J.'s petition, without explanation. In effect, the California Supreme Court violated Article VI, of the United States Constitution, by shamefully avoiding one man's plea—O.J. Simpson. This singular, most important event not only screwed O.J., but the criminal justice system, with the blessings of a controlled and censored media, invited all Americans and the world in general, to kiss their ass.

They have the prerogative to do that, you know.

CONCLUSION

It's not over 'til it's over. The "Trial of the Century," the O.J. Simpson tragedy, played out in the media, in the scheme of time, saturated our lives with distorted trivia. It was a perfect example of how an event, which has marginal significance on one's life, can be manipulated to have a major impact on society. The most distressing aspect of the media presentation of the trials draws from the bias in reporting, which begs the question, how can we afford to trust what we are bombarded with in times of real crises?

O.J.'s petition to the California Supreme Court served not only to demand his rights guaranteed by the U.S. Constitution, but to guard the immunities of all people, all citizens affected by the laws in California and across the U.S. When those in service to the citizens, after taking an oath to uphold the laws of this Country and State, violate those laws with impunity, along with their oath, it is tantamount to treason. It leaves those that have abdicated a degree of liberty to be governed by democratic ideals in a state of lawlessness.

O.J.'s humility as a father remains unquestioned. As an ex-athlete and a man who has dedicated his life to entertaining people and making them happy, he did not possess the professional expertise or eyes in the back of his head, to watch everything that was going on around him. He did the best job he could to defend himself. In his fight to clear his name, he has always been impeded by those professionals who receive tax dollars to investigate and solve crimes.

The media, in the process of denying O.J. a fair hearing in the

297

court of public opinion, while the courts impeded his right to completely exhonerate his name, failed all Americans as well. The implications of the judicial travesty which O.J. endured is repugnant to American values embodied in our sense of fairness. O.J. was reduced to petition the Highest Court in California to protect his right to prove his innocence. He has always and still proclaims his innocence in the deaths of his ex-wife Nicole Brown Simpson and Ronald Goldman. The Supreme Court had the power to order the telephone records and resolve this question created by double jeopardy, but they chose not to. The day they denied O.J.'s request will be remembered as the darkest hour in California's judicial history.

One day the truth hidden in darkness will come to light. You know, an apple pie is only as good as the apples. You can't remove the apples and still have pie. If the apples are as rotten as Mark Fuhrman, it is clear why the plaintiffs resisted swallowing his testimony. Worse yet, the telephone records are plump, juicy worms infesting the apples. O.J.'s antagonists have cooked up the pie, and the court should have made them take the first bite. Principles should always reign over procedure, as good over evil.

How much time and energy must we expend to maintain a facade? What cosmic force impels us to drift from reality, when life and the pursuit of serenity commands us to embrace humanity? In our quest to attain a higher quality of life, we seem to forget that harmony, like a fine-tuned engine, reduces friction and drag. In order to foster an environment which enhances our chances to succeed obstacles, we must admit our failures and learn from them.

A subtext of this story has been a war of words, so to speak. You might say a David vs. Goliath epic, to bring awareness to issues which directly impact our perceptions of each other and how the world looks upon us as Americans.

The "Trial of the Century" truly allowed us to measure where we have come as a civilization supposedly based on a Judeo-Christian ethic. The case of the People vs. Orenthal James Simpson was not merely a murder trial, but an examination of our collective insecurities. It remains inescapable to assume that freedom exists in the face of injustice.

Our forbearers' blood, sweat, and sacrifices to sustain the principles of liberty and justice, which has made America great, becomes inconsequential in the frame of this hypocrisy. Honesty reinforces the foundations of democracy and provides us a compass to chart a course in times of violence, suffering, degradation, and insecurity. That is why progress demands resolution.

The facts we have exposed may or may not help O.J., yet clarity of the real issues will start the healing process for society. I, for one, strongly believe in O.J.'s innocence, but as a scientist, I know that very few things in life are absolute.

"*I told them that it is not the custom to hand over any man before he has faced his accusers and has had an opportunity to defend himself against their charges.*"

Acts 25: 16 N.I.V.

BOOK AVAILABLE THROUGH
Milligan Books, Inc.
An Imprint Of Professional Business
Consulting Service

DOUBLE-CRO$$ED FOR BLOOD $19.95

Order Form

Milligan Books
1425 West Manchester, Suite B,
Los Angeles, California 90047
(323) 750-3592

Mail Check or Money Order to:
Milligan Books

Name _____ Date _____

Address _____

City_____ State _____ Zip Code_____

Day telephone _____

Evening telephone_____

Book title _____

Number of books ordered ___ Total cost .... $ _____

Sales Taxes (CA Add 8.25%)............................... $ _____

Shipping & Handling $4.50 per book.....................$ _____

Total Amount Due.. $ _____

_ Check   _ Money Order   Other Cards _____

_ Visa   _ Master Card   Expiration Date _____

Credit Card No. _____

Driver's License No. _____

_____   _____

Signature   Date